Tehran's Vengeance

Dave Austin

A Thriller

Tehran's Vengeance is a work of fiction. Names, characters, places, and incidents are products of the author's imagination or are used fictitiously. Any resemblance to actual events, locales or persons, living or dead, is purely coincidental.

Copyright © 2018 by David Austin

ISBN: 9781790295654

Acknowledgements

I want to thank my family for putting up with me being away much more than the average husband and father.

To my parents, who were great role models and fostered a spirit of service to our country.

And last, but not least, to my editors, Max and Claire Sutton who corrected my many mistakes and were instrumental in making this book happen. I can't wait to start working on the next one with you.

Prologue

The most sophisticated cyber weapon ever created was released in mid-2009 and sped across the Internet like a school of hungry piranha looking for their next meal. The virus ignored the overwhelming majority of computers and systems it encountered as it traveled through the ether and optical fiber of the World Wide Web. Unlike the indiscriminate appetite of the fanged fish, this malicious string of code zeroed in on a very specific target – a top-secret underground fuel enrichment plant in central Iran – a plant the world didn't even know existed until its presence was revealed in 2002 by a man who had emigrated to the United States twenty-three years earlier.

The Natanz Uranium Enrichment Facility is located approximately three hundred kilometers south of Tehran, Iran. Encompassing nearly twenty-five acres of land, the plant is surrounded by a concrete wall two-and-a-half meters thick. Buried under layers of steel, concrete, and earth, and defended by a ring of anti-aircraft batteries, the complex is fortified against the best bunker-busting bombs the West had to offer.
Those countermeasures, supplemented by forces of the Islamic Revolutionary Guard Corps, or IRGC, made Western and Israeli generals alike believe an overt military strike on Natanz was futile.

On several previous occasions, Israel's Air Force had bloodied the noses of its larger neighbors Iraq and Syria with air strikes against their nuclear facilities. Because of those successes, elements within the Israeli government lobbied for a similar strike on Iran. Debates raged in the Knesset, and many in the tiny country were concerned a military attack on Iran would trigger an all-out war in the Middle East. With air and ground attacks all but ruled out, Western intelligence agencies, namely the Central Intelligence Agency and Israel's Mossad, needed to find another way to disrupt Iran's nuclear ambitions.

To this day, many experts and nuclear scientists believe the United States and Israel, possibly with help from Great Britain and Germany, had been working on a covert plan to attack the computer systems in and around Natanz. The virus, named Stuxnet by computer security specialists who had analyzed the code after the attack, specifically targeted the German-made Siemens controllers that monitored centrifuges enriching the uranium Iran's scientists hoped to use to create a nuclear weapon.

Brilliant in its design, the virus didn't attack all at once but worked in stages. The first stage consisted of recording normal centrifuge readings for playback at a later time. It was during the second stage of the attack, when the centrifuges would accelerate for a short period of time and then return to normal, that the actual damage would take place.

The virus would lay dormant for about thirty days before attacking again, this time slowing the centrifuges. The varying speeds would cause the aluminum tubes to expand and contract to the point that some of the internal parts collided, destroying the centrifuges. The normal readings recorded during the first stage of the operation were then fed into the monitoring sensors, making it appear as if everything was running smoothly. By the time the Iranian technicians became aware of the malfunction it was too late. Experts estimated a thousand centrifuges, roughly ten percent of the equipment at Natanz, were destroyed.

No one is quite sure how the virus got into Natanz in the first place. Some believe Siemens was a willing participant, providing the Iranians with contaminated or defective equipment. Others think a shipment of the German-made controllers were intercepted in the United Arab Emirates by a foreign intelligence agency and altered there. There's also a theory that the systems at Natanz weren't connected to the Internet and the virus was introduced through USB thumb drives belonging to unwitting Russian contractors. For obvious reasons, the Americans and Israelis have been tight-lipped about the cyberattack, offering only cryptic answers when asked to comment.

Regardless of how the virus penetrated one of the most secure facilities in Iran, the incident was a major embarrassment to the Islamic Republic and a significant setback to the country's nuclear program.

With the populace clamoring for a response and forces inside the government hungry for revenge, Ayatollah Ali-Khamenei granted permission for multiple attacks against Israel and its citizens. The Supreme Leader had only one condition: no direct links to Iran. The Revolutionary Guards were not trained for this type of work so these assignments usually fell to the al-Quds Force, the IRGC's elite hit squad responsible for operations outside the borders of Iran.

At the time, Major General Qasem Suleimani was the commanding officer of the Quds Force. He'd celebrated the successes his men had achieved in the region but knew they were not ready to deploy and execute on a global scale. He lacked the right people with the requisite skill set to operate outside the familiar surroundings of the Middle East.

Being the commanding officer of the Supreme Leader's personal covert action force afforded General Suleimani a few perks, one of which was direct access to the Ayatollah himself. Making the most of his special access, Suleimani lobbied for permission to form a unique outfit within the Quds Force that would be capable of carrying out operations across the globe. His goal was to make this unit the equal of any covert-action team in the world, and he began by seeking out the best and brightest Iran had to offer. The recruits were provided with specialized training in hand-to-hand combat, close-quarters battle, assassination techniques, espionage, and tradecraft.

With visions of American and Israeli officials falling prey to Iranian assassins, the Ayatollah gave Suleimani the green light and provided the additional funding necessary to move the project forward.

Hamid Farzan, a young man from Bandar Anzali, a seaport town on the southern coast of the Caspian Sea, was one of the unit's first recruits. He excelled throughout his training and was selected as the class Honor Graduate. The award came with a promotion to the rank of major and the opportunity to lead the unit on its first operational mission. Major Farzan's father had served honorably as the commander of a tank battalion in the Iran-Iraq War, and now, thirty years later, it was the son's turn to serve the Islamic Republic.

Over the years General Suleimani had compiled a list of over five hundred individuals that were targeted for assassination. This newly promoted major was going to be given his chance to start crossing names off that list.

CHAPTER 1

With Regional Security Officer Tim Carter riding shotgun in the right front seat, and Assistant RSO Marcus Jacobs behind the wheel, the black Chevrolet Suburban transporting Ambassador Jonathan Lewis and the embassy's press officer, Gene Moynihan, sped east on Highway 10. A second Suburban carrying four heavily armed diplomatic security agents followed closely behind.

The motorcade cleared the outskirts of Fallujah and eased onto the exit ramp, merging smoothly onto Highway 8. Their destination was the enormous and heavily fortified American Embassy in Baghdad, forty-five miles to the east.

Ambassador Jonathan Lewis's mind wandered as he watched the desert speed by through the green tint of the Suburban's bullet-resistant window. *How the hell did a career diplomat with a resume like mine end up being posted to Iraq?*

This was exactly the type of assignment he had done his best to avoid over the last twenty-odd years. He hadn't joined the Foreign Service to serve in war zones and third world hell-holes. Lewis enjoyed the finer things in life and had spent his career striking deals with his counterparts on the cocktail circuit of the civilized world in places like Paris and Madrid.

The State Department did its best to accommodate the creature comforts a government official of Lewis's rank and status merited. But even after this many years, some of those comforts were still hard to come by in Iraq. Due to the instability of the security situation – compliments of the Islamic State of Iraq and the Levant, or the Islamic State of Iraq and Syria, or ISIS – the State Department had designated Iraq as an unaccompanied post. The designation meant the environment wasn't safe enough for its employees to have their spouses and dependents join them in country. The policy applied to all American diplomatic personnel, even the ambassador. The long separation from Barbara, the love of his life for the past forty years, made Lewis's time in Baghdad that much more unpleasant.

With four months remaining on this godforsaken tour, Lewis hoped to be rewarded with one last prime assignment, maybe London, to put a bow on his distinguished twenty-seven-year career before he and Barbara retired to their home in Virginia's horse country.

The motorcade was returning to Baghdad after a full day of meetings with Iraqi officials and military leaders in Fallujah. He was there to emphasize America's commitment to helping the Iraqi military and a mish-mash of assorted militias fight the Islamic State and put a halt to their dream of establishing a Caliphate across the region.

After meeting with the local officials and military commanders, he was more convinced than ever that they were straddling the fence, playing both sides of the conflict. They would act like devout Muslims in order to gain favor or survive an encounter with ISIS, then pocket the millions of dollars in cash and aid flowing into the country, much of which made only a brief stop in Iraq before ending up in a numbered Swiss bank account. *God, it was frustrating dealing with these people,* Lewis thought.

CHAPTER 2

Over the last few days, Tim Carter had spent a considerable amount of time in the ambassador's office urging Lewis to host the meeting at the embassy instead. "Have the Iraqis come to us, sir. That way we can conduct the meeting on our terms."

Gene Moynihan, the embassy's press officer, was in on most of the meetings and was doing his best to undermine Carter and his concerns. "You obviously don't see the bigger picture here, Tim. The whole point of the trip is to show our support for the Iraqi forces. It's going to be pretty damn hard to rally the troops and bolster their confidence from our protected compound here in Baghdad."

Carter did his best to keep cool and remain professional in front of Ambassador Lewis but felt he was fighting a losing battle. "Gene, you know as well as I do that those guys are going to run for the hills at the first sign the fight isn't going their way.
Hell, the Iraqis have only stood and fought when they were backed by our troops calling in airstrikes or when the Iranians of all people were embedded with their units. The Iranians, Gene. The goddamned Quds Force! Do you even get the irony in the situation?"

The fact that Carter and Moynihan despised each other was the worst kept secret in the embassy. Most of the diplomatic staff shared Carter's opinion when it came to the press officer, but few, if any, were willing to challenge Moynihan directly because of his closeness to the ambassador. Carter's position on the protective detail earned him more equity than most with Lewis, which allowed him to go toe-to-toe with Moynihan on occasion.

Finally, after a tense silence, Ambassador Lewis stepped in

to break the stalemate. "Tim, I understand your concerns, but this time I agree with Gene. It's tough to lead from the rear, and I'm afraid it will send the wrong message to the Iraqis if we don't show. I'm sure they'll have the situation well under control for the visit, and to this point, ISIS hasn't conducted an attack on anyone as high profile as a foreign ambassador."

"You're right, sir. They haven't. I just don't want you to be the first," Carter cautioned. Realizing the discussion on the matter was over, he continued, "If you'll excuse me, I have to put together the security plan for the movement."

That had been three days ago. Now, slumped into the plush leather seat next to Ambassador Lewis, the press officer massaged his temples. Moynihan hated leaving the safety of Baghdad's Green Zone, and the stress of today's trip had manifested itself as a pounding migraine.

After spending the better part of the day outside the wire, the press officer was kicking himself for insisting Lewis meet with the Iraqis on their turf. He'd won the argument earlier in the week with Tim Carter, but after the day they'd had, Moynihan was thinking the ambassador's diplomatic security agent-in-charge might have been right after all.

CHAPTER 3

Lewis thought he'd made some progress with the Iraqis today but the uneasy feeling in the pit of his stomach told him otherwise. *Tim might have been right about the people pretending to lead this country. And why wouldn't the military stand and fight to protect their homeland from a group of fundamentalists who wanted to kill their way back to the fourteenth century? Had the divide between Sunni and Shia grown to such an extent that they couldn't live together on the same piece of land? After all, weren't they Iraqis first and foremost or had the sectarian violence eroded that solidarity to the point that loyalty to sect or tribe had overtaken their allegiance to the nation?*

As much as he hated to admit it, there were times when Lewis thought the United States had made a mistake in removing Saddam Hussein from power. Never afraid to use his military's power, Saddam would have ordered his Republican Guard to crush any Islamic State fanatic who dared set foot across the border from Syria. The dictator had no qualms about using poison gas on his own people and tortured others he'd seen as a threat to his power base. He wouldn't have given a second thought to doing the same or worse to a bunch of fanatics trying to incorporate Iraq into a larger Caliphate.

Ambassador Lewis broke the silence inside the Suburban. "How long until we get back to the embassy, Tim?"

"About an hour and a half, sir."

Lewis exhaled in frustration. "There's got to be a more efficient way to do this."

Tim Carter and Marcus Jacobs exchanged a quick glance thinking, *we wouldn't be here if you'd listened to us in the first place.*

Tired, dusty, and desperately in need of a stiff drink, Lewis cringed at the thought of an additional ninety minutes in the back of this armored behemoth. The extra layers of armoring and thick bullet-resistant glass significantly reduced the amount of space in the Suburban's cabin, and at times the closeness made him feel a little claustrophobic.

He made a mental note to have a talk with the military attaché or Scott Garrett, the CIA's station chief, about getting a helicopter for some of these longer trips outside the Green Zone. He and Scott got along well and the Agency had a substantial air operation in the country. Maybe Garrett could free up one of their Bell 412s or an MI-17 on occasion.

In the meantime, he would make the best of today's commute by working up a draft of the cable Washington would no doubt be requesting on the results of his meetings in Fallujah.

Feeling the SUV slow, he looked up and saw traffic coming to a halt as the motorcade approached a busy truck stop. "What's up, guys?"

"Looks like a bit of a traffic jam up ahead, sir," Carter offered.

Lewis peered out at the hive of activity. At first glance, it looked like any other truck stop along most interstates in the U.S. The most noticeable difference was the hundreds of shipping containers stacked in neat rows off to the side. Some were empty and rusting, while others were full of goods waiting to be transported to their final destinations like Baghdad or Nasiriyah. Shifting his gaze to the parking lot, he counted twenty or thirty vehicles whose drivers had pulled over for gas and a snack or to use the restroom before continuing their journey.

The scene brought back childhood memories of the road trips his family used to take over summer vacations. Lewis and his sister Maggie would sprint into the gas station and grab an ice-cold Coke from the cooler while their dad filled up the station wagon. Lost in the moment, he could almost feel the chill of the cold glass bottle on his lips as he chugged the soda and munched on a snack before piling back into the family roadster for the next leg of the trip.

A smile crept across his face, enjoying the pleasant snapshot of his childhood. Lewis reached for his phone, overcome with an urge to share the moment with Barbara, and dialed the number for the house in Georgetown. Baghdad was seven hours ahead of Washington, and Barbara would probably be beginning her day playing a round of golf with the girls or working on one of the many charities that were near and dear to her heart. With his unpredictable schedule, and the seven-hour time difference, it had been a couple of days since they'd talked. Even after forty years together, Lewis still cherished the sound of her voice, and felt a schoolboy's anticipation as he waited for her to answer the phone.

His moment of reverie was obliterated when a blinding flash of light and an ear-splitting explosion rocked the Suburban. Lewis lost his grip on the phone and it tumbled to the floor, coming to a rest under Tim Carter's seat. He never got the chance to hear Barbara's voice as the call connected on the other end.

CHAPTER 4

The enormous Mitsubishi's diesel engine coughed, expelling plumes of thick black smoke from the exhaust stacks behind the cab, as the driver pressed the starter button. Idling in neutral, the man behind the wheel could feel the engine's vibrations through the soles of his shoes as he waited for the order to move.

The big cargo truck was identical to many others using the truck stop's services. But instead of transporting goods to a variety of destinations, this truck was going to make a much shorter trip today, probably no more than a hundred meters or so.

The driver uttered a quick prayer and gripped the steering wheel a little tighter than normal while his right foot revved the engine, ensuring it didn't stall. Several years had passed since the driver had been operational and he was having a hard time maintaining his composure. Sweat stains soaked through his light-green dress shirt, even though the truck's air conditioner kept the cab cold enough to hang meat.

The driver pressed the clutch and shifted the big rig into gear. But instead of merging into traffic, he pulled straight across the road and stopped, completely blocking all three southbound lanes. Panicked drivers stood on their brakes, trying their best to stop in time. A few were successful, but a combination of worn tires and a light layer of sand blowing across the blacktop worked against most of them. The air was filled with the sound of screeching tires and bending metal as cars slid into one another.

Marcus Jacobs saw the truck pull out and anticipated the mayhem its action would cause. He called back to the follow car to give them a heads-up and the motorcade came to a stop. The good news was that they were able to avoid a collision. The bad news was that the Americans found themselves surrounded by a sea of vehicles.

Two men wearing black-and-white-checked keffiyehs rose from behind the parapet running along the perimeter of the truck stop's flat, sunbaked roof. Each man shouldered an RPG-7 rocket-propelled grenade launcher and centered the viewfinders' crosshairs on the second SUV. The American security team had to be neutralized before they could bring their weapons to bear or call in reinforcements that would affect the outcome of the attack.

The men fired in unison and the rockets leaped from the launch tubes with a familiar whoosh. White smoke trails marked their trajectory as the warheads sped toward their target. Having honed their skills fighting against U.S. and Coalition forces as members of the insurgency, the men's aim was true. Designed to destroy tanks, the rockets easily penetrated the SUV's armor and detonated inside the cabin. The four American agents didn't stand a chance.

Ambassador Lewis's vision was blurred by the concussive force of the blast and his ears shut down in an act of self-preservation. The sensation was odd and reminded him of being underwater in his backyard pool. Tim Carter, Gene Moynihan, and Marcus Jacobs were enduring a similar experience. Except for the ringing in their ears, the four men were dazed but otherwise unhurt.

It took a moment for Carter to clear the cobwebs and regain his senses before he turned in his seat to get a good look at Lewis. He ran his hands over the ambassador's upper body, then down each arm and leg, looking for blood or other telltale signs of trauma. "Are you injured, sir? Do you feel pain anywhere?"

"I...I think I'm fine. Just a bit shaken up," Lewis responded.

Putting their differences aside for the time being, Carter turned to the press officer and repeated the same procedure. "How about you, Gene? Are you hurt?"

Moynihan pushed Carter's hands away, annoyed at being manhandled by the agent. "I'm fine. What the hell happened?"

Returning his attention to their current predicament, Carter began searching for the cause of the explosion. "Not sure yet. You see anything, Marcus?"

"No, not with all the smoke and dust in the air."

Carter strained to get a good look through the thick, bullet-resistant windows. But pockmarks from shrapnel and flying debris, combined with a dense cloud of thick, black smoke, reduced visibility to a few feet at best. After what seemed like an eternity, the ever-present winds blowing across the Iraqi desert began to disperse the cloud. Gradually, the men were able to get a better view of the scene outside their armored cocoon.

Surprised at the lack of chatter from the rest of the protective detail, Carter radioed back to the follow car. "Hey, Derrick, gimme a sitrep. What's going on back there?" When he didn't get a reply, he tried again but got the same result.

Wondering if the limo's radio had been damaged in the blast, he gave his hand-held a try, but there was still no response, only silence. Carter was dialing Derrick's cell phone when he heard the ambassador mumble something from the backseat.

"Uh, guys…," Lewis said, his voice trailing off as if his brain was having a hard time registering what his eyes were seeing.

Carter and Jacobs turned in unison and their eyes followed his gaze out the rear window to the charred remains of what had once been the follow car. Its armored roof had been peeled back like the lid on a can of tuna.

"My God!" Moynihan whispered, feeling bile rise in the back of his throat as he fought the urge to vomit.

The grisly sight of their dead colleagues temporarily stunned the two agents before the gravity of the situation sank in and they realized what was happening.

"We're under attack! Reverse! Reverse! Reverse!" Carter ordered.

The realization dawned on Jacobs at the same time, and he went to work trying to clear a path out of the traffic jam. He slammed the Suburban into reverse and mashed the gas pedal to the floor. The SUV moved about two feet before the rear bumper slammed into the remains of the follow car.

"Shit!" Jacobs hissed.

Throwing the truck into drive, he hit the gas again. The big American vehicle lurched forward a few feet before smashing into a van belonging to an auto parts store, from the looks of the fading logo painted on the side panel. Jacobs tried using the V8's power and the weight of the Suburban to push through the mass of cars, but it was no use. There was nowhere for them to go.

All too familiar with the sounds of two decade's worth of violence, terrified Iraqis had abandoned their vehicles and run for safety. Empty cars and trucks littered the highway, completely surrounding the Americans.

The attackers took advantage of the confusion and pulled a second large cargo truck across the lanes behind the traffic jam. The vehicular barricade prevented panicked drivers from reversing out of the chaos and eliminated any opportunity for escape.

"We're sitting ducks if we stay in this truck," Carter said. "Marcus, when I give the word, you and I will go out your door. I'll provide cover while you see if any of these vehicles are still running. When you find one we can use, I'll bring the ambassador and Gene out of the Suburban and we'll make a run for Baghdad."

Jacobs press-checked his Sig Sauer P-229, looking for the shine of brass to make sure he had a round in the chamber. "Roger that. I'll find us some wheels."

Carter turned in his seat to face Ambassador Lewis and began the evacuation briefing. "Sir, Marcus will signal us when he's found a vehicle. When I give the word, be ready to bail out on the left side of the Suburban. Once we're outside, stick with me and do exactly as I say. Is that clear?"

Lewis had been briefed on the emergency action drills and took the procedures seriously. And unlike many of his peers, he had even taken the time to run through the drills with the guys on occasion. But he was still having a hard time coming to grips with the fact that they were actually doing this for real. "Aren't we safer staying in the armored Suburban?"

"I agree with Jonathan," Moynihan said, incredulous that Carter would even think about going outside. "There's no way in hell I'm going out there."

Carter dismissed Moynihan and looked the ambassador in the eyes. "Sir, you saw what they did to the follow car. If we stay in this truck the same thing is going to happen to us. We've got to move if we're to have a chance of surviving this attack."

Lewis still felt safer in the Suburban, but the gruesome scene of the destroyed follow car kept playing over and over in his head like a video on a loop. He deferred to Carter's experience and training. "Alright, Tim. Whatever you say."

Stunned at Lewis's response, Moynihan said, "Jonathan, you can't be serious? You're going along with this madness?"

"Gene," Carter said, putting a hand up to cut him off. "You can stay here if you like. It makes no difference to me. But we're leaving, with or without you as soon as Marcus finds us a ride."

Turning back to the front, he hit the emergency distress button on the truck's GPS tracker.

CHAPTER 5

The distress signal registered in the State Department's Diplomatic Security Operations Center in Washington, D.C., where it caught the attention of the supervisor. She leaned over the duty officer's shoulder and asked, "What do you have?"

Her blood ran cold as the duty officer pulled up the GPS coordinates on his monitor and they listened in on the live feed of the radio traffic. Having been on duty the last time a call like this came into the Ops Center, she whispered, "Not again." The attack on the U.S. Consulate in Benghazi, Libya, and the ensuing scandal over the State Department's response still resonated through the halls of Foggy Bottom.

Lance Corporal Stevenson was on duty in the Marine Security Guard command post at the embassy in Baghdad when the alarm went off. Using the call signs for the motorcade and the embassy, he tried to raise the protective detail on the radio. "Stagecoach this is Palace, we've received your alert. What's your status, over?"

Stevenson tried the radio again but there was still no response from any member of the team. Next, he tried Carter's and Jacobs' cell phones, but both went immediately to voicemail. Fearing the worst, he turned to the other Marine on duty and ordered, "Get the Gunny…now!"

The Marine's boots squeaked on the waxed floor as he sprinted down the hall lined with framed photographs of the commandant of the Marine Corps, the secretary of state and the president. Without hesitation, and against his better judgment, the young Marine burst into the gunnery sergeant's office.

"What the hell?" snarled Gunnery Sergeant Leland Page. A combat veteran of multiple tours in Iraq and Afghanistan, Page was currently assigned to the Special Activities Forces, the parent unit of the Marine Security Guard Detachments that protected diplomatic posts overseas. Everyone in the embassy, especially his Marines, knew better than to barge into his office unannounced.

The young Marine cringed, certain he'd experience Page's wrath at some point, but said, "We've got a situation, Gunny. You're needed in the CP right away."

Page stormed into the command post and growled, "What's so goddamned urgent, Stevenson?"

"Gunny, the distress beacon on the ambassador's Suburban has been activated. Its GPS tracker puts their last recorded position about five miles southeast of Fallujah."

"Any word from Carter?"

"Nothing, Gunny. I've been trying to raise him or any member of the detail on the radio or their cell phones but haven't had any luck yet."

Page rubbed his right hand over the bristles of his flattop. "Have we got any assets in the area?"

"We're checking. Should have something for you in a couple of minutes."

Gunny Page walked over to a nearby desk, snatched the phone's handset out of the cradle, and dialed the number to Carter's office.

Three rings later he heard the voice of Tim Carter's assistant on the other end of the line. "RSO's office, how may I direct your call?"

"Teresa, it's Lee. Who's in charge over there while Tim's out with the ambassador?"

"Josh Gordon has the duty this afternoon," she replied.

"Could you get him on the line please? And hurry. It's important."

Thirty seconds later, Page heard Gordon say, "Hey, Lee, you get the alarm in your CP too?"

"Yeah, we did. They're stationary so it could be nothing more than a traffic accident or a breakdown. But if that were the case, we should have heard from Tim or one of the guys by now."

"Agreed. I've got two choppers spinning up and we should be lifting off in about five minutes. I'm taking four of my agents plus three contractors and a couple of medics in case there are casualties. And I got word an Iraqi Special Forces team was in the air heading back to Baghdad. They've been rerouted to the scene and will meet us there."

"Sounds like a good plan, Josh," Page agreed. "We'll continue to monitor the situation from here and update D.C. on your progress." He was pleasantly surprised with the young DSS agent as he hung up the phone. *That college puke seems to have his shit together.*

Page desperately wanted to send some of his Marines with Gordon. Hell, if he had his way, he would kit up and lead the quick reaction force himself. But diplomatic agreements prevented the Marine detachment from operating outside the walls of the embassy compound. So, Gunnery Sergeant Page and his Marines were forced to sit this one out and watch from the sidelines. The conflict between his orders and his desire to help Americans in need was eating him up on the inside.

CHAPTER 6

Carter press-checked his own Sig, then gave the command, "Move!"

"Moving!" Jacobs responded, using his legs to push the Suburban's heavy door open. He exited the vehicle, then sprinted to his right and took a knee behind the trunk of a beat-up sedan.

Carter slid across the front seat and out Jacobs' door. He closed it behind him to maintain the integrity of the armor, then turned the opposite direction and made his way to the rear of the SUV.

Jacobs searched the area, looking around for a car big enough to hold the four men. Spotting one that might fit the bill, he crawled to it on his hands and knees. The door was left open, probably an afterthought as the driver ran for safety, so Jacobs stayed low and slithered onto the driver's seat. He ducked his head under the steering wheel, hoping to see a set of keys dangling from the ignition, and cursed.

"No luck on this one," he said over the radio. "Driver must have taken the keys with him out of habit."

Jacobs glanced out the door, first to the left and then the right, but didn't see anything promising. Using the sedan to conceal his presence, he stole a quick peek over the doorframe, hoping to spot a gleaming chariot ready to whisk him away from this craziness. What he saw made his heart sink.

Two men carrying Russian-made PKM machine guns walked out from behind the truck stop. They advanced to within twenty-five meters of the corralled embassy vehicle, then stopped, as if they were waiting for someone to issue further orders.

Jacobs knew he was outgunned and that it would be suicidal to take on the heavy weaponry with nothing more than his pistol. But if he could draw the gunners' attention, get them focused on him, Carter might have a chance to get the drop on the pair. *You better nail at least one of those assholes, Tim.*

Jacobs backed out of the car and tried to close the door as quietly as he could, but years of rust and neglect caused a metal-on-metal screech that instantly drew the men's attention.

Seeing the man on the right turn toward his partner, Carter screamed, "Marcus, get down!" as he raised his pistol, acquired a good sight picture, and fired two rounds.

Machine-gunner number one dropped to his knees and released his grip on the weapon. The big gun swung like a pendulum from the strap around his neck as he groped at the holes in his chest. Carter lined up his sights and drilled two more rounds into the side of the man's head.

Machine-gunner number two spun toward the sound of gunfire and let off a long burst. Carter dove behind the Suburban, scraping his knees and elbows, as the deadly barrage pelted the truck's rear quarter panel.

Ambassador Lewis and Gene Moynihan instinctively ducked below the windows as the heavy rounds thumped against the side of their armored sanctuary.

Jacobs peered over the hood of the sedan and squeezed off three quick shots. The rounds went high and to the right, passing over the man's left shoulder.

Surprised by Jacobs' volley, the man turned and fired a sustained burst into the old sedan. Roaring like an angry jackhammer, the machine gun spewed a stream of death at the American agent. Empty shell casings littered the ground, tinkling like a glass chandelier as the bullets passed effortlessly through the car's sheet metal bodywork.

The first two bullets hit the strike plate in Jacobs' body armor. Their impact knocked him onto his rear end and he fell back against the passenger door of a white Volkswagen Beetle. He felt as if he'd been smashed in the chest with a sledgehammer and was trying to catch his breath when a third and fourth round entered his stomach just below his vest. Feeling gut-punched, Jacobs looked down at his blood-covered lap as a fifth and final round went through the top of his head.

Ambassador Lewis and Gene Moynihan watched the destruction of Marcus Jacobs in abject horror from the back seat of the armored Suburban.

Seeing his partner die before his eyes, Carter experienced a fury he never knew existed. Moving from his position of cover, he led with his weapon, firing as he advanced on machine gunner number two. Round after round hit the man's torso, making him jerk and twitch as if he were having a seizure. The man's body collapsed in a heap as the slide on Carter's pistol locked to the rear on an empty chamber.

Muscle memory took over, and he ejected the spent magazine while retrieving a spare from the pouch on his belt. He inserted the fresh mag and thumbed the slide's release, sending it forward to chamber a round. With his weapon reloaded and ready for action, he scanned the area for additional threats. Seeing none, he sprinted back to the Suburban.

As badly as things had gone up to this point, Carter still believed deep in his heart that he could evacuate the ambassador and survive this encounter. Thinking the explosion that wrecked the follow car had been caused by a car bomb or an IED, not by a couple of guys firing RPGs from the truck stop's roof, Carter had forgotten he was operating in a three-hundred-and-sixty-degree environment. Threats weren't only to his left or right, his front or rear, but also above and below.

One of the rocketeers leaned his launch tube against the low wall surrounding the roof and reached for the AK-47 slung across his chest. He placed the rifle's iron sights in the middle of the American's back and pulled the trigger.

Carter was two steps away from the Suburban, his arm outstretched, reaching for the ambassador's door, when the rounds hit his strike plate like a freight train. The impact caused him to stumble forward and his head bounced off the bullet-resistant window with a sickening thud. Tim Carter fell to the ground and his world went dark.

CHAPTER 7

A black Mercedes S550 sedan pulled around from behind the truck stop and eased to a stop just short of the American SUV.

The front passenger door opened, and a large, muscular man stepped out of the car. He held a compact AK-74 assault rifle in his right hand. Built like an Olympic weightlifter, Yousef Mehrdad topped the scales somewhere in the neighborhood of two hundred and fifty pounds. His black hair was cut short and a dark, perpetual five-o'clock shadow covered the lower half of his face. He wore desert brown combat boots, khaki tactical pants, and a loose-fitting linen shirt that concealed a Makarov pistol and two spare magazines.

The shooting had stopped for the time being and the situation seemed to be under control. A sense of uneasy calm hung in the air, mixing with the smell of acrid smoke and burnt gunpowder.

Satisfied the scene was secure, Mehrdad moved to the rear of the Mercedes and opened the door.

A man wearing a tailored black Armani suit emerged from the back seat of the luxury sedan. Polarized Persol sunglasses shielded his eyes from the sun's blinding glare as he surveyed the carnage.

He was proud of his men's performance. They had inflicted a significant amount of damage on the diplomatic convoy and innocent motorists alike. But he wasn't worried about the civilian casualties. His reward for the weeks of painstaking planning and the tremendous amount of violence unleashed today was the man inside the disabled SUV – the American ambassador.

Walking past twisted chunks of metal, the man stepped over the dead and dying as if he didn't have a care in the world. With his designer suit, coiffed black hair, and neatly trimmed beard, he looked as if he should have been window-shopping at Harrods instead of leading an assault in the heart of Iraq. A satisfied smile appeared on his face as he approached the American vehicle and positively identified the silver-haired diplomat in the back seat.

He glanced down at his Panerai watch. "How much time do we have, Yousef?"

"Twenty minutes, maybe a little more. It all depends on whether or not they were able to call for help."

Mehrdad shaded his eyes from the sun as he turned to look at the men on the roof. "Keep an eye on the approach from the southeast. If a response force is on the way, it will most likely come from the capital."

With the lookouts in position, Mehrdad retrieved a crowbar from the sedan's trunk and began to assault the back door of the Suburban. Its occupants weren't going to open it for him, so he took matters into his own hands. Pulling with his full weight and considerable strength, the big man managed to pop the damaged locking mechanism on his third attempt.

Pleased with his effort, he stood back and took a second to admire his handiwork while beads of sweat dripped from his nose and chin. In the extreme heat, the salty drops almost evaporated before they hit the sand. Using the bottom of his untucked shirt to wipe the sweat from his face, Mehrdad stepped back and held the door open to give the man in the suit a better view into the SUV's cabin.

In perfect English, with the accent of someone educated at Oxford or Cambridge, the man said, "Good afternoon, Ambassador Lewis."

Still dazed from the events of the last few minutes, Lewis asked, "Who...who are you? What do you want with us?"

Motioning to Moynihan, the man drew a black pistol from the small of his back and said, "With him? Nothing at all."

"Wait!" Moynihan screamed as he retreated farther into the confined space in a futile attempt to escape his fate. "You don't have to do this!"

Disgusted by the overt display of cowardice, the man took aim and the pistol barked once. The bullet entered Moynihan's head just below his right eye, and his skull exploded against the bullet-resistant window. His lifeless body slumped against the seat with a shocked expression of disbelief frozen on his face.

Lewis couldn't believe what was happening. First, the four men in the follow car were killed, burned to a crisp in the explosion. Then he watched as his personal protectors Jacobs and Carter were gunned down before his eyes. Now this man had just killed a member of his staff in cold blood, showing no more emotion than if he were finishing some mundane chore like taking out the trash.

In a patient and respectful tone, the well-dressed man said, "Mr. Ambassador, my name is Hamid Farzan and I am a major in the al-Quds Force of the Sepah Pasdaran. You are my prisoner."

It took a moment for the last part of the man's sentence to sink in. As it did, an incredulous look spread over Lewis's face. "Your...prisoner? You can't be serious?"

"Quite serious, Mr. Ambassador. Now, if you would be so kind, we need to move this along before your rescuers arrive."

Tim Carter let out a low moan as he began to regain consciousness. Summoning his last remaining ounces of strength, he managed to get up on his hands and knees. The world was spinning, and he shook his head back and forth, trying to clear the cobwebs. The motion only made his head hurt worse and a wave of nausea came over him.

Noticing the movement, Mehrdad closed the distance with two quick steps and put a boot into the middle of Carter's back, forcing him back down to the ground. He looked to Farzan for confirmation and received a slight nod in return.

The big man knelt next to Carter, leaning in so his mouth was close to the American's ear. "You acquitted yourself well today, agent. You managed to kill two of my men and fought hard to the very end. For that, you have earned my respect."

Yousef stood as he drew the Makarov from under his linen shirt, thumbed off the safety, and shot Carter in the back of the head.

Seeing his AIC put down like a wounded animal shook Lewis to his core. The two men had grown close, and he wondered how he was going to explain today's events to Tim's family, to the families of all the men who died today.

After what seemed like several minutes, Lewis snapped back to reality and fought to regain his composure. He climbed out of the vehicle, buttoned his suit coat, and ran his fingers through his wispy white hair. Regardless of what was going to happen next, he was still the president's personal representative to Iraq, and was damn well going to act like it.

Resigned to his fate, Lewis said, "Alright, Major Farzan. Let's get on with it."

CHAPTER 8

Joe Matthews sat alone in a dark office in the basement of the Central Intelligence Agency's Original Headquarters Building. His face was lit by the glow of the twenty-seven-inch computer monitor on the desk. The only other light in the office emanated from the flat-screen TV mounted on the wall across the room. Joe's icy blue eyes darted back and forth between the monitor and the TV. Three intelligence reports on the abduction of Ambassador Lewis vied for his attention with the ongoing news coverage of the event.

Matthews' official job title listed him as a paramilitary operations officer. As a member of the Special Activities Division, he had conducted covert missions all over the world in hostile or "non-permissive or denied" locations, as they were called in Agency terminology. Joe and his team had targeted terrorists for assassination, conducted snatch and grabs – officially known as extraordinary renditions – and performed reconnaissance and surveillance on a wide variety of targets.

But Carl Douglas, the chief of SAD and a veteran of the Cold War who had gone toe to toe with the best the KGB had to offer, thought it would be good for Joe and his team to gain a different operational perspective. So, he worked out a deal with his counterpart in protective operations that would bring two groups of the Agency's top operators together to share their knowledge, skills, and tactics.

As a result, Joe's team would split time between the Director's Protective Staff, protecting the Director and Deputy Director of the CIA, and the Protective Resource Group, which was responsible for supporting case officers and chiefs of station assigned to high-risk posts overseas.

The importance of what Douglas was trying to do wasn't lost on Joe, but to a man, his team wasn't thrilled with the assignment. Not that they had anything against their colleagues or their protective mission. Those men and women were highly trained operators and the cream of the crop when it came to personal protection.

The issue was that Joe's men preferred to be the ones doing the assaulting. To them, running around the world's most dangerous vacation spots waiting to be attacked didn't sound like a whole lot of fun.

He often thought of the quote, "We sleep soundly in our beds because rough men stand ready in the night to visit violence on those who would do us harm." The members of his team were those rough men, and they lived for the express purpose of visiting violence on the bad guys. It took a different mindset altogether to spend your waking hours doing everything possible to keep from getting hit in the first place.

In return, a team from the DPS would learn to operate in the dark world of the Directorate of Operations. The exchange would end up making both teams better as they traveled the world on their respective missions.

Joe flipped through the news channels, spending a minute or two on CNN International before flipping over to Fox News, BBC, and finally Al-Jazeera. All the talking heads were spewing the same canned commentary and pseudo-analysis of the attack, which is why he had the volume was muted. At this point the only people who actually knew what happened were the bad guys and the diplomatic security agents in the ambassador's motorcade. Everything else was just speculation.

He was scrolling through the intel reports when a tall man with a mop of sandy blond hair – looking more like a surfer than a paramilitary officer – entered the office.

"We're just about finished loading the gear. Should be ready to head out to Andrews in about fifteen minutes."

Joe's team was to be part of a larger group bound for Iraq to investigate the attack on Ambassador Lewis. "Thanks, Chris."

Chris Ryan was a former Navy SEAL and Joe's best friend. They had joined the Agency around the same time and forged a bond through the mutual suffering inflicted on trainees at the CIA's facility commonly known as the Farm. In fact, the two men worked so well together that their instructors recommended they be assigned to the same unit upon graduation. Carl Douglas heeded their advice and the guys had been teamed up ever since.

Chris was a great operator, but his real passion shone through when he got into a vehicle. It didn't matter if it had two, four, six, or eighteen wheels. The guy could drive the hell out of anything that moved across the surface of the planet. If he hadn't decided to join the Navy after high school, Chris imagined he would have had a bright career racing on the NASCAR or Formula One circuit. It was an opinion he wasn't shy about sharing with anyone who'd listen.

Chris leaned forward and shoulder-surfed, glancing at the report displayed on the computer monitor, then turned his attention to the news coverage on the big screen TV. It was tuned to Al-Jazeera, which, in his opinion, had captured the best footage of any of the major networks. The Qatar-based network was not concerned with the West's broadcast regulations or of offending the general public's sensibilities by airing grisly images. In fact, its willingness to air such images often provided a unique view into an event no Western network could or would offer.

"Anything actionable in the reports?" he asked.

Joe continued scrolling through the pages and shook his head. "Nothing yet. The media seems to think ISIS is the prime suspect but I'm not buying it. There's no way those meatheads are capable of pulling off something like this."

"And it's been a long time since they've been seen operating that far south," Chris added.

"Yeah, they've been scattering like roaches when the light is flipped on after getting their asses kicked out of Mosul. No way they would've had time to think about, much less, put together an attack this complex."

Agreeing, Chris continued, "Well, it'll be interesting to find out who did plan this hit because they did a helluva job. You gotta give credit where it's due."

"Yeah, I'd like to sit down with him sometime and discuss it over a beer."

"Then put a bullet in his head," Chris added for good measure.

CHAPTER 9

As disastrous as the attack on the ambassador's motorcade and his subsequent disappearance had been, the situation outside Fallujah had only gotten worse once the quick reaction force arrived.

The Iraqi MI-17 helicopter orbited the truck stop in a lazy circle as the crew surveyed the area. The leader of the Special Forces team moved forward and crouched between the pilots to get a better view. Finding a spot to his liking, he pointed to an open stretch of sand across the highway from the gas pumps and asked, "How about there?"

The pilot scanned the area, considering the request. After a minute or so he agreed it would be as good a place as any. "That should work. Prepare your men to deploy."

With the landing zone confirmed, the team leader removed his headset and turned back into the cabin. He shouted in order to be heard over the roar of the engines. "Two minutes!"

In unison the men repeated the two-minute call to acknowledge the order and began performing a final check of their gear.

Assuming the attackers were long gone by now, the men hoped their detour to Fallujah would be short and sweet – just lock down the area long enough for the Americans to come in and recover their dead – then, with a little luck, make it back to base in time for dinner. The best laid plans….

The downdraft from the MI-17's rotors blasted the sand outward in a wide circle. When it touched down, the troops disembarked through the open doors on either side of the helicopter and fanned out across the landing zone. When they were clear of the rotors spinning overhead, each soldier took a knee with their rifles at the low ready and formed a secure perimeter.

Josh Gordon, the assistant regional security officer from the embassy in Baghdad, took in the bird's-eye view of the action from the open door of a UH-60 Blackhawk. The pilot stopped the helicopter's forward momentum and hovered two hundred feet above the truck stop while they waited for the other American helicopter, also a Blackhawk, to land. The diplomatic agents on the lead Blackhawk checked their weapons and unhooked their safety harnesses so they could hit the ground running.

Two men in a small van parked on the shoulder of Highway 10 a kilometer north of the truck stop watched with anticipation as the helicopters approached the deadly trap they had set for the responding force.

Their excitement continued to build as their prey edged ever closer to the kill zone. The man in the driver's seat watched the Blackhawk approach through a set of high-powered binoculars. "Patience, my friend. Wait for the American helicopter to land."

As the lead Blackhawk's wheels touched the hard-packed sand, the passenger punched a series of numbers into his mobile phone and hit the send button.

The call activated several remote detonators attached to blocks of high explosives placed in and around the gas station's fuel tanks. They had also thought to wire the two tanker trucks that had ensnared the American motorcade earlier in the day.

A wall of fire from the massive explosion swept across the sand and engulfed the four Iraqi soldiers unlucky enough to be positioned between their helicopter and the truck stop.

Pieces of metal ripped from the tanker trucks penetrated the thin skin of the Iraqi MI-17 and tore jagged holes in the internal fuel bladders that had been installed to increase its maximum range.

The jet fuel ignited on contact with the open flames and the helicopter exploded, sending pieces of the rotors spinning like giant buzz saws toward the soldiers forming the right side of the perimeter. One soldier was fortunate and died instantly. The other three were nearly cut in half by the blades but remained conscious as blood from their gaping wounds turned the sand black. The roar of the explosions drowned out the men's screams as they prayed for a quick and merciful end to the pain.

The initial explosion mixed gasoline from the fuel pumps with the thick crude oil in the tanker trucks parked nearby. Forming a poor man's napalm, the combination of fuel and oil coated everything within a hundred meters. When the fiery mixture rained down on the mortally wounded soldiers, their end was neither quick nor painless.

The blast hit the left side of the lead Blackhawk with the force of a hurricane. Disconnected from their safety harnesses in preparation for landing, the American agents and their medic were blown through the open door on the right side of the fuselage.

Opening the throttle to the stops, the pilot summoned every ounce of power the helicopter's General Electric turboshaft engines could produce in an attempt to save his doomed aircraft. As the wheels left the ground the superheated wall of air lifted the Blackhawk, causing it to bank hard to the right. Lacking the altitude for such a maneuver, the rotor's composite blades dug into the sand and sheared off at varying points, adding to the deadly debris flying through the air like a tornado in the Oklahoma countryside. The stricken bird crashed down on its right side, crushing the unconscious agents lying in the sand, then exploded.

Seeing the mushroom cloud rising from the downed Blackhawk, the pilot of Gordon's helicopter banked hard to the left, attempting to avoid the fireball heading his way.

The maneuver was so violent that Gordon lost his balance and began sliding feet-first toward the open door. His rifle banged across the metal deck as he reached for anything to slow his momentum. Still buckled in their seats, the other men onboard tried but failed to grab him and stop his slide toward the abyss.

Gordon was terrified by the prospect of falling to his death but simultaneously pissed off at the thought of dying under such idiotic circumstances. As the gaping hole of the open door grew larger, he closed his eyes and waited for the weightless sensation of the free-fall. His feet had cleared the threshold on his way out the door when he felt a sudden jerk as the safety line attached to the carabiner on his belt went taut. In stunned disbelief, Gordon stared down at the blur of the desert racing below as his boots dangled out the door.

CHAPTER 10

A white, unmarked Boeing Business Jet belonging to the CIA's Directorate of Operations landed at Joint Base Andrews three hours after the decision to deploy the Incident Response Team to Iraq was made. Thanks to its extended range capability, the BBJ-737 made the fifty-four-hundred nautical-mile trip from the suburbs of Washington, D.C. to Baghdad in eleven and a half hours.

Landing under the cover of darkness, the pilot taxied the passenger jet into a large hangar near the VIP section of Baghdad International Airport.

As Joe neared the bottom of the BBJ's stairs he was greeted by the chief of air operations and escorted across the tarmac to a waiting Bell 412. While Chris and the rest of the team unloaded their kit, Joe climbed aboard the helicopter and strapped himself in for the fifteen-minute flight to the Green Zone.

The ground crew at the embassy's helipad slid the door open, and the space was filled with the hulking frame of an enormous black man. Ron Foster, a former Marine from Waco, Texas, was the Protective Resource Group's team leader in Iraq.

"Holy shit! If I'd known it was you on this flight, I wouldn't have bothered to drag my sorry ass out of my air-conditioned office," the man deadpanned in his trademark Texas drawl.

"At your advanced age, I hear just getting out of your chair takes a lot of effort. Do you have one of those motorized recliners that raises up and dumps you out of it when you need to take a piss?" Joe asked, giving it right back to his longtime friend.

"Damn, it's good to see you," Ron said, wrapping his arms around Joe in a powerful bear hug. "How long's it been? A year, maybe two?"

"At least," Joe replied as they crossed the helipad and headed for the consulate.

They entered the main lobby and approached the Marine Security Guard station, commonly referred to as Post One in the diplomatic community. Aiming a thumb at Joe, Ron said, "He's with me, Sergeant Johnson."

"No problem, Mr. Foster."

Joe exchanged his diplomatic passport for a temporary badge, then he and Ron took the elevator up to the fourth floor. As they stepped out, both men placed their smartphones on a wooden shelf before passing through the station's vault door.

Ron introduced Joe around the office, and Joe stopped to say hello to a few familiar faces he'd worked with in the past. With the introductions and reminiscing complete, they grabbed a cup of coffee and headed back to the Sensitive Compartmented Information Facility, or SCIF.

When Ron opened the heavy door, they were greeted with a hiss of escaping air. Scott Garrett, the chief of station, and Assistant Regional Security Officer Josh Gordon sat around a generic, government-issue conference table with their own steaming mugs of coffee.

Joe entered and shook hands with Garrett. "Hey, Scott. It's good to see you again."

"You, too. I just wish it was under different circumstances."

Joe had known Garrett for several years but was meeting Gordon for the first time. He extended his hand, "Nice to meet you. I'm Joe Matthews."

"Josh Gordon," the man from State replied. "Scott, here, has told me a lot about you."

Joe gave Garrett a sideways glance before turning back to Gordon. "I reserve the right to dispute anything he said while not in my presence."

The four men laughed as they waited for a green light mounted on the wall to illuminate, indicating the room was sealed and impervious to electronic penetration.

With a nod from Garrett, Josh Gordon began the briefing with a little background information on the ambassador's movement to Fallujah and then fast-forwarded to the point they had received Tim Carter's distress call.

Impressed by Gordon's recollection of the smallest details, Joe listened intently to every word and jotted down notes as the man spoke.

Gordon described the scene as they had approached the attack site from the air. His account of the events painted a vivid picture of the explosions and raging inferno that had engulfed the two helicopters and their occupants. He paused occasionally to gather his thoughts and take a sip of coffee as the horrific images flashed through his mind.

Almost an hour had passed before Gordon fell silent – confident he'd shared everything – except for the part where he had almost fallen out of the helicopter.

Joe asked a few follow-up questions, then checked his notes one last time to make sure he had everything he needed. Confident he did, Joe thanked Gordon for recounting the events and offered his condolences for the men he had lost in the attack.

With his role in the briefing over, Foster escorted Gordon out to the elevators.

Back inside the SCIF, Garrett asked, "Well, what do you think?"

Joe took a moment to think over his answer. "This was an elaborate operation that had to have taken months to plan. And that secondary attack on the responders," he continued, "it's not something you throw together a few minutes before bugging out. That was some next level shit."

"Yeah, I agree. That means we can probably eliminate any of the local militias as suspects. They just don't have the ability to pull off something this complex."

"How about ISIS?" Joe asked. "Have you seen anything since you've been in country to suggest they were this capable – where they've displayed this level of expertise?"

"No, I don't think it was them for a couple of reasons." Garrett said. "First, it's been a while since Islamic State fighters have been this close to the capital. They're busy up north getting killed by the Iraqi army and our airstrikes."

"And the second?" Joe asked.

"They do have a few professional military commanders who've joined the cause, so I guess it's not out of the realm of possibility that one of them could have planned an attack this sophisticated. But the guys who conducted this operation showed real skill and that's not something we've seen from ISIS as a whole. Their rank and file are average guys who drank the jihadist Kool-Aid and went over to the dark side. Most of their training was on the job, raping and pillaging their way through local villages and towns. Islamic State fighters with actual military training and expertise are few and far between. I really doubt Baghdadi could muster enough guys good enough to carry out this attack."

Joe nodded in agreement as a thought entered his mind. *Would a country actually sanction an attack on someone as high ranking as an ambassador? Intel services routinely conduct surveillance on diplomats and maybe even try to catch one in a compromising position on occasion. But assassination? That would be a game changer on an international scale.* "Can't argue with your logic, Scott. So, if it wasn't them, then what about another country? Could it have been state sponsored?"

"There's only one country in the region brazen enough to try something like this. I'll give you three guesses as to who that might be."

"Iran."

"Got it on the first try. Apparently, there's some brains behind those rugged good looks of yours. But like ISIS, we really haven't seen the Quds Force execute an external mission with this level of sophistication or planning either. They're pretty damn good at operating when they have the home field advantage, but their track record outside their borders hasn't been very impressive."

"It does seem like they've shot themselves in the foot a few times in recent memory."

"And in a very public manner," Garrett added. "They've cocked up attempts on Israeli diplomats in Georgia and India. Not to mention the bus attack in Bulgaria."

"But what if it was the Quds Force? What if they have totally revamped their training program? Say, with the help of an ally?"

Garrett thought about that last statement for a moment. "Well, it wouldn't be anyone in the Middle East, that's for sure. None of Iran's neighbors wants anything to do with them. There's no way one of them would provide any support that would make the Islamic Republic even more of a menace to the region than it already is. And the Sunni Arab states wouldn't give the Shias in Tehran the time of day on sheer principle. Their hatred for each other goes back centuries."

Garrett fiddled with his mug for a minute, then downed the remaining coffee in one long pull. He'd lost track of time and the once-steaming hot coffee was cold and stale. He grimaced as he choked it down.

The green light above the door dimmed as Ron Foster re-entered the SCIF. He closed the door and all three waited for the light to go green before continuing the conversation.

Joe filled him in on their idea that Iran had been working with a foreign benefactor to upgrade their training and operational capabilities.

Foster thought about that statement as he took a seat at the conference table. "If I were chasing down that thread, I'd have to look at the Russians."

"That would make sense," Joe agreed. "Tehran and Moscow have been best buds since they teamed up in Syria to support Assad."

"Yeah, and a mission training a foreign service would be right up the SVR's alley. Not so different than what our SF teams do with indigenous forces." Ron concurred.

Feeling they had come to a consensus, Garrett said, "I'll send a cable to Langley and run this up the flagpole. I want to put the bug in their ear and get them thinking about the Russian and Iranian angle."

Turning to Joe, he said, "You'd better get on up to Fallujah and check out the scene for yourself."

"Will do. Chris and the guys should have the helo loaded and ready to go. I'll call once we have something to report."

Back down in the lobby, Joe swapped the temporary badge for his passport at Post One, then made his way back to the helipad and the waiting Bell 412.

CHAPTER 11

Joe surveyed the scene from the roof of the truck stop. Below him, the roadway was littered with broken and burned-out vehicles. It looked like a kid had dumped a bunch of Matchbox cars on the driveway, smashed them with a hammer, then set them on fire.

Judging by the dusty boot prints left behind, Joe guessed he was in the spot where the RPGs were fired to initiate the assault on the motorcade. Scenes of the attack unfolding on the street below ran through his head as he visualized each phase of the operation. Lost in the moment, he could almost feel the heat of the rocket's exhaust and hear the ear-splitting booms as their warheads decimated the follow car.

After seeing the destruction with his own eyes, Joe knew instantly that they were dealing with an extremely dangerous adversary. This attack was professional. There was no way a local militia or roving band of ISIS gun-toters had the skill, much less the imagination, to carry out an attack of this complexity.

The sound of rusty hinges groaning as the roof's access door opened drew Joe's attention away from the imaginary battle running through his mind. Looking over his shoulder, he saw Chris Ryan emerge from the darkness of the stairwell.

Chris adjusted the assault rifle hanging from its sling, then took a long pull of water from his Camelbak's drinking tube. Looking down at the wreckage, he muttered, "What a fucking mess."

"Yep," Joe replied, still deep in thought. "The news coverage didn't do it justice. It's even worse in person."

The conversation was interrupted by the familiar voice of John Roberts crackling through their earpieces. "Hey, boss, there's a woman down here that says she might have some info for us. Wanna talk to her?"

Joe said, "Absolutely. Do me a favor and bring her up here. She might be more comfortable talking to us without all the bystanders giving her the evil eye."

Even though it had been nearly seventy-two hours since the attack, there were still dozens of people at the site. Iraqi security forces had set a perimeter but seemed to have more important things to do than enforce it. The news cycle had not moved on yet, so a few crews were still around filing follow-up stories.

And for the local population, the truck stop had become a must-see, like some sort of macabre tourist attraction. People, young and old alike, milled around taking photos and videos with their cellphones. Joe thought he actually saw a couple of people take selfies with the destruction in the background. Those shots would be up on Twitter or Facebook within minutes if they weren't already. The thought disgusted him.

A minute later John and the woman appeared in the doorway. He stepped forward, leading the way to Joe and Chris, but the woman refused to cross the threshold. Instead, she remained in the shadows, hidden from onlookers and the Iraqi security forces on the ground below.

She wore a hijab decorated with colorful flowers and appeared to be in her mid-fifties. Wisps of salt-and-pepper bangs spilled out of the traditional head covering and blew across her forehead. Dust and dried blood covered the front of her dress that might have been a nice shade of yellow before the attack. Both hands were a dark brownish color, caked with that same combination of dust and blood. Exhaustion and grief deepened the lines that creased her face.

Joe approached her and said, "As-Salaam-Alaikum." *Peace be upon you.*

In a soft voice, the woman replied, "Wa-Alaikum-Salaam. You are Americans?"

"We are," Joe replied, surprising the woman with his command of her language. Noticing the dried blood on her hands and dress he asked, "Are you injured? Do you need medical attention?"

She looked down, seeming to notice her appearance for the first time. "The blood is not mine. It belongs to my brother-in-law. He was killed in the attack."

Chris walked over to the woman and sucked on the

mouthpiece of his drinking tube to get a good flow going and splashed the cool water across her hands. It dissolved the dried blood and grit, forming a red puddle at her feet that instantly began evaporating in the severe heat.

She thanked him, then searched her dress for a clean spot to dry her hands.

When she was finished, Joe pulled a bottle of water from his pack and handed it to her. "I'm Joe and this is Chris. We're from the embassy in Baghdad. It's been quite a while since the attack. Why are you still here? Do you live nearby?"

"My name is Siyana Ashwaq and I am from Baqubah." she replied. "I was traveling to Ramadi with my sister and her husband Mohammed. We had stopped for fuel and a snack when the attack occurred." She paused to take a sip of the water before continuing. "We're still here because the investigators haven't released Mohammed's body and my sister refuses to leave without him."

"We're very sorry for your loss." An uncomfortable silence fell over the three of them before Joe asked, "What can we do for you, Mrs. Ashwaq?"

She looked at both men for a long time, as if she were deciding if they could be trusted with the information she possessed. But who would she give it to, if not these kind Americans? Certainly not the Iraqi police or military.

Finally, she said, "Gentlemen, it is I that may be able to help you."

CHAPTER 12

Mrs. Ashwaq went on to explain that she'd been traveling with her sister to visit her nephew in Ramadi. Mira's husband Mohammed had pulled into the truck stop for fuel and the two sisters had gone inside to use the restroom and get a soft drink while he topped off the tank. They were enjoying the break in the journey, and the truck stop's air conditioning, when the attack began.

The explosion shook the building like an earthquake. The overhead fluorescent lights flickered briefly before the damaged electrical lines gave out and darkness enveloped the interior of the building.

The shockwave shattered the truck stop's large plate glass windows, sending millions of tiny glass razors hurling through the building. Shards of metal ripped from the bodywork of several vehicles combined with the glass to shred everyone in its path. Except for the two sisters, who were in the restroom and protected from the direct line of the blast, everyone inside the building was either killed or severely wounded.

Exiting the toilet, Siyana and her sister inched their way to the corner of the hallway, leaned back against the wall, and took deep breaths to try and steady their nerves. Looking at one another for reassurance, the women braced themselves before peeking around the corner. Their minds ran wild imagining the horror that must be awaiting them.

Bright sunlight poured in through the empty spaces where the windows had been, making it difficult to see until their eyes made the adjustment.

Mira stumbled when her foot brushed up against the lifeless body of a woman who appeared to be roughly their age, but Siyana's grip kept her from falling. They stepped carefully around the bodies of two other men were also lying in the hallway. From the severity of their injuries, it was obvious they were dead. The sisters continued moving forward and entered the main area of the truck stop.

What they saw had the makings of nightmares. Blood and gore were everywhere, splashed across the walls as if an artist had dipped his brush in bright red paint and slung it against a canvas. Most of the bodies lay quiet and motionless in thick pools of blood, their own mixing with that of others. There were so many victims, at least twenty by Siyana's count, that their blood covered nearly every worn linoleum tile on the floor. Those still moaning and writhing in pain were beyond help and would be joining the others in death soon enough.

Desperately looking for Mira's husband, the sisters searched the faces of the stricken. They breathed a short sigh of relief when he wasn't among them until they realized Mohammed had probably still been pumping gas when the explosion occurred.

Mira started for the door as a burst of gunfire erupted outside. Siyana grabbed her by the shoulders and dragged her away from the door. Retreating back into the relative safety of the truck stop, they hid behind a counter.

Heavy automatic fire answered by the occasional pops of a handgun filled the air outside. They heard a single gunshot, then everything went eerily quiet.

Mira got to her knees and stole a quick look over the top of the counter. Thinking the attack was over she stood and bolted for the door. With three long strides, she was gone. Without thinking, Siyana got to her feet and followed her sister into the unknown.

Oblivious of what was going on around her, Mira ran through the wreckage to the spot where she'd last seen Mohammed. Frantically, she called out his name, becoming more and more hysterical as each second passed without an answer.

Continuing the search, she darted between cars like a running back. Mira let out a shriek when she caught a glimpse of Mohammed's broken body wedged between two sedans thrown together by the explosion.

Panic-stricken, she ran to her mortally wounded husband. His neck had been sliced open by a piece of shrapnel and with each beat of Mohammed's heart, a steady stream of blood spurted from the severed carotid artery.

Siyana tore a strip of fabric from the bottom of her dress and pressed the makeshift bandage onto the wound, but the effort was too little, too late. The injury was too severe.

Mira let out a wail of sorrow as the last of Mohammed's blood spilled onto the ground and his body went limp. Her shoulders heaved as the grief left her body in great sobs.

"I got up and backed away," Siyana said. "They deserved a moment together to say goodbye. As I turned to leave I came face to face with a large man. He was pointing a gun at me. I believe he was about to pull the trigger when a smaller man, who seemed to be in charge, gently put a hand on his arm and guided the gun toward the ground. He told the big man he thought I had suffered enough loss for one day." She continued, "I believe the large man was going to shoot me because I might be able to identify them. But once again, the smaller man observed that many people had survived today's attack and asked the big man if he would kill us all."

A confused look spread across Chris's face. "A terrorist with a sense of decency?"

"The big man didn't argue and returned to what he was doing. The man in charge gave me a slight, almost apologetic nod, then turned and walked away. The last time I saw them, the big man was pushing an older white-haired foreigner into their car."

"The ambassador survived the attack," Joe said in amazement, starting to feel a glimmer of hope that the odds were about to break their way. "Do you remember what type of car it was?"

"A black Mercedes. It left with another vehicle, a white SUV, like the UN and aid organizations use," she added.

Great, Joe thought, that glimmer starting to fade a little. *There are only about ten thousand black Mercedes in Iraq. And white Toyota Land Cruisers are a dime a dozen around here. Talk about a couple of needles in a haystack.*

"If it helps, the two men weren't Iraqi," she continued.

"What makes you say that?" Joe asked.

"Because they spoke Farsi."

"Iranians," Joe muttered under his breath. Siyana Ashwaq had just confirmed that this was not a run of the mill terrorist attack. It was state sponsored after all.

"But what the hell do the Iranians want with a U.S. ambassador?" Chris asked.

"I don't know. But if he's still alive, it's our job to get him back."

Joe reached into a cargo pocket for his phone. When the call connected he briefed Scott Garrett on what they had learned. "Looks like it was the Iranians after all."

"How confident are you in her story?" Garrett asked.

"She came forward on her own and doesn't have any apparent reason to lie to us. Plus, she lost a family member in the attack. I think she wanted to share what she knew, just not with the Iraqi authorities."

"Then you guys ride up like knights in shining armor and she has this overwhelming desire to tell you everything she knows?"

Joe grinned. "Pretty much. Chris says I have a trustworthy face. Maybe he's right. Regardless, it's clear we were her best option and she probably figured we'd damn sure take some action if her intel pans out."

Garrett let out a sigh, "Alright. I'll brief headquarters when we're done. The president's going to shit a brick when the director drops this bit of intelligence on his desk. The good news is that I have a Reaper in the area. It's returning from a mission, but I'll have flight ops re-task it to see if we can find the vehicles. Have your guys prepped and ready to go if we get a target."

"Just get us something actionable and we'll take care of the rest." As Joe disconnected the call, a wicked smile spread across his face.

"Uh-oh. I know that look," Chris said. "What's running through that head of yours?"

CHAPTER 13

Their second break of the day, the Iraqi woman coming forward being the first, came when the Reaper flew over an abandoned cement factory, three kilometers east of Fallujah.

In its heyday, the factory had been the primary supplier of cement and building materials for Saddam Hussein's massive palaces. Its owner was from the dictator's hometown of Tikrit, and because of that tribal familiarity, was rewarded with a steady stream of business. The relationship had been extremely profitable and made the owner a very wealthy man. But like so many others in Saddam's inner circle, he packed up his family, and his money, and fled the country as the regime came to an end.

Without competent management in place to drum up new business, the factory was forced to close its doors. Machinery and buildings that had once been a hive of activity sat idle, deteriorating rapidly in the harsh desert conditions.

A packed dirt and gravel access road ran down the center of the sprawling two-acre complex. Two retention ponds, a couple of rusting corrugated metal warehouses, and a dilapidated maintenance shed surrounded by heavy machinery occupied the east side of the compound. Across the road, the west side of the compound consisted of an office building and a residential area that had housed the factory's foremen.

Imagery analysts in Baghdad and Langley had been glued to their monitors for hours watching the Reaper's live feed as it flew a standard grid search pattern over the area. They were on the verge of repositioning the UAV, thinking the attackers had moved out of the area, when something caught the lead analyst's eye.

Joe's smartphone vibrated and he saw Scott Garrett's number appear on the screen. He hit the button to answer the call and said, "Please tell me you found them?"

"A definite maybe. The Reaper found two vehicles matching the woman's description at a cement factory east of Fallujah. Infrared sensors picked up at least six heat signatures around the house but there may be more inside we couldn't see. There's no way of telling if one of them is Ambassador Lewis."

"Are we a go?" Joe asked, feeling the adrenaline start to flow through his body.

"Yep. You've got the green light. But Joe, do me a favor."

"What's that?"

"Don't kill them all. It'd be nice to have a couple to interrogate."

"We'll do our best," Joe said with a grin. "But that'll be up to them. I'll call you once we've secured the compound."

"Make your own luck," Garrett said.

***

Sitting in a climate-controlled trailer, Travis Mullin, call sign Warrior One Seven, was on his second shift at the controls. Darkness had descended over the desert landscape, but the lack of sunlight meant nothing to the unseen MQ-9 Reaper flying lazy circles high above Fallujah.

Its fuel-efficient Honeywell engine propelled the unmanned aerial vehicle effortlessly through the cool night air. The combination of the drone's customized engine and its sixty-six-foot wingspan enabled the Reaper to stay aloft for up to twenty-seven hours. Its electro/optical infrared video cameras allowed the pilots and imagery analysts to see in the dark and through other conditions the human eye could not.

Having completed its mission along the Syrian border, the Reaper was beginning its journey back to the clandestine landing strip in the Jordanian desert when the ambassador's motorcade was hit. Scott Garrett had immediately rerouted the UAV to the attack site, and the Reaper had been in the area of operations ever since.

"Spartan, this is Warrior One Seven," Mullin said, over the encrypted radio link.

Spartan was Joe's call sign from his days with 1st Group. "Warrior One Seven, go for Spartan."

"Bad news, I'm afraid." replied Mullin. "I'm running low on fuel and have to return to base."

"Is a replacement bird on station?"

"Negative. The back-up Reaper is having mechanical

problems and can't fly. I'm sorry to say you're gonna be without coverage for a while."

"Damn," Joe said, shaking his head. Murphy's Law was well known to everyone in this business – if something could go wrong, it would. The mission hadn't even kicked off yet and old Mr. Murphy was already raising his ugly head. "Thanks for the heads-up, Warrior One Seven. Do me a favor and get back up here as soon as you can."

"Roger that, Spartan. Warrior One Seven is returning to base," Mullin said, as he eased the joystick to the right. The Reaper responded immediately and began a graceful turn, heading away from Fallujah and the team of operators on the ground. A sick feeling began to develop in the pit of Mullin's stomach. He hated leaving the team without air cover and would have a tough time forgiving himself if anything happened to them, whether it was his fault or not.

CHAPTER 14

Thick cloud cover blotted out the moon as Chuck Jamison brought the MI-17 in, maneuvering the big helicopter as if it were a sports car. Coming in a mile east of the compound allowed the prevailing winds to carry the sound of the rotors away from the cement factory and any sentries who might still be awake at this ungodly hour. The helicopter's landing gear barely registered the contact as it touched down on the hard-packed sand. *Nothing to see here. Just another on-time delivery of an assault team to their designated landing zone.*

Jamison was arguably one of the most talented pilots in the Agency's stable. He could fly just about anything that left the ground and had the type ratings to prove it. He was a favorite among operators and case officers alike because of his willingness to fly through hell and back to get them out of bad situations. Stories of his runs into hot landing zones to snatch friendlies from the jaws of death were quickly becoming the stuff of legend.

The mechanics, on the other hand, had mixed emotions about his exploits. While they admired his determination to bring the guys home safely, they weren't so thrilled when he returned with their planes riddled with fresh bullet holes.

For the assault, Joe's team was being supplemented by Ron Foster and four members of the Protective Resource Group stationed in Baghdad. Joe did a quick headcount to make sure everyone was accounted for, then the ten operators moved out from the landing zone in a standard patrol formation. Given their extreme levels of fitness, and night vision goggles illuminating the landscape, the men covered the distance to the eastern wall of the compound with ease.

Each of the compound's four walls was roughly two hundred and fifty meters long and four meters high. They were constructed from thousands of cinderblocks that were most likely handmade in the same factory they surrounded.

After a brief pause to listen for sounds of activity, Joe whispered over his inter-team radio, "Randy, bring up the ladder."

Randy Esposito unfolded the lightweight aluminum ladder and held it steady against the wall.

Joe was the first one up the ladder, and when everyone was on the other side, Randy scampered up the aluminum rungs and spider dropped to the ground below without making a sound. With another headcount complete, the team stuck to the blackness of the shadows as they moved along a low wall that ran perpendicular to the one they had just scaled.

Mike McCredy, the point man and former college linebacker from Poughkeepsie, New York, navigated the team around the retention ponds and through several pieces of rusting machinery. They crossed the gravel road dividing the complex and entered the residential area.

Fifty meters from the target house, a soft but serious "Stand by, Mike." came through his earpiece. Stopping on a dime, he eased back into the safety of the shadows and took a knee, his weapon at the ready. The rest of the team did the same.

Tim Shannon was providing overwatch from a water tower six hundred meters to the east of the house. He scanned the darkness through the night vision scope on his sniper rifle, a Special Operations version of the highly accurate Knight's Armament SR-25. Shannon was one of the best snipers the SEAL's ever produced and had brought his talents to the CIA when he retired from the Navy. Whenever Joe needed someone to watch his back, Tim was always at the top of the list. As the old telephone commercial used to say, he could reach out and touch someone.

Keying his mic, Tim said, "A guy just came through an access door on the roof of the target house. No, correction, make that two. I've got two Tangos, both armed. Looks like they decided to step out for a quick smoke break."

The two men had in fact stepped onto the roof for some fresh air and a nicotine fix. The first man leaned his AK-47 against the low wall that formed a border around the flat roof and fished a crumpled pack of bootleg Marlboros from his shirt pocket. The second man's contribution to the effort was a cheap plastic lighter. He thumbed the starter wheel and the flint sparked, bathing the men's faces in the warm glow of the butane flame.

From his perch, Shannon observed, "They must not be expecting company because their light discipline is for shit. Am I clear to engage?"

The team had been briefed on the rules of engagement before boarding the helicopter. "These fuckers killed fifteen Americans and more than twice as many Iraqis in the attack on the truck stop," Joe had said. "Anyone carrying a weapon is a legitimate target. Do not hesitate to put them down. Are we clear?" Each member of the team acknowledged the order, and Joe had continued, "That being said, we don't know if the ambassador is in the house, so make sure you positively identify your targets and be selective with your fire."

Kneeling in the shadows with the rest of the assault team, Joe responded over the radio, "Whenever you're ready, Tim."

Shannon took one last calming breath as his thumb moved the selector switch from safe to semi. He placed the tip of his index finger on the trigger and pressed in a smooth relaxed motion. The suppressed rifle coughed once, sending the 7.62-millimeter round through the left side of the first man's head just above his ear. Before his body hit the ground, Shannon re-sighted on the man still holding the lighter and repeated the action. He drilled a hole through the right side of the man's head with the same deadly precision.

Having dispatched the two men, he scanned the area for additional threats. Confident there were none, he said, "Two Tangos down. You're clear to proceed."

With Tim's reassuring voice in his ear, Mike left the comfort of the shadows. The team fell in behind him and advanced on the rear of the house as quietly as ghosts moving through a graveyard.

With the possibility of Ambassador Lewis being in the building, Joe didn't plan on taking any chances. Stealth was going to be the key to this assault. The last thing he wanted was to alert the bad guys to their presence and give them a chance to execute the ambassador.

If this had been a straight-up kill mission, Joe might have decided to make a dynamic entry, going in loud from the start with breaching charges and flash-bang grenades – certainly effective, but not appropriate for this situation.

Shannon continued his overwatch as the entry team stacked up on Mike at the back door.

Ron Foster and his PRG operators took up positions around the perimeter of the house. They were responsible for covering the doors and windows in case any squirters decided they weren't up for the fight and tried to make a run for it. When his men were in place, Foster relayed, "Joe, we're in position."

Joe clicked his mic twice to acknowledge the transmission.

Mike stood motionless with his suppressed HK416 trained on the door in case some knucklehead decided to take a walk in the middle of the night. He waited for Joe to squeeze his shoulder, letting him know they were ready to enter the building.

From atop the water tower, Shannon confirmed, "No movement boss. Everything looks quiet. You're a go for entry."

Joe clicked two more times before reaching up with his left hand and gently squeezing Mike's shoulder. Keeping his weapon trained on the door, Mike reached for the knob with his left hand and turned it as gently as he could. He cringed in anticipation of the loud metallic screech that was sure to come from the years of neglect and rust that covered the hinges. Surprising everyone, the door opened without so much as a squeak.

Props to the guy who made that door, Mike thought as he entered the house and turned right. He moved along the wall making sure some jackass wasn't hiding in the corner waiting to gun down the team as they entered one by one.

Joe glided through the door on Mike's heels, turning left to dig the opposite corner. Chris, Randy, and John flowed into the house, alternating left and right as they scanned their fields of fire for threats. The team moved with the grace and precision of a deadly ballet and dominated the room in less than five seconds.

The interior of the house was dark – and that suited the guys just fine. With their night vision goggles locked in position, the Americans had a huge advantage. They could see in the dark.

Through his NVGs Joe could see the infrared lasers attached to each man's rifle sweep methodically around the room in search of targets. Finding none, each member of the team gave a barely audible "Clear."

The element of surprise was still on their side. So far, fortune was smiling on the bold tonight.

From his position on the left side of the room, Joe whispered, "Move," and the five men advanced on line, closing down the room.

Even in the dark it was obvious that the house had been abandoned for quite some time and the current occupants had not done anything to improve its condition. A couch with threadbare cushions sat along the long wall of the living room. A battered coffee table covered with overflowing ashtrays and carry-out food cartons jutted into the center of the floor, and four faded plastic lawn chairs sat in a semicircle around an old dust-covered television set.

The floor was littered with empty water bottles and old newspapers, as if they'd been put there to act as an early warning system. The debris on the floor forced each member of the assault team to carefully plot each footstep as they moved through the living room. No one wanted to be the guy who started a firefight or got the ambassador killed because he accidentally crushed an empty water bottle and woke up every terrorist in the neighborhood.

The smell of food hung in the air as they approached the kitchen. Two half-eaten plates of rice and spicy meat were on the counter and dirty dishes filled the sink.

Someone had been in the house recently. Joe just hoped they were still here.

On the other side of the kitchen, a long hallway led to the rear of the house. He figured the two doors on either end of the corridor had to be the bedrooms. With any luck, the ambassador would be secured in one and the bad guys would be snoring like lumberjacks in the other. The team would sneak in, untie Ambassador Lewis, and sneak back out without even waking up the terrorists. Easy day.

With his suppressed rifle at the ready, Joe led his team down the narrow hall in a single file. He hated hallways. They sucked, and everyone knew it. Without any cover to speak of, the team was totally exposed. If a bad guy emerged from either of the rooms, it would be up to Joe to drill him before he could get any rounds off.

As the last man in the train, Randy was responsible for covering the team's six o'clock. It was his job to make sure no one sneaked up from behind and shot them in the back.

Reaching the end of the hall, Joe and Chris stacked on the door to the left. Mike and John did the same on the right. Randy knelt and pulled security, facing back the way they'd come. When everyone was in position, Joe gave a nod and they entered the rooms.

CHAPTER 15

Faint rays of moonlight streamed through the tattered curtains covering the windows. Joe and Chris crept into the room with their NVGs on thermal mode, which made warm objects appear white and cool objects black or dark grey. The room was black except for two bright white figures lying on the floor.

The men snored quietly as they slept on some old mattresses and blankets left over from the previous tenants. The heat was stifling even though the temperature had dropped at least twenty degrees from the previous day's high, and the room reeked of body odor. Apparently, the men made use of every amenity in the house except the shower.

An AK-47 and chest rig containing eight spare magazines lay on the floor next to each man's bed. Chris noticed a couple of RPG-7 launch tubes propped against the wall in the far corner of the room and pointed them out with his laser.

The American operators slung their rifles and drew identical Glock 19 pistols as they approached the sleeping men. Tubular SureFire suppressors made the handguns look abnormally long.

Joe knelt and placed a gloved hand over one of the men's mouth to prevent him from calling out when he woke up. Total shock registered on the man's face when he saw the alien-like figure with night vision goggles protruding from his face hovering over him.

Pressing the pistol's suppressor to the man's forehead, Joe whispered in flawless Arabic, "Unless you are prepared to be martyred this instant, my friend, I'd advise you to be quiet and do exactly as I say."

The terrified young man nodded his head up and down in acknowledgement. He wasn't ready to die for his cause, at least not right now, or under these circumstances.

Chris went through the same routine with the second man, only his language was a little more colorful. He always preferred to learn the curse words in a foreign language first and he'd become quite proficient at insulting people in their native tongue.

His prisoner responded similarly to Joe's but without the same level of nervousness. Pure hatred burned in this guy's eyes. He could tell the man was prepared to die and would try to take Chris with him if presented with the opportunity. "I'll be keeping my eye on you, buddy."

The men sat cross-legged on the floor with plastic flex-ties securing their hands behind their back. Strips of duct tape were placed across their mouths and matching black hoods covered their heads. The momentary pause in the action allowed the disappointment of not finding Ambassador Lewis to settle in.

Chris whispered, "I hope John and Mike have better luck across the hall."

"Yeah, me too," Joe replied. He pressed the push-to-talk button attached to his plate carrier. "We're clear. Two Tangos secure."

Randy acknowledged Joe's call, and the three of them held tight waiting for the all clear from John and Mike. What they really hoped to hear was, "Jackpot! We have the Precious Cargo," and they could exfil and call it a night.

John and Mike had entered the room on the right side of the hallway. They were greeted with the same heat and stench of sweat their teammates had experienced across the hall.

In the military, troops learned to sleep in some inhospitable conditions because they never knew when the next opportunity might present itself. But even John had to admit this was bad. He could have handled the heat, but the smell of the unwashed men was horrible. Sure, he'd been pretty rank after a couple of weeks in the field on long-range patrols or missions behind enemy lines, but at least he'd been outdoors where a stiff breeze could carry the body odor away.

The layout of this bedroom was almost a mirror image of the one across the hall. An AK-47 leaned against the wall and a PKM machine gun resting on its bipod confirmed the bad guys' presence. Two beds, rummaged from long discarded mattresses and blankets, were arranged on the floor. But even with all the similarities, there was one glaring difference. One of the beds was empty.

John went to work securing the man while Mike searched the room for any nook or cranny where the other guy could be hiding. *But that was ridiculous.* he thought. *There was no way these guys had any idea we were even in the house, much less in the room with them.*

"Shit!" Mike whispered. "Where's the other guy?"

"Hell if I know. Think he might've been one of the dudes Tim smoked on the roof?"

"Maybe. Doesn't feel right though." Over the team net Mike said, "Heads-up, everyone. We might be one guy short in here. Keep an eye out for a squirter."

Joe and Randy acknowledged the call and Ron replied with a quiet, "Roger."

With the flex-ties and duct tape securely in place, John pulled a black bag from his cargo pocket and slipped it over his captive's head. "He's ready to move," John said, as he helped the man to his feet.

As they headed to the door, neither man noticed the blanket hanging vertically on the room's back wall. The green hue of their goggles made it tough to distinguish between the wall and the fabric.

Mike was leading the way to the door when they heard a toilet flush. "What the…?"

Both men turned toward the sound as the blanket was pulled to one side and an expanding sliver of light revealed a small bathroom. Mike flipped his NVGs up to keep from being blinded by the abundance of light amplified by his goggles. John's left hand was directing the man he'd secured and his right remained on the pistol grip of his rifle. Unable to turn away in time, he was blinded before the NVGs automatic shut-off kicked in.

"Shit! I'm blind!" John said, kneeling to make himself a smaller target as a man wearing a sweat-stained undershirt and baggy boxer shorts stepped into the room.

Having just answered the call of nature, the man was shuffling back to bed when he noticed the dark figures in the room. Thinking it was a bad dream, he closed his eyes and rubbed them with his knuckles. But when he reopened them the odd-looking men were still there, and they had weapons. The sight of armed strangers in his bedroom jolted the man instantly awake.

"Intruders!" the man screamed as he lunged for the assault rifle. His alarm went unanswered because everyone capable of responding was already bound and gagged – or in the case of the two men on the roof – dead.

Mike stepped in front of his blinded partner to shield him from the threat. In one fluid motion, he raised his weapon and pressed the trigger four times in rapid succession. As the lifeless body slid to the floor, Mike pumped two more rounds into the man's forehead for good measure. He checked the bathroom to make sure they weren't in for any more surprises, then pressed the transmit button. "Clear."

Joe waited a beat, hoping to hear Mike follow up with the Precious Cargo call. When it didn't come, he responded, "Roger. Any sign of the ambassador?"

"Negative. Just two Tangos. One down. One secured."

"Copy that." Joe grabbed his prisoner and led him to the door as Chris and his captive fell in behind them. Joe paused at the door and said, "Coming out," letting Randy know they were about to enter the hallway. The frustration in Joe's voice was evident to anyone within earshot of the transmission.

Randy replied, "Come out," signaling the hall was clear.

Joe opened the door and led the hooded and bound man back up the narrow hallway to the living room. Chris followed with his prisoner.

John and Mike repeated the procedure and entered the hallway with their own insurgent in hand.

John hesitated, and said, "Thanks for what you did in there."

Mike slapped his friend on the back and said, "Don't worry about it, brother."

CHAPTER 16

Sunlight peeked over the horizon, signaling the end of a long night, and Joe welcomed the warmth of the sun on his face as it ushered in the new day.

As he stood in the front yard discussing the events of the last few hours with Ron Foster, their feelings about the raid were mixed. Garrett would be happy to have three prisoners to interrogate, and the assault team hadn't suffered any casualties in the operation. Those were two wins for sure. But the fact that they hadn't found the Iranians or the ambassador made the mission feel like a failure to everyone involved.

The familiar sound of rotor blades chopping the air announced the arrival of one of the Agency's MI-17s as it approached the compound – a member of the flight crew was visible through an open window keeping an eye out for threats and obstacles as they neared the ground. A cloud of sand blossomed from the helicopter's rotor wash as it touched down just inside the cement factory's western wall. Anyone not wearing a pair of Oakleys was forced to turn away and shield his eyes. Anticipating a quick turnaround, the pilots kept the rotors spinning.

Two forensics specialists and a technical exploitation expert up from Baghdad hopped off and passed Foster's PRG team as they climbed aboard for the short ride back to the Green Zone.

"Thanks for your help last night, Ron," Joe said.

"Anytime. I'm just sorry we didn't finish the job. You sure you don't want us to hang around until you wrap up here?"

Joe nodded toward the house. "Better not. I'm about to start interrogating the three stooges in there. You and your guys won't have to answer any tough questions from D.C. if you're back in Baghdad getting a hot meal and a shower."

They shook hands, then Foster turned and jogged over to join his men on the helicopter.

Joe looked on as it lifted off, hovered a few feet, then rotated on its axis. The pilot dipped the nose to pick up speed and headed east into the rising sun. Next stop, Baghdad.

It's going to be a long day, Joe thought, as the helicopter faded in the distance, *might as well get on with it.*

***

Three bound and hooded men sat quietly on the living room's battered couch. None of the Americans had spoken to them since they were awakened in the middle of the night by the nudge of a suppressor against their foreheads. Being alone with their thoughts allowed fear and uncertainty an opportunity to eat away at the bravado gained from the success of the attack on the motorcade.

Joe had removed the tape from their mouths in hopes of picking up on some conversation that would help him get a feel for which of the three might be most willing to talk. He had been impressed with their discipline since the hoods went on, but could tell the guy in the middle was beginning to feel the pressure. Sweat soaked through the man's dingy undershirt even though the morning was relatively cool and the heat of the day was still several hours away. Both knees bounced up and down in a rapid-fire motion due to the nervous energy and adrenalin flowing through his system.

Who were these men that came like djinns in the night? the man thought. They seemed to materialize out of thin air like the devilish mythological creatures, and it scared the hell out of him. *If Allah is at all merciful they would be military.*

When a series of abuses at Abu-Ghraib prison had been made public, the American military instituted a new set of regulations and procedures to ensure the humane treatment of prisoners and detainees. Publicly, there had been reports that the CIA had instituted similar rules, but no one thought they were true, especially when the Agency had experienced so much success with their interrogation protocols.

The man knew he would be in for a much different experience if these men were with the dreaded American intelligence agency. The mere thought sent a chill coursing through his body.

As he sat in silence, the man pictured himself being whisked away to a black site for what the Americans called enhanced interrogation. After the media reports broke the story of the CIA's extraordinary rendition program, Congressional hearings forced the closure of the prisons. In the wake of the hearings the American president had publicly denounced the CIA's methods as un-American and promised to halt the interrogations. But the man was sure the sites still existed. It was inconceivable to him that the CIA would close all their facilities. They had to have some quiet out-of-the way place to interrogate their captives.

He imagined himself wasting away in a dark cell in some foreign country, never to be seen or heard from again. His family would never know what happened to him and the thought of his parents not knowing his fate was almost too much to bear.

If he cooperated, and told the Americans what he knew, maybe they would send him to the detention center at Guantanamo Bay instead. He'd heard through the terrorist grapevine that detainees at Camp X-Ray had access to the International Red Cross. He'd be able to send word to his family through the IRC's representatives and at least they would know he was alive. But after what his team had done, he wasn't sure any amount of information could keep him from enduring a long, bleak future.

Breaking the long silence, the man to his left growled, "Sit still, you imbecile! You will say nothing to these men, do you understand? The Americans are weak. Remain silent and no harm will come to us."

The nervous man's knees bounced a little slower as he thought about what the man to his left said. He wasn't convinced these Americans were weak, especially from what he'd seen of their cold-blooded efficiency during the night. "Are you sure, Mustafa?"

"Quiet!" the man snarled. "Speak again and I will cut out your tongue!"

Before Mustafa could say another word, the hood was ripped off his head. He turned away from the bright morning sunlight streaming in through the windows and cursed at his unseen captor.

"Now, Mustafa," Joe said in Arabic, "that's no way to talk to one of your comrades."

Mustafa's eyes gradually adjusted to the light and he stared up at the American.

"So, are you the leader of this rag-tag group of assholes, or just the most senior guy still breathing?"

Mustafa's blood boiled with fury at the insult.

"C'mon, Mustafa, work with me here. It's been a long night

for both of us. We already know you guys were involved in the attack on the American motorcade in Fallujah. But from what we saw of your crew's performance last night, there's no way you pulled off that hit by yourselves. Your guys are sloppy and unprofessional but it's not their fault, Mustafa. It's because they have poor leadership. And that's a direct reflection on you."

Despite Joe's attempts to bait the terrorist, he remained silent, never once breaking eye contact.

Joe paused for a minute as he considered which direction to go with his next question. *Maybe it was time to validate what Siyana had told them about the two men speaking Farsi.*

"Well, it appears we've established you aren't capable of conducting an attack this creative or sophisticated. Why don't you tell me about the Iranians since it's obvious they were the brains behind the operation?"

Mustafa didn't say anything, but he didn't have to. The shocked look on his face told Joe the woman's assessment had been spot on.

The nervous man in the middle was stunned to hear the American ask about the Iranians. *How could he have known? If he knew about Farzan and Mehrdad, what else did he know?*

"Look," Joe said. "I can appreciate you not wanting to give up the Iranians. They can be some nasty bastards when you cross them. But you know what, Mustafa? Your loyalty to them is misguided. They don't give a damn about you or your men. If they did, they would be here with you right now. But they're not, are they? I'll bet the two of them are already back in Tehran enjoying a nice cup of tea while you're sitting on this moldy couch talking to me."

Mustafa said nothing. He just continued staring at Joe.

"Let me explain the situation as I see it, just so there's no confusion on your part. Your life, as you know it, is over. No more living the high-life fighting on behalf of the Iranians or profiting from renting your skills out to the local militias. As things stand, the best-case scenario you can hope for is to spend the rest of your days rotting away in one of our black sites. And the worst-case is, well, let's just say, it's worse."

Joe let those last words hang menacingly in the air for a moment before continuing. "But you still have an opportunity to influence the outcome of those two scenarios, Mustafa. Your level of cooperation in the next few minutes will go a long way toward determining your immediate future."

Sensing the tension building in the room, the young man's knees started bouncing up and down again.

Joe changed the subject, "Alright, you don't want to talk about the Iranians. How about we talk about something else, like, for instance, the American ambassador."

Cracking under the pressure, the nervous man in the middle of the couch pleaded, "Just tell him! He obviously knows what happened."

Even if the American did know what happened, Mustafa wasn't about to give him the satisfaction. Instead, he just stared up at Joe, looking as if he were imagining all the ways he'd like to kill him if their roles were reversed.

Joe returned the stare, coming to the realization that Mustafa wasn't going to talk, at least not without some serious pressure applied by professional interrogators. That process would take time, and time was something he didn't have a lot of at the moment.

"Last chance, my man. Where is Ambassador Lewis?"

Without warning, Mustafa reared his head back and spat a wad of phlegm at Joe. The mucus-filled projectile stuck to Joe's chest and slid down his body armor like an oversized slug. Pleased with his aim, a grin began to pull at the edges of the Iraqi's lips.

Joe used the hood to wipe the slime from his body armor. "If that's how you want to play this," he said, slipping the snot-smeared hood back over Mustafa's head. "Don't say I never gave you the opportunity to do this the easy way."

If Joe hoped to get anything out of the other two men on the couch it was time to make an example out of Mustafa. He drew his pistol, unscrewed the suppressor, and stowed it in a pouch on his vest.

Joe grabbed Mustafa by the arm and helped him to his feet. "Let's go, my friend. If you're not going to talk, you're of no use to me."

As they turned to leave, Mike McCredy's muscular frame filled the doorway. "Hey, boss. Can you step out for a minute? It's important."

The timing of the interruption annoyed Joe until he noticed the distraught look on his buddy's face. He sat Mustafa back down on the couch, holstered his pistol, and followed Mike outside. "You okay? What's going on?"

Mike led his team leader across the grounds to a dilapidated warehouse. He pulled a corrugated metal door open and stepped aside. "We were clearing some of the outbuildings when we came across this."

It took Joe's eyes a few seconds to adjust to the darkness of the interior of the warehouse. But the smell that greeted his nostrils and the buzzing of the flies filled him with a sense of dread. A knot formed in his stomach as he entered the house of horrors.

A lifeless figure was strapped to a chair in the center of the warehouse. Even before he saw the tortured face, Joe knew in his bones that the dead man was Ambassador Jonathan Lewis. He slowly circled the scene, forcing himself to take in every detail, no matter how gruesome. Those details were necessary for the investigation's report, but they would also serve as motivation to track the two Iranians to the ends of the earth and make them pay for their actions.

When he had seen enough of the sights that would haunt his dreams for years to come, Joe said, "Mike, do me a favor and get the forensics guys in here."

Rage flowed through Joe's body as he returned to the house and his three prisoners. Any good will or thoughts of concern he might have had for them earlier in the day were gone. After he'd seen what had been done to Ambassador Lewis, these guys deserved whatever the interrogators had in store for them.

CHAPTER 17

Everyone stood when Lawrence Sloan, the director of the Central Intelligence Agency, strode into the conference room deep within the heart of the Counterterrorism Center. Located in the basement of the CIA's New Headquarters building, the CTC was a multidisciplinary unit that cut across the Agency's traditional regional boundaries.

In 1996 a unit named Alec Station was created within the CTC to track Osama bin Laden, disrupt al-Qaeda's finances and operations, and warn policymakers of impending attacks by his organization. It was from here that the nation's war on terror was planned and directed after the devastating attacks of September 11, 2001. CTC officers led the way into Afghanistan, developed relationships with the Northern Alliance, and fought alongside Special Forces soldiers to rout the Taliban and al-Qaeda.

Over the next eleven years those same operatives continued the search for the attack's mastermind. Through their tireless dedication to duty, the men and women of the Counterterrorism Center were ultimately responsible for providing the intelligence that allowed the U.S. Navy's SEAL Team Six to assault a compound in Abbottabad, Pakistan, and put a few bullets in Osama bin Laden's head. As the CIA moved into the twenty-first century, the CTC was the sharp tip of the spear when it came to capturing, interrogating, or killing terrorists.

Harold Lee, the CTC's chief, Carl Douglas, the chief of the special activities division, and their boss, Katherine Clark, the deputy director of operations, were all in the conference room. A high-definition image of Joe Matthews and Scott Garrett occupied the center of three monitors mounted on the wall. They were joining the meeting by videoconference from the station in Baghdad. The monitor to their left was partitioned, displaying drone footage of the attack site and the abandoned cement factory. Still photos of what was left of the ambassador's motorcade were on the monitor to their right.

"Good afternoon," Director Sloan said as he took a seat at the head of the long oak conference table. Looking to the CTC's chief, he asked, "Harold, what do we know?"

"Well, sir," Lee began, "as you're aware from the initial reports, Ambassador Lewis had just concluded meetings with local government officials in Fallujah and was returning to Baghdad when his motorcade was attacked. The ambassador was abducted, but Gene Moynihan, the embassy's press officer, and all six members of the protective detail were killed in the assault. It only got worse from there with the secondary attack on the quick reaction force."

Director Sloan asked, "Has anyone claimed responsibility for the attack?"

"One or two fringe groups have posted some ramblings online but no one we're taking seriously at this point. In fact, we believe the postings might be a ploy designed to get us looking in the wrong place."

"What led you to that conclusion?"

"Our working theory was initially based on a tip from a local Iraqi woman who was present at the time of the ambush. Her description of the men leading the attack and their vehicles was instrumental in helping us identify a location we believed the attackers were using as a safe house." Motioning to the monitor, Lee said, "I believe you know Joe Matthews."

The director's protective detail was pretty small compared to the number of agents deployed by the Secret Service or the State Department's Diplomatic Security Service. This gave Sloan and his senior staff more direct contact with the agents and an opportunity to get to know them personally. He liked and respected Joe and his men.

Lee continued, "Joe was in Iraq with the response team investigating the attack when the imagery analysts reviewing a Reaper's feed spotted the suspected vehicles at an abandoned cement factory. It was his team that assaulted the safe house. Three terrorists were killed and another three were captured during the operation."

"Nice work," Sloan said, with a nod of approval.

"I'd like to have him take over the briefing since he

conducted the initial field interrogation of the captives."

Joe cleared his throat, then began. "While we were able to confirm that the guys we encountered at the safe house were involved in the attack, it was obvious they didn't have the skills necessary to pull off the operation by themselves. Based on the Iraqi woman's eyewitness account, which was corroborated by my conversation with the attackers, we've determined they had help, and that help came from Iran."

"Sepah Pasdaran?"

"Yes, sir, al-Quds Force specifically."

The director continued with his train of thought, almost as if he was thinking out loud. "The IRGC takes its orders directly from the Ayatollah. That would mean this operation was sanctioned at the highest levels."

Joe continued, "It turns out that six of the men had been part of an IRGC Special Group that carried out attacks against U.S. and Coalition forces after the invasion. This particular group had been dormant for several years and only went operational when they received orders from an old but valid activation code. An al-Quds Force major by the name of Hamid Farzan showed up to run the mission with his second in command, Yousef Mehrdad."

"What do we know about this Major Farzan?" Sloan asked.

"Not much," Katherine Clark, the deputy director for operations, interjected. "Either he's new to their organization or General al-Massoud has done a good job keeping the guy under wraps." General Amjad al-Massoud was the commanding officer of the al-Quds Force.

"Sir, if the attack on Ambassador Lewis is any indication, Tehran has significantly upped their game. This hit was far more sophisticated and well-executed than anything we've seen out of the Quds Force in recent memory. If the Iranians have developed the ability to operate at this level, they'll be a serious problem for anyone unlucky enough to land on their target list."

Sloan sat deep in thought, unhappy with this new development. "So, we don't think these are the same guys who screwed up the attacks on Israeli diplomats in New Delhi and Tbilisi, or that bizarre plot the Bureau disrupted here in D.C. a few years back?"

He was referring to an al-Quds plan to assassinate the Saudi ambassador while he was dining at the Palm Restaurant near DuPont

Circle. An Iranian-American had attempted to set up a deal with a man he thought was a member of Los Zetas, one of the most feared drug cartels in Mexico. The Iranian wanted to hire the cartel to kill the Saudi ambassador, then blow up the Israeli Embassy in Washington. When that mission had been completed, they were to bomb the Saudi and Israeli embassies in Buenos Aires. Unfortunately for the al-Quds officer, the man he was dealing with was an informant for the DEA.

It was Carl Douglas, the chief of the special activities division, who answered this time. "No sir. We don't believe these men came from the same unit as those other attacks you mentioned."

"Why not?" Sloan asked, "other than the fact that this attack was successful."

"Except for activating a recycled Special Group, Farzan's team used tactics we haven't seen from the al-Quds in the past."

The disembodied head of Scott Garrett spoke from half a world away. "We also have a pretty good grasp of the usual players al-Massoud uses for this sort of assignment, sir. As Katherine said, this is the first we've heard of Major Farzan. This unit is something new, and apparently, very deadly. With a success like this notched in his belt, I'm afraid the Ayatollah will be emboldened to begin using it regularly."

Director Sloan nodded his agreement and asked, "What else do we have on the attack?"

Joe took a quick sip from a bottle of water, "After the hit, Ambassador Lewis was taken to an abandoned cement factory east of Fallujah. From what we found, it appears Farzan and Mehrdad used one of the empty warehouses to subject the ambassador to a brutal interrogation."

"How bad was it?" Sloan asked, wanting to know the full extent of the horror Jonathan Lewis experienced.

"As bad as I've ever seen, sir. When we found the ambassador's body, it was strapped to a chair. His feet were submerged in a bucket of water and electrodes wired to a car battery were attached to his chest. Jagged holes in his shoulders, elbows, and knees indicate he'd been tortured with a power drill, among other things. A workbench next to the chair was littered with bloodied tools and other instruments that looked as if they were used to put him through a living hell. He was finally put of out his misery with a single bullet to the head."

Sloan rose from his chair, deep in thought as he absorbed every detail of Joe's description, and walked over to a table that had been set up with a coffee service. He poured himself a cup and stirred in a couple of artificial sweeteners and some creamer. He stared into the steaming mug for a few seconds before taking a long sip. "Do we know what the Iranians wanted with Lewis?"

"No, sir," Joe replied. "The men we captured weren't allowed in the warehouse during the interrogation. They were outside pulling perimeter security. But it's a pretty good bet the ambassador gave up whatever information the Iranians were after."

Returning to his seat, Sloan directed his next question to Garrett. "What do you think, Scott?"

"I'm in agreement with Joe's assessment, sir. We know from conducting our own interrogations that everyone breaks at some point, it's just a matter of when. Plus, it would have been pointless for Farzan to kill Ambassador Lewis before he got the information he was looking for."

"Do we have any idea where Farzan and Mehrdad are now?"

"According to the captives, the Iranians departed immediately after they killed the ambassador. Farzan didn't share their exfiltration plan with the men but my guess is they made a run due east for Iran."

"They might have returned to the al-Quds headquarters in Ahvaz, but for an operation of this nature, Farzan may have been ordered directly to Tehran to brief the mullahs," Clark added.

"What support can we leverage in Iran, Katherine?" Sloan asked.

"I've already alerted some deep cover assets in Ahvaz and Tehran and reached out to the Brits and Israelis for help. NSA is monitoring all phone and Internet traffic into and out of Iran, and the National Reconnaissance Office has satellite coverage of the al-Quds compound in Ahvaz and the Beit Rahbari Presidential Palace in Tehran. If Farzan shows up in either location, we'll find him."

Sloan stood, signaling the meeting was coming to an end. "Good work, everyone. I'm heading to the White House to brief the president and want to have some options ready in case he wants to retaliate against the Iranians. Start thinking about how we can hit back at Farzan and his bosses. I want the response to be severe enough that they'll think twice about ever pulling a stunt like this again."

With the meeting over, Sloan headed to the door, then paused. "Katherine, would you walk with me for a moment?"

The two senior intelligence officers made their way through maze-like corridors to the ground floor atrium of the New Headquarters Building, passing under large models of the U-2 and A-12 spy planes hanging from the ceiling.

Sloan guided Clark to a secluded spot away from the other employees. When he was sure they were alone, he asked, "What do you think the Iranians wanted with Jonathan Lewis?"

"I'm interested to find out why they went to the trouble of torturing him. While ambassadors are our highest-ranking officials in a given country, they don't typically have access to the sensitive classified information floating around in the head of, say, a chief of station."

"Agreed," Sloan said, his voice trailing off as a thought worked its way forward from the recesses of his mind.

Noticing the change in his demeanor, Clark asked, "What is it?"

Sloan looked around to confirm they were alone, then lowered his voice to a whisper and said two words, "Project Wraith."

She took a step back as if the words were somehow threatening. "There were only a handful of people read in on that operation. How on earth could the Iranians know Jonathan was one of them?"

"I'm not sure. But at this point we have to assume the operation is blown."

"If Joe is right, and Jonathan broke, then General al-Massoud just added a few names to his target list," Clark said. "Namely, ours."

Sloan checked his watch, then headed to the escalator. "I've got to get downtown. If we're right, this incident just turned into much more than the assassination of an American diplomat."

CHAPTER 18

Lawrence Sloan stood when he saw the light above the door flash, giving him an early warning that someone was about to enter what was perhaps the most secure conference room in the world. The lock disengaged, and a Secret Service agent held the door open as President Andrews and his national security advisor, Julia Maxwell, entered the White House Situation Room. The warning light stopped blinking once the agent closed and secured the door.

Brad Andrews had come to the highest office in the land from humble Midwestern roots and a desire to make life better for the average American. He was a warm, genuine man, which could be considered a rarity for a politician.

"Good afternoon, Lawrence," Andrews said, giving his CIA director a firm but friendly handshake.

"Good afternoon, Mr. President. Thank you for making the time on such short notice."

"Actually, I should be thanking you. Your call managed to get me out of the most God-awful budget meeting I've ever had the misfortune of attending."

Sloan greeted the national security advisor and shook her hand as well.

President Andrews took his customary seat – the one with the presidential seal embroidered on the headrest – at the head of the long conference table. Julia Maxwell and Director Sloan chose to sit across the table from each other, Maxwell on the President's right and Sloan on his left.

"Well, Lawrence," Andrews said in a casual tone that was sure to become more serious any minute. "What's up?"

"Sir," Sloan began, "we have a developing situation you need to be made aware of."

The tone in Sloan's voice gave the president the feeling he

wasn't going to like what he was about to hear.

"Do you recall receiving a briefing on Project Wraith, the operation to attack Iran's nuclear program using the Stuxnet virus?"

"I think so," Andrews replied, unsure if he was recalling the classified briefing, what he'd read in the paper, or had seen on one of the cable news networks.

"It was right after you'd taken office," Maxwell interjected, refreshing his memory. "Director Sloan and Katherine Clark briefed us on it at Camp David during your first trip up there."

Both men turned and looked at her in unison, amazed at Maxwell's ability to recall even the most obscure detail relating to the president's participation in national security briefings.

"Julia is correct, sir," Sloan said, as his thoughts drifted back to the day in 2008 when Paul Foley, the deputy director of science and technology, had introduced him to a brilliant technical intelligence officer named Fred Jackson. The young man had come up with a plan to do what the military and intelligence communities of several nations had failed to accomplish on multiple attempts. Jackson called the plan to disrupt Iran's ability to develop a nuclear weapon "Project Wraith."

Although technical intelligence officer was his official title, Fred Jackson liked to think of himself as a hacker with access to the best equipment and bandwidth the world had to offer. The resources at his fingertips would have been the envy of every engineer at Microsoft or Google if they had possessed the security clearance necessary to get a peek at the Directorate of Science and Technology's digital arsenal.

The hackers that made up the bulk of the cyber-ops cell worked out of a nondescript steel and glass office building on the corner of Lynn Street and Lee Highway in Rosslyn, Virginia. Jackson and his colleagues loved being away from headquarters and the prying eyes of upper management. And the bar scene in Georgetown, just a short walk across Key Bridge, was an added bonus.

Surrounded by office buildings belonging to the likes of Deloitte and Boeing, the cyber-ops cell and their covert facility were doing a pretty good job of hiding in plain sight. The only noticeable government building in the area belonged to the State Department's Bureau of Diplomatic Security, a block farther down Lynn on Nineteenth Street.

Jackson had been intrigued the day his supervisor walked into the office and threw out a challenge, wanting to see if anyone could come up with a way to use their digital skills to interrupt Iran's quest for the bomb. Jackson let the challenge simmer for a couple of weeks as ideas began to form in his mind. He was determined to design a more elegant solution than dropping tons of high explosives on fortified bunkers.

Fueled by an endless supply of Red Bull or any other energy drink within arm's reach, Jackson banged away at his keyboard for hours on end. Strings of code scrolled endlessly across his setup of four, thirty-two-inch, high-definition monitors. To the uninitiated, the seemingly random lines of words, numbers, and characters looked like a child might have sat down at the computer and banged away on the keyboard while mom was in the kitchen cooking dinner. But to those who could read and understand the complexity displayed on his monitor, the code was a pure work of art.

Jackson had created a digital masterpiece, a weapon made of ones and zeroes that could do as much if not more damage to the Iranian nuclear weapons program than a two-thousand-pound bunker-busting bomb.

CHAPTER 19

The CIA, along with Israel's Mossad and Britain's Special Intelligence Service, commonly known as SIS or MI-6, had been searching for a solution to the Persian nuclear problem for years. Even though Israel's Air Force had conducted successful air strikes against nuclear facilities in Syria and Iraq, analysts from all three countries had concluded that the losses of pilots and planes in an air strike on Iran would be unacceptably high. Neither of the IAF's previous targets were as heavily defended as the Iranian plants at Natanz or Fordow.

So rather than conducting a brutish physical attack on the Iranian nuclear plant, Jackson's idea was to come at them from the inside, or behind the firewall, as he put it. The intent was to attack the computers programmed to run and monitor the sensitive equipment inside the enrichment facility.

His code would attack the Iranian's centrifuges by altering the speeds at which the tube's rotors would spin, first slowing them down and then speeding them back up. Over time, the vibrations caused by the varying changes in speed would damage the centrifuges. Cracks would form in the precisely machined aluminum tubes, ruining them and the uranium they were enriching.

The primary obstacle to Jackson's plan was the very real possibility that the computers at Natanz weren't connected to the Internet, eliminating the opportunity for his code to reach their systems from the outside. He needed to find a way to get the virus inside the heavily guarded facility.

A couple of ideas came to mind, but they would require people on the ground to install the code. That meant he'd need help from other parts of the Agency for the plan to succeed. Accustomed to working at the speed of the Internet, Jackson didn't fully comprehend how long it would take or how complex the rest of his plan really was.

Months of planning and leveraging relationships with several key foreign intelligence services and an international corporation or two would be needed to pull this thing off. But if it worked, this attack would deal the most severe blow to Iran's nuclear program to date without ever firing a shot. And although very few people would be aware of his achievement, Fred Jackson would have the knowledge that he had conducted perhaps the greatest cyberattack in history.

Knowing he'd need help to move his plan forward, Jackson pitched the idea to his boss, Paul Foley. The deputy director of Science and Technology knew his way around a string of code, being an accomplished computer scientist in his own right, and was impressed with his young hacker's work, so much so that he decided to have Jackson tag along when he pitched the idea.

When Jackson learned he was going to a meeting with Director Sloan and Katherine Clark, he was equal parts excited and terrified. Very few people at his level ever set foot inside the director's suite on the seventh floor, and even fewer still were given the opportunity to brief the man in person.

A large desk and conference table filled the left side of Director Sloan's office. An American flag recovered from Ground Zero after the attacks of September 11, 2001, hung on the wood-paneled wall behind his desk, a constant reminder of the sacrifices so many made that day, and in the years since. To the right, a couple of armchairs and a small sofa were arranged around a coffee table. A door near the armchairs provided quick access to Sloan's executive assistant, Paula Hanson, and his chief of staff, George Owens.

Paul Foley and Fred Jackson sat on the couch with their backs to the wooded view of the Potomac. Director Sloan and Katherine Clark chose the armchairs and listened intently as the men from the DS&T laid out their plan. When they'd finished, a contemplative silence fell over the room.

Sloan sat back in his chair and gazed out over the woods separating the headquarters building from the George Washington Memorial Parkway, mulling the idea over in his head. Clark stared into her cup of Earl Grey like a gypsy reading the tea leaves as she thought about the various resources they'd need to make this work. "We'll need help," she said, breaking the silence. "It'll be much more difficult if we try to go it alone."

"I'd start with the Brits," Sloan agreed. "They have a long history of conducting successful operations in the Middle East, and their embassy in Tehran is up and running, although with a limited staff."

Clark was intrigued. "Use of their embassy would come in handy. If we ended up inserting operatives it would provide them with a legitimate cover and make a good safe haven if things went bad. Plus, we could use the diplomatic pouch process to get some sensitive equipment into the country."

Sloan nodded, adding, "The Israelis too. We could probably task some of their assets in Iran for support, and then there's always Dimona."

"Dimona?" Jackson asked, looking around at the group as if they were speaking a foreign language. The conversation had quickly moved away from the technical aspects of the operation, making him feel even more out of his element than he already did.

"Dimona, my young hacker, is a highly classified Israeli facility located deep in the Negev Desert. It may be useful because it's where some of the most brilliant minds in the Israeli government conduct their electronic signals intelligence and cyber operations," Foley said. "They've been hacking into Tehran's systems for years and may be able to provide some insight on the best way to get your code through the Iranians' firewalls."

Jackson was noticeably disappointed that his boss thought he might need help hacking the Iranians. "I see."

Picking up on Jackson's tone, Director Sloan said, "It's not that we don't believe in your abilities, Fred. What you've proposed here today is brilliant and audacious. We wouldn't be discussing it if it weren't." He paused a minute to let the bit of praise sink in before continuing in a fatherly tone. "But the operational side of the plan is going to require massive resources and partnerships with our allies for it to have the best chance of success."

Jackson realized Foley's comment wasn't a slight, just one of the realities of conducting an operation of this scope and scale, once again proving to him how they were moving farther and farther away from his area of expertise. He didn't want to push his luck but felt the need to take full advantage of the rare opportunity before him. "In that case, the Germans would be helpful as well."

"Go on."

"Well, sir, the controllers running the Iranian's centrifuges are made by the Munich-based Siemens corporation."

"The sale of sensitive equipment to Iran is banned in accordance with the U.N. sanctions. Are you implying the Germans have been selling the equipment to Tehran for use in their nuclear program?"

"Not at all, sir. According to my research, Iran bought most of the equipment through cutouts and shell companies. My point is that it would really save a lot of time and effort if I could work with the engineers at Siemens to test my code on their actual systems. That way, if I found any bugs I'd have time to tweak the code before we initiate the operation."

CHAPTER 20

There was a lull in the conversation and the office fell silent again. Director Sloan stood and walked to the large window, taking in the panoramic view as a plan began to form in his head. "Fred, what if we could get you access to a shipment we knew was headed to the Iranian program?"

Jackson's face lit up at the thought. "That's a no-brainer, sir. If I could get my hands on a batch of controllers, or any computer systems headed to Natanz for that matter, I could really throw a monkey wrench into the Ayatollah's turban."

Clark and Foley looked up as they caught on to what Sloan was thinking. "Do you think Siemens will cooperate?" Foley asked. "If their participation in this operation ever became public, I have no doubt the company's executive leadership would rocket to the top of the Quds Force hit list."

"Not to mention the potential damage to their brand reputation and stock price," Clark added.

Sloan turned away from the window and bent down to retrieve his coffee cup. He gave Clark and Foley a look, asking if either wanted a refill. When they declined, he walked over to the service on the conference table and poured himself another cup.

"There is a legitimate risk, I'll grant you that." He paused to take a sip of coffee. "What do you think? Will Siemens work with us?"

As the deputy director of operations, Katherine Clark met with corporate CEOs more often than one might think. "Hard to say," Clark said. "In my experience dealing with corporate CEOs I've found them to be patriotic and willing to help, but ultimately they have to weigh that desire against their fiduciary responsibility to the company and its shareholders."

"Do we know anyone with a connection to Siemens who could make the pitch, or would it be better to work this through our counterparts in the BND?" Foley asked, referring to Germany's foreign intelligence agency, the Bundesnachrichtendienst, or BND.

Sloan thought for a minute before responding. "We'll certainly have to notify Gunther of our intentions to approach Siemens, but I'd prefer we try someone on our side first." Gunther Reinhold was Sloan's counterpart at the BND. "I seem to recall hearing somewhere that Senator Isaacson was close to their CEO."

"Samuel Isaacson? The senator from New Jersey?" Jackson asked. "Isn't he also the chairman of the Senate Select Committee on Intelligence?"

"One and the same," Clark said. "I think Sunday's *Washington Post* ran a picture of the two of them at a recent charity function here in D.C. Something about Siemens offering job-training programs for at-risk youth in the area."

Sloan shook his head. "I'm not sure I want to ask a sitting congressman for a favor of this magnitude. The price might be a little more than I'm willing to pay."

The room went quiet again as the three senior intelligence officers racked their brains for another name.

"How about Jonathan Lewis over at State?" Clark asked.

Making the connection, Sloan smiled at his DDO. "Lewis and Isaacson are best friends. Have been since they went to Princeton together."

Foley was beginning to catch on. "So, it would be reasonable to expect that Lewis would know the guy from Siemens as well?"

"Exactly," Sloan said. "And I'd feel much better about having Jonathan make the approach. I'd prefer we owe the State Department a favor rather than be in debt to the esteemed senator from New Jersey." Looking to each person around the room, Sloan said, "This seems like a good start. Anything else we should be considering?"

Jackson was afraid he might be pushing his luck but decided to go for it. "Uh, sir...there is one more thing."

"Jesus, Fred," Foley said with a laugh. "What we've agreed to so far hasn't been enough?"

Director Sloan chuckled as well. "Don't mind him. What is it?"

"There's one last group I'd like to target. On a monthly basis, Russia sends the same group of engineers to Iran. They claim the team is working on the country's Internet and cellular infrastructure."

"You don't think their story is legit?" Clark asked.

"No, ma'am, I don't. Even though Russia's largest mobile phone companies are locally owned, they rely heavily on foreign providers like Nokia, Siemens, and Ericsson to upgrade their technology and services. Hell, they even use the Chinese company Huawei on occasion. If they had their own internal capability, they wouldn't be paying billions of dollars to Nokia and the others to keep their cell and Internet service up and running. I think the IT angle is the cover story Moscow is using to generate plausible deniability for the engineers' work on Iran's nuclear program."

"It's not a bad hypothesis," Clark said. "We've suspected someone stepped in to fill the void after we busted Pakistan's A.Q. Khan for selling nuclear tech to rogue states. Maybe it was the Russians. It's not out of the realm of possibility that those engineers could be providing the Iranian scientists with technical support on issues like warhead design and delivery options."

Jackson gathered his thoughts before presenting the final portion of his plan. "Sir, I've been able to track the engineers through the GPS in their mobile phones and most of them spend a considerable amount of time in and around Natanz."

That last statement took the three senior officials by surprise. "You did what?" Foley asked.

"I was following up on a hunch about the Russians. I wasn't going to ask you to approve this portion of the plan until I could confirm they had access to the nuclear facility. So, I tracked their phones," he said a little sheepishly, not sure if he was going to be praised or punished for his initiative.

Director Sloan laughed. "Paul, do all of your people show this total disregard for the approval process?"

"Well, I'm not sure. But I sure as hell hope so."

Director Sloan asked, "Okay Fred, what exactly would you have us do with these Russian advisors?"

Somewhat confident he wasn't going to be fired, Jackson continued. "I was wondering if we could somehow infect the equipment they're carrying into Natanz? This would be the third phase of the attack, giving us the highest probability for success."

Knowing his man's plan was solid, Paul Foley backed him up and said, "A three-phased attack. First, the virus goes out on the Internet. It's specifically programmed to ignore the greater web and won't affect any system outside the Iranian nuclear program. Second, we identify the cutouts and tamper with the Siemens products bound for Iran. And third, we infect the Russian engineers' equipment, so the virus is released when they plug into the Iranian network."

Six months of long nights and meticulous planning finally paid off when, with a little persuasion from Jonathan Lewis and the director of the BND, the CEO of Siemens agreed to work with the CIA and allowed Jackson to test the virus at their headquarters in Munich.

Jackson's successful test set a series of events into motion. Britain's Secret Intelligence Service and sailors of the Royal Navy's Special Boat Service boarded vessels underway on the high seas, claiming they were conducting antiterrorism operations. It was no coincidence that each of the ships they chose to inspect carried cargo with bills of lading for Iran. While the crew's passports were being inspected on deck, SIS technicians went below to inject Fred's code into certain pieces of the ship's cargo.

Mossad agents working in Moscow befriended some of the Russian engineers and cemented the relationships by throwing them a going-away party two nights before they departed for Tehran. The thought of going a month without a drink was all the motivation the engineers needed, and with the help of a powerful sedative called Ketamine added to their vodka, the Russians quickly drank themselves into a stupor. While the engineers were sleeping it off, the Israeli agents downloaded Fred's virus onto anything electronic the men might carry inside the Iranian nuclear plant at Natanz.

On a sweltering midsummer day in 2009 all the pieces were finally in place, and it was time to release Stuxnet into the wild. Director Sloan, Katherine Clark, and Paul Foley gathered around Fred Jackson's work station as he loaded the program into the virtual chamber, ready to be fired onto an unsuspecting Internet.

Fred looked up at Director Sloan, "Sir, would you like the honor of launching it?"

"No. This whole project was your idea, your creation. The honor should be yours."

Touched by the director's sentiment, Jackson hit the Enter button on his keyboard and unleashed a digital missile aimed at the computer networks in Iran.

CHAPTER 21

"As you know, Mr. President, the attack on Natanz was considered a success," Director Sloan said. "Jackson's virus resulted in the destruction of approximately one thousand centrifuges and the uranium they were enriching. And the rest of the enrichment process, to include the centrifuges that weren't damaged, was halted when the Iranians shut down the facility to investigate the incident."

"A success, but not the result you were looking for," Julia Maxwell interjected.

"You are correct, Julia," Sloan replied, taking the subtle rebuke in stride.

"The operation set the Iranians back a few years but was hardly the knock-out blow you were after."

"Once again, I cannot argue with that statement. However, in the wake of the attack, the Iranian security services launched a massive mole hunt, believing the operation had to be an inside job. Tehran couldn't comprehend that Natanz might be vulnerable to attack from the outside, so the IRGC's ensuing witch hunt set the program back even further."

"Didn't they actually execute a few of the scientists as an example to the others?" Maxwell asked.

"Yes, they did," Sloan agreed. "The interrogations were medieval. The Iranians acknowledged a handful of executions, but our sources indicated there were many more that were never made public. Multiple reports from our friends in the region and various human rights groups estimated the number of scientists put to death at around a hundred or so. The actual number may even be higher, but I doubt we'll ever know the full story."

"I don't mean to be rude, Lawrence," President Andrews interjected, "but what's the point of this conversation? Why are we talking about an operation that took place before I even came into office?"

"Sir, there were nine individuals who played integral roles in

Project Wraith. For operational security reasons, everyone else involved only knew about the part of the operation they were working on."

"Sounds reasonable," President Andrews said. "Same as most of our covert actions. A small group of decision makers with the access necessary to run the operation and need-to-know for everyone else, right?"

"Exactly, sir. These nine knew the details of the entire project and were instrumental in its success."

"So, what's the problem?" Maxwell asked.

"Jonathan Lewis was one of those nine decision makers."

The new implications of Lewis's kidnapping instantly crystallized in Maxwell's mind. "Good God."

"We think there's a high probability Jonathan divulged what he knew about the operation, to include the names of the others involved, when he was interrogated in Fallujah," Sloan continued.

President Andrews rose from his chair and began pacing the length of the Situation Room as he and his national security advisor took in the gravity of Sloan's revelation. "Based on what?"

"There's no other explanation for his kidnapping and interrogation, sir. If this was a simple assassination, Jonathan would have been killed on the spot with the rest of his protective detail. The Iranians went to a lot of trouble to make sure he survived the attack."

"Could they have been after something else he was working on?" Maxwell asked.

"Unfortunately, no. I spoke to Claire Nichols on my way here." Claire Nichols was the secretary of state. "She said there was nothing sensitive in Jonathan's portfolio that would rate an operation of this magnitude. We're early into our investigation but the evidence leads us to believe Jonathan was specifically identified and targeted by an Iranian-backed hit team. This was not a random act of violence."

"But how on earth could the Iranians have known about Jonathan's involvement in Project Wraith?" Maxwell asked. "And if they knew about Jonathan, wouldn't it be a reasonable assumption to think they would have already known the identities of the others as well?"

Sloan watched the president's body language as he paced the room, looking for any indication that would give him some insight into what his boss was thinking or how he was going to react to this news.

"We're not sure how the Iranians became aware of Jonathan's role. As I said, we're still in the nascent stages of the investigation. At this point, there's no way of knowing the extent of the information the Iranians had prior to the attack. But there had been whispers floating around town for years about Jonathan's work as a back-channel liaison between the Intelligence Community, State, and several private corporations."

"Rumors that were apparently true," Maxwell said.

"Yes, they were." Sloan admitted.

"Is it possible the Ministry of Intelligence heard the same rumors and decided to snatch Jonathan and see for themselves?" President Andrews asked.

"That's certainly a possibility, Mr. President. But if I were the one authorizing the kidnapping of a high-ranking government official, I'd need something more solid than a hunch before green-lighting the operation."

"Me, too." Throughout his first term as commander in chief, Brad Andrews had postponed plenty of high-risk – high-reward operations because he wasn't comfortable with the quality or quantity of the targeting intelligence. As a former battlefield commander who saw action in the first Gulf War as a Marine infantry officer, he was more qualified than most of his predecessors when it came to making decisions that would put the lives of his fighting men and women at risk.

Sloan continued. "That means they had to be confident enough in their intelligence to move forward with the kidnapping. If the men who took Jonathan possess the same level of skill in interrogation as they displayed on the ambush, then we have to assume they were able to extract whatever it was they were after."

"What makes you think Jonathan gave up any information?" Andrews asked.

"When Jonathan's body was discovered it was clear from his injuries that he'd been tortured," Sloan replied. "Real torture, sir. Not the kid gloves techniques we used to employ in the enhanced interrogation program."

"Real torture?" Maxwell asked with a quizzical look on her face. "What exactly does that mean, Lawrence?"

Sloan looked the national security advisor directly in the eye before he answered. "As I'm sure you know, Julia, our program consisted of breaking an individual down through sleep deprivation, keeping them in stressful positions, and occasionally, in very rare instances, waterboarding. All of which are techniques used on our own service men and women in Survival, Evasion, Resistance and Escape, or SERE training."

"I'm aware of the program."

"Real torture, Julia, means we found Jonathan's naked body strapped to a wooden chair in an abandoned warehouse." Sloan went on to detail the extent of the injuries, then paused a moment to give Maxwell a chance to absorb just how horrific and pain-filled the last hours of Jonathan Lewis's life had been.

She recoiled in disgust at the mental picture Sloan had just painted for her.

"Fucking animals!" President Andrews said, slamming his fist down on the polished oak conference table. "I wish I'd come across these guys back when I was in the Corps. What I wouldn't give to have these bastards in my platoon's crosshairs."

Sloan continued. "Jonathan's pain and suffering finally came to an end when one of the Iranians put a bullet in his head."

"Savages," Maxwell hissed, thinking of Jonathan and what his last moments on earth must have been like.

"So, as you can see, Julia, those who find our enhanced methods distasteful really have no idea what constitutes real torture."

Wanting to change the subject, the president settled back into his leather chair at the head of the table and asked, "So, Lawrence, who are the other eight individuals?"

"At the top of the list was your predecessor, President Williams, the man who signed the finding authorizing the covert action. I was obviously involved, as were Deputy Directors Clark and Foley. And of course, Fred Jackson, the Agency officer who came up with the idea and wrote the code. Those are all of the Americans. The remaining three are foreign nationals from the countries that had a role in the operation."

"The Brits?" Maxwell asked.

"One," Sloan said. "A very good operative with SIS at the time. He rose through the ranks at Vauxhall Cross and was on the fast track to run the place before the prime minister appointed him as the foreign secretary."

"Nigel Craig?" President Andrews asked, referring to the

United Kingdom's equivalent of the secretary of state. "He was involved in the operation?"

"Yes, sir. At the time, Nigel was MI-6's chief of Middle East operations and their foremost expert on Iran. He'd spent a couple of tours in Tehran before they closed their embassy and is fluent in Arabic and Farsi. Quite a natural choice for this assignment."

"Who else?" Andrews stated more than asked.

"A Mossad officer named Daniel Golan. He also ran their Iran desk and had command and control of all assets working inside the Islamic Republic. Most important were three teams from the Israeli Defense Force's Sayeret Matkal who were seconded to Mossad for just such a mission."

"Israeli Special Forces?" Maxwell asked.

"Yes," Sloan continued. "They are based on Britain's Special Air Service and specialize in gathering strategic intelligence behind enemy lines and conducting hostage rescue missions on foreign soil. That last part would have come in handy if Project Wraith had required the insertion of operatives into Iran, or if their extraction had been compromised. Like our relationship with the Joint Special Operations Command, they work hand-in-hand with Mossad. Daniel is currently the chief of Mossad's equivalent of our Counterterrorism Center. He's also the primary liaison with our station in Tel Aviv."

"And the last one was…?" Maxwell asked.

"Friedrich Voigt, the president and CEO of Siemens AG. He provided Fred Jackson with the opportunity to study Siemens' systems firsthand and test the virus on the actual controllers the Iranians use at Natanz."

"President Williams lost his battle with pancreatic cancer and passed away two years ago," Andrews said. "And with Jonathan's death in Fallujah, that leaves seven of you."

"Indeed it does, sir."

"What do you think Tehran has in mind?"

"It's hard to say. But at this point we must assume the Iranians have the names of Project Wraith's leadership. And if that is the case, then interrogating the rest of us would be pointless. Their motives could be nothing more complex than vengeance. Kill anyone who played a significant part in the operation."

CHAPTER 22

Major Hamid Farzan of the IRGC's elite al-Quds Force sat in the back of the black Mercedes S450 as the driver maneuvered the luxury sedan through Tehran's rush hour traffic. The car and driver had been idling inside an unmarked hangar at the western end of Mehrabad International Airport's main runway to greet the IRGC helicopter that had plucked Farzan and Yousef Mehrdad from a rally point near the Iraqi border.

A light rain fell, making the temperature feel at least ten degrees colder than the number glowing on the sedan's dashboard as the car merged with the other commuters into the Azadi Tower traffic circle. The one hundred-sixty-four-foot monument at the center of the circle was a major tourist attraction and marked the western entrance to Iran's capital city.

Farzan took in the sights of the city as the driver flipped on his turn signal and made a right onto Hafez Avenue. Streetlights made the raindrops on the sedan's windows sparkle like yellow diamonds as they passed the expansive compound belonging to the Russian Embassy. He wondered if there might be a time when the Russians living and working behind those fortified walls would face the same fate as the Americans who were held hostage for four hundred forty-four days back in '79. Iran and Russia were allies today, but that didn't guarantee the relationship would remain that way indefinitely.

Even inside the car he savored the many aromas saturating the air as the sedan passed by coffee shops brewing freshly ground beans and street vendors grilling lamb or chicken on revolving spits. Farzan loved the Sangelaj section of Tehran more than any other place on earth, even on a cold, dreary night like tonight. It was the reason he'd decided to rent the two-bedroom flat across the street from Shahr Park. He'd been seduced by the expansive park's gravel paths and wide cobblestone sidewalks that were intermingled with colorful rows of red, orange, and yellow tulips.

Fascinated with his country's history, he found this location perfect for a man of his tastes. Tehran's Peace Museum and the Park-e-Shahr Library were both located inside the park's borders, and other cultural landmarks were within easy walking distance in every direction. The National Museum of Iran was a short walk to the north, and he could see the top of the Golestan Palace, a World Heritage Site and Tehran's oldest historic monument, from the east-facing windows of his apartment. Imam Ali University was across the park to the west, and his favorite, the Grand Bazaar, was to the south. Farzan spent hours wandering the bazaar's ten kilometers of corridors, walking the same paths his ancestors had for over a thousand years.

Due to the nature of his work, he was keenly aware that each time he deployed on a mission, it might be the last time he set foot in his country or laid eyes on its capital city. Yes, it was good to be home, and he planned to make the most of the well-deserved time off he had been granted. It wouldn't be long before he would be back in Ahvaz, planning the next steps of the operation.

Riding in the back of the luxurious Mercedes, Farzan exhaled a deep, cleansing breath and let his mind wander, reflecting on the mission and the interrogation of Ambassador Lewis. The American was a diplomat, not a trained operative or soldier, but he'd resisted to the best of his abilities. Lewis had been determined to hold out as long as humanly possible, and Farzan respected him for his efforts. But time had been of the essence, and he needed the information stored inside Lewis's head sooner rather than later if they hoped to have any chance of escaping before an American response team arrived. That condensed time frame meant the Iranians had to forego traditional interrogation techniques and jump ahead to more extreme measures in order to expedite the process.

Farzan wasn't a squeamish man, but he was convinced he would hear the ambassador's pained screams in his sleep for years to come. It was a desperate wail he could not un-hear, and he was thankful when Lewis finally broke. With the coveted information in his possession, he was able to put the old man out of his misery.

Farzan was a soldier, a trained killer of men, but he was put off by the torture. It was one thing to face a man in battle or take a shot through a sniper's scope, but he wasn't sure anyone deserved what they'd just done to the American. However, the information Ambassador Lewis revealed had been invaluable and he knew his masters would feel the same way. *Perhaps the ends do justify the means, after all,* he thought.

With the interrogation complete, he had lit a cigarette and taken a long drag, then stepped outside and left the gore of the warehouse behind. When Farzan finished the cigarette, he flicked the butt and watched it arc end over end before landing on the hard-packed sand. He exhaled the last of the smoke then reached inside the coveralls he'd donned to protect his clothes from the ambassador's blood and retrieved a Thuraya XT-PRO satellite phone. Farzan powered it up and dialed a number from memory.

"It's done," he said, before giving a quick synopsis of what they'd learned. "It seems our asset's information was correct after all."

"Excellent," the disembodied voice said. "When are you heading back?"

"Soon. We'll be leaving within the hour."

"Good. We must incorporate this new information into planning the next phase of the operation. Make sure you get home safely. You will play a vital role in unleashing our vengeance against the West."

"Yes, sir," Farzan said before ending the call and powering off the phone.

Yousef stepped out of the warehouse sucking on a cigarette of his own and asked, "Everything alright, sir?"

An uneasy feeling rose from the pit of Farzan's stomach. "I fear we may have gone too far with the ambassador, Yousef. When the Americans' discover his body, I have a feeling they're going to come after us with a determination like nothing we've seen before."

Yousef took one last drag before dropping the cigarette to the sand and crushing it out with his boot. A smile spread across his face as he said, "Good. If they come to us, we won't have to waste time looking for them."

Farzan didn't share Yousef's confidence but smiled and said, "Let's prepare to leave. It's a long way to the border."

CHAPTER 23

The C-17 Globemaster rolled across the ramp and came to a stop in front of a hangar to the left of Joint Base Andrews' VIP terminal. As the pilot shut down the engines, the ground crew sprang into action, chocking the wheels and attaching an auxiliary power unit to keep the plane's electronic systems up and running.

Receiving the all-clear over the in-plane intercom, the crew chief unbuckled his harness and moved to a control panel midway down the fuselage. With the press of a button, the hydraulics hissed and lowered the giant loading ramp at the rear of the plane. Bright sunlight flooded the cavernous cargo bay.

A Joint Service Honor Guard stood at parade rest next to a black Cadillac hearse as the stars and stripes rippled majestically in the breeze blowing across the tarmac. The crew chief gave the officer in charge of the Honor Guard a nod and a thumbs up, letting him know the ramp was secured and the team could begin their solemn duty.

On the officer's command, the eight pallbearers snapped to attention and entered the cargo bay. Moving smoothly back down the ramp, they slid the casket containing Jonathan Lewis into the back of the hearse, and the officer ensured it was properly secured in place. He closed the rear hatch and the driver pulled away, slowly maneuvering the long black car into the hangar.

The protocol team at Joint Base Andrews had done a magnificent job of transforming the massive space into a makeshift auditorium. With approximately eighty-seven thousand square feet of floor space, the hangar was capable of housing two wide-body jets with room left over for maintenance workshops and offices. There was no way that much room would be necessary for today's event, so the protocol team partitioned the steel frame structure with pipe and drape.

A podium emblazoned with the presidential seal sat atop a

small stage at the south end of the hangar. An enormous American flag, bracketed by crests representing the various squadrons based at Andrews, served as the backdrop. Ten rows of folding metal chairs, two hundred in all, faced the stage and were backed by risers to support the multitude of news crews on hand to cover the event.

The group gathered in the hangar was a virtual who's who of Washington's political elite. President Andrews and Vice President John Curtis sat solemnly with their spouses in the front row. Their respective Secret Service agents occupied the four seats directly behind them. The remainder of the president's Cabinet, members of Congress, and fifty or so State Department employees were also in attendance. Several foreign ambassadors and diplomats who had developed deep friendships working with Lewis over the years filled the remaining rows of folding chairs.

Accompanied by his agent-in-charge, Doug Kelly, CIA Director Lawrence Sloan stepped through the black drapes at the rear of the hangar. He avoided the limelight the other men and women in the audience craved, and chose a spot out of the media's line of sight to watch the proceedings.

Barbara Lewis sat in the front row with her grown children occupying the seats to her left. She was a strong woman, determined to represent her husband's sacrifice with grace and dignity. She'd be damned if she would break down in front of everyone in the building, much less the members of the media, and have the images broadcast on national TV. No, any tears she would shed would be behind closed doors in the privacy of her home.

Samuel and Elizabeth Isaacson, the Lewis's closest and dearest friends, sat to Barbara's right. Samuel Isaacson was the distinguished and long serving senator from New Jersey who chaired the Senate Select Committee on Intelligence. He and Elizabeth were doing their best to console the grieving Lewis family while dealing with their own profound shock and sadness.

Jonathan and Sam had met while attending Princeton and remained close after graduation, when government service drew both men to the nation's Capital. Lewis chose the Foreign Service, lured by the attraction of a career traveling the world. Isaacson stayed closer to home, and moved to Washington after being elected as the junior senator from New Jersey.

The two Ivy Leaguers were regulars on the diplomatic and congressional cocktail circuits when Lewis was in town between overseas assignments. They were living the dream of every young up and comer in Washington, D.C., but their lives changed dramatically, for the better, the night the two confirmed bachelors met Barbara and Elizabeth at an event at Congressional Country Club in Bethesda, Maryland. Falling in love with the amazing women changed Lewis and Isaacson's priorities, and the barhopping public servants began to settle down and get more serious about their careers. Marriage and kids came along for both couples, and nights out on the town turned into backyard cookouts and trips to the beach along the Jersey shore.

Jonathan Lewis went from posting to posting, rising through the ranks of the State Department, while Samuel Isaacson, beloved by his constituents back home in New Jersey, continued winning re-election. Over the years, the two friends would get together to discuss issues and seek each other's counsel on a wide range of subjects. Their favorite spot for these world-changing conversations was the Hawk 'n Dove, a dive bar that had been a fixture on the Hill since the late sixties. They'd find a booth in the back, order something to eat, and then spend a few hours helping each other solve various problems over a few beers.

They didn't always see eye to eye, but the one issue where they were always aligned was the Middle East. From a diplomatic standpoint, Lewis recognized the need to support Israel, the only democratic, non-Muslim country in the region. He spent a good portion of his time working with Jordan and the other more moderate Arab states to keep the fragile peace in place. As a devout Jew and staunch ally of Israel, Samuel Isaacson worked the back channels between Washington and Tel Aviv, using his influence to ensure the United States was doing everything in its power to support the tiny country's long-standing battle for survival.

CHAPTER 24

President Andrews joined Secretary of State Claire Nichols on stage, both lauding Jonathan Lewis for his long and distinguished career in the Foreign Service. With their remarks complete, they left the podium and offered Barbara and the Lewis family their most sincere condolences.

As the ceremony came to an end the attendees gravitated to like-minded tribal groups based on political party or agency affiliation. Murmurs of hushed conversations could be heard emanating from each group.

President Andrews looked over at Senator Isaacson and said, "Can I get a minute of your time, Sam?"

"Of course, Mr. President."

The two men walked out of the hangar surrounded by a phalanx of Secret Service agents toward the Sikorsky Sea King helicopter designated Marine One. Wind blew across the tarmac whipping at the men's hair and ties as they walked.

"I'm sorry about Jonathan. I know you two were close," the president remarked.

"Thank you, sir."

"We'll get these guys, Sam. Lawrence assures me his team over at CIA has some good leads and may have narrowed down the list of likely suspects."

Isaacson's face lit up. "That's great news. You know I hold Lawrence Sloan in the highest regard. If there's anything I can do to support him in the hunt for Jonathan's killers...."

"As a matter of fact, there is," Andrews responded, as he stopped just short of the folding stairs leading into the helicopter. "The minute we have some actionable intel, we're going to hit back, and I mean hard. I don't care who's involved or where they are. I will not have the world thinking our people can be killed without suffering any consequences."

"I agree completely, Mr. President."

"That's good to hear because we're going to give these goddamned characters a taste of their own medicine. I want them to know and feel the same kind of terror they've been inflicting on innocent people for years." Andrews paused a moment to get his emotions under control.

Once more the statesman, he continued, "Lawrence Sloan and his people over at Langley are taking the lead on this operation. I would consider it a personal favor, Sam, if his folks didn't have to look over their shoulders worrying about being put through the wringer of public hearings or summoned to the Hill by the oversight committees on this one."

"Mr. President, if Lawrence can keep me up to speed, I can guarantee there will be no issues from my committee in the Senate. Unfortunately, I can't make the same promise about the House. As you know, Cynthia Drake is no fan of the Agency. I can speak with her if you like, but I'm not sure how receptive she'll be to your request."

The congresswoman from California was Isaacson's counterpart in the House of Representatives and served as chair of the House Permanent Select Committee on Intelligence, or HPSCI.

She had graduated from Cal-Berkeley with honors and plans to attend law school until she scored a minor coup by landing a position in Governor Gray Davis's administration. Witnessing firsthand the power, authority, and respect afforded elected officials was a life-changing event for Drake, and she thirsted for that power like an alcoholic desperate for her next drink.

She worked her way up the ladder, topping out as Governor Davis's chief of staff. The position provided her with valuable insights into the inner workings of big government and experiences dealing with issues like crime, unemployment, and health care. As chief of staff, she also had a hand in writing new laws and building the necessary relationships to get them passed through the state's legislature. But she had bigger, more far-reaching aspirations than leading California's government. Drake wanted, no, she needed, to go to Washington because that's where the real power resided.

Deciding it was time to strike out on her own, she ran for and won California's Twenty-Eighth Congressional District. With her move to Capitol Hill complete, Drake began lobbying the leadership for a seat on several high-profile committees. She was hoping for Appropriations or Ways and Means but ended up on the House Committee on Foreign Affairs. It wasn't her first choice, but she quickly became fascinated with the committee's responsibilities and jurisdiction.

She recalled her International Relations professors at Berkeley railing about U.S. foreign policy and how America should stop meddling in the affairs of other countries. Their harshest criticism was directed at the CIA and the intelligence community at large. Now here she was, reading background materials and attending classified briefings on the topics of national security and the deployment and use of America's armed forces.

Her committee also had oversight of legislation relating to international law, something Drake felt previous administrations had violated too many times to count, with programs like extraordinary renditions and drone strikes. She was determined to use her position and expanding influence to guide America's foreign policy in a direction that agreed with her educational and belief systems.

With two successful terms on the Foreign Affairs Committee under her belt, Drake was nominated to fill a vacancy on the Intelligence Committee when the senior congressman from Virginia did not seek reelection and decided to retire. With her appointment, life became exponentially more difficult for any member of the intelligence community unfortunate enough to be called to testify before the HPSCI.

"Let me know how it goes with Cynthia," President Andrews said as the two men shook hands. "I'll step in and talk to her if necessary."

Returning the crisp salute from the Marine posted at the helicopter's folding stairs, the president hurried up the steps and buckled in for the short flight back to the White House. The helicopter lifted off into the bright summer sky and took its place in formation with two other identical Sea Kings, playing a virtual shell game in the sky to thwart an attack on Marine One. The president's departure was a signal to the assembled crowd of Washington's elite that they were free to leave and head back to their daily routines of meetings and power lunches.

The massive hangar emptied out quickly. It was practically deserted except for a few members of the media putting the finishing touches on their stories and a couple of camera crews breaking down their equipment.

Surrounded by the expanse of the empty space, Barbara Lewis and her kids huddled around the casket and shared a few quiet moments with Jonathan before they drove out to Loudon County, Virginia, where a private family service would be held at a cemetery near their home.

Barbara looked up and noticed Lawrence Sloan for the first time. She excused herself and strode confidently over to him. Extending her hand, she said, "Hello, Director Sloan. I'm Barbara Lewis."

He shook her hand, appreciating the firmness of her handshake, and said, "I'm very sorry for your loss, Mrs. Lewis."

"As am I, Director."

"I didn't know Jonathan well but I do know he was very highly regarded among his peers."

"He was a good husband and father but he was an even better man," she said, looking out the hangar doors at a random point across the airfield.

Sloan remained silent, giving Mrs. Lewis as much time as she needed.

The moment passed and she said, "So, Director Sloan, as I'm sure you're aware, I've been around this town a long time."

Sloan nodded his head in agreement but didn't say anything, interested to see where she was going with the conversation.

"I've seen administrations come and go and have been at Jonathan's side through one diplomatic crisis after another."

"Yes, I'm quite sure you have."

"I would never expect you to divulge classified information, but I have to ask if you have any idea who did this to Jonathan?"

He took a moment to consider his response before saying, "Yes, I do."

Appreciating his candor and willingness to share even the smallest nugget of information, she asked, "And are you planning on bringing these suspects to justice?"

"Mrs. Lewis, as I'm sure you're aware, the CIA is not in the business of arresting our nation's enemies. That responsibility falls under the purview of the FBI." He paused a moment before continuing, "But I can assure you the people responsible for your husband's death will be punished. It just won't be in a court of law."

Barbara Lewis thought about his answer, comprehending the

underlying message. "In that case Director Sloan, I would ask you to do me one favor…for Jonathan."

"And what would that be?"

"Promise me you will use the full power and resources of the Central Intelligence Agency to rain down fire and brimstone on the heads of the sons of bitches who killed my husband."

Sloan liked this woman. Jonathan Lewis was a lucky man to have been married to her for over forty years. A sly smile spread across his face as he said, "Rest assured, Mrs. Lewis. My people are stoking the fires as we speak."

CHAPTER 25

Hamid Farzan admired the view of the Karun River from the balcony of his apartment on a tree-lined stretch of Saheli Boulevard in Ahvaz, Iran. He sipped coffee and scanned the pages of the *International Herald Tribune*, stopping occasionally to read a full article when an item caught his attention. While the digital version of the newspaper was available on his tablet or laptop, he still liked the smell of the ink and the feel of the paper in his hands.

His two-bedroom apartment was tastefully decorated in what an interior designer might call elegant minimalist with a Persian twist. Farzan was rarely home so he had no need for an abundance of furnishings or material possessions. But the items he did have were top of the line and displayed an appreciation for his heritage. Persian rugs covered the hardwood floors and several works by Iran's finest artists hung from the walls.

The building's prime location overlooking the river provided its residents fortunate enough to have an apartment facing west with a spectacular view of the sunset every evening. Farzan loved the apartment in Tehran but most of his work and training were conducted at the nearby Quds facility, so the flat here in Ahvaz served as his primary residence.

A text message chimed on Farzan's phone at eight o'clock sharp. He grabbed his bag, filled a couple of travel mugs with freshly brewed coffee, and took the elevator down to the lobby. Yousef Mehrdad was waiting patiently in the driver's seat of the black staff car. Seeing Farzan descend the steps, he popped the trunk.

Farzan tossed his bag inside and closed the lid with his elbow. He bent over and passed one of the cups to Mehrdad through the window, then used his free hand to open the door and settle into the front seat.

"Good morning, Yousef. Are you ready to get on with the next phase of the mission?"

"Definitely, sir," nodding his thanks for the coffee. I'll be putting the finishing touches on our load-out while you're in with the general. Barring some unforeseen issue, everything should be ready by the time your meeting breaks up."

He took a sip of the coffee, appreciating Farzan's choice of a rich Arabian blend, then set the travel mug in the cup holder. He put the car in gear and pulled away from the portico. As they reached the neighborhood's exit, he merged the black staff car onto the southbound lanes of the Modares Highway.

"Excellent," Farzan said. "Our infiltration into the area of operations will be considerably more challenging than getting into Iraq. I want to make sure everything is prepared for our insertion, and more importantly, our extraction."

"It would be a shame to get wrapped up just as the operation is getting under way," Mehrdad added.

Farzan took a sip his coffee and said, "That it would, Yousef. That it would. We still have so much more to accomplish."

They continued south toward the traffic circle at Chahar-Shir and joined in with the morning's rush hour traffic. Exiting at the circle's six o'clock position, Mehrdad continued southeast, past the Khouzestan Gas Company and the Azadi Sport Complex. Recent renovations to the sports complex, with the addition of a new indoor pool and diving platform, had transformed the aging stadium into one of the premier sporting venues in the country.

He slowed the car, made a right turn to leave the highway, and pulled up to the gate of what was very likely the most strategically important Quds Force base in the country. With multiple live-fire ranges and complete mock-ups of intended targets, the Fajr Garrison served as a training facility and logistical replenishment depot for the Quds Force and other proxy units fighting on Iran's behalf. The sprawling compound also housed the Sepah Yekkom, a secret detention facility specifically designed for the torture and interrogation of the regime's political prisoners.

A soldier on guard duty approached the car as Mehrdad eased to a stop. The chevrons and unit patch on the dark green sleeves of the soldier's uniform indicated he was a sergeant in the Islamic Revolutionary Guard Corps. He walked toward the car in a manner that could be considered confident bordering on arrogant, but his demeanor changed dramatically when he bent down to get a better look at its occupants. Instantly recognizing the two men inside, he snapped to attention and offered his best salute, then grabbed the radio from his belt and instructed the men in the guardhouse to open the gate.

CHAPTER 26

General Malek Ashkan sat behind his ornate desk, taking long, deliberate drags on a cigarette as he consumed the overnight reports from the Ministry of Intelligence and Security. The MOIS, Vezarat-e Ettela'at va Amniat-e Keshvar, or VEVAK, as it's known in Farsi, was the most powerful and well-supported ministry in the Iranian government. Considered by many to be one of the most dynamic intelligence agencies in the Middle East, the MOIS oversaw all Iranian covert operations. The organization conducted most of the internal operations itself but relied on the IRGC's Quds Force for sabotage, assassination, and espionage operations outside the Islamic Republic's borders.

A knock at the door broke Ashkan's concentration, and he looked up from the intelligence reports. Mildly annoyed at the interruption, he took another long drag, burning the cigarette down to the filter. He stubbed it out in a half full ashtray and took his time before saying, "Enter."

His executive officer opened the door and announced, "Sir, Major Farzan is here to see you."

Realizing he'd lost track of time, Ashkan said, "Of course, send him in."

Farzan strode briskly through the door, stopping two feet in front of the desk. He stood at attention and saluted. "Good morning, General. Major Farzan reporting as ordered, sir."

Ashkan stood and returned a casual salute, then walked around from behind the desk to greet his young major. The two men shook hands and Ashkan ushered Farzan toward a sitting area in the corner of the office. "Tea?" he asked, motioning to a setting on the coffee table as Farzan took a seat on an oversized leather couch.

"Thank you, sir."

General Ashkan poured the tea and added two sugar cubes to

each cup before handing one to Farzan. He eased into a matching leather chair and said, "So, Hamid, I've read the official after-action on the operation in Fallujah but I want to hear it in your own words."

Farzan took a sip of the steaming tea, then set the cup and saucer on the polished teak coffee table. "Well, sir, it went about as well as could be expected. The men of our Special Group were a bit rusty. It had been several years since they had seen action, but they managed to take out most of the ambassador's security team with the first volley of RPGs. Two of the Iraqis were killed by one of the ambassador's agents, but the Americans never had a chance to put up any meaningful resistance."

Dismissing the Iraqi deaths as insignificant, Ashkan asked, "And the ambassador? What can you tell me of him?"

Thinking back to the events and the interrogation at the cement factory, Farzan's tone changed ever so slightly as he responded to the general's question. "Once the reality of the situation sank in, Ambassador Lewis was remarkably calm even though it was obvious he was not going to survive the encounter." Taking another sip of tea, he added, "He earned my respect that day."

"Very interesting, Hamid. You still respect him even though he revealed some of the U.S. government's most sensitive information?"

"As you know, sir, a man can only hold out for so long. Everyone breaks at some point." *I shouldn't have to explain that to you after all the people you've tortured on the grounds of this facility,* he thought.

"I suppose you're right," Ashkan conceded. Sipping his own tea, he continued, "So, Hamid, I'm sure you can imagine how excited Tehran is about the information you extracted from Lewis. VEVAK has been searching for evidence of the West's complicity in the cyberattack on Natanz for years, but you, my young major, are the one who acquired it. Truly, a job well done."

"Thank you, sir. But we wouldn't have known where to start looking if it hadn't been for the asset's information."

"His assistance in identifying Ambassador Lewis as a starting point was invaluable, but you are the one who obtained the intelligence that will drive this mission forward. News of your accomplishment has reached the highest levels of the government," Ashkan paused a few seconds to let that sink in, then continued, "because of this new information, the Supreme Leader himself has taken more than a passing interest in your mission."

"The Supreme Leader?" Farzan asked. He imagined the Quds chain of command would be briefed on the mission but was surprised it had gained the attention of the politicians and religious leaders in the capital, much less the Ayatollah himself.

"Indeed, Hamid. He has personally amended the target list and you will now focus exclusively on the individual names provided by Ambassador Lewis. The Ayatollah has decided it is time the West and their Zionist stepchildren in Israel learn they cannot attack our nuclear program, kill our scientists, and interdict arms shipments to our allies in the region."

The more he spoke, the more Ashkan's voice filled with emotion. He leaned forward, resting his elbows on his knees. "How long do our enemies think they can continually meddle in our affairs without a substantial response?" he continued, slamming his fist on the coffee table so hard the impact rattled the cups and saucers. "You, Major Farzan, you and your men will be our response!"

It was well known around the IRGC that Ashkan was one of the borderline zealots. Farzan knew it was wise to toe the party line when his boss worked himself up like this, so he bowed his head in deference and said, "We are but humble servants of the Republic, General."

Farzan loved his country dearly and would willingly lay down his life if necessary, but he was a trained professional and preferred to operate without the emotion and ideology of religious fanaticism.

Touched by Farzan's sentiments, Ashkan said, "I admire your humility, Hamid, but even you must admit your team is so much more. You are the hammer that will strike a blow against the West – a blow they will never forget."

Both men fell silent for a minute, and the general took advantage of the opportunity to regain his self-control. "Is there anything you need before departing on the next stage of your mission?"

"Actually, sir, and I'm a little hesitant to bring it up, but there is one thing."

"Tell me, Hamid. What can I do for you?"

"As you said, sir, the West, most notably, Scott Garrett, the CIA's station chief in Iraq, has been interdicting our arms shipments to Hezbollah and our other friends in the region. Before we undertake our mission for the Supreme Leader, allow us to return to Iraq to kill Garrett."

"Garrett has been quite the thorn in our side," Ashkan agreed. "The losses of our shipments moving overland through Iraq are making us look weak and ineffective to our partners in Syria and Lebanon. Something needs to be done about that clever American."

"Then do I have your permission to eliminate Garrett?"

"I'm afraid not."

"But sir...." the words came out a little more vigorously than Farzan had planned, and he sounded like a petulant child arguing with a parent.

"But nothing, Major!" General Ashkan interrupted in a raised voice, cutting Farzan off before he could finish the sentence. He was not accustomed to having his decisions questioned. "Do not let your early success cause you to forget your rank or position, young man."

Realizing he'd overstepped, Farzan immediately backtracked, "Yes, sir, please accept my sincerest apology."

Ashkan swirled the tea in his cup, allowing his temper a chance to cool down. When he felt enough time had passed for his young protégé to absorb the rebuke, he continued. "Apology accepted, Major. I understand and appreciate your passion. But as I said earlier, your operation has been assigned by the Supreme Leader himself. Fulfilling that mission is your only responsibility at this point."

He crossed his legs and brushed a piece of lint from his uniform's dark green trousers. "Don't lose sight of the big picture, Hamid. We – no – you, will avenge the unprovoked attacks on our nuclear program. Each of the individuals involved with that cursed Stuxnet abomination will pay the severest of prices."

Ashkan had begun plotting his country's revenge the moment he learned of the cyberattack. VEVAK's investigation into the incident was reminiscent of something out of the Inquisition. Believing there was no way that Natanz could have been penetrated by outside elements, its agents turned their attention and brutality to those inside the program. Anyone with even the most remote access to the covert facility was considered a suspect, and as such, treated as a traitor. At the end of the bloodletting, the VEVAK was no closer to solving the mysterious cyberattack than when they started.

CHAPTER 27

"Rest assured, Hamid," Ashkan continued, "we will kill Garrett."

Farzan felt reassured by the general's promise, but that feeling vanished when he heard what Ashkan had to say next.

"Captain Shazhad and the back-up team will conduct the assault on Garrett while your team continues with your mission as scheduled."

Farzan almost came up off the sofa at the mention of Shazhad's name but managed to keep his emotions under control. He'd already drawn the ire of his commanding officer once this morning and didn't want to push his luck by doing it a second time. *That imbecile Shazhad barely made it out of training and he's leading the assault on Garrett?*

His mind wandered back to the difficult days and nights he and the others had endured as they went through the selection process and follow-on training. The course had been loosely based on the U.S. Army's Ranger School, where rank meant nothing and officers and enlisted men were trained and tested to the same standard.

Shazhad's performance stood out from the others but not for reasons that would make anyone proud. He consistently struggled to meet even the minimum standards, passing various tests and weapons qualifications by the slimmest of margins. His poor performance led the other students to wonder how he had even made it through selection in the first place. The fact that Shazhad was put in charge of a team assigned to lead a mission boggled the mind.

Farzan considered telling General Ashkan what he really thought of Shazhad, but after his earlier flare up, decided to keep his opinion to himself. Besides, if natural selection came into play, Shazhad would probably be killed in the attack. However unfair it might be to the men who would die alongside him, at least the unit would be rid of his incompetence once and for all.

Now that he thought about it, the general's decision might work out well for everyone in the long run. *Then Yousef and I can clean up Shazhad's mess and kill Garrett ourselves.* Pleased with his realization, Farzan said, "I know Captain Shazhad well, sir. As you know, Arash and I were in training together. I wish him nothing but success on his mission."

"Excellent," General Ashkan concurred. He finished the last of his tea, then stood, a clear indication that the meeting was over.

Stepping out into the bright sunlight, Farzan saw Mehrdad leaning against the staff car, its engine running to give the air conditioner a chance to battle the midday heat. The big man pushed his bulky frame off the car and noticed the troubled look on his commander's face. "Are you okay, sir?"

Lost in his thoughts, it took Farzan a moment to reply. "I'm fine, Yousef."

As they settled in the car, Mehrdad asked, "Any word on your request? Is the general going to allow us to kill Garrett?"

Farzan had only been outside for a minute but appreciated the frigid air blowing through the AC's vents. "No. Captain Shazhad and his team will handle the hit on Garrett."

Mehrdad went silent and stared straight ahead with a dumbfounded look on his face.

Knowing his lieutenant had something to say, Farzan asked, "What's on your mind, Yousef?"

He turned and looked at Farzan, unsure if he should really say what he was thinking.

"It's alright. Please. Speak freely."

"Shazhad? Seriously?"

"I was equally surprised when General Ashkan informed me of his plans. You know as well as I do that Shazhad has no business being a part of this unit. But I doubt he'll be a problem much longer. He doesn't stand a chance in hell of succeeding against Garrett. It's much more likely the American, or members of his protective detail will end up killing Shazhad instead."

Mehrdad put the car in gear and pulled away from the headquarters building. "Well, if he does fail, maybe we'll end up getting our shot at Garrett after all."

"My thoughts exactly," Farzan replied.

CHAPTER 28

Congresswoman Cynthia Drake entered the Omni Shoreham's Marquee Lounge radiating the confidence that came with knowing she was one of the most powerful people in Washington. Several patrons sitting at the bar recognized her and immediately reached for their smartphones, vying to see who could be the first to post their celebrity sighting online.

Drake ignored the gawkers and paused in the entryway, scanning the crowd in search of the person she was there to meet. Dismissing those she identified as hotel guests or in for an after-work cocktail, her eyes landed on a distinguished looking gentleman sitting alone at a secluded table.

Senator Samuel Isaacson sipped a martini while browsing the front page of the *Wall Street Journal*. His calm, unassuming demeanor betrayed the amount of influence he wielded in the nation's Capital. With every strand of his salt and pepper hair in place and the form-fitting Saville Row suit from his favorite tailor in London, Sam Isaacson looked like someone who belonged in this setting. Movement caught his attention, and he glanced up from the newspaper as Cynthia Drake gracefully worked her way across the crowded floor.

He stood to greet her and said, "Thanks for agreeing to meet me here, Cynthia."

"You're welcome, Sam. But why here? Couldn't we have just met in one of our offices and saved the drive across town?"

"I thought it would be nice to get away from the Hill and meet on neutral ground, so to speak. Besides, this hotel has a long and distinguished history as a place where people in our profession came together to strike deals," he said with a genuine smile spreading across his face. "I hope you don't mind but I took the liberty of ordering you a glass of wine, a nice Pinot from Sicily."

He helped her with her chair, then moved around the table

and eased back into his own. Drake took a sip of the chilled white wine and nodded her approval. "Very nice, thank you. So, tell me, what kind of deal are you looking to strike?"

"The president came over to offer his condolences after Jonathan's ceremony at Andrews," he began.

"I remember seeing the two of you together. I know you and Jonathan were close. I'm so sorry about his death."

"Thank you," Isaacson said. "As I sure you can imagine, the president's top priority is to determine who killed Jonathan, and why. And once we have the suspects identified, he intends to make them pay such a terrible price that it will act as a deterrent to other individuals or groups planning future attacks on our diplomatic personnel around the world."

"Sounds reasonable, as long as it's done within the boundaries of the law. But you didn't arrange this meeting just to tell me the president is pissed off. Why are we really here, Sam?"

"You're right, of course," he replied, taking a sip of his martini before continuing. "Lawrence Sloan over at CIA has information leading him to believe the Iranians were behind the attack, and his people are in the process of locating the primary suspects."

"That's great news, but it still brings me back to my original question. Why are we here?" Drake asked.

"Cynthia, the president wants to take the leash off the Agency and allow them to inflict some serious pain on the Iranians. Enough to make them think twice about ever kidnapping and torturing an American diplomat again. To do that, Sloan's people are going to need to operate in real time, pulling threads and following leads wherever they may take them. Due to the fluid nature of the operations they'll need to have the authority to take whatever action they deem necessary without calling back to Washington for approval. In some cases, there may not even be time to notify the Gang of Eight of impending action."

Drake's jaw dropped at that last sentence and she felt the warmth in her cheeks, a sure sign the anger welling up inside her was looking for a way out. If the meeting had been held in one of their offices on the Hill, Drake probably would have exploded and told Isaacson that while she was sorry for his friend's death, there was no way she would give the CIA a blank check and a license to kill. This wasn't some James Bond movie. But because they were in a public setting, she maintained her composure. The last thing she needed was a cell phone video of her screaming at a colleague hitting the nightly news or spreading across the Internet like wildfire.

She couldn't believe her hears, "So let me get this straight, you're saying you want my support to allow Lawrence Sloan and his spooks at Langley to conduct unilateral operations without congressional approval or oversight?"

"As it relates to the investigation and retaliation for Jonathan's murder, yes."

"Sam, you of all people know how I feel about this issue, not only as it relates to the CIA but the entire intelligence community. And you can also throw in those Neanderthals over at JSOC for good measure. I've dedicated a good portion of my career to revoking the Gang of Eight provision and requiring full committee notification for all covert action."

When she had been appointed to the House Permanent Select Committee on Intelligence, Drake immediately took advantage of her newfound access to the nation's most classified material. She and her staff spent hours digging though file after file looking for anything that could be used to rein in the seventeen agencies that make up the U.S. intelligence community. But the more she read, the more furious she became. In her opinion, it seemed as if there was a blatant pattern of activity by the intelligence community, the CIA in particular, of skirting the laws requiring congressional notification of impending covert action.

For years, the full intelligence committees in both the House and Senate had to be notified of covert actions. But in 1980, legislation was passed authorizing the executive branch, namely the president, to limit notification of especially sensitive covert actions to a select group of individuals in Congress. The group consisted of eight people, the chairmen and ranking minority members of the two congressional intelligence committees, the Speaker and minority member of the House, and the Senate majority and minority leaders. This exclusive group was referred to as the Gang of Eight.

The new law provided the president with a greater degree of operational security when it came to the planning and execution of the country's most sensitive operations. Limiting notification to the Gang of Eight would apply only to covert actions of such extraordinary sensitivity or risk to life that they could possibly be compromised by widespread knowledge of the operation. The idea was to still provide notification to Congress, but have it restricted to as few people as possible.

In 2009, the House of Representatives, led by Cynthia Drake, attempted to introduce language into the Intelligence Authorization Act that would strip the president of the Gang of Eight provision and require notification to the full intelligence committees. Senior White House staffers countered with a promise to Congress that the bill would be vetoed if the new language remained in the final version sent to the president. To avoid a prolonged stalemate and the threat of the presidential veto, the Senate submitted a bill that kept the Gang of Eight option in place but put tighter controls on certain aspects of the requirements for reporting covert action. The House eventually gave in, approved the new language, and the bill was passed into law.

It was Cynthia Drake's opinion that the Gang of Eight option was no longer the exception but had become the rule. Although she couldn't prove it, Drake was certain there were occasions when the eight members of Congress were being bypassed altogether. She intended to revoke the president's ability to hide behind the Intelligence Authorization Act and reassert the power and authority she felt the American people bestowed upon her and her colleagues in Congress.

After a long pause, Drake shook her head and said, "I'll give you credit, Sam, you've got some balls asking me of all people to give Sloan a pass on this operation."

Isaacson remained silent, hoping she would blow off some of the initial steam so they could get back to the point at hand.

"Jonathan was my best friend, but this is not strictly about our relationship and my desire to see his killers brought to justice. Iran has been pushing the envelope for years, poking and prodding the West, all the while exerting its influence throughout the Middle East without any substantial response or repercussions. They've been emboldened by our lack of action, not to mention the revocation of the sanctions that released billions of dollars in previously frozen assets, money that most likely funded the team that attacked Jonathan's motorcade. Our inaction has emboldened them to the point where they feel confident enough to attack a senior U.S. official in broad daylight. How many others are going to have to pay a similar price before some meaningful change takes place?"

***

Back at her corner office in the Rayburn building, Drake recounted her conversation with Senator Isaacson. While other members of her staff were appalled by the president's request, Todd McCutcheon sat quietly, his mind racing with excitement over the news.

He was probably the only person in government who had more disdain for the intelligence community than his boss. Those common feelings were one of the reasons they had such chemistry and that she had hired him as her chief of staff. But they also contributed to a level of frustration between them as well.

Sure, Cynthia talked a good game, but when it came to taking action – real, meaningful action – she faltered every time. Drake thought holding hearings and sponsoring legislation was the way to rein in what she considered to be a borderline illegal intelligence gathering apparatus. But to McCutcheon's way of thinking, the CIA and the other organizations that made up the community had gamed the system over the years, rendering the traditional means of regulation and oversight ineffective.

The action McCutcheon was looking to take would not just affect budgets or legislation but would cause actual pain to the individuals who had risen to the highest levels of the IC. Maybe their loss, and the ensuing press coverage revealing their activities, would be enough to finally reform the community and bring some meaningful change to its member agencies.

He and Drake had been searching for that piece of kryptonite since coming to Washington early in their careers. So far, they had come up empty at every turn, but not for a lack of trying. McCutcheon knew the piece of ammunition they were looking for had to exist. It was just buried too deep under layers of classification or the mysterious shadows of need-to-know.

Frustrated by their lack of success, McCutcheon decided to change tack and go it alone. There had been rumors floating around D.C. for years that Ambassador Jonathan Lewis had acted as a back-channel conduit between the CIA and groups that would prefer not to be seen meeting with the spy agency in the light of day. What if he passed that nugget along to an aggrieved party and let them figure out if the rumors were true?

Many in this town would consider what he was planning an act of espionage – treason even. But McCutcheon felt differently. In his mind, he would be performing his patriotic duty. It had been almost a year since he had cleared that first hurdle and made the decision to act. Like the men prospecting for gold in the early days, Todd McCutcheon lit a fuse and could not wait to see what the ensuing explosion uncovered. It sounded to him like the first stick of dynamite had just gone off. *So, it's begun.*

CHAPTER 29

With the investigation into Ambassador Lewis's murder turned over to the analysts at headquarters, Joe's team had slipped into the Protective Resource Group's rotation and were currently deployed to Iraq as Scott Garrett's protective detail.

Chris Ryan was behind the wheel of the fully armored Mercedes G550 and Joe occupied the seat to his right. Scott Garrett had his choice of the two bucket seats in the back of the silver SUV, but standard operating procedures dictated he sit directly behind Joe. A similarly armored Toyota Land Cruiser manned by John Roberts, Mike McCredy, and Randy Esposito followed behind the Mercedes.

Heat waves shimmered across the black strip of asphalt as the two-vehicle motorcade sped towards Baghdad sixty kilometers to the south. They were returning to the capital after spending the last three days paying a visit to the CIA's base in Baqubah.

The temperature outside was nearing one hundred and thirty degrees, and a hot wind blowing in from the west covered the road with a fine layer of sand. To combat the heat, the air conditioners were cranked full blast, making the interior of the armored SUVs feel more like a fall day back home in D.C.

Joe was the first to spot the two beat up Toyota Corollas on the left side of the highway about five hundred meters ahead. "Heads-up," he said, pointing in the cars' direction.

Three men in slacks and collared dress shirts had their heads under the raised hood of the lead sedan. They appeared to be working on the engine, either broken down from a lack of preventative maintenance or overheated from the day's scorching temperatures.

But to the trained eye of the American operators, it looked like the men were pretending to have a breakdown to identify their target as it passed by. It was quite possibly the oldest trick in the book.

Joe spotted two more men, one sitting in the back seat of each car, who didn't seem to be doing much of anything other than chain smoking while their friends suffered in the heat trying to get the car running again. Chris eased the Mercedes to the right, giving the Corollas a wide berth. He was careful not to drift off the shoulder and get the truck bogged down in the soft sand. Mike McCredy accelerated and pulled the Land Cruiser into the vacated space, so it acted as a shield between the Corollas and Garrett in the back seat of the Mercedes. Randy Esposito was in the back seat, watching their six while John Roberts sat up front and handled the radio duties.

Instantly alert, Joe started running through their options as the powerful SUVs closed the distance on the Corollas. He considered turning around and heading back to Baqubah. They could return to the safety of the base and have a helicopter fly up to transport Garrett back to Baghdad. That would take care of Scott, but the guys would still have to drive the vehicles back at some point. Or he could have the Iraqi military clear the road and they could resume the journey south with the military escort. But that would probably take a day or so to set up. They'd already been out of town longer than expected and Garrett needed to get back to the station in Baghdad.

He decided to take his chances and continue along their current route of travel. Turning to Chris, he ordered, "Pick up some speed and give them as much room as you can when we go by." He then radioed the guys in the follow car, "Keep an eye on the Corollas and let me know if the guys do anything stupid."

Mike accelerated to match the Mercedes' speed, and the armored SUVs kicked up a cloud of sand as they sped past the idle sedans. He glanced down at the men and their cars as they went by. "There's an RPG in the back seat of the second sedan."

"AKs, too," Randy added.

John relayed the message to the guys in the Mercedes as the convoy cleared the Corollas and fell back into their original formation.

The three men pretending to work on the lead car's engine slammed the hood down and scrambled into the vehicles. The Corolla's front wheels were spinning on the sandy highway before all the doors were closed. When the worn tires finally gained some traction, the cars shot off in pursuit of the Americans.

Randy spun around in the back seat, not liking what he saw. "Shit! They're comin' hard and fast."

John was on the radio to the limo, "Joe, we've got company. The Corollas are closing on us."

Sonofabitch. "Alright. Get on the horn to the office. Let them know we may have a problem."

"Roger that." Switching from the inter-team channel on his MBITR secure multiband radio, John relayed the motorcade's situation to Baghdad station's Telecommunications Unit.

Under his breath Joe muttered, "Too bad the military pulled out back in 2011. We could really use a QRF right about now."

"Those were the days," Chris agreed, thinking back on those days with a touch of nostalgia. "We were runnin' and gunnin' all over this damn country. When someone called for help the entire fucking cavalry showed up ready for a fight."

The lightweight sedans closed quickly on the heavier armored SUVs and fell in behind the Land Cruiser. When the left lane cleared of on-coming traffic, the drivers pulled around and came up alongside the trucks.

Joe hoped the men were going somewhere else with their carload of weapons, but in his gut, he knew that was wishful thinking. These guys had bad intentions and were here for a fight. "Slow down a little and give them a chance to pass."

Chris eased off the gas a little, but the sedans' drivers slowed to match his speed, paralleling the American vehicles. Glancing down into the lead car, he made eye contact with the man in the back seat. There was no fear or nervousness in the man's eyes. He was calm, as if this were something he did on a daily basis.

The man held Chris's gaze for four or five seconds, then gave the American the slightest nod of his head. As the man's head came back up, Chris saw his hands were busy charging an AK-47 assault rifle that had been hidden out of sight in the floor well.

The man shifted his body in the back seat to get a good firing angle and shouldered the rifle. Chris saw the AK's barrel and curved thirty-round magazine protrude from the open window as the man clicked the selector switch from safe to full auto.

CHAPTER 30

"Hold right here," Captain Shazhad ordered, eyeing the American driver as he worked the action of his AK-47's charging handle and chambered a round.

A slight smile spread across his lips as he thought of the accolades he'd receive for successfully completing his mission to kill Scott Garrett. Farzan had quickly become General Ashkan's golden boy after kidnapping the American ambassador. But the ambassador was a soft old man, a diplomat, not a seasoned intelligence officer like Scott Garrett. The two men's capabilities could not have been on more opposite ends of the spectrum. Shazhad thought the general would surely see the difference in this mission's degree of difficulty and reward him appropriately. The grin faded as he forced his thoughts back to the task at hand and raised the weapon, lining up the iron sights on the driver's head.

Chris yelled, "Contact left!"

Joe repeated the call over the radio for the guys in the follow car even though he knew it was unnecessary. They'd be watching their sectors like hawks and would have seen the rifle long before they heard Joe's voice over their earpieces. But the words left his mouth nonetheless, more out of reflex and training than necessity.

For most people, the sight of having an assault rifle pointed at their head would cause them to flee, to gain as much distance between themselves and the threat as possible. But instead of swerving away from the danger, Chris moved toward it and the small sedan.

The unexpected move took Shazhad's driver by surprise and he jerked the steering wheel hard to the left, wanting to avoid a collision with the big, armored Mercedes.

The sudden change in direction threw Shazhad off balance, and he experienced a weightless sensation as he floated toward the open window. His upper body was already far enough outside the car that his rifle's flash suppressor scraped along the pavement, sending up a shower of sparks. He let go of the weapon with his left hand and desperately reached for anything that would stop his forward momentum. His hand brushed across the front passenger seat's headrest and his outstretched fingers clamped down on it with every bit of strength he could muster. With a firm handhold, he managed to pull himself back inside the Corolla.

Shazhad was furious with the driver's reaction to the American's maneuver but he was even more embarrassed by his ridiculous near-death experience. Fighting to be heard over the wind rushing through the open windows and the screech of tires on the asphalt he shouted, "Get me back up to the lead vehicle!"

Chris's move gave the protective detail a few precious seconds of breathing room, so John called the station again to confirm they were under attack and activated the distress button on the vehicle's Blue Force Tracker. The BFT was used extensively throughout the war when multiple units of Coalition forces were operating near one another. The system acted like a transponder on an airplane and identified friendly forces to prevent units from firing on each other by accident.

In case of an emergency, such as being attacked by armed men in two piece of shit Toyota Corollas, the BFT would also pass along the exact GPS coordinates of the vehicles to assist with the QRF's response. Today, the alarm was received in the embassy, as well as by the CIA Operations Center on the sixth floor of the headquarters building at Langley. But without a military QRF to respond to the call for help, and with their own Agency assets at least thirty minutes away, it looked as if, for the time being, Joe and his small team of operators were on their own.

The driver regained control of the Corolla and moved back into position alongside the American Mercedes. Repositioning himself in the sedan's open window, Captain Shazhad raised his AK and pulled the trigger. The Quds man sitting in the front passenger seat heard the chattering of automatic fire and opened up with his own rifle.

The long bursts of heavy rounds tore into the left side of the Mercedes with dull metallic thuds. The bullets punched through the outer skin of the bodywork, but the armor did its job and kept them from penetrating into the SUV's cabin. The men in the second

Corolla were giving McCredy's Land Cruiser the same treatment.

There was a pause in the firing as the attacker's rifles ran dry and the men retreated into the cars grasping for fresh mags.

Chris accelerated, moving ahead of the Corollas with Mike's Land Cruiser hot on his tail. Once again, Mike and the guys in the Toyota SUV played the role of human shields, placing themselves between the attackers and Scott Garrett in the Mercedes.

The Iranians' resumed firing and the full brunt of the attack now fell on the Land Cruiser as it absorbed round after round from their assault rifles. Each impact to the bullet-resistant glass resulted in a small circle with a spider's web of cracks expanding out from its center. The Land Cruiser's rear window was covered with so many pockmarks and cracks that Mike couldn't see out the rearview mirror.

"We can't take much more of this shit!" Randy yelled as small glass particles began breaking loose on the inside of the rear window, sparkling like fairy dust as they floated around inside the Land Cruiser's cabin. "Rounds are going to start penetrating any minute."

John hailed the limo, "Boss, we're taking a beating back here. The Cruiser's doing a great job as a bullet sponge but it can't take much more punishment." He looked to Mike and Randy before continuing, "You guys take off. We'll keep these assholes off your back so you can make a break for Baghdad."

Everyone in this line of work acknowledged it was risky and knew the time might come when they would have to put themselves in harm's way to protect their principal. Joe was honored to work with men willing to sacrifice everything for their protectee and the teammate to their left or right. But the thought of abandoning his men, leaving them to fight a force that outnumbered them two to one, was one of the toughest decisions he'd ever have to make.

John's voice came through his earpiece again, "Besides, we're sick and tired of getting lit up back here. We want to see how they like having some hate coming back at them for a change."

Torn between his responsibility to protect Scott Garrett and the thought of leaving his friends behind to handle this fight on their own, Joe made the only decision his training and duty would allow. He gave the order and Chris mashed the accelerator to the floor.

CHAPTER 31

Each member of the CIA protective detail carried an HK416 assault rifle and a Glock handgun. But the guys in the follow car usually brought along a little something special in case things went pear-shaped and they were having a particularly bad day.

Randy Esposito released the clasp on his sling and set his rifle aside. Choosing to go with something a little more substantial, he reached into the cargo space normally occupied by the third-row seat and hefted up an M249 Special Purpose Weapon. The light machine gun fired the same 5.56-millimeter rounds as his assault rifle but at a much higher rate. He had a two-hundred-round-box magazine loaded on the weapon and two more stored in the ammo pouches on his load-bearing vest.

As an added bonus, John Roberts never went on a movement without his trusty HK69A1 40-millimeter grenade launcher. All in all, the three operators in the Toyota Land Cruiser made up a formidable fighting force.

There was no need for a drawn-out discussion to come up with a game plan. The men had run through countless attack-on-principal, or AOP scenarios, on the training range, and the procedures were seared into their brains.

Mike accelerated to gain some distance between the Land Cruiser and their pursuers and asked, "Ready?"

Completing one last check of his weapons and equipment, John answered, "Absolutely."

"Then grab something and hang on!" Mike said as he cranked the steering wheel to the left and pulled up on the emergency brake.

The move caused the Land Cruiser's back end to swing around in a one-hundred-and-eighty-degree arc. The tires screamed in protest as they tried in vain to grip the asphalt and prevent the vehicle from making the unnatural movement. Aided by the thin layer of sand blowing across the highway and Mike's skill behind the wheel, the top-heavy SUV managed to perform the maneuver without rolling over.

It was time to turn the tables on the situation. Mike and John kicked open the heavy armored doors and braced them in position with a booted foot. The armor in the Land Cruiser's doors and bullet-resistant glass in the windows and windshield would protect the men from incoming rounds while they used the V formed by the door and the frame of the windshield as a firing port. They shouldered their rifles and were cracking off well-aimed shots two at a time before the attackers even realized what was happening.

On television or in the movies, people always try to stop a moving vehicle by shooting the engine. But in real life, a car will continue to operate even after the engine has taken a considerable amount of damage. That's why operators believe the best way to stop a vehicle is to shoot its driver.

Mike placed the reticle of his sight on the forehead of the lead car's driver and pressed the trigger. The first pair of rounds spiderwebbed small holes in the glass as they passed through the Corolla's windshield. The double tap hit the man in the face, snapping his head back against the headrest as a third and fourth round went low into his exposed throat.

Blood sprayed from the grotesque neck wound, coating the other men in the car. The dead driver's right foot fell to the side, releasing the pressure on the gas pedal, and the Corolla coasted to a stop, seventy-five meters from the Americans' Land Cruiser.

To his right, Mike could hear John's rifle was alive and well, popping at a regular cadence as it sent a steady stream of lead at the man in the Corolla's front passenger seat. John's fire forced the Iranian to dive behind the dashboard or risk suffering the same fate as his buddy.

Seeing the back of his friend's head explode, the driver of the second Corolla stood on the brake pedal with both feet. The worn tires locked up and the sedan slid forward on the sandy highway until it slammed into the back of the lead car. Both cars came to a stop perpendicular to the American Land Cruiser.

Dazed from the collision, the driver and his two passengers bailed out and stumbled behind their sedan for cover. Shazhad and his man in the lead car did the same. The captain moved to the front wheel well of the second Corolla and organized his remaining men into two fire teams. He sent a team of two to the left and the others to the right.

Using the lull in the action to his advantage, Randy opened

the back hatch of the Land Cruiser, dropped the tailgate, and climbed out of the battered SUV. He unfolded the M-249's bipod as he stood up on the tailgate and placed the light machine gun on the truck's roof, using it as a stable firing platform.

He pulled back the charging handle, then let it go forward to chamber a round. "I'm up!" he shouted over the sound of the gunfire. With the press of his right index finger, the M-249 came to life, removing any doubt he was in the fight in case John and Mike hadn't heard him. The weapon spit a stream of armor-piercing rounds toward vehicles that were built for running errands or a commute to work, not military operations.

The sedans' thin metal skin offered little resistance to the high-velocity bullets as they tore through the cars and one of the Iranian's legs. The man screamed in agony and fell onto his back as he clutched his shredded thighs. With every beat of his heart, the punctured femoral arteries spilled their contents onto the sandy pavement. At the current rate of blood loss, the man had less than a minute to live.

Shazhad heard the screams coming from his right but refused to leave his position of relative safety to aid a man he knew to be mortally wounded.

The three other Quds men looked on as the dark red pool of blood continued to expand and their friend's cries faded to silence. Losing two members of their team in such a short timespan seemed to give the Iranians some renewed motivation and spurred them back into the fight.

Two of the men positioned on the left popped up over the hood of the lead Corolla and began firing at the American vehicle. Their rounds peppered the Land Cruiser's windshield and open doors, sending Mike and John diving back inside the safety of the SUV's cabin.

"Keep up the suppressive fire!" Shazhad ordered. Hoping to end this fight in one fell swoop he yelled, "Get the RPG!"

With the two Americans taking cover inside the Land Cruiser and his teammates drawing the fire of the third CIA man, one of the Quds operatives crawled to the Corolla's open door. He reached into the back seat and retrieved the RPG launch tube and a backpack of spare warheads. As his friends laid down a withering cover fire, he inserted a rocket into the launch tube, stood, took aim, and fired.

CHAPTER 32

Randy screamed, "RPG!" hoping the guys heard him over the roar of the gunfire, but he doubted they could. Hell, his own ears were ringing so badly from the machine gun's reports that he barely heard himself shout the warning.

"Aw shit!" Mike hissed as he hunkered down and braced for the impact.

In his rush to get the shot off, the Iranian's aim was a little high and the rocket skipped off the Land Cruiser's roof. Had it been a foot to the left, Randy probably would have been impaled or decapitated by a direct hit. He ducked out of instinct, but the rocket was moving so fast it was already past him. The spent warhead spiraled out of control before exploding in the desert with an ear-splitting boom.

Before the Americans had a chance to regroup, Shazhad demanded, "Again!"

Cursing himself for the errant shot, the man reloaded the launch tube and muttered, "I missed once. You won't be so lucky the second time." A confident smile spread across his face as he centered the launcher's crosshairs on the Toyota badge affixed to the Land Cruiser's grill, and fired. Once again, the rocket shot from the tube and screamed toward the American's SUV.

John and Mike peeked up over the dashboard, thanking their lucky stars the rocket went high when they saw the Iranian taking aim with a fresh round in the tube. They both figured there was no way in hell the guy could miss twice from this distance and made the decision to abandon the doomed SUV.

"Evac! Evac! Evac!" John yelled as he and Mike dove out the open doors and sprinted away from Land Cruiser.

Still deaf from the gunfire, Randy didn't hear the call to evacuate and was just getting back up on his gun when the rocket penetrated the truck's grill. The blast lifted the heavy SUV into the air, sending razor sharp pieces of the bodywork in every direction as the tank-killing projectile shredded the front end of the truck.

The force of the impact blew Randy off the tailgate and his unconscious body landed in the middle of the street. Blood leaked from a gash along the right side of his head, and his left arm was bent at an unnatural angle, obviously broken in several places. But the most serious wounds were from the three large pieces of shrapnel that had pierced his body armor and were embedded deep in his chest.

Separated by the stretch of highway after bailing out of the Land Cruiser, John found cover behind a boulder on the right side of the road, and Mike went prone in a low ditch on the left. They would have preferred to be together, with the ability to fight as a team, but being spread out the way they were made it harder for the Iranians to flank them from one side or the other.

When life gives you lemons, Mike thought, trying to put the best spin on a really bad situation.

John peered out from behind the boulder and saw the Iranians enjoying a moment of self-congratulation for the direct hit on the SUV. He reached for the grenade launcher, dropped a round into the breech, and fired. With an audible thump, he watched the high-explosive grenade sail through the air in a gentle arc before it exploded harmlessly fifty meters behind the attackers.

At first the Iranians thought they were being attacked from the rear and turned to see where the fire was coming from.

"Dammit! Too far." John chastised himself. He reloaded the weapon, adjusted his aim and fired again. The second HE grenade was on its way, and the attackers could see the slow-moving round spiraling toward them.

"Incoming!" Shazhad screamed – his warning sending the men scrambling for cover. The grenade landed on the roof of one of the Corollas and exploded, showering the Iranians with bits of metal and glass.

With their attackers distracted, Mike rose from the ditch and yelled, "Moving!"

"Move!" John replied, knowing exactly what his teammate was doing. He shouldered his rifle and fired short bursts until the bolt locked back on an empty chamber. Wanting to maintain the covering fire, John decided to forego the mag change and transitioned to his Glock to continue the barrage. He felt a little silly using his handgun at this distance and wasn't really expecting to hit anyone. He just wanted to keep their heads down long enough for Mike to get to Randy.

Mike sprinted across the road, and without breaking stride, reached down and grabbed the drag handle on his teammate's plate carrier. He fired his rifle in the Iranian's general direction with his right hand while dragging Randy behind him. He made it across the road, pleasantly surprised he hadn't been shot, and took refuge behind the boulder with John.

"What took you so long, brother? Lose a step or two in your old age?"

"Screw you," Mike gasped, breathing heavily from the exertion. "That little dude is heavier than he looks."

Even though their situation was dire, both men had a smile on their faces. Sure, they still had a few issues to overcome, like four shitheads trying to kill them, but they were happy to be reunited and able to finish this fight together.

"How are you doing on ammo?" Mike asked.

"Two full mags for my rifle and one grenade for the launcher. Plus two mags for my Glock. You?"

"About the same."

Ammunition was rapidly becoming a problem for the two operators, so Mike rolled Randy on his back and rifled through the mag pouches on his plate carrier. Finding four that weren't damaged in the explosion, he took two for himself and handed the other two to John.

A fresh volley from the Iranian's assault rifles interrupted the Americans' resupply. Rounds snapped overhead and whistled into the desert as they ricocheted off the boulder and dug grooves in the pavement.

Now that both men were on the same side of the road, the four Iranians advanced from behind the Corollas, attempting to trap them in a pincer move. Confident that the end was near, all four Quds men fired from the hip as they closed in on their prey.

With rounds impacting all around them, a little doubt started to creep in from the dark recesses of Mike's mind. For the first time, he began to wonder if they were going to make it out of this firefight alive. Never one to give up or go down without a fight, he peeked around the boulder and fired at the Iranians to slow their advance. John was doing the same and ducked back behind the big rock just as a burst struck six inches from where his head had been.

In between trigger pulls, Mike thought he heard the sound of a helicopter's rotors off in the distance. *Nah, couldn't be,* he thought, figuring the combination of stress and the onset of heat exhaustion were causing him to hear things. *What's next, full blown hallucinations?*

Badly in need of a sanity check, Mike asked, "Did you hear that?"

"Hear what?" John said, peeking back around the boulder to get a fix on their attackers.

"Rotors. I could have sworn I heard a helicopter."

John chuckled, "Dude, you sure that's not just wishful thinking?" as he squeezed off a few rounds.

Hearing it again, Mike said, "Shut up and listen. There...," he said, picking up the faint sound again. "I think it's getting closer."

It may have been a shift in the wind or the break in the firing as the Iranians paused to reload, but this time John heard it, too. "Think it's one of ours?"

The rhythmic beat of the rotor's blades grew louder by the second as the sound of the helicopter neared their location.

"Hard to tell...," but before Mike could finish the sentence, he heard Joe's voice come over his earpiece.

"Keep your heads down, boys. We're comin' in hot!"

CHAPTER 33

Before the two American operators could fully comprehend what was happening, an MI-17, with none other than Chuck Jamison in the left seat, flew so low overhead they thought the landing gear might hit the roof of the destroyed Land Cruiser. The rear cargo doors were locked in the open position and they could see their team leader strapped into the gunner's seat as the big helo passed overhead. The six barrels of an electric mini-gun were spinning, waiting for Joe's permission to unleash their fury.

Jamison banked hard to the left and came to a hover, one hundred feet off the ground. He auto-rotated the ship so the business end of the aircraft faced the attackers.

Captain Arash Shazhad's heart sank. The mini-gun's barrels seemed to be staring at him from the cargo bay of the helicopter suspended over the highway. He knew he had failed in his primary mission when Garrett's vehicle escaped their ambush. But he had hoped to redeem some measure of respect by killing the three Americans who stayed behind to fight. Then this damned helicopter arrived just as they were advancing for the kill, denying him even this small victory.

Realizing they were caught in the open, Shazhad and his men retreated and took refuge behind the Corollas. Hoping to salvage some semblance of victory from this imminent defeat, Shazhad gave the order for his men to open fire on the flying beast. Confident he couldn't miss from this distance, the man with the RPG loaded his last rocket and sent it skyward toward the MI-17.

Rounds peppered the fuselage as the crew chief manning the port side gun port called out, "RPG, six o'clock," in the same calm manner an airline pilot might use when asking passengers to "secure their tray tables and return their seats to their upright positions."

"Breaking right," Jamison replied over the intercom as he dipped the nose and banked to the right, easily maneuvering away from the unguided rocket. "Stand by, Joe. I'm bringing her back around."

Once again in position to put a quick and final end to this fight, Joe depressed the trigger and the electric powered mini-gun belched, sending a maelstrom of lead down at the doomed men.

Captain Shazhad saw the flame erupt from the six-barreled gun as his own weapon ran dry. There was no place to run. Nowhere to hide. The fusillade of bullets ripped through the thin-skinned sedans, drilling into the pavement as they passed through the cars and the Iranians' bodies. In a span of seconds, the fight was over and the four men lay dead on the sweltering asphalt, their bodies twisted in unnatural poses.

Unbuckling his harness, Joe leapt from the chopper before Jamison even had it on the ground. Adam Elliot, the team's medic, was on his heels, running for Randy's motionless body.

Chris Ryan slid into the vacated gunner's seat to keep an eye out for anyone else who might want to have a go at the Americans, even though the carnage strewn about the highway should have been more than enough warning to discourage even the most dedicated fighter.

Six members of the Protective Response Group, acting as the makeshift quick reaction force, streamed out of the MI-17's cargo bay and set up a perimeter around the helicopter. John and Mike looked on as Adam examined Randy's injuries. Their teammate was pale and pasty from the loss of blood, and the shrapnel sticking out of his chest was a horrific sight, even to someone who had seen his fair share of combat.

"We got to him as soon as we could," Mike said apologetically. With their attackers no longer a threat, he had a chance to focus on his teammate's condition and tears began to form in his eyes. Joe put a reassuring hand on Mike's shoulder as they all waited for Adam's prognosis.

Seeing the look of despair and responsibility on Mike's face, the medic said, "There's nothing you could have done. His injuries were just too severe. If I had to guess, he was probably dead before he hit the ground."

The news hit the three men like a sucker punch to the gut, and Mike dropped to his knees in a state of shock. He hadn't come to the Agency from the military, so this was the first time he'd lost a friend in battle. While the men were dealing with the initial shock,

Adam began prepping Randy's body for the flight back to Baghdad.

Joe knew what it was like to lose a friend or a member of the unit, so he gave his guys a few minutes to get their heads wrapped around the fact that Randy was dead. He wanted to give the men some time but didn't want them dwelling on their teammate's death, so he retrieved a small kit from the helicopter and handed it to Mike. "Why don't you and John go check the bodies for intel? Grab some fingerprints and DNA while you're at it."

Mike was slow to move, so Joe knelt next to him and put an arm around his friend's muscular shoulders. "Mike, the best way we can honor Randy is to identify these guys and find out who ordered the hit."

"Then we find them and exact some revenge?"

"Then we find them and exact some revenge," Joe echoed.

With that reassurance, Mike got to his feet and joined John for the short walk over to the dead men.

The medic looked up and said, "Good call. He needed something to do to get his mind off Randy."

John photographed and fingerprinted each of the bodies while Mike checked them for pocket litter. The process was called Sensitive Site Exploitation, or SSE. They were looking for anything that might shed some light on who attacked their convoy. There was no way these guys were just some locals looking to jack a couple of SUVs. The American motorcade had been specifically targeted and they wanted to know why.

Joe joined his men over by the Corollas. "Find anything?"

John said, "When we get back to the station we'll run these guys through the facial recognition software and fingerprint analysis. We'll also run the serial numbers on the weapons. My money says they came from Syria or Iran."

Adam's voice broke up the conversation. "Can someone give me a hand? Esposito is ready to be transported."

A couple of the PRG operators began moving toward the body bag but Mike yelled, "Thanks guys, but we've got him."

He and John rushed over and gently lifted their teammate into the helicopter, then placed Randy's body on a stretcher secured along the right side of the cargo bay. Chris reached down to give Joe a hand up, hauling him and the SSE kit into the helicopter. With everyone onboard, Jamison lifted off, hovering for a moment to take one last look at the carnage, then headed for Baghdad.

CHAPTER 34

Relishing the thought of some extra shut-eye, Daniel Golan rolled over and hit the snooze button on his alarm clock. But only a minute or two had passed before the nagging voice in the back of his head began chastising him. *"Come on, Daniel,"* the voice said. *"Get your ass out of bed. You're not getting any younger, you know."*

Feeling guilty about hitting the snooze, Golan threw off the covers and let out a big yawn as he sat up on the side of the bed and stretched in an attempt to chase the sleep from his body. He walked over to the dresser and put on a pair of shorts and a t-shirt, then laced up his favorite pair of running shoes.

Dressed, he moved to the large window and pushed the curtains apart, allowing the morning's sunlight to flood the bedroom. A view of the Mediterranean's bright blue waters greeted him as he gazed out over the old seaport of Jaffa. The sight never got old or failed to bring a smile to his face.

Golan had purchased the two-bedroom apartment in the old city south of Tel Aviv after completing his mandatory stint in the military twenty years earlier. The location hadn't been a problem until he joined the Mossad and had to make the long daily commute from the southern end of Tel Aviv to the spy agency's headquarters north of the city. He had considered selling the apartment on a couple of occasions to cut thirty minutes or so off his drive time but managed to resist the temptation each time.

He loved the feel of Jaffa's old narrow streets and alleyways. Any number of coffee shops and bakeries were within easy walking distance, and the restaurants were amazing. The food scene in and around Tel Aviv was as good as any city in Europe or the U.S. Jews who had emigrated from countries across the Middle East and North Africa had brought with them a variety of dishes to go along with those of the Arabs, Druze, and Bedouins who had long been a part of Israeli culture. Then there were the Eastern Europeans and the unique cuisine they brought from the old country that always seem to be washed down with plenty of alcohol. Jaffa was a real melting pot of cultures and ethnicities where Jews, Christians, and Muslims enjoyed a peaceful coexistence.

Golan grabbed his smartphone off the nightstand, inserted the earbuds, and scrolled through his playlists. He hit the Play button and AC/DC's "Back in Black" assaulted his ears as he headed out the door.

Skipping down the short flight of stairs to the sidewalk, he made a right onto Nemal Yafo Street and ran past the port, watching the fishermen tending their boats and offloading the day's catch. Golan continued past St. Peter's Franciscan Church, which, as if to confirm Jaffa's status as a haven of peaceful coexistence, was no more than two hundred and fifty meters up the road from the Al-Bahr Mosque. Just past the mosque he abandoned the pavement and hopped down onto the powdery sand of the beach, heading north to his turnaround point at the Tel Aviv Marina.

***

Three days earlier, Hassan Nasrallah, the leader of Hezbollah, had been asked to support a Quds Force mission into Israel, he had jumped at the chance to take part in an operation against his neighbor to the south, not only for the ideological reasons he shared with the Islamic Republic, but also because he feared the inevitable repercussions that would come from declining a request from Tehran.

Nasrallah had just the man for the assignment. A farmer for most of his life, the man grew an assortment of fruits and vegetables in the fertile soil of southern Lebanon and made regular trips into Israel to sell his crops. Many years ago, he decided to supplement his meager income by transporting illicit goods across the border and outfitted his truck with a false floor.

It was in that smuggler's compartment that he would conceal Hamid Farzan and Yousef Mehrdad. The trio crossed into Israel near the town of Metula because he was well-known both to the border guards and the soldiers deployed along the Blue Line as part of the U.N. Interim Force in Lebanon, or UNIFIL. The unit's familiarity with the old man, and his crossings on a regular basis for the past several years, meant he and his truck were given only a cursory look before being permitted to enter the country.

Farzan's peers thought his plan to assassinate an Israeli government official in Tel Aviv was pure insanity. General Ashkan, on the other hand, loved the idea of hitting the Israelis in their own backyard. But was he in love with the idea enough to approve the mission? Especially if something went wrong and Farzan was killed or captured? Ashkan was well aware that he would probably pay for the failure with a bullet to the back of the head, his body dumped in a shallow, unmarked grave.

However, if the mission succeeded, Ashkan would be the toast of Tehran and could see himself leapfrogging other officers to the top of the promotion list. With personal ambition in his eyes and hopes of additional stars on his shoulders, the temptation was too great to resist.

***

Having made the turn at the Tel Aviv Marina, Daniel Golan dodged people strolling along the promenade that paralleled Ha-Yarkon Street. With several major hotels and foreign embassies occupying the high-priced beachfront real estate, the area was a hive of activity.

As he wound his way through the grassy hills of the Charles Glore Park, his mind drifted back to the surf club he'd passed a few minutes earlier and wondered how in the world they managed to stay in business. Having lived in Tel Aviv for most of his life, Golan had never recalled seeing any waves big enough to surf, especially with the breakwaters built along the beach to help combat coastal erosion. He made a mental note to talk to one of his friends at work who was big into the local surf scene.

Leaving the pavement at the park's southern edge, his long, powerful strides propelled him through one last stretch of sand. He was heading back towards the Al-Bahr Mosque when he noticed the sun reflecting off something in the dark recesses of its minaret. His pace slowed to a jog, then to a walk as he studied the tower in the distance.

***

Yosef Mehrdad saw the man slow his pace to a walk and look up in their direction. Observing his target through the magnified lens of a spotter's scope, it seemed as though the man was staring directly at him.

"Range?" Farzan asked, from his perch behind the scope of a

Russian-made Dragunov SVD sniper rifle.

"Six hundred meters."

"Wind?"

"Ten miles per hour. Full value. Moving left to right off the sea." Full value meant the wind would be moving at ninety degrees, or straight across the flight of the bullet.

At ten miles per hour, the wind would move the bullet three feet to the right as it traveled the six hundred meters to its target. Farzan adjusted the scope three and a half minutes of angle to the left. He'd already dialed in his dope for the distance and anticipated bullet drop.

A long list of possibilities ran though Golan's head as he stared at the minaret. *Was it my imagination? Did the sun glance off a window near the tower? Maybe it reflected off one of the spotlights mounted near the top.* Then, for some reason he couldn't explain, a picture of Jonathan Lewis popped into his head. *It couldn't be. Not right here in the middle of downtown Tel Aviv.*

He frantically scanned the area looking for something he could use for cover but there was nothing along this stretch of beach except for some low hedges to his left and the blue waters of the Med to his right. Golan realized that his daily run, along the same route at approximately the same time, a routine that he'd never consider falling into when he was operational, might have just cost him his life.

"Ready," Farzan said, placing the scope's crosshairs in the center of Golan's chest. No need to be greedy and go for a headshot.

Mehrdad keyed his radio. "Now, Basir."

The operative who'd picked the men up from the smuggler and driven them to Tel Aviv was downstairs in the mosque's parking lot. He reached through the car's open window and pressed on the center of the steering wheel.

Even though the rifle was suppressed, it was by no means silent. The blaring horn masked any sound that escaped Farzan's rifle, and the morning's traffic swallowed up the crack of the round as it broke the sound barrier.

The breeze coming in off the sea guided the hardened steel projectile from left to right as it covered the six hundred meters to its target in under a second. The impact of the center-mass shot obliterated Golan's heart, and his body collapsed onto the hot sand with a look of utter disbelief etched on his face.

CHAPTER 35

Bad news travelled fast, and word of Esposito's death had spread like wildfire throughout the embassy complex. A somber mood greeted Joe Matthews and his team as they entered the station's secure fourth floor office space. Everyone stood and approached the four men, shaking hands and offering condolences in hushed tones for the loss of their teammate.

Keenly aware of the risks they faced on a daily basis, the men and women of the CIA knew the same fate could befall them on any given day. The death of a colleague in the line of duty was a loss felt by every Agency officer, whether in the field or at headquarters in Langley, Virginia.

With his death a few hours ago, Randy Esposito had become a member of an exclusive group, joining over one hundred other intelligence officers who had given their lives in the line of duty. A black star representing his sacrifice would be engraved among the others on the marble Memorial Wall in the lobby of the Original Headquarters Building. It was not an honor anyone set out to accomplish when beginning a career at Langley.

Scott Garrett was waiting for the men in the SCIF. Feeling an indescribable appreciation for the sacrifice Joe's team had made to protect him today, he shook each man's hand and thanked him for his actions as they entered the room.

It was standard protocol to conduct a debriefing and after-action report, routinely called a hot wash, after a mission. But this meeting took on the additional level of significance due to Esposito's death. The images of Director Sloan, deputy director of operations Katherine Clark, chief of the special activities division Carl Douglas, and the chief of the Counterterrorism Center, Harold Lee, were displayed on a high-definition monitor so large it dominated the far wall of the secure conference room. Joe had expected Lee and

Douglas since they were in his direct chain of command but was a little surprised to see the Director and DDO on the monitor. *Makes sense though. The death of an Agency officer was bound to draw the attention of the seventh floor.*

He propped his rifle in the corner, then stripped off his plate carrier before taking a seat at the table. Following Joe's lead, the three other members of his team did the same, the mental and physical exhaustion of the firefight evident on their faces. Garrett grabbed four bottles of ice-cold water from a small refrigerator and offered one to each man. "We'll swap these out for beers later," he said before activating the videoconference's audio. Then, he turned to the camera mounted below the monitor, "Ready on this end, sir."

Director Sloan took the lead. "Everyone here at headquarters is mourning the loss of Randy Esposito. He gave his life serving his country and will be afforded the appropriate recognition and honors. Katherine will personally ensure his family has every resource at our disposal to help them cope with his death."

The men sitting around the table nodded in solemn agreement. Joe nodded as well, but it was more of a robotic response than actual comprehension of what the director had just said. His demeanor did not go unnoticed by the leadership group assembled in Sloan's conference room several thousand miles away.

Douglas asked, "What's on your mind, Joe?"

Lost in his thoughts, Joe was silent for a long moment. Finally, he said, "I just can't shake the feeling that if I'd made a better decision, or done something differently, Randy might still be alive."

Harold Lee barked, "That's bullshit, Joe, and you know it. We've all lost people in the field, and it sucks. But the decisions you made today saved Scott's life. You made the right call."

"We're all in agreement, Joe," Director Sloan added. "You and your men performed with extraordinary valor today."

Joe appreciated the reassuring words. When push came to shove, he knew he'd made the right decision, but it didn't make losing a teammate any easier.

They discussed the attack for another forty-five minutes acknowledging the good and the bad, learning from any mistakes so they wouldn't be repeated in the future. With the hot wash complete, Joe asked, "Sir, do we have any new leads on the Iranians who killed Ambassador Lewis?"

Director Sloan said, "As a matter of fact, we've developed a working theory as to why Jonathan Lewis was targeted. And if we're right, there are seven more names on the Iranians' hit list for this operation."

Joe and his guys sat up in their chairs and looked at one another. If Sloan didn't have their full attention before, he surely did now. In a departure from protocol, Sloan went on to explain the details of Project Wraith, to include the names of the key players in the operation who had found themselves in the Iranians' crosshairs.

Appreciating Sloan's candor, Joe said, "That explains the why, sir. But at this point I'm more interested in finding Farzan and Mehrdad so I can put a couple of my bullets in their heads."

"We all share that same interest, Joe," Sloan agreed, speaking for the group.

"Do we know where Farzan and Mehrdad are now?" Joe asked.

"No, we don't," Clark offered. "I know it sounds callous, but we were hoping it was their team that attacked you today. Unfortunately, the remains of the men you killed don't match the descriptions of Farzan or Mehrdad."

"Then the guys that hit us today must have been a secondary or stand-by team," Joe interjected. "Which means, if Farzan didn't attack us today, then he and Mehrdad must be setting up on one of the other targets on their list."

"Agreed," Clark added. "The only question is which one."

A knock on the conference room's door forced a pause in the conversation and Sloan turned away from the camera to address the intrusion. His annoyance evaporated when he saw the familiar face of Doug Kelly, the agent-in-charge of his protective detail, enter the room. He knew Kelly wouldn't have interrupted the meeting unless it was necessary, so whatever the reason, it had to be important.

Kelly handed Sloan a flash message. "Sorry for the interruption, sir, but this just came in from the Operations Center. The Watch Officer said you needed to see it right away."

Sloan's brow furrowed and a grave expression crossed his face as he read. When he finished the document he said, "Daniel Golan of the Mossad was assassinated in Tel Aviv an hour ago. I'd say our Major Farzan is currently in Israel, but he probably won't be there for long."

Katherine Clark was the first to speak after the shock of the message's contents wore off. "Daniel was a good man and a friend of the Agency."

"The Israelis are going to go apeshit," Douglas said, then turned to the director to apologize for his language. "Sorry, sir. What I meant to say is that they're going to turn the planet upside down looking for the shooters."

"I agree," Garrett added, "it will be like the killing spree they went on after the Munich massacre at the Olympics in '72."

Joe asked, "Sir, do the Israelis know about Farzan and Mehrdad?"

"Not yet. Due to the sensitivity of Project Wraith, President Andrews hasn't authorized me to share any of our findings."

"We might want to keep it that way for the time being," Joe suggested.

"Why is that?"

"Well, sir, I'm assuming or at least hoping we're going after the Iranians. And if we are, I'd like to volunteer for the mission right here and now." Before Joe could continue, the other three members of his team chimed in as well.

A slight smile spread across Sloan's face at the display of camaraderie among the team.

"I would imagine the Israelis will send out a fully operational Kidon team to track down Golan's killers. So far, Farzan and Mehrdad have demonstrated that they are very capable operators."

"And your point is?" Sloan asked.

"That the team you assign to track and take down Farzan and Mehrdad will have a hard enough time trying to find them, much less kill them. If the task falls to us, I would prefer we didn't have to look over our shoulders worrying about getting caught between the Iranians and the hit team sent to exact Israel's revenge."

"That makes good sense," Director Sloan said. "I'll set aside some time during the president's briefing in the morning to try and convince him of the merits of keeping the identity of the assassins to ourselves, at least for the time being."

"So, what's our next move?" Clark asked, throwing the question out to the assembled group.

Routinely working four or five moves ahead of any problem, Director Sloan was the first to speak. "With the death of Daniel Golan, there are six names remaining on the target list. Katherine, Paul Foley, Fred Jackson, and I are all here in the D.C. area. I'll brief Doug Kelly on the situation we're facing and have him put the appropriate security in place."

"That leaves Sir Nigel Craig, the British Foreign Secretary, and the CEO of Siemens, Friedrich Voigt," Clark said.

"I'll call Nigel as soon as we finish here," Sloan said. "He'll need to notify Special Branch of the threat and inform the Prime Minister."

"What about Friedrich?" Clark asked. "Would you like me to call him?"

Sloan thought it over for a minute, then said, "That would be helpful, Katherine, thank you."

With the notifications taken care of, Director Sloan turned back to the camera and addressed Joe and his men. "Now, gentlemen, earlier in this conversation you volunteered to take on the mission of tracking down our two Iranians and putting an end to their reign of terror. Does that offer still stand?"

Joe looked at Chris, John, and Mike and received three affirmative nods. With a smile on his face and vengeance in his eyes, Joe Matthews said, "Yes, sir. It certainly does."

CHAPTER 36

The tiny municipality of Grünwald sits on the east bank of the Isar River. A mere twelve kilometers southwest of Munich, the town is home to the Bavaria Filmstadt, one of Germany's largest movie studios. But the Burg Grünwald, or Grünwald Castle, is very possibly the town's most popular attraction. It was built on top of a hill overlooking the Isar River and is believed to have begun its existence as a single Roman guard tower.

Modern-day Grünwald is glamorous and sophisticated, with neighborhoods consisting of large, walled compounds with emerald green yards, tennis courts, and in-ground swimming pools. In stark contrast to the grey concrete of Munich, well-tended gardens and manicured parks, playgrounds, and an outdoor skating rink provide plenty of lush green space throughout the town. With a population of just over eleven thousand, mostly prominent businessmen and women, professional athletes, actors, and actresses, Grünwald is an exclusive community of Munich's elite. It would be a perfect setting if a German studio ever decided to make a Bavarian version of "Lifestyles of the Rich and Famous."

Friedrich Voigt, the president and CEO of Siemens AG, was one of the elite who made his home in Grünwald. While many of his counterparts chose to live closer to their offices in Munich, he enjoyed the quiet atmosphere of living in a small town.

Voigt made the most of the thirty-minutes spent in the backseat of his BMW sedan each morning to get a headstart on any emails that had landed in his inbox overnight and to prepare for his first meetings of the day. Conversely, he used the afternoon commute home to wrap up any outstanding issues so that he could devote his evenings to spending time with his family.

To the untrained eye, Voigt's BMW looked like any other 7 Series on the road. Practically indistinguishable from the production 760Li one might see on a local dealer's lot, Siemens had chosen to purchase what BMW calls the 7 Series High Security. The special-order sedan is outfitted with a variety of security enhancements that can protect its occupants from armor-piercing ammunition and even certain types of explosive devices.

Along with the armored BMW, Siemens also provided its CEO with a full-time security detail. Gerhard Albrecht, a retired federal police officer, was Voigt's driver. And Hans Schleck, a former member of the Federal Border Guard's Grenzschutzgruppe 9, or GSG-9, Germany's premier counterterror unit, was Voigt's head of security. In another era, say eighty or ninety years ago, Schleck's cobalt blue eyes and closely cropped blond hair would have guaranteed him a spot on a recruiting poster for the Third Reich.

The door to Voigt's office opened and he stepped out at five-thirty on the dot. In typical German fashion, he was unbelievably punctual and efficient as he fulfilled his duties throughout the workday. Schleck often thought Deutsche Bahn's high-speed trains might have set their watches by his boss to make sure they were running on schedule.

As a security professional, Schleck hated the fact that his boss insisted on maintaining such a strict routine. The predictability of it made them vulnerable. He'd spoken to Voigt more than once about the reasons behind the need to vary his arrival and departure times but had been rebuffed on each attempt. Schleck eventually accepted defeat and dropped the subject. After all, Voigt was the boss. And if the boss wanted to leave at exactly five-thirty every day, who was he to tell him he couldn't?

Schleck was chatting with Voigt's executive assistant Elsa while he waited in the executive suite's outer lobby. Lost in the conversation, they were both startled by the sound of Voigt's voice when he said, "For heaven's sake, Hans, why don't you just get it over with and ask her out?"

Elsa blushed and turned away, as if she were looking at something on her computer screen to avoid making eye contact with her boss. Both men laughed because they could see her monitor and there was nothing on it except the screensaver.

Rising to the challenge, Hans replied, "Perhaps you're right, sir. What do you say, Elsa, dinner on Saturday?"

Looking back up at the muscular blond, she said, "Sounds great. Pick me up at seven-thirty?"

Schleck winked at Elsa, "Seven-thirty it is."

"Now that I've played the role of Cupid and arranged for you lovebirds to finally go on a date, may we go home, Hans?"

"Of course, sir. Gerhard is waiting downstairs." They crossed the lobby and Hans entered the private elevator car ahead of Voigt. He pressed the button for the garage level, then radioed Albrecht to let him know they were coming down.

Hans heard the familiar voice of the driver's reply over his earpiece. "Copy. All clear."

Schleck's thoughts kept drifting back to Elsa and their upcoming date as he and his boss descended to the garage in silence. He couldn't remember the last time he'd gone out on a Saturday night that didn't involve too many beers with his former teammates at the local biergarten.

A chime sounded, breaking the silence as the elevator reached the garage. The doors slid open and Schleck exited the elevator ahead of Voigt, leading the way to the idling BMW. With everyone in place, Albrecht put the car in gear and headed up the ramp.

CHAPTER 37

Joe Matthews and his team had scored seats on one of the CIA's King Air B200s making the routine run from Baghdad to Amman, Jordan. A few hours of sleep, a hot shower, and a change of clothes later they were on their way to Queen Alia International Airport to catch a Lufthansa flight to Munich.

Rental vehicles and hotel reservations had been made with an assist from the CIA's local office. After checking into their rooms, the team had gone to work setting up a tactical operations center, or TOC. They had been in the city for a week, putting together a full surveillance package on Friedrich Voigt, and had been keeping an eye on him ever since.

Given the first attack in Iraq, the second in Israel, and now a possible third individual being targeted in Germany, the Iranian assassination team seemed to be working their way westward. Was Munich the next stepping stone on Farzan's path of destruction? Sloan and the brain trust back at Langley thought so, believing Voigt to be the next logical target on the list. And if that was the case, it meant Farzan and Mehrdad would be coming to town if they weren't there already.

Prior to their departure from Baghdad, Joe's marching orders had been to do everything possible to take the men alive so they could be subjected to an interrogation. Then, with the president's approval, they would be paraded before the world as absolute proof of Tehran's involvement in Jonathan Lewis's murder. However, if the Iranians put up a fight, Joe doubted Director Sloan would shed a tear if he put them down like a couple of rabid dogs.

Kevin Chang was in the TOC, monitoring the radio traffic and tracking Voigt's movements on a laptop. He had joined the team in Munich, filling the vacancy created by the death of Randy Esposito in Iraq. The guys knew Kevin and respected his abilities from previous assignments so the transition had been seamless.

Chang's grandparents had emigrated to the U.S. from China forty years ago and settled in Vermont, of all places. As a result, people tended to do a double take when they heard an Asian guy with a heavy New England accent asking for extra maple syrup on his pancakes and referring to everything as "wicked." Growing up with great ski resorts like Stratton Mountain practically in his back yard, Kevin had learned to ski and snowboard at an early age. Even now, he was still a daredevil on the powder and dreamed about competing in the X Games someday.

He loved his job, but being from New England, despised operating in the Middle East. The people were okay when they weren't trying to kill you, but the heat was ridiculous, and the God-forsaken sand chafed like a sonofabitch. "If I have to operate in some shithole, it might as well be Afghanistan," he'd said on more than one occasion. "At least they have mountains and plenty of snow. If we could get rid of the Taliban, I'd think about opening up a wicked awesome ski resort in the Hindu Kush."

Katherine Clark had called Voigt to warn him of the impending danger prior to the team's arrival in Munich. Since they were speaking on an unsecure line Clark wouldn't go into the specifics of the Agency's working theory, namely that the killing of Jonathan Lewis was Iran's opening salvo in a war against the individuals involved in Project Wraith. Even so, she did manage to get her point across by referring to a technical project Voigt had worked on many years ago, a project that was successful in no small part due to his company's contribution.

The German CEO immediately understood the reference to Project Wraith and why his friend would have been targeted if certain parties became aware of his involvement in the operation. And based on the project's intended target, it wasn't difficult for Voigt to determine who the suspects were.

"We believe all the key people involved in the project are at risk, and we are urging them to take the necessary steps to ensure their safety," Clark said.

Assuming the Americans' theory was correct, Voigt was certain that he would occupy a prominent spot on the target list. And if that was the case, he had no doubt the Iranians would send someone to visit violence upon him and his family.

Clark continued, "I've already spoken with my counterpart at the BND to make them aware of our concerns," referring to Germany's Federal Intelligence Service, their equivalent of the CIA. "For obvious reasons, I didn't go into details regarding why we believe you may be in danger, just that some information came to us through a trusted asset in the Middle East."

"I appreciate your discretion, Katherine. I certainly do not need or want the scrutiny my involvement in the project would draw to the company or my family," Voigt replied. "Please don't misunderstand, I'm proud of the part I played in the operation. I just don't think any good would come from having it exposed to a wider circle of people. In fact, I've been pleasantly surprised it's stayed quiet this long. Usually, information like this is too big to keep secret."

"I agree wholeheartedly, Friedrich. Best we keep this information to ourselves and the trusted few who've been involved from the beginning."

Voigt was happy they seemed to be thinking along the same lines. "I'll be equally vague when informing my head of security. I have the utmost respect for his abilities and am confident he'll take the appropriate precautions. He'll need to know what the threat is but not why it has come about."

"Excellent. How about your family? How are they?"

"Marthe and the kids are well. Thank you for asking."

"You may want to consider moving them for a few weeks. At least until we get a fix on the suspects."

Voigt considered the suggestion for a moment and said, "I suppose a holiday wouldn't be out of the question. I'll discuss the idea with Martha. She and the kids will be disappointed I won't be joining them, but they'll understand. Unfortunately, it won't be the first time I've missed a vacation because of work."

"It might be good for you to get out of town for a while as well," Clark suggested.

He sighed before answering, "If only that were possible, Katherine. We're in the final stages of negotiations on two very lucrative contracts, which I hope to wrap up in the next week or so. And members of our Board of Directors are coming together for a meeting here in Munich next month. I'm sure you can imagine the amount of work to be done ahead of that gathering. It is just not possible for me to get away right now. But as I said before, I have the utmost confidence in my security team and I'm sure everything will be fine."

Clark understood Voigt's situation. It was nearly impossible for a person in his position to take off for a few weeks on a moment's notice. She faced the same problem every time she tried to take a vacation, even one that was scheduled months in advance. And when she did get away, it wasn't really a vacation. As the person responsible for America's clandestine service, there was always one crisis or another requiring her attention.

As a result, she traveled with a secure communications package to maintain contact with Langley and the CIA's stations around the globe. The never-ending stream of secure calls and classified emails meant she just ended up working from an off-site location, whether she was sitting on the beach or by the fire at a ski lodge in the mountains. Maybe one day, after she'd retired and her service to the country had come to an end, she and her husband would take off on a whim and vacation like normal people. But Clark knew that day was nowhere in sight.

"I understand, Friedrich. The burden of responsibility."

A smile crossed Voigt's face, knowing the woman on the other end of the line felt a similar burden – admittedly, on a different level, because lives hung in the balance with some of the decisions she was forced to make. "Thank you for the call, and your concern, Katherine. It is very much appreciated."

CHAPTER 38

John Roberts and Mike McCredy had drawn the short straw, earning the misfortune of working the overnight shift, so they were back in their rooms getting some well-deserved sleep.

Sitting in an idling Volkswagen Touareg they'd acquired from the consulate's motor pool, Joe and Chris were in position, waiting to tail the German CEO when he left the office. Like most if not all vehicles in the consulate's inventory, the SUV was fitted with license plates bearing a unique number and letter combination that identified it as a diplomatic vehicle. The combination on the Volkswagen's plates told the world it belonged to the U.S. diplomatic mission in Munich.

Chris had worked his charm on a helpful logistics officer who happened to have several spare sets of local license plates in her possession. With a little encouragement and an offer to buy a round at the next happy hour, the officer was more than happy to provide him with a clean set of plates.

Joe's phone vibrated and he checked the screen for the incoming text message. It read, "Just cleared the garage. Heading your way in a black BMW 7 Series."

The text was from Meg Murphy, a case officer based in Munich who had been assigned to assist Joe's team. He had never met the tall blond from Washington, D.C., but after working with her the last couple of days it was obvious she knew her shit. Meg was a natural at conducting surveillance and had an uncanny ability to hide in plain sight. She was like a freaking ghost and could practically disappear in broad daylight. Joe had a hard time picking her out of a crowd even when he knew exactly where she was supposed to be. He'd never seen anyone with abilities even remotely close to Meg's, and that level of tradecraft had him wondering what other skillsets she might possess.

Joe could count on one hand the number of females currently serving in the Protective Operations Division, and the number of women occupying operational roles in Special Activities was even smaller. He made a mental note to have a conversation with the division chiefs when this Farzan saga was over. *Someone should seriously consider recruiting her.*

Meg appeared to be studying the bronze statue in the center of the Wittelsbacher Platz, which was conveniently located across the street from Siemens' corporate headquarters. With the workday coming to an end, workers heading home for dinner or on a mission to find their first beer of the evening filled the plaza. The mass of people, combined with Meg's unnatural powers of invisibility, shielded her from the security cameras monitoring the perimeter of the Siemens building. Positioned near the statue, she was afforded a clear view of the exit ramp leading up from the building's underground parking garage.

He and Chris were parked under a row of trees along Kardinal Döpfner Strasse, a one-way street that would funnel drivers leaving Siemen's offices their way. Joe was starving, and the aromas emanating from the Italian restaurant on the corner weren't helping matters. Italian was one of his favorites, so he looked up the Perazzo Ristorante's website on his smartphone and saved the address in its map application. Next, he searched the site and downloaded the menu, planning to come back and try the linguine if he had the chance.

Chris was watching traffic in the rearview mirror when he caught sight of Voigt's BMW. "Here they come."

"You know the drill. Let them have some space. Voigt's team is supposed to be pretty high-speed, so we don't want to spook them."

With an appreciative smile spreading across his face, Chris looked around at people laughing and enjoying a post-work beer at the sidewalk cafes and pubs. "Man, it's nice being back in the civilized world. You ever get tired of running around the ass cracks of the planet?"

"Yeah, it does get old after a while."

"You know what I'm enjoying the most?" Chris asked, keeping an eye on Voigt's car. "It's the simple things, like people obeying traffic laws…and the color green. I really miss seeing green when we're over in the sandbox. How nice is it to see actual trees and grass? Plus, that damn sand gets into everything. You don't have that problem with grass."

Joe just shook his head and laughed along with his friend.

Chris continued his riff, "And how about the women? My God, it's great seeing them walk down the street in heels and a short skirt."

"That is a wonderful thing," Joe agreed. "If I never see another woman in a burka it'll be too soon."

"You ever wonder what they're wearing underneath those black tents?" Chris asked.

"I'm sure it's something sexy," Joe said, positive that every guy who'd traveled to the Middle East has had that same thought at some point. "They probably all look like Victoria's Secret models, and the burkas help them get around without being stalked by guys like you."

They laughed as the BMW went by and Chris pulled out into traffic. He fell in behind Voigt and his security detail, always keeping a buffer of at least four or five vehicles between them.

Making a right on the Oskar von Miller Ring Road, he followed the luxury sedan through the Altstadring tunnel. Traffic exited onto Prinzregenten Strasse and the enormous Englisher Garten was on their left. With seventy-eight kilometers of trails, it was a prime training ground for Munich's runners and cyclists.

"I heard this park has its own beer garden that looks out over a lake," Joe observed, as they drove past the lush groves of trees.

"Sounds nice. Maybe we can swing by and down a pint or two if we ever get a day off."

"Wishful thinking," Joe said, keeping his eyes on Voigt's car as they talked. "Looks like they're making a right."

The BMW did in fact turn right, and paralleled the left bank of the Isar River with the American operatives discreetly shadowing its every move.

Chris turned serious, which was unusual for the habitual smart ass. He glanced over at his friend and asked, "So, how are you holding up?"

Joe knew where Chris was going with his question but didn't want to get into it right now. "I'm fine. Why?"

"Why?" Chris countered, a little annoyed. "Don't pull that tough guy shit with me. It's been a little over a week since Randy was killed and our operational tempo has been balls to the wall. Other than the debrief, we haven't had time to discuss what happened because we've been spending all of our time and effort chasing these two assholes across the Middle East and Europe."

Joe had to admit there was some truth to what Chris was saying. He and the guys had been briefing Director Sloan and the leadership team in the SCIF when the Mossad agent was assassinated. They had been dispatched to Munich later that same day, and once they landed in Germany, everyone's focus had been on setting up the surveillance effort on Voigt. *Jesus.* Chris was right.

Chris continued, "We've both lost men in battle, but we also usually had time to process and mourn the loss. Hell, with everything going on we didn't even have a chance to do a proper hot-wash after the attack."

A hot-wash was a team meeting routinely conducted after a mission where everyone's actions were scrutinized down to the smallest detail. Regardless of rank or position, everyone was expected to speak up and self-report, detailing the good and the bad, whether it was the most senior operator on the team or a wet-behind-the-ears recruit straight from the Farm. It wasn't meant to be a finger-pointing session but a learning experience designed to prevent the same mistakes from being repeated in the future.

Joe turned and looked out his window as the outskirts of Munich blurred past. "Yeah, you're right. We didn't even get the chance to hoist a beer in his memory before we took off. We'll have to make a point to do that when we get some downtime."

Chris was glad his friend acknowledged the burden he'd been carrying. He felt Joe might have turned a corner and was ready to absolve himself of any guilt for Esposito's death. He wanted his team leader to have a clear mind when they came face to face with the Iranians.

Admittedly, Joe felt a little of the weight lift from his broad shoulders. "Thanks, Chris. I guess I did need talk it out a bit."

"That's what I'm here for. But truth be told, my motives were a little self-serving."

"Really? How?"

"Well, you really are kind of a downer to be around when you're all mopey like that. And the thought of spending the foreseeable future cooped up in a car with you had me contemplating driving us straight into the next telephone pole I could find."

Joe shook his head and laughed, "Well, if you're done with your Dr. Phil impersonation, how about we get our heads refocused on taking down Farzan and Mehrdad?"

"Sounds like a plan, my friend."

CHAPTER 39

Gerhard Albrecht continued guiding the BMW south along the Isar River, following the route he and Schleck had chosen earlier in the day. Knowing they'd have to cross the river at some point, the men studied the routes they'd used recently for patterns or routines that might have developed unintentionally.

Bridges, like tunnels, were best avoided if possible. They were natural chokepoints that left the protective detail with few options should an attack occur while on or in one. If there was no other choice, which was the case here in Munich, it was necessary to get across the river and away from the chokepoint as quickly as possible.

But unlike many cities with only one or two bridges, no fewer than seven spanned the river between Munich and Grünwald, so they had several options. For this evening's trip home, the men chose the Reichenbach Bridge for the crossing. It was a not-so-hidden gem of unusual activity in one of Munich's suburbs.

Built of grey stone and concrete with supports resembling castle towers, the bridge spans a length of the Isar where the currents formed a nice stretch of white water.
When the water was flowing down from the Tyrolian Mountains, residents from the surrounding neighborhoods would line the bridge to catch a glimpse of surfers. Most tourists would probably never think of Munich being a hotbed of surfing, but they would be wrong. It was not at all unusual to see surfers and kayakers carving up the water as people crossed the bridge on their daily commute. During the summer months, sunbathers took advantage of the grassy park along the banks for picnics or catching a few rays on the weekends.

As Albrecht turned left onto the bridge, Schleck saw the results of the torrential rains the region had experienced the last couple of days. The water was high and the current swift. He imagined there would be quite a few people eager to take advantage of the conditions.

Once they were safely across the bridge, Albrecht wound his way through the southern portion of Au-Haidhausen, an old neighborhood of townhomes and apartments. The suburb was a picture-book community, with manicured lawns and red-tiled roofs that looked like a German version of a Norman Rockwell painting. Kids played in the yards, kicking soccer balls to one another, and couples were out enjoying an evening stroll, leashes in hand with their dogs leading the way.

It was hard to imagine the possibility of such a tranquil scene after the devastation wrought across the country during World War II. People's ability to rebuild, whether here in Germany or in other countries similarly devastated by war or natural disaster, never ceased to amaze Schleck. Their resiliency made him proud of his country but at the same time sad that previous generations had endured such hardship in the first place.

Voigt looked up from his tablet as Albrecht turned onto Martin Luther Strasse and approached the Grünwalder Stadium. For years, the stadium had been the home pitch for Bayern Munich, the city's professional football team that played in the elite Bundesliga. The team moved to their new home, Allianz Arena, at the beginning of the 2005 season, but the red, white, and blue banners still surrounded the crown of the old stadium. Voigt liked it when they took this route home because the sight of the old stadium brought back some of his favorite childhood memories of attending the games and cheering on the team with his father.

Voigt broke the silence in the car as they passed the stadium. "So, Gerhard, do you have plans for the weekend?"

"Not that I'm aware of, sir, but it's been a few hours since I've spoken to my wife. Knowing her as I do, there are probably a few chores she'd like me to take care of around the house."

Voigt chuckled. "Sounds familiar. Marthe probably has a very similar list for me."
The security men exchanged a look, stunned that a man of his stature had to take care of a honey-do list like every other working stiff.

"The reason I ask is FC Bayern is playing at home Saturday night. With Marthe and the children out of town I don't feel like going to the game alone. However, my loss is your gain. You're welcome to use my box seats if you can convince your wife to let you push the chores off until Sunday."

Voigt's generous offer took Albrecht by surprise, and he didn't know what to say. He desperately wanted to go to the game but felt a little awkward accepting the tickets in front of Schleck. He glanced over at his partner, wondering why the boss hadn't given him the prime tickets instead.

Noticing the nervous look, Voigt said, "It's alright, Gerhard. Hans is busy this weekend and won't be able to attend the game."

Now Albrecht was really confused. *Was Hans working Saturday and Sunday? And if so, why wasn't he?*

Voigt continued, "I have it on good authority that our man Hans has a hot date Saturday night. So, don't worry about him. He'll be just fine."

Schleck squirmed a little in the BMW's leather seat as his cheeks flushed with embarrassment, still not accustomed to his boss's good-natured ribbing.

Enjoying the big man's discomfort, Albrecht asked, "Really, Hans, a date? Who, pray tell, is the lucky girl?"

"Maybe you can ask Elsa when you pick up the tickets in the morning," Voigt chimed in from the back seat, clearly enjoying the opportunity to stir the pot.

Albrecht shook his head and let out a low whistle. "Elsa? Well done, Hans. Well done."

The thought of her brought a grin to Schleck's face. "Thank you, my friend, but I would appreciate you focusing more on your driving and less on my social life."

"I'm sure you would. But giving you a hard time about your date is so much more fun. I had no idea you even knew what a social life was, or that you were interested in having one yourself."

All three men laughed, enjoying the lighthearted moment. Determined to finish up this last bit of work before they arrived at the house, Voigt turned his attention back to his tablet. The two security men up front returned to their duties, although you couldn't blame them if their minds continued to wander a little. Schleck couldn't stop thinking about Elsa and their date on Saturday night, trying to decide what she'd like to do and where he should take her. Albrecht's mind was already on the game, trying to remember who Bayern Munich had on the schedule and picturing the view from the luxury box.

Both men pushed the thoughts to the back of their minds as they entered the outskirts of Grünwald. They knew most attacks took place near the home or office, locations where the target's time and place were most predictable, and the men in the BMW were rapidly approaching one of those locations.

CHAPTER 40

Reaching the outskirts of Grünwald, Albrecht took a left at the Bavarian Film Studio, then a right onto Gabriel von Seidl Strasse. Finished with his email, Voigt switched off his tablet and slid it into his leather shoulder bag. Less than a kilometer from home, he could see the slate-grey tiles of the roof and its three white-brick chimneys come into view.

Voigt had purchased the property when he was promoted to the chief executive position ten years ago, and it had been his family's primary residence ever since. The home was a rectangular two-story structure made of the same white brick as the chimneys that rose so prominently over the neighborhood. A paved driveway led from the solid-wood privacy gate to the front of the house, where a large spruce tree acted as the centerpiece of a circular drive that doubled as parking for guests. The driveway continued past the front door to the large four-car garage attached to the far end of the house.

The back of the home opened onto a half-moon patio set up with an elaborate food prep and grilling area. Comfortable outdoor furniture was arranged around a fire pit that looked out over the expansive yard and in-ground swimming pool. As the CEO of one of Germany's most prestigious companies, Voigt had a very public profile, so one of the features he appreciated most about the home was the ten-foot ivy-covered walls surrounding the property. They provided a measure of privacy from the prying eyes of the media, but most of all they afforded his children with a safe place to play. Countless games of football and hide-and-seek had taken place inside the grounds when they were little.

Albrecht slowed the car and came to a stop as Schleck activated the remote to open the gate. Made of wood sections, similar to railroad ties stacked vertically, the gate was incredibly heavy. Even with an optional upgrade to the motor, it still took an eternity to open. Schleck had initially been a fan of the gate's construction. appreciating the security provided by the heavy wooden sections. But he had begun having second thoughts lately, due to the length of time they were left exposed on the street.

Drivers sat patiently behind Voigt's BMW as traffic on Gabriel von Seidl Strasse had ground to a halt. They didn't seem to mind, though, because most of the homes along this street were gated compounds, and the motorists had grown accustomed to the routine.

While they waited to make the left into the compound, Schleck noticed a gleaming BMW motorcycle to his right. "Sir, did your neighbors buy a new motorcycle?"

Looking over at the bike, Voigt said, "Not that I'm aware of." Thinking it was odd, he continued, "I've never even heard them express an interest in riding."

Albrecht leaned over to get a better look at it and said, "It wasn't here when we left for the office this morning. If it is theirs, why isn't it parked inside the grounds?"

***

Albrecht was right. The motorcycle hadn't been there when they headed into work that morning. As the sun rose over Grünwald, filling the sky with brilliant streaks of pink, purple, and orange, an operative from the Iranian Consulate on Mauerkircher Strasse was in the neighborhood observing their departure.

Satisfied Voigt and his security team were heading north into the city, the man unlocked his smartphone and tapped in a message. A second operative's phone chimed at the arrival of the text bubble on his screen. Receiving the "all clear" from his colleague, the man left the consulate and rode south toward Grünwald on a recently purchased BMW R1200GS motorcycle.

Most of the town's residents were still asleep or just beginning to stir as the operative, his identity hidden by the helmet and visor, entered the town and approached Voigt's residence. He had to look closely in the dim light but eventually found the "X" Farzan had placed on the wall directly across the street from Voigt's gate. Marked with white chalk, it designated the exact spot where Farzan wanted the big motorcycle parked.

The rider wondered why Farzan wanted it there, but shrugged off his curiosity as he dismounted and used his right foot to push the bike's center stand down until it contacted the pavement. He pulled back on the handlebars with all his strength, using the momentum to lever the heavy motorcycle to the rear until it came to rest on its center stand. His orders had specifically requested the motorcycle be parked on the center stand to keep it perfectly vertical, at a ninety-degree angle to the street, preventing the lean to the left that resulted from using the kickstand.

With his part of the mission complete, the rider climbed into the watcher's sedan and was driven directly to Munich's International Airport. Less than two hours after parking the motorcycle in Grünwald, the operative was on a flight to Istanbul. He watched Munich disappear under the wings as he sipped a cup of strong Turkish coffee from the comfort of his business class seat. He'd spend a couple of days of R&R in Turkey before catching a flight back to Tehran. Not a bad reward for a few hours of work.

The motorcycle parked across from Voigt's gate was outfitted with aluminum cargo boxes that attached to each side of the bike's frame. Normally used to carry luggage or camping supplies for a cross-country ride, the box on the left side of this bike contained something far more lethal.

Explosively Formed Penetrators, or EFPs, were an efficient and deadly type of roadside bomb that made their debut on the battlefields of Iraq in 2003. Western intelligence services believed Iran's Quds Force provided the munitions to Shiite militias and insurgent groups, along with the know-how to construct them, in order to carry out attacks against U.S. and Coalition forces.

Fairly simple to build, an EFP is made by packing a short section of metal pipe with explosives and fitting it with a concave, dish-shaped cap made of copper or steel. When the charge is detonated, the force of the explosion partially melts the cap, transforming it into a projectile that travels at speeds of more than a mile per second. A one-pound projectile is capable of piercing over four inches of hardened steel armor, then spraying the inside of a vehicle with flesh-shredding shrapnel. Up-armored Humvees were incapable of protecting the servicemen and women they carried, and even America's main battle tank, the M-1 Abrams, was not immune to the destructive forces of an EFP. It was one of these devices that was packed into the motorcycle's cargo box, waiting to unleash its devastation.

***

The gate was about halfway open, not quite wide enough for the car to enter the grounds, when Schleck's attention was drawn away from the motorcycle. A white panel van was idling approximately one hundred meters south of Voigt's residence. It was emblazoned with the large pink "T" of Deutsche Telekom, the largest mobile phone service provider in the Europe. The company also offered its customers Internet access and television programming, so it wasn't unusual for one of their service vehicles to be seen in a residential neighborhood.

Orange cones surrounded the van, standard company procedure when on a service call, but Schleck didn't see any outward signs of activity. Maybe the technicians were inside the neighbor's home, installing new service or troubleshooting a glitch in the network. They might even be in the back of the van taking a break, but it was a little late in the day for that. Schleck imagined the techs would be anxious to finish their work so they could wrap up their shift and head home.

Movement in the van's darkened cab drew Schleck's attention, and he noticed a man in the passenger seat for the first time. An uneasy feeling in his gut told him something was wrong.

Albrecht was getting the same vibe from the van when Schleck ordered, "Back up. Make a U-turn and head to the police station. I'll call and let them know we're coming."

Albrecht put the car in reverse, planning to back into the next available driveway to make the turn. The only problem was the four cars waiting patiently behind them for the gate to open.

CHAPTER 41

Hamid Farzan was keeping an eye on the street, having chosen a location that gave him a clear view of traffic entering the exclusive neighborhood from the north. Yousef Mehrdad busied himself in the back of the van, readying their assortment of weapons. There would be no need for them if everything went according to plan, but a plan was only good until first contact. At that point the enemy, or in this case the target, had a vote, and anything could happen once the attack was initiated. He wanted to be prepared, just in case.

"Just a little farther," Farzan whispered as he armed the remote trigger. He was about to initiate the attack when Voigt's sedan stopped short of the motorcycle. His finger hovered over the remote trigger while they waited on the laborious process for the gate to open. Farzan's eyes and full attention were locked on a chalk mark he'd made on the street that corresponded to the motorcycle's placement. If his calculations were correct, Voigt's door would be perfectly aligned with the EFP inside the aluminum cargo box when the sedan's front wheel hit the chalk.

Satisfied the weapons were in order, Mehrdad had just settled into the driver's seat when he saw Voigt's security man eyeballing them. "Do you think he's seen us?"

The Quds men watched as the BMW's driver turned, looking over his shoulder out the rear window, and attempted to reverse out of the danger zone. From their vantage point, it was clear the driver's action was futile. The cars waiting in line left him with no place to go. Farzan saw the security man in the passenger seat frantically shouting orders he couldn't hear, and the driver returned his attention to the front in an apparent attempt to move forward and get off the X. The driver barely had time to shift back into drive and press the gas pedal when Farzan's finger fell, activating the remote trigger.

***

"What the hell?" Chris asked as he saw the BMW's white reverse lights come on. "Why's he trying to back up?"

"I don't know," Joe said. "Maybe something spooked him. Keep your eyes open for anything out of the ordinary."

The words had barely left his mouth when a blinding flash was followed a split second later by a deafening explosion. Instinctively, he and Chris ducked behind the dashboard as the shockwave barreled down the street. It swept over the vehicles and shattered their SUV's windshield, covering the interior of the cabin with tiny bits of glass.

The vehicles between the Americans' SUV and Voigt's BMW didn't fare nearly as well. Blaring car alarms and the screams of frantic and possibly injured people filled the air. Joe had seen the results of far too many car bombs throughout his career and knew there had to be multiple casualties on the street. It was usually the innocent bystanders who took the brunt of an attack of this nature.

Still tucked behind the relative safety of the dashboard, Chris asked, "What the fuck just happened?"

Joe and Chris inched their way up in unison and peered over the dash. The scene that greeted them was more reminiscent of Iraq or Afghanistan than Germany. Smoke rose from the burning remnants of the obliterated motorcycle and the street was littered with damaged vehicles. Stunned people wandered around in a daze after experiencing a level of violence they never imagined would visit their peaceful hamlet.

The explosion had blown Voigt's heavily armored sedan across the oncoming lane of traffic and it had come to rest against the compound's wall. Joe could make out the sedan but the dust and debris hanging in the air made it impossible to tell if any of the occupants were still alive.

Movement beyond the car caught Joe's eye, and he thought he saw two figures running through the smoke and haze towards the stricken vehicle. *Were they first responders? How did they get here so quickly? Plenty of people had been on the street when the explosion occurred, maybe they were good Samaritans coming to the aid of their neighbors.* "Let's get up there and see what the hell is going on."

Chris reached into the back seat and grabbed his ruck, which contained a basic trauma kit, before bailing out and following Joe up the street. As they approached Voigt's sedan, Joe got a better look at the two men he'd seen through the smoke. They were wearing some type of utility uniform. Hoping for the best, he thought they might be paramedics. But the explosion happened less than a minute ago. There was no way they could respond that fast. Besides, where was the ambulance? And why weren't they carrying any advanced life-support equipment?

His eyes moved from the men's uniforms to the dark objects in their hands, objects that were all too familiar in Joe's line of work. Looking up from their hands to their faces, he immediately recognized the men. "Chris, it's them!"

Confused, Chris asked, "Them who?"

"Farzan and Mehrdad."

"No shit? You sure?"

"Yep. Looks like they're moving in to finish off any survivors."

Without saying another word, the American operators drew their Glocks and continued moving toward the Iranians. To say they were eager to take these guys down was the understatement of the year. Farzan and Mehrdad were leaving a trail of dead bodies in their wake and had to be stopped. Joe thanked God he wasn't a cop because he had no intention of reading the Iranians their rights or placing them under arrest.

Farzan and Mehrdad beat the Americans to the sedan, having jumped out of the van and sprinted toward the stricken car before the echo of the explosion had faded into the distance. The Iranians were determined to confirm their kill and ensure there were no survivors.

The entire right side of the armored BMW was caved in from the impact of the projectile. Its rear door and bullet-resistant window were still intact, but were jammed in place by the car's bent frame. Mehrdad went to work immediately and began yanking on the door in a rhythmic motion.

Joe couldn't believe his eyes. The big man seemed to be making some progress prying the door open with his bare hands. He decided then and there that the proposition of going hand-to-hand with this guy was a nonstarter.

Farzan took up a position near the BMW's hood where he could cover Mehrdad's back and keep a lookout for any first responders or do-gooders who might interfere with their operation. Blood seeped through Mehrdad's fingers as the metal frame cut into his hands, leaving long red streaks running down the sedan's armored skin. Unhappy with his progress, or lack thereof, he decided to change tactics. He put his left foot on the car's rear quarter panel and used the strength in his leg to assist in the effort. He fell into a push-pull rhythm, pushing with his leg and pulling with his arms. The new tactic seemed to be working and the door opened a fraction of an inch with each iteration. Seeing his victory on the horizon, Mehrdad let out a great primal scream and pulled for all he was worth. The effort seemed to give him the extra bit of power he needed, and with one last heave, the metal creaked and the door swung open.

CHAPTER 42

Mehrdad drew a Makarov PMM pistol from a shoulder holster concealed by his utility uniform. The weapon's grip was slick with the blood from his hands as he aligned the sights on Voigt's head. His right index finger began taking the slack out of the trigger, but before the weapon fired he was distracted by an unfamiliar voice calling his name.

He could see Farzan standing at the front of the BMW and knew his boss hadn't said anything, so he was momentarily confused as to where the voice was coming from. He looked to his left and saw two armed men emerge from the smoke, moving in his direction. One had close-cropped red hair and the other looked like pictures he'd seen of California's surfers. His hair resembled a shaggy, blond mop.

The man with red hair yelled at him again in Farsi, "Drop the gun, Yousef!"

As shocked as Mehrdad was to hear a stranger calling his name, the fact that the man was speaking to him in his native language was even more surprising. He had no idea who the man was, but he was clearly armed and posed a threat to their mission, so Mehrdad raised his weapon to fire at the mystery man.

Using the split second of confusion to his advantage, Joe pressed the trigger four times. The Iranian dropped to a knee and rolled to his left, simultaneously lowering his profile while getting out of the line of fire. The four rounds missed their intended target and struck the inside of the open door's bullet resistant window.

Chris snapped off two shots as well, but Mehrdad was up and moving with surprising agility for a man of his size. He spun around on the balls of his feet and took cover behind the open door, using its armoring as a protective shield.

Smoke obscured Farzan's view of the attackers, but he heard the gunfire and the metallic thuds of the bullets impacting the BMW. He rose from behind the sedan's hood and fired all twelve of his weapon's rounds toward the sound of the gunshots. The most he'd hoped to achieve with this initial volley was to suppress the men's fire, or at the very least, slow their advance. Hitting one of them would have been pure luck. The slide locked to the rear on an empty chamber, so he ducked back behind the hood to reload. Mehrdad popped up, firing his own Makarov over the top of the door, adding to the stream of lead flying toward the advancing men.

The sound of the gunfire sent the two Americans scrambling for something solid to hide behind. Chris dove to his right, around the corner of a neighbor's wall and landed hard on his left shoulder and hip. Joe chose to go the opposite direction, crouching behind the wheel well of an abandoned but still idling car.

He was shuffling from side to side in search of an angle that would allow him to return fire when he felt a burning sensation in his right thigh. Looking down, he saw a horizontal rip in his jeans that was surrounded by a rapidly expanding bloodstain. Joe spread the denim apart with the thumb and forefinger of his left hand to get a better look at the wound. A round had creased the outside of his thigh, carving a half-inch deep groove in the muscle, but it hadn't penetrated his leg. Seeing the extent of the damage, or lack thereof, he let out a sigh of relief. It would hurt like hell but shouldn't affect his mobility if he could suck up the pain. That wouldn't be an issue.

With the lull in the action, Farzan decided to forego confirmation of the kill and make a break for it. Both men turned and bolted toward the Deutsch Telekom van.

Joe saw the Iranians take off down the street. He acquired a good sight picture on the center of Farzan's back but didn't take the shot. There were too many bystanders in the way. Some were dazed, stumbling around aimlessly like zombies in the Walking Dead. Others were curious neighbors who had heard the commotion and come out to see what was going on. There was no way he could take the shot and risk hitting one of the innocent civilians.

He desperately wanted to chase the bastards down but couldn't leave Voigt and his security guys if there was a chance they were still alive. Letting the Iranians go for the time being, they sprinted to the demolished BMW. Chris was the first to reach the car and slid headfirst into the back seat. Voigt's head was slumped forward, with his chin resting on his chest. He was unconscious, but Chris could tell he was breathing. It was shallow and ragged, but it was there.

"I have no idea how, but he's alive," Chris said in the same calm manner a paramedic or trauma doc in the ER might use with an injured patient. That calm only comes to those who have spent a considerable amount of time walking the razor's edge between life and death. The two operators had seen plenty of death and destruction and, on occasion, had even caused their fair share of it. But it was times like this, when chaos reigned supreme and things were going to shit, that the two Agency men displayed the unique ability to keep their heads when those around them were losing theirs.

Pink, frothy spittle dripped from Voigt's mouth, staining the trousers of his tailored suit. More blood trickled from his nose, and a clear liquid oozed from his ears. A sure sign his eardrums had burst from the overpressure of the explosion.

Chris reached under Voigt's suit coat searching his torso for hidden wounds requiring immediate treatment. When he withdrew his hands, they were covered in blood. He ripped open Voigt's shirt and found too many puncture wounds to count, undoubtedly caused by shrapnel as the projectile passed through the car. None of the wounds were particularly large or gruesome, but it was clear from Voigt's symptoms that his lungs and maybe even his heart or an artery had been damaged. There was a distinct possibility he was bleeding internally, but there was nothing Chris could do with the limited resources of the basic trauma kit he was carrying.

While Chris was evaluating Voigt, Joe pried the front passenger door open to check on the protective detail. What the veteran operator saw turned his stomach. The front of the cabin had taken the brunt of the blast and was coated with blood and the remnants of the security team's internal organs.

Tracking the path of the projectile, he saw the hole where it had penetrated the door's armor and entered the right side of Schleck's torso just below the ribcage. It missed his spine, which was basically the only thing that kept the German from being cut in half. With nothing substantial to halt or alter the EFP's trajectory, the driver suffered the same fate as his partner.

Continuing on its path through the driver and his door, the projectile left a softball-size hole in the twelve-inch thick wall of Voigt's compound. Joe figured the police investigators would probably find it somewhere on the grounds, once they started processing the crime scene.

"Jesus," Joe said stepping away from the gore. He could only hope that the trauma was so violent and the injuries so severe that the men had died instantly, saving them from experiencing the unimaginable pain that might accompany this amount of damage to the human body. He'd witnessed this kind of scene too many times during his tours in Iraq and Afghanistan. Images of burning vehicles and soldiers with devastating injuries, many no more than eighteen or nineteen years old, flashed through his mind.

Joe heard Chris calling his name and was snapped back to the present. "Yeah?"

"You ok?" Chris asked, noticing the look on Joe's face and the expanding dark stain on his thigh. "Want me to take a look?"

"It's just a scratch. I'm fine."

"So, what's our next move?"

"Is there anything more you can do for Voigt?"

"Not without advanced life support. And even then, he probably wouldn't make it."

"Then grab your stuff. We're going after the Iranians."

CHAPTER 43

Joe shouted, "Move, dammit! Get outta the way!" as they waded through the mass of onlookers who'd gathered around the destroyed sedan. When no one did, his frustration hit the boiling point, so he drew his Glock and fired two rounds into the compound's wall. The sound of gunfire sent the people scurrying like roaches when the light was turned on, looking for a safe place to hide from the madman with the gun.

"I guess that's one way break up a crowd," Chris said, shaking his head in disbelief.

They took off at a jog toward the van and slowed as they approached the vehicle, not wanting to run headlong into an ambush. Joe took the left side of the van and Chris took the right, crouching as they moved, to expose as little of themselves as possible. On the count of three, Chris covered the windshield as Joe stood and peeked in through the side window.

Joe used the flashlight mounted on his pistol's rail system to illuminate the cargo area. It was empty. He moved forward between the compound's wall and the side of the van until he met up with Chris at the rear bumper. "I know we had to clear the van but there's no way they'd hole up in there. Farzan would know they'd be trapped, and he's way too smart to make a mistake like that. Any idea where they went when they took off?"

"No. I just saw them running toward the van, then lost them in the smoke."

"Well, they've gotta be around here somewhere," Joe said, looking down the street and thinking about where he'd go if he were being chased. As if on cue, the echo of a loud crack reverberated up the street. "That way."

***

One after another, a series of questions flooded Farzan's mind as he and Mehrdad raced past the van. *Who were those men? German police? There was no way a response could have occurred so quickly unless they were nearby when the explosion went off. But the men weren't in uniform and didn't look like policemen. Could they be Americans? If so, how did they find us? There were no records of our entry into Germany. The only people who knew we were here worked in the consulate. The redhead spoke Farsi, and spoke it well. Could these possibly be the men Ashkan failed to kill in the attack on Scott Garrett? It's bad enough that imbecile failed in his mission and got his entire team killed. But his incompetence may have just affected my mission as well.*

Farzan shook his head as he ran, trying to banish the seeds of doubt that were creeping into his psyche. He had to focus on their current predicament and stick to the escape plan.

A gate opened to their right, and the sudden movement startled Farzan. A woman and her son emerged from the compound accompanied by Max, the family's German shepherd. The unexpected sight of two strangers running past his family kicked Max's protective instincts into overdrive. Baring his teeth at the men, Max let out a low, guttural growl and lurched forward. The woman yelled for Max to heel as she pulled his leather leash, leaning back to put the full weight of her body into the effort to control the big dog. She lost her balance and stumbled forward, letting go of the leash to free her hands and break the fall.

Fixated on the mouthful of teeth snarling at him, Farzan found he was more afraid of the untethered beast than the men chasing them. Mehrdad had never cared much for dogs in the first place, so he raised his pistol and placed the sights between the dog's eyes.

The boy saw the man pointing the gun at Max and yelled, "Nein!" He dove forward, putting his body between his best friend and the man with the gun just as Mehrdad pulled the trigger. The boy grunted and his knees buckled. He slumped across the dog's back, and Max, sensing something was wrong, supported the boy's weight until his mother gathered him in her arms. She collapsed to the ground and, fearing the worst, erupted with great sobs of grief while Max took a protective position between his family and the strangers.

Mehrdad looked down at the grieving woman cradling her injured son. He felt a small amount of remorse for accidentally shooting the boy. But before the emotion could take hold he reminded himself there were always casualties of war. The boy was just collateral damage.

Looking to his left, Farzan saw the gate belonging to the compound adjacent to Voigt's. During their pre-attack reconnaissance, he'd noticed it had a pedestrian door, allowing people to enter and exit the compound without having to open the main gate. He'd incorporated this tidbit of information into their escape plan, and was glad he had.

The gate and its pedestrian door were locked, so Farzan placed a small breaching charge near the handle and set the ten-second fuse. He and Mehrdad moved a few steps to the right and pressed their bodies flat against the compound's wall. The charge exploded with a loud crack, splintering the center of the door and blowing the deadbolt off its mount.

Farzan stepped through the opening with his weapon at the ready in case the owners happened to have a large dog of their own patrolling the grounds. Mehrdad followed a moment later, keeping an eye on the hole in the gate for the men he assumed wouldn't be far behind. Hearing and seeing nothing, Farzan said, "Time to move," and they jogged along the gentle curves of the gravel driveway.

***

Joe and Chris ran down the street toward the sound of the gunshot and small explosion until they came upon a woman sitting on the ground wailing hysterically. Her cries for help had been drowned out by the chaos up the road. She held a child in her lap, a boy no more than seven or eight years old, bleeding from what appeared to be a gunshot wound. A huge German shepherd stood guard, and turned his razor-sharp teeth toward the men as they approached.

"Damn," Joe said, skidding to a halt. "That's a big dog."

"Not a problem. I've got this."

"Seriously? What are you, some kind of dog whisperer?"

"As a matter of fact…."

Frightened by the sight of more men with guns, the woman grasped her son even tighter, determined to protect him from further harm. Her fears began to ease when Chris holstered his pistol and raised his empty hands for her to see. He slowly reached into his ruck and pulled out the trauma kit. Sliding the zipper around its perimeter, he opened it wide, allowing the woman to see the medical supplies packed inside. In his most charming doctor voice Chris said, "It's okay. We're here to help."

She didn't understand a word he said, but the tone of his voice and the sight of the medical equipment convinced her he wasn't going to harm her son. Turning to Max she said, "Hinlegen." The command from his master to lie down seemed to flip a switch in the dog's brain. He instantly transitioned from the ferocious guard dog ready to rip their face off to the family pet. His entire demeanor changed, and he curled up next to the woman, keeping a wary eye on the two men, even though his owner seemed to trust them.

Chris reached over and scratched Max behind the ear. "See? No problem. The only species I get along with better than women are dogs."

"And here you are working with both at the same time," Joe said eyeing the big shepherd, not totally sure he still wasn't going to try to rip his face off.

While Joe pulled security, Chris knelt next to the woman and her child. She looked up at him as he set the trauma kit on the ground next to her. Seeing the empathy in his eyes, the woman loosened her grip on the boy, giving Chris a chance to begin examining his wound.

"Looks like he took a round in the back," Chris said as he sealed the entry wound below the boy's shoulder blade and began packing the exit wound with combat gauze to help stop the bleeding.

"Is he gonna make it?"

"Honestly, I don't know. The round broke some ribs and probably collapsed his right lung. If no other organs were damaged, he stands a good chance, but he needs to get to a hospital right fucking now."

Joe pulled out his phone and dialed Meg Murphy's number. She answered on the second ring.

"Voigt's detail has been hit outside his residence. We're in pursuit of the Iranians, but they shot a kid during their escape."

"What do you need?"

"Chris is treating the kid but he needs to get to a hospital. Can you call an ambulance and let them know the boy and his mom are about two hundred meters south of Voigt's place?"

"Consider it done. I'll also let the chief of base know what's happened so she can alert headquarters. What are you going to do?"

"Once Chris gets the kid stabilized, we're going after Farzan and Mehrdad."

"By the way," Meg asked, "What kind of asshole shoots a kid?

CHAPTER 44

Joe was about to hang up and put the phone back in his pocket when the woman, perhaps beginning to feel better about her son's situation, became extremely animated. With vengeance in her eyes and fury in her voice, she began screaming at Joe and Chris while pointing vigorously across the street.

"What's she saying?" Chris asked, trying to calm the woman while still tending to her son.

"How the hell would I know? I speak Arabic and Farsi." Joe said as an idea popped into his head. He put the phone back to his ear, "Meg, you still there?"

"Yeah."

"You speak German?"

"No. I'm fluent in Mandarin. That's why the government saw fit to send me to Munich." She paused, then said, "Of course I speak German, why?"

Kneeling to get on the woman's level, Joe said, "I need you to talk to someone and tell me what she's saying."

He offered the phone and the woman took it, looking at him quizzically while continuing her rant. Hearing Meg's voice on the other end of the line seemed to temper some of the rage, but the woman was still pointing emphatically across the street.

Following her gaze, he finally saw it. The gate belonging to the compound next to Voigt's was damaged. A splintered hole was all that remained where the locking mechanism used to be. *Farzan.*

The woman handed the phone back, and Joe heard Meg say, "Man, that woman is pissed! But I guess I would be too if some douche bag shot my kid."

"What did she say?"

"Two guys, she thought looked Middle Eastern, ran by as she and her son left the house to walk the dog. Apparently, the guys startled the dog and he lunged at them. The bigger of the two, probably Mehrdad, aimed his weapon at the dog but her kid jumped between them as the gun went off. She says the guys ran off and disappeared through a hole they blew in the neighbor's gate."

"Thanks, Meg. Get that ambulance on the way."

"Will do. Let me know if you need anything else."

Joe was fuming as he disconnected the call and put the phone back in his pocket. He had no tolerance whatsoever for men who hit women or harmed children. Laser focused on the hole in the gate, he said, "Take care of the kid. I'm going after them."

"Wait…what?" Chris turned to say something else but he was too late. Joe's long powerful strides propelled him toward the shattered gate in pursuit of his prey.

***

The crunch of the Iranians' footsteps on the gravel as they crossed the circular drive in front of the red brick house was drowned out by the wail of sirens. An incident of this magnitude in such an exclusive neighborhood was bound to draw every policeman, firefighter, and paramedic in greater Grünwald.

They are too late. Farzan thought. *It would have been impossible for anyone to survive that explosion.* Running past the house, he saw what he was looking for – the detached building at the far end of the grounds.

Imagery of the area provided by the intel analysts back in Ahvaz had come in handy, not only for the attack-planning purposes but also for identifying their exfiltration route. The structure he'd been seeking turned out to be a four-car garage nestled against the compound's east wall. For the briefest of moments Farzan considered breaking in and stealing a car. But that would force them to drive back toward their pursuers, not to mention all the police and first responders who must have arrived on the scene by now. And all the responding vehicles on Gabriel von Seidl Strasse would have brought traffic to a grinding halt. No, they'd stick to the original plan.

Farzan picked up speed, certain the two men chasing them couldn't be far behind. He leaped as he neared the wall, placing the ball of his foot against the bricks, and pushed off, using the strength in his leg to vault high enough to grasp the top with both hands. He pulled himself up and straddled the wall, waiting for his lieutenant to join him.

Mehrdad looked around for something he could use to climb the wall and spotted a cord of firewood stacked neatly to his right. *This will do nicely.* He veered toward the stack of firewood, and using it as a stepladder, reached up and grabbed the top of the wall. He pulled with the considerable strength in his arms and used the balls of his feet to run up the wall. The push-pull combination did the trick, and the big man crested the top.

Farzan looked back, half expecting the men to be breathing down their necks, but instead saw only a single form passing through the hole in the gate. Pleasantly surprised to see they had a decent head start, the two Iranians dropped over the side of the wall.

***

Joe burst through the splintered pedestrian door as if he'd been shot out of a cannon, fueled by pure adrenalin and anger. He paused for a split second, permitting his eyes and brain to take a quick inventory of his surroundings before penetrating farther the compound. *Where are they?*

He caught a flicker of movement out of the corner of his eye and snapped off two quick shots at a leg as it slithered over the top of the wall. He fired two more rounds, hoping for a lucky shot, but the bullets did nothing more than gouge divots into the bricks.

"Shit!" Joe took off at a dead sprint across the grounds, the bullet wound on this thigh throbbing with every stride. As he approached the spot where Mehrdad had gone over the wall, Joe elevated like an NBA player going up for a slam-dunk. He planted his right foot on top of the firewood, and used his momentum to vault himself up and over the wall.

A bed of pine needles cushioned his landing, but he was unable to stifle a grunt as a lightning bolt of pain shot through his injured thigh. Rolling to his right, Joe took cover behind a thick pine tree, pausing to catch his breath and get a feel for his surroundings. He looked around, surprised to find himself in the middle of a dense forest. *What the hell?* It was like he fell down a rabbit hole and landed in a different dimension. One second he was in the center of town, and the next thing he knew he was in the middle of the woods.

Not exactly sure where he was, Joe pulled out his phone and opened the map application. He tapped the current location indicator and waited while the phone's GPS searched for his position. The app finally locked on to his location and the indicator flashed on the screen. Joe switched to satellite view and saw he was in fact in the middle of a forest. He touched the screen and moved his thumb and index finger together, zooming the map's view out to get a better look at his surroundings.

The expanded view confirmed his suspicions. He was in the woods all right, but it also showed a road no more than fifty meters straight ahead through the trees. Forsthaus Strasse ran perpendicular to the wall he had just scaled, then bent gently to the left, leading back into Grünwald. Maybe this rabbit hole hadn't taken him quite as far from town as he had initially thought.

That sneaky bastard has a getaway car stashed around here somewhere. This must've been their escape plan all along.

Joe stood and began working his way toward the road. He moved quickly but at a pace that still allowed him to maintain good sound discipline. With his Glock at the ready, Joe swept the weapon's muzzle back and forth, moving in sync with his eyes and head like the turret of a tank. In the silence of the woods, his hearing was hypersensitive as he listened for anything that sounded manmade or out of the ordinary.

Reaching the edge of the forest he took a knee, allowing the foliage to conceal his presence. He looked up and down the road hoping to spot something, tire tracks, a dirt road, anything that would tell him where the Iranians might have hidden their getaway car.

When Joe couldn't wait any longer he decided it was time to make his move. One way or another, he had to get across the road. Feeling like the butt of some chicken joke, he rose and had taken only two steps when he heard the shot. Bark exploded from the tree to his right as the round burrowed into the trunk, showering his head and neck with splinters. He dove behind the tree and felt a stinging sensation under his right eye. Joe reached up and pulled an inch-long sliver of wood out of his cheek. He gave it a quick look, thanking his lucky stars that it hadn't gone and inch higher and impaled itself in his eye. Tossing the splinter aside Joe peeked around the tree just in time to see Mehrdad sprinting into the woods. *Bingo! Thanks for giving up your position, asshole.*

As the big man retreated, Joe crossed the road and ducked behind another thick tree. He listened for movement hoping to get a fix on the Iranians' location. As he was about to move deeper into

the forest, he heard a car engine start, then rev at a high rate.
They're making a run for it!

A black Audi A3 came flying down a dirt road to Joe's left.
He raised his pistol, tracking the vehicle from right to left, and
opened fire. Bark splintered in every direction as most of Joe's
bullets hit the trees between his position and the Audi. But a few of
his rounds managed to find a way through the forest and he heard the
distinct sound of two or three impact the car.

The driver's side rear window shattered as Joe's slide locked
back on an empty chamber. He turned and sprinted for the road,
running as fast as his injured leg would carry him. While on a dead
sprint, he dropped the empty mag, inserted a fresh one into the well,
and sent the slide forward.

The Audi shot out onto Forsthaus Strasse and slid sideways
as the tires transitioned from dirt to asphalt. Mehrdad countersteered
and eased off the gas, dumping speed to keep the car from rolling as
the tires grabbed at the newfound traction. He saw the redheaded
man in the rearview mirror burst from the trees and leap over a
drainage ditch, simultaneously impressed and annoyed with the
man's tenacity.

Joe slid to a stop in the middle of the road, thankful there
wasn't much traffic at the moment. If there had been, he might have
ended up splattered like a bug on someone's windshield. He looked
to his right and saw the Audi accelerating down the road and opened
fire again. This time all of his rounds struck the car, chipping paint
off the bodywork as they entered the trunk and rear quarter panels.
The rear window shattered, and he thought he saw the big Iranian in
the driver's seat lurch forward as if he'd been hit, but the Audi
continued north toward Munich.

CHAPTER 45

While the rest of the team was back at the hotel breaking down the TOC, Joe was on a video conference in the SCIF, providing Director Sloan and the other leadership at Langley with a thorough after-action report.

When he finished, Director Sloan said, "Friedrich Voigt died from his injuries on the way to the hospital."

Hearing the words come through the speakers, Joe nodded his head in acceptance. From the moment he saw Voigt slumped over in the back of the BMW, he knew the CEO's odds of surviving were slim.

"According to our explosives experts, there's no way he should have survived the blast in the first place, much less still been alive by the time you made it to him," Carl Douglas, the special activities division chief said.

"After seeing the inside of the car and what happened to the two guys up front, I couldn't believe it either," Joe agreed. He paused a moment to give the gruesome image a chance to fade, then asked, "Any word on the kid?"

This time it was Katherine Clark, the DDO, who answered, "I checked in with my counterpart at the BND. It was touch and go for a while, but it looks like he's going to make a full recovery. The treatment Chris provided probably saved the boy's life."

A visible wave of relief spread over Joe's face. "That's great news."

Clark continued, "His mother still has no idea who you guys are, but she's eternally grateful for what you did for her son."

Joe was happy the kid would be alright but wanted nothing more than to get his hands on the men who hurt him. "Do we have any idea where the Iranians are now? Or if they're even still in the country?"

"After the assassination of three of their citizens, especially one as high profile as Voigt, the Germans are pulling out all the stops," Clark said. "They've blanketed the international airport in Munich as well as the city's train stations and bus terminals. Roadblocks have been set up around the area, but there's been no sign of them yet."

"And the Iranian Consulate?"

"The German's are all over it. So far, there have been no reports of Farzan, Mehrdad, or their bullet-ridden car anywhere near it."

"The bullet holes and broken windows would draw too much attention, so they'd have to ditch it at some point." Joe said. "I'd steal a car at the earliest opportunity, then dump the Audi in some obscure spot off the beaten path that would make it hard for the police to find. We might want to check for any reports of stolen cars in the immediate aftermath of the attack."

"Munich's a big city. They probably have any number of thefts a day, but it's worth a shot," Director Sloan said. "Would you do me a favor and ask the chief to check with the Munich police?"

There was a pause in the discussion as Joe stood and exited the SCIF.

It was an unusual move, but Director Sloan had decided to keep the station in Berlin and the base here in Munich in the dark regarding Joe's team and their mission in Germany. As far as the chief of base was concerned, this was a typical terrorist hunt, and the team of operators were in town chasing a couple of high-value personalities.

Joe returned to the SCIF a few minutes later and relayed what the chief had been able to find out. "There were six stolen cars in the greater Munich area today. Of the six, only three took place after the attack on Voigt. One was to the west of the city, but two of the cars were stolen from locations just north of Grünwald. One of those, a burgundy Mercedes sedan, was found in the parking lot of a small airport southwest of the city. The police and BND are on scene, searching the airport's grounds and going through the flight plans of any plane that took off in the wake of the attack."

"Then I'm afraid Major Farzan and Lieutenant Mehrdad are literally in the wind," Director Sloan said, as the look of disappointment on his face was projected across the monitor in high definition.

"But shouldn't the Germans be able to track the planes and give us an idea of where they were heading?" Joe asked. "We could have multiple teams waiting at the various destinations to interdict each one upon arrival."

"If Farzan is half the operative I believe him to be, their flight plan would be a ruse," Sloan said. "The pilots would have plotted a domestic flight plan to some place like Frankfurt or Dusseldorf to avoid having to deal with customs and immigration at the airport. Farzan wouldn't risk having their documents scrutinized or having to speak with the authorities, especially if Mehrdad was, in fact, wounded. A domestic flight would expedite their access to the plane and their departure from Munich."

He paused to take a sip of coffee and give everyone a chance to examine his thought process for flaws. The last thing he wanted at this point was for the team to fall into group think. Sloan wasn't looking for a bunch of yes men who agreed with whatever he said just because he was the boss. He wanted his people to be critical thinkers and challenge each other on the merit of their experience and ideas. "And secondly, once they were in the air, the crew could turn off the transponder and change course for any point on the compass."

Clark added, "If the pilots took a northerly heading, they could be out over the North Sea and into international air space without even having to cross another country's border."

The Agency's fleet of aircraft fell under the chief of SAD's purview, so Carl Douglas was accustomed to dealing with aviation issues. He did some quick math in his head and added, "At a business jet's average cruising speed, they could cover the four hundred miles to the coast in less than an hour. In fact, I'd wager a substantial sum of money Farzan is already clear of Europe and out over the open water by now."

Joe was furious he'd let the Iranians escape. He had replayed the events in Grünwald over and over in his mind, searching for anything, no matter how small, that he could have done differently. But unlike Farzan and Mehrdad, he and his men were not cold-blooded killers. There was no way he could have bypassed Voigt and his guys without checking for survivors.

And Joe couldn't imagine a scenario where he'd leave an injured child to die. His moral code demanded they stop to render aid and he knew he would make that same decision every time. Just knowing the kid would make a full recovery was the one positive he could take from the attack – that, and the fact that he'd gotten rounds on target. He was positive he'd hit Mehrdad with that shot through the rear window.

Joe came to the realization they'd done everything possible, given the set of circumstances he and Chris had faced, but it still didn't make him feel any better. The Iranians had escaped and were probably developing a pattern of life on their next target. His failure in Grünwald meant someone else's life was now in danger.

"Are you still with us, Joe?" Director Sloan asked.

The sound of Sloan's voice snapped Joe out of his private mental hot wash. "Yes, sir. Sorry."

Sloan continued, "I was saying I'd like you and your team to come home for the time being."

"But sir," Joe protested, "the Iranians are still on the loose. We can't just give up and call it quits."

"The last thing in the world we're going to do is quit pursuing these guys. They will be out top priority until we either have them in custody or they've been put in the ground." Sloan shifted in his chair and leaned into the camera, "But your team has been operating nonstop for an extended period, not to mention all the action you've been involved in lately. We'll keep running down leads on the Iranians' whereabouts, but your guys need some down time and a little home cooking. I want you recharged and ready to deploy when we get a spike on their location."

Joe nodded his agreement. You couldn't argue with the director's logic. As things stood at the moment, there were no leads to follow, no needle in a haystack or thread to pull that would offer a reasonable chance of finding the Iranians. For now, maybe it was best to go home and let the considerable capabilities of the U.S. intelligence community continue the search for Farzan.

Joe looked up at Director Sloan's image on the monitor and said, "Sorry, sir. I get it."

"I'm not sidelining you or taking you out of the fight, Joe. Just give the rest of us a chance to find the Iranians. And when we do I want you locked and loaded. Clear?"

"Crystal, sir."

CHAPTER 46

Located twenty-two kilometers from Munich, the Special Airport Oberpfaffenhofen is one of the oldest airfields in Bavaria. It was founded in 1936 by Claude Dornier, the pioneer in German aircraft design and manufacturing. Aviation research and development was a big part of the operation at Oberpfaffenhofen, but the airport also offered charter flights, full fixed-based operations, and handling and refueling services as well as immigration and passport control. And with a seventy-five-hundred-foot runway, the airport could accommodate a wide variety of aircraft.

Farzan planned from the beginning on using Oberpfaffenhofen to get out of the country after killing Voigt. Heightened security at the international airport would make it next to impossible to transit without being spotted and detained by the authorities. He had considered taking a bus or train, but they would be much slower and the police would be monitoring those stations as well. Farzan wanted to get out of Germany as quickly as possible, so he'd arranged for a business jet, a Bombardier Global Express, to be waiting on Oberpfaffenhofen's tarmac as their means of escape.

The two men charged with flying the Global Express wore the ubiquitous uniforms of private pilots the world over – dark slacks and white shirts adorned with wings pinned over the left breast pocket and shoulder boards that distinguished the captain from the first officer. Dark ties and gold-rimmed Ray-Ban aviator sunglasses completed the ensemble.

To the casual observer, they looked like every other crew one might expect to find at any FBO around the world. But these men were actually members of a small unit buried deep within the IRIAF, the Islamic Republic of Iran Air Force, tasked with supporting covert Quds Force operations.

A third man, wearing the same uniform as the pilots, chose to remain on the plane, only stepping off occasionally to stretch his legs and fill his lungs with a breath of fresh air. Iranian by birth, he had moved to Germany to attend university and study medicine. He had decided to stay in the country after graduation, applied for permanent resident status, and eventually gained employment in the emergency room of one of the largest hospitals in Munich.

Unlike the pilots, he wasn't on the Iranian government's payroll, but the MOIS knew his name and of his specialty in trauma and emergency medicine. While he was no fan of the regime, it was concern for the wellbeing of several family members still living in Iran that convinced the doctor to assist when requested from time to time.

The pilot's cell phone vibrated and the text message that appeared on its screen spurred the crew into action. The first officer strode quickly across the apron and entered the FBO while the captain began working his way through the preflight checklist. With all indicators showing green, he asked the ground crew to disconnect the auxiliary power unit and contacted the tower for permission to spin up the engines.

Watching the flurry of activity through the Plexiglas window next to his seat, the doctor saw the first officer escorting two men across the tarmac. The contrast between the men was not lost on him. One was lean and fit, the other massive and overly muscular. But despite his musculature, the bigger man seemed to be struggling to walk. He would stutter step in a manner that made his legs appear weak and unable to support his weight. Or he would list from side to side like a drunk staggering down the sidewalk after the bars had shuttered their doors for the night. When the big man looked as if he couldn't take another step, the smaller man would wrap his arm around the man's thick waist to help steady him. There were no outward signs of the man's injury, but the doctor assumed he was the reason for his presence on this flight.

Once onboard, the first officer directed the men to the rear of the plane. When they were settled, he retracted the stairs and secured the port-side door. The men barely had time to strap themselves in before the captain applied thrust and taxied to the runway. Two minutes later, the nose began to rise as the sleek business jet accelerated down the smooth concrete, and the plane streaked into the sky. The pilot banked to the right, straightening out on a northerly heading and pointed the Global Express toward the coast and international airspace.

As they reached cruising altitude, Farzan looked around the cabin, taking in his new surroundings and noticed the other passenger for the first time. Curious about the man in uniform he asked, "Why aren't you up in the cockpit with the others, my friend?"

"I…I'm not a pilot," the doctor answered tentatively, unsure why he was so nervous. The man seemed friendly enough, but there seemed to be an air of danger and violence lurking just under the surface, waiting to be unleashed when the time was right. "I'm a physician."

"Excellent!" Farzan exclaimed, clapping his hands together, "because I just so happen to have a patient for you."

The doctor unbuckled his seatbelt, then moved around to assess Mehrdad. He was awake but incoherent and kept fading in and out of consciousness, most likely due to the amount of blood he'd lost on the way to the airport. "I was told he had a gunshot wound. Where was he shot?"

Farzan unzipped Yousef's jacket and said, "He took a bullet in the top of his right shoulder."

The doctor leaned in and pulled the front of the jacket open, trying to get a better look at the wound. Yousef's shirt was soaked with blood and the wet material clung to his muscular torso. A makeshift bandage was taped to the spot where his overdeveloped trapezius muscle met his neck. The gauze had absorbed so much blood that it was saturated and couldn't hold any more. The doctor put on a pair of surgical gloves before peeling back the bloody mess of fabric and let out a low whistle when he saw the wound.

"What is it?" Farzan asked.

"Your friend was very lucky."

"Why do you say that?"

The young man nodded toward Mehrdad's shoulder, indicating Farzan should take a look. "See the hole?"

"Yes. What about it?"

"Well, one more inch to the left and the bullet would have hit his spine. The best he could've hoped for would be paralysis from the neck down, but most injuries of that nature end up being fatal."

Farzan had been so busy attempting to stop the bleeding after Yousef had been shot that he hadn't taken the time to fully comprehend the extent of his man's injury. He'd also been laser-focused on escaping the attack site, only stopping along the way to the airport to take over driving when Mehrdad started fading in and out of consciousness.

Now that they were in the relative safety of the luxury jet, the gravity of Mehrdad's situation began to sink in. "I see your point, doctor, he was indeed quite fortunate."

The door to the cockpit opened, and the captain walked down the carpeted aisle to greet his passengers. Careful to refrain from using Farzan's name or rank in front of the doctor, he said, "Good to have you aboard, sir. Any changes to the flight plan?"

"None, Captain. Proceed as scheduled."

"Yes, sir. By the way, the galley is fully stocked in case you're hungry or thirsty. The first officer will prepare a meal in a couple of hours."

"Thank you," Farzan said, as the pilot pivoted and made his way back to the cockpit. Before he closed the door, Farzan asked, "What's our flight time?"

"We're looking at about twelve hours, give or take a few minutes, depending on the winds."

Twelve hours? Where in the world are we going? the doctor thought. Resigned to the fact that it was out of his control, he looked at Farzan and said, "I need to get to work on your friend. Help me get his jacket off."

CHAPTER 47

It was early by congressional standards, but Congresswoman Cynthia Drake had already been at her desk in the Rayburn House Office Building for a couple of hours while most of her colleagues were just finishing breakfast or mired in their commute to the office.

Located on Independence Avenue between South Capitol Street SE and First Street SW, Drake's fourth floor office occupied some of the most coveted real estate in the building. Large plate glass windows filled the wall behind her desk and provided a spectacular view of the Capitol and its manicured grounds.

Knowing she would need the extra kick of caffeine to finish the document currently displayed on her laptop, Drake had sent one of her staffers on a coffee run – the second of the morning – to the Starbucks down the street. She was in one of those zones where the words seemed to flow straight from her brain to her fingertips as they typed in rapid-fire bursts on the MacBook Pro's keyboard. When the staccato of fingers on keys finally stopped, she leaned back and smiled with satisfaction at her work.

Drake reached for the coffee, a rich Colombian blend, and absentmindedly took a big swig. Immediately realizing her mistake, she sprayed the scalding liquid into the trashcan under her desk. "Godammit! Why do they have to make it so fucking hot?"

Regaining her poise, the chair of the House Permanent Select Committee on Intelligence refocused on her work. The document displayed on the screen was a blueprint, a silver bullet she intended to fire at CIA Director Lawrence Sloan in a public hearing.

A couple of weeks ago she had met with her counterpart, the chairman of the Senate Select Committee on Intelligence, Sam Isaacson, at the behest of the president, to get her onboard with the swift and violent response to the killing of Ambassador Jonathan Lewis. Drake had no idea how Sloan had acquired the information that pointed the finger at the Iranians, but she was certain it was done without congressional approval, or at a minimum, notification to the Gang of Eight.

A knock at the door interrupted Drake's train of thought, and she looked up from her laptop. "What is it?"

Todd McCutcheon, Drake's chief of staff, cracked the door and stuck his head through the opening. "Sorry to disturb you, Cynthia, but Senator Isaacson's in the outer office. He would like a few minutes of your time."

Drake had been anticipating this conversation. She did owe Sam and the president an answer but would have preferred he made an appointment, rather than just show up out of the blue. Nudging the trashcan back under the desk with her foot, she closed the laptop and said in an exasperated tone, "Fine. Send him in." She stood and moved around from behind the desk to greet her unexpected guest.

McCutcheon opened the door and moved aside as the senior senator from New Jersey strode confidently past him, then returned to his own office and closed the door. He sat at his desk and counted to ten, giving Drake and Isaacson a moment before he picked up his phone and activated the direct line to the identical handset on Drake's desk. With the phone on his boss's desk acting as a listening device, he could hear every word as if he were in the room.

"Good morning, Sam. What brings you over to this side of the Hill?"

Isaacson shook her hand. "I was in the neighborhood, meeting with a couple of other representatives and thought it would be rude if I didn't drop by to say hello."

"How considerate," she replied, thinking it was much ruder to drop in unannounced. "Would you like some coffee, or maybe a cup of tea?"

"I appreciate the offer, but I've already hit my limit for this morning."

Motioning toward a sitting area, Drake said, "Shall we sit while we talk?"

Taking a seat on the sofa against the wall, Isaacson looked out the windows, "I always forget what a beautiful view of the Capitol you have."

Drake chose one of the chairs across from the sofa and looked back over her shoulder. "I have to admit, it is probably my favorite thing about this office." She paused to take a sip of her coffee, careful to remember its scalding temperature. "But you're not here to talk about the view, Sam, so what can I do for you?"

Isaacson crossed his legs and straightened the crease on his trousers before answering. "Actually, I came by to see if you'd made your decision regarding the president's request."

"I was wrapping up some work on that very subject when you arrived. Your sense of timing is impeccable."

"And?" Isaacson asked in anticipation.

"I've given the president's request a lot of thought, and I've concluded that I will not, no, make that cannot, subjugate my core beliefs regarding the CIA and the intelligence community, just so the president can exact his pound of flesh for Jonathan's murder. I know Jonathan was your friend, and I'm sorry about his death, but we have a rulebook for a reason, and I'm not willing to throw it out or bury it in a desk drawer whenever the president feels those rules have become inconvenient."

Isaacson was momentarily taken aback by her seemingly outright refusal to work with the White House on the matter. "But the evidence Lawrence Sloan and his operatives at CIA have uncovered is incontrovertible. It clearly implicates the Iranians in the death of Jonathan and the members of his protective detail. They must be punished for their crimes."

Neither Isaacson nor Drake had been read in on Project Wraith, so they had no idea that Farzan and the Iranians were also responsible for the wave of violence that had swept through Israel and Germany.

"I'll concede that on face value the evidence is damning. But I'd be interested to find out exactly how Sloan and his spooks happened to come into possession of the information. Was it through normal sources and methods or did he give his operatives the green light to act unilaterally?" She paused a moment before continuing, "If Sloan did undertake some new covert action, he did it without notifying my committee. How about you, Sam? Did he notify yours?"

"You can't be serious, Cynthia!" Isaacson's temper was beginning to boil and it was taking every ounce of his self-control to prevent a full-blown eruption.

"Serious as a heart attack. Did they get this information from Electronic Intelligence? Signals? How about HUMINT? Has he managed to penetrate the Quds Force or MOIS? Did he convince an

Iranian government official to turn over a file on the attack?"

Furious with her line of questioning, Isaacson shot back, "I believe the information was gleaned from the interrogation of several suspects captured during a raid in Iraq."

The look of surprise on Drake's face made it obvious this was a piece of information she hadn't been aware of until just now. Seeing her response, Isaacson immediately regretted the revelation.

"A raid and an interrogation? Really? Who did the questioning? I certainly hope it was the FBI because the CIA's Extraordinary Rendition program and black sites are supposed to be a thing of the past."

Sam Isaacson realized he'd stuck his foot in his mouth, and it was time for some serious damage control. Trying to change the tone of the conversation, he said, "Now, Cynthia, you know as well as I do that the nature of intelligence work is often free flowing. You come across one piece of information and it leads you to another, then another. It's my understanding that is how this operation unfolded. Sloan's people were sent over to investigate the attack, and in the course of their investigation, discovered the location of a safe house. The attackers were still there, so Sloan's paramilitary officers took the initiative and conducted an in-extremis assault on the location. The CIA officers managed to capture some of the attackers, and in the interest of time, interrogated them on the spot. There was no time to call back to Washington to ask for approval."

Drake couldn't believe her luck. It would have taken her staff months to uncover the kind of information Isaacson was revealing this morning. Whether he realized it or not, he was providing her with additional ammunition that she would use to take that kill shot at Lawrence Sloan and the CIA.

"You said the CIA officers captured some of the attackers, not all of them? What happened to the others, did they escape?" Drake felt she knew the answer but wanted to hear Isaacson say it out loud.

"They didn't escape. Three of them were killed in the assault."

Jackpot! "Let me get this straight, Sam. A team of Sloan's paramilitary officers assaulted a suspected Quds Force safe house in Iraq, killed three of the six men they found on the premises, and then interrogated the rest? Does that about cover it?"

Resigned to his mistake of bringing up the subject in the first place, Isaacson admitted defeat and said, "I believe it does, Cynthia."

"And what happened to the prisoners who were interrogated? Any idea where they are, Sam?"

Isaacson shook his head. "I have no idea as to their whereabouts or current disposition."

"That's okay. I'll have an opportunity to ask Director Sloan in person when I summon him before my committee."

"You really plan on bringing Lawrence up to the Hill? You do realize nothing good can come from a hearing, don't you?"

"Maybe nothing good for Sloan, or the president for that matter. But that's not my concern. The intelligence community needs to be reformed, and I'm going to be the one to do it."

"So," Isaacson said more as a statement than a question, "I suppose I have your answer for the president."

Cynthia Drake stood and walked toward the door indicating the meeting was over. "I suppose you do. And when you see President Andrews, please tell him he should never ask me to compromise my principles again. Especially when it comes to the intelligence community."

Isaacson knew he'd lost this round. He didn't like it, but this was the nature of politics. You win some. You lose some. And when you lost in this town it was important to lose graciously. Politics made for strange bedfellows, and he knew there might come a time when he would need Drake's support on a bill or a piece of legislation in the future. He had nothing to gain by burning this bridge, even though he'd like nothing better than to set the bitch's office ablaze. He stood and followed her lead as she opened the door.

Business hours on the Hill were in full swing, and Drake's outer office was full of constituents hoping to get a few minutes with their representative, so Isaacson struck a cordial tone and said, "Thank you for your time, Cynthia. Don't hesitate to stop by the next time you're in the Russell Building."

"Same to you, Sam. My door is always open." As he walked away, she turned to people waiting in the foyer and said, "Good morning, everyone. If you'll give me just a moment to wrap up a few things, I'll be happy to visit with each of you."

Drake closed the door then leaned up against it, letting out a deep breath as a Cheshire Cat smile crept across her face. She gave a victorious fist pump, then made a beeline for her laptop. Lawrence Sloan's reign at CIA was about to come to an ignominious end.

Todd McCutcheon broke the connection and put the handset back in its cradle. He leaned back in his chair, lacing his fingers behind his head as he stared up at the ceiling, deep in thought.

CHAPTER 48

Five men and two women were assembled for the meeting in the Situation Room. President Andrews occupied his customary seat at the head of the oak conference table. His chief of staff, George Owens, and national security advisor, Julia Maxwell, sat to the president's right. Senator Isaacson, Keith Hultsman, the director of national intelligence, along with CIA Director Lawrence Sloan and Katherine Clark, the deputy director for operations, sat to the president's left. There were a couple of empty seats at the table, but for the most part, the select group formed the nucleus of America's intelligence and national security apparatus.

Andrews glanced at each person in the room and asked, "What's so urgent that I had to be pulled out of a meeting? Is it safe to assume we haven't come together because of something positive that's happened in the world?"

George Owens said, "That would be an accurate assumption, Mr. President. Senator Isaacson met with Congresswoman Drake this morning and it didn't exactly go as we'd hoped."

The president turned his attention to Isaacson. Always preferring the direct approach when receiving bad news, he said, "Okay, Sam, lay it on me."

Despite his status as the senior senator from New Jersey and his position as chairman of the Senate's Intelligence Committee, Isaacson felt a bit out of his element briefing the president and his National Security team in the Situation Room. He took a sip of water, cleared his throat, and jumped in with both feet. As he neared the end of the briefing, Isaacson relayed his inadvertent disclosure of the information she had not been aware of previously.

He concluded by saying, "I'm sorry I wasn't able to persuade Cynthia to join us on this quest for justice. I also want to apologize for letting my temper get the best of me." Isaacson took another sip of water, then continued, "Cynthia told me she's planning on calling Lawrence to testify before her committee in the not too distant future. I don't know what her exact agenda is but it's clear she's intending to end his career as the director of the Central Intelligence Agency."

Owens said, "What the hell is Drake thinking? She must know the damage a hearing like this will cause."

In a calm, almost bored tone, Lawrence Sloan said, "Cynthia Drake has a hatred and distrust of the intelligence community stemming from her education, you could almost say radicalization, at Berkeley. She's been working for years to attain her current position, one where she would have some sway over those of us in the IC." He spoke without referring to any notes, seeming to have committed Drake's biographical details to memory. "Frankly, I'm surprised it's taken her this long to make a move. I suppose the circumstances since Jonathan's death have provided the congresswoman with the opportunity she has been waiting for."

President Andrews looked at the DNI and asked, "What do you think, Keith?"

Having been appointed to his position at the beginning of Andrews' second term, Hultsman wasn't aware of Project Wraith's existence. As a result, he had no idea the killings of Daniel Golan and Friedrich Voigt were related to the attack on Jonathan Lewis, or that an Iranian kill squad was actively targeting several people in this very room. To the best of his knowledge, the news seemed to be routine business as usual for the beltway insiders.

"Sir, I'm really not sure what all the fuss is about. We get requests to appear on the Hill all the time." He paused and looked across the table at Isaacson. "No offense, Senator, but more often than not the hearings are a waste of our time. Your colleagues seem more interested in using them to posture for the press and advance personal agendas than getting answers to any meaningful questions."

Senator Isaacson did in fact take a measure of offense at Hultsman's remarks but didn't feel he was in a position to protest too vigorously. He simply nodded at the DNI and said, "None taken."

Lawrence Sloan spoke next, "I agree with Keith, sir. Thanks to Senator Isaacson, we're aware of the game Drake is playing. I'll be ready for her and the allies she has on the committee when I'm summoned to appear on the Hill."

President Andrews knew if there was anyone in Washington who could handle himself in front of a congressional committee it was Lawrence Sloan. "Alright, Lawrence. Just do me a favor and let Julia know when you get the summons."

"Of course, sir."

Andrews turned to Senator Isaacson. "Thank you for getting us up to speed, Sam. Now if you'll excuse us, we have a few other matters to discuss."

"Of course, Mr. President," Isaacson said as he stood and made his way to the door. "Don't hesitate to call if there's anything else I can do to help."

George Owens disengaged the Situation Room's door, and led Isaacson through the foyer and out onto West Executive Drive. A member of the Capitol Police's Dignitary Protection Unit was waiting patiently for the senator next to a spotless black Chevrolet Suburban.

Back in the Situation Room, DNI Hultsman said, "Sir, if there's nothing else, I'm off to a meeting at Liberty Crossing with the leadership of the NCTC." The National Counterterrorism Center was formed in 2003 to bring together the various government agencies responsible for fighting terrorism. Its offices were in a heavily guarded complex in McLean, Virginia, a few short miles from CIA headquarters.

"No problem, Keith. We're just wrapping up a few details. Lawrence can fill you in on anything pertinent that comes up."

"Very good, sir." The door closed behind the DNI, and the green light went solid once again.

President Andrews turned to the remaining group with a look of relief on his face. "Thank God for that meeting at Liberty Crossing. I was beginning to wonder how we were going to get him out of the room without things getting awkward." The comment drew a few chuckles, then Andrews turned serious. "So, where the hell are Farzan and Mehrdad?"

CHAPTER 49

"At this point, sir, we really don't know," Sloan said.

President Andrews was astonished by the lack of progress finding the Iranians. "It's been two weeks since they flew out of Munich. We haven't had one sighting or picked up any chatter at all?"

"Unfortunately, they are doing a good job of flying under the radar. Literally and figuratively, sir."

Andrews was having a hard time believing that anyone could fall completely off the grid the way these two had. So far, Farzan and Mehrdad had managed to elude the considerable resources and technology the United States and a couple of other governments had thrown at them.

Visibly frustrated with the situation, he said, "I get it. The world's a big place and that makes it easy for a couple of guys to get lost in the wash. But we haven't heard a thing? A single call or email? Not even a text message? How is that possible?"

Sloan leaned forward in his chair, "Their task would be much more difficult if they were private killers for hire. But the fact that Farzan and Mehrdad are highly trained operatives belonging to a country's intelligence apparatus makes it infinitely easier for them to evade our search."

"How so?" Andrews asked.

"The biggest challenges for someone attempting to operate without drawing the attention of the security services are funding, secure communications, and documentation – passports, visas, and the like. But since Farzan belongs to the IRGC, the support structures of Iran's diplomatic community, its embassies, consulates, and those of their allies will be at his disposal. He's smart enough to know we'll be watching the buildings and will undoubtedly keep his distance. But if his escape from Germany was as well planned as his previous operations, then he may well have pre-positioned caches of materials, safe houses, and human support set up along the intended route to his next destination."

Andrews nodded his understanding. "Makes sense." A short pause followed before he asked, "So if we can't find the men, have we had any luck tracking down the plane?"

Katherine Clark fidgeted in her seat. "We found the plane, sir, but it turned out to be a dead end."

"Explain."

"The jet belongs to a charter service based in Marseille, France. Two days prior to the Voigt operation, a company in Jakarta, Indonesia, called to set up the reservation."

"So, what's the problem? Can't the French just provide us with the flight plans? Or give us the opportunity to interview to the pilots and see where they went?"

"The problem, sir, is that the Indonesian company insisted on a rider to the charter agreement that would allow them to provide their own pilots."

"Sounds a little odd, doesn't it? That can't be standard operating procedure for a charter company. I mean, I can't imagine they'd go for turning over a multimillion-dollar airplane to an unknown entity."

It was Sloan who spoke this time. "You're quite right, sir. It is unusual. The French would agree to the charter only if the Indonesian company took out an insurance policy with Lloyds of London, assuming all responsibility for the plane if it was not returned in pristine condition. Apparently, the Indonesian company agreed and even paid a bonus to expedite the paperwork."

"So, this French company turned over a perfectly good plane that cost how much, thirty-five or forty million dollars…."

"More like forty-five to fifty million, sir," Clark interjected.

"To some total strangers to do who knows what?"

"Yes, that about sums it up."

"And the flight plans?" the president asked, growing increasingly impatient with the lack of a break in the case.

Director Sloan took over to divert the president's growing frustration away from Clark. "The data, as it relates to the time the Indonesian company had possession of the plane, had been deleted from the onboard computers and in-flight navigation systems."

President Andrews pushed his chair back from the

conference table and began to pace back and forth along the far wall. "And the Indonesian company, what do we know about them?"

"It turns out the company based in Jakarta was a front, a shell company set up by Iran's Ministry of Information and Security, probably for the express purpose of supporting covert operations throughout Southeast Asia. It was most likely used in this case because they thought its distance from Europe would minimize any trackbacks to the Islamic Republic."

The president sighed, "That damn Farzan seems to be a couple of steps ahead of us at every turn."

"I agree, sir. But there's no telling how long these plans have been in the works. The Iranians could afford to be meticulous in their planning because they had all the time in the world. The only deadlines or timelines on their operation were self-imposed. I'll admit, we've been a step or two behind, but that's to be expected. We just have to keep pulling the threads and something will break our way."

"I hear you, Lawrence," President Andrews said. Refocusing on the plane, he asked, "So, how far could they have gone in the...remind me what type it was again?"

"It was a Bombardier Global Express, a fairly common long-haul business jet. It has an effective range of around seven thousand miles."

"Seven thousand miles? Jesus, they could be anywhere."

"Very true, sir. If the fuel tanks were topped off before the plane left Germany it would be able to reach any point in Africa and could make it as far east as Japan or Singapore."

"And if they flew west?" the president asked.

"He has plenty of options. All of Central and South America are in play. An easy choice might be Venezuela. With Caracas on the northeast coast, the flight would be shortened dramatically. The Venezuelans would relish an opportunity to assist in a strike against the United States, even if it is just expediting Farzan's entry into the country. Then they could travel by sea through Puerto Rico to the Dominican Republic and on to Cuba, where they would be only ninety miles from the Florida Keys. Another option would be the Tri-Border Area," Sloan said, referring to the area where Argentina, Brazil, and Paraguay came together. "Hezbollah has a presence in the area and would be a natural ally for support."

"But it's unlikely Farzan would head to the Tri-Border

Area," Clark added. "It would be too obvious, and he would have to assume we'd have it blanketed with surveillance."

Andrews continued pacing. "Anywhere else?"

Sloan paused a minute before delivering the truly bad news to a president who was already frustrated by a lack of results. "If they flew west, and had favorable headwinds, it is conceivable the Global Express could have made it as far as Mexico without having to refuel. That would effectively put them right on our doorstep."

Clearly unhappy with this bit of information, Andrews cursed under his breath, then walked over to a credenza and grabbed a bottle of water.

Julia Maxwell spoke for the first time, "So, with basically the entire planet within his range, where do you think Farzan is headed?"

Clark said, "Other than Scott Garrett in Baghdad, the only remaining targets involved in Project Wraith are to the west. Nigel Craig in the U.K...."

"And you, Lawrence, and Paul Foley here in the United States," Maxwell said, finishing Clark's sentence.

"That's right. Farzan will want to capitalize on the momentum until he's crossed every name off his target list. I'd lay odds he's heading in our direction," Clark agreed.

President Andrews took a break from the pacing and stopped behind his chair. He leaned both elbows on the headrest adorned with the presidential seal and looked at Sloan, "Is it safe to assume you've put extra precautions in place for your safety? I don't want anything happening to the three of you."

"I appreciate the concern, Mr. President," Sloan said. "The head of my protective detail is aware of the threat and is taking the necessary steps."

"Good. Let me know if your people need any help. I'll have the Secret Service standing by to provide whatever support they might need." Content their safety was being addressed, the president turned back to the task at hand. "Do you think Nigel Craig is Farzan's next target?"

Sloan thought for a minute. "From a strictly geographic standpoint an attempt on Nigel certainly makes sense before coming to the United States. But at this point, I don't think so."

"Why not?" the president asked.

"First, we believe one of our men wounded Farzan's

lieutenant, Yousef Mehrdad, when the Iranians made their escape from the scene of Voigt's assassination. Depending on the severity of the injury, Mehrdad would need medical attention and time to heal. Plus, with Nigel in England, Farzan probably wouldn't want to carry out another attack in Europe until the heat in Germany had a chance to die down. With the injury to his man, Nigel may be too close, too soon."

"And second?"

"Well, sir, the attack on Scott Garrett in Iraq was carried out by a second Quds Force team. All the Iranians were killed in the ensuing firefight, but their existence and deployment leads us to believe Farzan and Mehrdad are not the exclusive hitters on this operation. The Quds leadership appears willing to put multiple teams in the field. There's always the possibility that another team will be sent to go after Nigel, especially if Farzan faces a delay because his man is wounded."

Maxwell directed the conversation back to finding out where the business jet dropped off the Iranians. "If, as you said, Farzan and Mehrdad did in fact head west, how will we find out where they landed? We need some idea to know where to direct our resources."

"We've plotted the airports and known runways that are capable of supporting a jet of that size," Clark answered. "With the risk of the next attacks taking place here in the homeland, we're focusing on airstrips in Central and South America and Mexico. We have people at headquarters going through the larger airports' electronic logs with a fine-toothed comb, and we've dispatched officers from our stations in the region to question staff and ramp workers. They'll also review hard copies of the arrival and departure logs for those airstrips that don't store their records electronically."

Director Sloan continued the train of thought. "Then there's the issue of private airstrips or those used by the drug cartels for smuggling flights. The National Reconnaissance Office is providing satellite imagery to help our analysts identify any stretch of pavement long enough for a Global Express to land. But as I'm sure you can imagine, the number of airfields within the jet's range is staggering, and checking out all of them is going to be a painstakingly slow process. Basically, what we're looking for is a single needle hiding in thousands of haystacks."

CHAPTER 50

Battery-powered lights the size of basketballs lined both sides of the nondescript runway in the countryside north of Cancun, the town best known for hosting drunk college students over spring break. It was cut out of a forest of Caribbean pine trees and royal palms adjacent to Yum Balam, a national park designed to protect native species and teach visitors about ancient Mayan traditions and practices.

Four Quds Force operatives, along with a dozen or so shooters belonging to the Gulf Cartel, had spent the better part of the last two hours preparing for an aircraft's arrival. Their final task involved activating a mobile transponder beacon to assist the crew in locating the airstrip.

With their work complete, the cartel men took pulls off large bottles of water from several cases loaded in the bed of a pickup truck. Refreshed and rehydrated, the men melted into the forest, taking up accustomed positions to form a secure perimeter around the airfield. It was a maneuver the men had performed hundreds of times in preparation for under-the-radar drug flights or the movement of cartel leaders determined to avoid arrest by the authorities or evade a rival's assassination attempt.

The heavy security presence was not concerned with the local police because most of those officers were already on the payroll or had long ago agreed to look the other way when cartel business was being conducted. With the life expectancy of an honest police officer in Mexico being relatively short, the motivation behind the inherent corruption went beyond a way to supplement their meager incomes. It was also the best way to stay above ground and continue breathing.

No, the gunmen in the forest tonight were in place to protect the Quds men and the incoming flight from the Mexican Marines.

The elite military force had been taking the fight to each of the cartels operating throughout the country and had been effective over the last several years, having successfully killed or captured scores of the drug runners' henchmen and even a few of their leaders.

The senior cartel representative at the airfield was a man who went by the name José. The Quds men didn't believe it was his real name but that hardly mattered as long as he fulfilled his end of the bargain. José's comfort with the heat and humidity of the forest, along with the insects and other nocturnal critters, seemed inconsistent with his appearance. With freshly manicured fingernails and highly polished loafers and linen slacks, José looked more like a wealthy businessman or successful lawyer. He certainly didn't fit the mental image one might have of a cartel fixer.

Turning to his visitors, José handed each of the Iranians a bottle of water and said, "Please, join me in the air traffic control center."

The four men looked at each other in confusion. *Air traffic control center? What was this crazy Mexican talking about?* All they saw was a small shack at the eastern end of the runway that looked like nothing more than a bunch of two-by-fours held together by some rusty nails. They were surprised a stiff breeze coming in off the Caribbean or the Gulf of Mexico hadn't knocked it over by now. Calling the fragile, wooden structure a shack was being generous. But an air traffic control center? No way.

Seeing the looks on the men's faces, José laughed. "I know it doesn't look like much, but it also doesn't draw any unwanted attention. We could easily spend the money to build something modern and substantial, but it would inevitably come to the attention of the government, and Marine or federal police helicopters would be landing on our airstrip before the cement dried. We're rather fond of this location and would hate to have to abandon it for another."

Mazdan, a Quds Force breacher and explosives expert, was the leader of the small group of foreigners. He'd been speaking English with José but switched to Farsi as he turned to his three countrymen. "Imad will come in with me." Then he motioned to the other two men, Hashem and Arman, "You two stay outside and keep an eye on our hosts."

Concerned by the change in the conversation, José asked, "Is everything okay?"

Switching back to English, Mazdan said, "Of course. I was just relaying instructions. The others don't speak English."

But that was a lie. Each of his men spoke English as well as he did. It was, after all, a prerequisite for participation on this mission. He just didn't want these drug-peddling scum to understand the orders he was giving in case things went south and he had to kill them.

"Please," Mazdan said, motioning toward the shack. "Lead the way."

José nodded and grinned like an accommodating concierge at the Ritz Carlton even though he didn't believe Mazdan's explanation as he led the two men into the shack. Over the course of his "fixing" career, José had dealt with all types of people and felt he had a pretty good sense of when someone was lying to him. It wasn't a problem right now, just a little nugget he would file away in the back of his mind as the night went on.

The interior of the shack looked exactly as Mazdan imagined it would, with one glaring exception. A young man, no more than twenty-one or twenty-two sat at a rickety table. A high-end laptop's power cord was zip-tied to a blue ethernet cable that ran down along one of the table's legs, across the floor, and out the shack's back door. Mazdan's eyes followed the cables, and he assumed the power cord was plugged into a small generator that was powering the shack. *But what was the ethernet cable plugged into?*

José noticed the curious look on his guest's face. "Aside from the small generator out back, we also have a satellite terminal for voice and data communication." He swung the back door open so his guests could see the small rectangular antenna. The system was one of many models offered by Inmarsat, a company based in Britain, that had become a favorite of maritime operators, aviation companies, and news outlets reporting from remote locations around the globe. "Not totally secure, but better than our mobile phones. And we don't have to rely on cellular towers for a signal. All we need is a clear view of the sky."

Mazdan began reconsidering his first impression of the cartel's operation. Even though these guys might be low-life drug dealers and criminals, they were unquestionably successful and had plenty of resources at their disposal. His attention turned back to the young man at the table when he heard a voice, presumably the pilot's, come across the laptop's speakers.

"We are locked on to the beacon and have the runway in sight."

The young man at the computer replied, "Roger. Good copy. Your welcoming committee is standing by for your arrival."

Farzan was in the cockpit, having donned a spare headset so he could listen in on the communication with the ground station. He stood with a hand on the back of each pilot's seat and leaned in between them to get a better look out the plane's windshield.

Covering the headset's boom microphone with his hand, Farzan ordered, "We need confirmation the situation on the ground is secure before we land. My men should be there to meet us, but we need to be sure. Ask them what the temperature is at their location."

The first officer pushed the transmit button on the yoke. "Requesting ground temperature at your position."

The computer operator turned to José with a quizzical look on his face. "Why would they be asking about the temperature?"

"Tell them it's clear and cool," Mazdan said.

"But that's not true. It has to be at least ninety degrees and humid," José said as he used a handkerchief to wipe beads of sweat from his forehead.

"Just relay the message. They'll know what it means." Returning to Farsi, he looked to Imad and said, "Let Hashem and Arman know we've made contact and the plane should be landing shortly." Imad nodded and left the shack without a word.

The three men in the cockpit heard the response through their headsets and Farzan grinned, now that he was confident the situation on the ground was secure. If there had been a problem the forecast would have been something like hot and humid or there was a storm brewing.

The jet's landing gear touched down on the airstrip that was originally designed to accommodate the smaller, twin-engine prop planes favored by the cartels. The runway's designers probably never considered the possibility someone would want to land a business jet this large in the middle of the forest. As a result, the runway wasn't meant to accommodate the Global Express's ninety-four-foot wingspan, and the tips of its wings barely cleared the trees on either side of the concrete strip.

The captain and first officer were clearly shaken by the tight fit as they turned the plane around and taxied back up the runway. Approaching the ramshackle control center, the first officer noticed a fuel truck emerging from the shadows of the forest. *They must have carved a spot out under the canopy to hide the truck from overflights. Clever.* It was a tactic the drug runners had used for years to avoid air strikes on their positions. A plane would land at a remote runway and taxi into a natural hangar carved out of the jungle's canopy, where a waiting ground crew would throw a tarp over the engines to hide their heat signature.

Two men in oily coveralls ran forward as the plane came to a stop and placed wooden chocks behind the wheels. The tanker truck eased to a stop next to the plane, and its driver hopped out to begin the refueling process. Mazdan was impressed with the fluid nature of the men's movements. They had this routine down, not unlike the pit crews on the Formula One teams he'd seen on television. The cartel's planes, and product, would be vulnerable when they were on the ground, and it probably made good sense to get them loaded or unloaded and back in the air as quickly as possible.

The first officer opened the plane's door and lowered the stairs. Warm, moist air filled the cabin as Farzan descended and extended his hand to Mazdan. "Good to see you, my friend."

"And you, Major." Turning to the cartel fixer, Mazdan continued, "I'd like to introduce you to José. He and his men have been most helpful this evening."

"Thank you for your assistance, José. I don't mean to be rude but how long until we can depart?"

"The vehicles are ready, so we can leave as soon as your gear is loaded."

"Very good." A smile crossed Farzan's face as he saw the other three members of his team approach the gathering. He shook hands with each of them, then said, "Yousef was wounded on our last operation. Could two of you help him down and into the vehicle?"

Mazdan and Imad took the stairs two at a time and disappeared into the cabin. They returned a short time later with Yousef, his big left arm thrown over Mazdan's shoulder for support as they carefully negotiated the stairs.

Imad followed behind with a duffel bag in each hand. A couple of changes of clothes and some toiletries had been prepared for each man when the flight had been arranged. Yousef's bag contained some extra dressings and medical supplies, compliments of the doctor onboard the jet.

With everything and everyone loaded into a combination of vans, SUVs, and pickup trucks, the makeshift convoy rolled away from the illicit airstrip.

"How far to the coast?" Farzan asked.

"About fifty kilometers," José replied. "The journey should take no more than an hour and a half."

Farzan's thoughts were already onto the next phase of the mission, as the Global Express lifted off the runway and climbed back into the sky.

CHAPTER 51

Deputy Sheriff Enrique "Ricky" Reyes had the radio in his patrol car tuned to his favorite talk station as he cruised west on Florida's Big Bend Scenic Byway. He preferred the late-night programming to what was on earlier in the day – less political rhetoric and more alien sightings and conspiracy theories. He didn't believe in either but the stories were entertaining and helped pass the time on the graveyard shift, not that he was complaining about the hours.

Before joining the Franklin County Sheriff's Office, Reyes had served eight years in the Marine Corps, spending much of that time deployed to Iraq or Afghanistan. People who've been in combat will tell you it provided enough excitement – and terror – to last a lifetime. He'd had his fill of both and relished the solitude of being one of the few Franklin County residents stirring in the wee hours of the night.

Reyes enjoyed working nights because it freed up his days to pursue his true passion of fly-fishing for tarpon and snook in the crystal-clear waters along Florida's Gulf Coast. When his shift ended, weather permitting, the former Marine would leave the station and stop by a local diner for a quick breakfast. Fortified with a hot meal and a couple of cups of coffee, he'd make the short drive to Carrabelle Marina. There he would stock the cooler, top off his boat's fuel tank, then fire up the engine and head out across the water.

Watching the sunrise fill the sky with pinks and purples as he ran full tilt for his favorite fishing spot near Dog Island was truly a sight to behold. Reyes would fish until early afternoon, then point his bow back toward the marina, dock his boat, and rush home to grab a few hours of shut-eye before it was time to report for his next shift. It was pretty much a routine of work, fish, sleep, repeat. Reyes didn't think life could get any better.

With little traffic to speak of at this hour, Reyes gunned his cruiser along the Big Bend Scenic Byway, also known as Highway 98. It was a beautiful drive during the day, with the waters of the Gulf on one side and Tate's Hell State Forest on the other. But at this time of night there wasn't much to see beyond the beams of his patrol car's headlights.

Reyes craned his neck to get a good look at the sky through his windshield, and he didn't like what he saw. Ominous looking clouds filled the sky, acting like a blackout curtain that prevented any light from the moon or stars to shine through. Except for the gentle breakers rolling onto the beach, the normally gin-clear water was black as ink.

"Damn," he said to no one in particular. "I'll have to be sure to check the weather forecast after work." He was not thrilled that Mother Nature might be wreaking havoc with his fishing routine.

Glancing at his watch he saw it was three fifteen. With a little less than three hours left on his shift, Deputy Sheriff Reyes decided it was time for a hot cup of coffee and a little human interaction. So he plotted a course for the nearest convenience store. *Maybe that cute blond Katie will be working tonight.* He could have sworn she was flirting with him earlier in the week. *It's probably about time I asked her out.*

***

While Ricky Reyes wasn't a fan of the overcast, moonless conditions, the seven men hunkered down in an inflatable Zodiac boat idling five hundred yards offshore couldn't have been happier. Waterproof cases and dry bags filled the centerline of the boat, and three men, each armed with AK-74 assault rifles, lined either side of the craft. The men lay on their stomachs to lower their profiles and reduce the chance of being silhouetted against the horizon. Weapons and eyes faced outward looking for threats. The seventh man sat at the stern with his hand on the idling outboard engine's throttle as the boat rocked gently on the waves.

Farzan had chosen this stretch of coastline for their insertion precisely because of its remote location. With just under twelve thousand residents, Franklin County was sparsely populated, and the presence of the state forest meant the area would be dark and undeveloped. The cloud cover on this moonless night was an added bonus.

Thinking back to the trip across the Gulf of Mexico, he

marveled at everything that had fallen into place to get to this point in the operation. Granted, the mission in Germany hadn't gone off as planned – mostly due to the interference of the two strangers – but it was probably unreasonable to think there wouldn't be some challenges along the way. Everyone's luck runs out at some point, and theirs almost had in the outskirts of Munich when Yousef took that round through the shoulder. Having the private plane on standby for the extraction had been a good plan, but the stroke of genius had been getting the trauma doctor on board to treat Yousef's wound on the flight to Mexico.

The transition from the jungle airfield to the fishing trawler had gone well, and the week spent aboard the ship had given Yousef's wounded shoulder some much needed time to heal. Truth be told, Farzan welcomed the down time as well. He was mentally and physically exhausted.

The remaining members of the team worked a rotating schedule, passing the hours by playing backgammon and studying their individual and team assignments. Even though they were making the most of the rest and relaxation, one of the men was always on duty, keeping a lookout for suspicious activity.

The ship's crew went through their daily routines and Farzan was happy the captain continued running his ship normally, even though he was on a covert mission assigned and paid for by a Mexican drug cartel. Since the trawler was a legitimate fishing vessel, the activity only served to reinforce their cover for action.

Farzan pushed the button on the back of his flashlight, sending a single burst of light toward the shore. This would be the moment of truth for the countless hours of planning and resources that had gone into this phase of the operation. The degree of difficulty he faced on the other missions, even the infiltration and escape from Israel, paled in comparison to this. He was about to lead a group of men onto the shores of the United States of America, and there was no doubt in his mind that their follow-on actions would be considered an act of war. Killing American officials on foreign soil was one thing. But sneaking into the United States and conducting operations in its capital city was another matter altogether.

Even with the meticulous planning, there were so many things that could go wrong. Farzan's biggest fear at this point was that his contact had been followed or worse, compromised. If that was the case, this mission would be over before he and his men set foot on dry land, especially if a hoard of FBI agents or a platoon of SEALs or Delta commandos were hiding in the darkness awaiting his arrival. A sheen of nervous sweat broke out over Farzan's body as he waited for the reply. Even though the night was relatively warm, the combination of the cool breeze off the Gulf and the fine layer of perspiration gave him a chill, sending an involuntary shiver down his spine.

Two quick flashes emanated from the blackness of the shoreline and Farzan breathed a sigh of relief. The signal was correct, two flashes to come ashore, one if there was a problem. He leaned in close to the Mexican's ear. "Okay, Captain, take us in."

CHAPTER 52

It was the time of year in Northern Virginia when the leaves were in the midst of changing from their summertime green to the reds, yellows, and oranges of fall. Some had lost their grasp on the oaks and maples surrounding the range and rustled across the firing line in the gentle breeze. The staccato of semiautomatic rifle fire crackled through the crisp autumn air as five men honed their skills at the covert facility on the outskirts of the Capital Beltway.

Joe Matthews stood in the center of the firing line and eyed his target twenty-five yards away. Spent shell casings, glinting in the early afternoon sun, covered the ground around his feet. He was dressed in full battle kit, with spare rifle magazines filling the pouches on the front of his plate carrier. His HK416 hung from its sling as he thumbed ammo into a thirty-round magazine. When the spring was fully compressed and the magazine couldn't hold another bullet, he inserted it into the mag well and pressed the bolt release with his thumb. The bolt shot forward, scooping the first cartridge into the chamber with a resounding thunk. Joe transitioned to his Glock and repeated the reload procedure on his handgun. A quick press-check of the slide verified the pistol was ready for action, so he slid it back into the holster on his right hip.

It had been three weeks since the shootout with Farzan and Mehrdad on the outskirts of Munich. Given the Agency's assets and the NSA's collection capabilities, Joe figured he would have been hot on the Iranians' trail by now, but that hadn't been the case. It was as if the Quds men had dropped off the face of the earth. He knew his brothers and sisters in the intelligence community were burning the midnight oil looking for even the smallest thread that would point him in the right direction. But each passing minute, much less the days and weeks without any tangible leads, was agonizing. After Director Sloan's mandated time off, Joe had quickly tired of sitting around headquarters reading intel reports and waiting for something to break.

202 / David Austin

It wouldn't hurt to have a little trigger time under their belts when Langley or Fort Meade found the Iranians, so he decided to shake things up a little and bring the team out to the range. The weather was perfect, and it had been a good day so far, lots of rounds sent downrange and even more laughs exchanged among the men.

Joe looked to his right and got a thumb's up from Chris Ryan and Kevin Chang. Satisfied they were ready for the next evolution, he turned to his left to check on the other two members of the team. Mike McCredy and John Roberts each nodded, letting him know they were ready as well. The four men wore basically the same kit as Joe but with minor modifications to meet their own personal preferences. All five operators shouldered their rifles in anticipation.

But instead of the familiar mechanical sound of the turning targets, they heard the rangemaster's voice over the tower's loudspeaker. "Stand by a minute, guys."

"What the hell?" Chris asked. "Mike, did you shoot the hydraulic system again?"

"Screw you, Chris," McCredy replied, as the other four men burst out laughing.

Three years ago, they'd been on the range for a pre-deployment workup when a bee landed on the back of Mike's neck. The sound of gunfire when the targets turned must have scared the black-and-yellow-striped insect, because it promptly buried its stinger deep in the flesh just above Mike's collar.

The unexpected jolt of pain caused him to flinch at the exact moment he pressed the trigger, sending the round diagonally across the firing line. The bullet ricocheted off a target's bracket and deflected downward into the system's pneumatic lines. No one was injured, but the errant round did effectively end that day's course of fire for everyone on the range…and create a story that Mike would have a hard time living down.

"How many times are you going to bring that up?" he said, still a little sensitive about all the ribbing he'd taken over the incident.

"As many times as it continues to be funny," Chris quipped, sending everyone into another fit of laughter.

The light moment was interrupted by the rangemaster's voice. "Matthews, you've got a phone call. You can take it here in the tower."

All five men looked at one another before Joe said, "Be right back. Get it? B-e-e right back?"

Chris, John, and Kevin burst out laughing again, enjoying some good-natured fun at their teammate's expense.

"What are you, in the third grade or something?" Mike said, as Joe turned and headed for the range tower. That just set the men off again and their howls echoed across the firing line.

Lee Wrobel's imposing figure appeared at the top of the stairs and he held the door open as Joe entered the tower. Wrobel was the senior rangemaster and ran the facility like a well-oiled machine. With a bushy Fu Manchu mustache and a pair of Oakleys perched atop his shaved head, he had the look of someone you didn't want to run into in a dark alley. Despite his imposing appearance, Wrobel was a big teddy bear, unless you were trying to kill him or anyone he was protecting. Once that line was crossed, there was no going back. He'd put an attacker down for a dirt nap without thinking twice about it.

"Sorry for the interruption, Lee."

"No problem." Wrobel motioned toward the desk. "It's on the green line." The green line was the CIA's secure internal phone network. The actual handsets were green to differentiate them from the normal, black desk phones.

Joe picked up the handset and said, "This is Matthews."

He immediately recognized the voice of Carl Douglas, the chief of the special activities division, on the other end of the line. "Joe, it's Carl. Having a good day on the range?"

"That we are. What can I do for you, boss?"

"I need you and the guys back at headquarters."

"What's up?"

"It's Farzan. He's here."

"Here as in the States or here as in D.C.?"

"The States for sure. And if we're right about him targeting Director Sloan and Katherine Clark, then it's a good bet he's in the area."

"Sonofabitch," Joe muttered, the significance of the information not lost on him. "We'll be rolling in ten minutes."

Joe hung up and turned to the rangemaster. "Something's come up and we've got to get back to headquarters. Sorry we won't be able to police our brass and clean up the range."

Understanding the nature of the business, Wrobel said, "No worries. There's a group of rookies coming in to qualify tomorrow morning. I'm sure they'll be happy to pick up the brass. Especially when I tell them it belongs to the guys who had to take off to save the civilized world from destruction."

"Thanks, Lee," Joe chuckled, closing the door on his way out of the tower.

Having had enough fun at Mike's expense, the guys gathered around the bottom of the stairs, eager to hear what their team leader had to say.

"So, what's the scoop?" Chris asked.

"Anything juicy?" Mike added, appreciative for the distraction from the harassment he'd been subjected to for the last ten minutes.

"Well," Joe began, "how would you feel about putting some rounds into live subjects instead of paper targets?"

Kevin Chang was the quickest on the uptake. "Those paper targets haven't done anything to me. I'd prefer to ventilate some bad guys...if you're offering that as an option."

Joe continued, "That was Carl on the phone. Apparently, there's reason to believe Farzan is in the country."

Slightly stunned by the comment, Chris asked, "What country? Here? In the States?"

"Yep. And they think he may be in the D.C. area."

"You gotta be shittin' me," John said, incredulously. "That guy's either got a death wish or he has a set of balls the size of grapefruits."

"If he's got that death wish I'll be more than happy to grant it for him," Chris said.

"Me, too," Joe agreed. "If there aren't any more questions, we need to get back to HQ in a hurry. Chris, you ride with me, and we'll go directly to the briefing with Carl." Turning to the other three, he said, "Do me a favor and head to the ready room. Get cleaned up and grab something to eat. We'll meet you there as soon as we know what the hell is going on with the Iranians."

With their long guns packed away and the rest of their gear stowed, the men loaded into two identical government-issue Chevy Tahoes. Gravel sprayed from the spinning tires as the SUVs left the range and headed for Langley.

CHAPTER 53

Dana Criswell was an analyst in the CIA's Operations Center. She was shy, bordering on antisocial. Had been ever since she could remember. It was one of the reasons why this job suited her so well. For the most part, it didn't require a lot of social interaction, and she rarely had to give presentations or speak in front of large groups of people. But the call from a friend at the FBI this afternoon changed all that.

An hour later, she was ushered up to the seventh floor by her supervisor and found herself standing in the director's conference room. Dana had never briefed anyone more senior than her boss but had the sinking feeling that streak was about to end. Her fears were confirmed when the door opened and Director Sloan entered the room.

The distinguished looking spymaster walked over and introduced himself. "Good afternoon, Dana. I'm Lawrence Sloan." Feeling slightly faint, she thought she might throw up, but Sloan's disarming manner helped ease her anxiety.

Hold it together, Dana. You can lose your lunch after the briefing. Finding her voice, she said, "G…good afternoon, Director Sloan."

"I hear you have something interesting to share with us."

Dana's stomach did a flip when she saw the others filing into the conference room.

"You probably know their faces but might not have had the opportunity to meet them in person." He went around the room introducing Katherine Clark, Harold Lee, Paul Foley, and Carl Douglas. Having been in Dana's situation at one time or another during their careers, each of the senior staff took a moment to shake her hand and offer a few words of encouragement.

Clark leaned in and whispered, "Stand up there and be confident in your presentation. If you don't believe in it, neither will they."

Dana was momentarily taken aback but appreciated the kind words from the DDO. "Yes, ma'am," was the only reply she could muster.

Director Sloan took his seat, and the others chose random chairs around the large oval conference table. With everyone seated, Sloan said, "Okay, Dana, ready when you are."

The young analyst cleared her throat and was about to begin, when there was a knock at the door.

Sloan held up his hand, indicating he wanted her to wait, then said, "Come in."

Joe stuck his head in the door with a questioning look on his face, wondering if he and Chris were still invited to the meeting. Sloan smiled and waved them in.

"Sorry, sir. We got here as fast as we could." He noticed the director looking them up and down and immediately became self-conscious about being in the executive suite in cargo pants and hiking boots.

Sloan looked at Doug Kelly, the head of his protective detail, who was standing by the open door. "Doug, I thought we had a policy regarding Agency officers' dress code when conducting business on the seventh floor."

"That we do, sir. Obviously these two mongrels have been spending too much time in the field. Forgot what it's like to operate in civilized environments."

"Mongrels?" Chris muttered under his breath.

"Would you like me to have them escorted from the building?" Kelly continued, barely able to keep from laughing. "I could take them over to the K-9 facility and hose them down."

"Absolutely not, Doug. I have entirely too much respect for our dogs to subject them to that sort of treatment."

Kelly couldn't keep it together any longer and burst out laughing. Clark and the others were enjoying the episode themselves. Even Dana let out a chuckle. The levity in the room helped her relax before the spotlight was shining directly on her once again.

"Excuse our attire, sir. We were at the range when we got the call."

Sloan seemed to take the explanation under consideration before saying, "Well, I suppose, based on your exemplary service to the Agency we can make an exception this once."

Joe and Chris entered the conference room and chose a couple of seats along the back wall. Kelly was closing the door when Sloan said, "Doug, why don't you join us. I think you may need to hear what Dana has to say."

"Yessir," Doug said, taking a seat next to Chris.

Leaning in close, Chris whispered, "Mongrels? Really?"

"Yeah. You smell like sweat and gun oil. It's actually kind of turning me on."

Chris almost pulled an ab muscle attempting to stifle his laugh.

Sloan turned his attention back to Dana, "Now that comedy hour is over, maybe we can get started. I apologize for the disruption, Ms. Criswell. This is not how we usually conduct business."

Dana took a deep breath and glanced at Katherine Clark, hoping for one more little shot of confidence. The DDO obliged with a smile and a nod. *Well, here goes....*

Moving to the side of a large high-definition screen mounted to the wall, she began the briefing. "I received a call from a friend at the FBI an hour or so ago. She was reviewing reports of police officers killed in the line of duty over the past few weeks. You may have seen some of the stories on the nightly news."

"While we all mourn the deaths of members of the law enforcement community, what does it have to do with us?" Lee asked.

"She came across one particular case of an officer who was killed responding to a couple of suspicious vehicles parked on the side of the road. In and of itself the incident, while tragic, isn't extraordinary. What drew her attention and prompted the call to me was the recording of the officer's radio transmissions with his dispatcher." Dana picked up a small remote and hit the Play button.

A young man's voice came over the speakers built into the conference room's ceiling. "Dispatch, this is unit twelve."

"Go for dispatch, twelve," a sleepy voice responded. "What's up, Ricky?"

"Glad to see you're still awake, Lonnie. I'm out on Highway 98, about a mile south of Lake Morality Road, and I've come across a couple of panel vans pulled over on the shoulder. I can only see one plate from my vantage point. Ready to copy?"

"Send it," the dispatcher said.

"It's a Maryland tag. 3NG5642."

"Copy. Maryland 3NG5642. Running it now."

"Kind of weird this time of night, don't you think?" Reyes asked.

"It is a little odd. You want me to send another unit your way, just in case?"

"Not yet. Let me take a quick look around, and I'll call you back."

There was a pause in the recording, and Joe closed his eyes, imagining what the officer was seeing as he got out of his patrol car to investigate.

A minute later, his voice come back over the speakers. "Hey, Lonnie, you still there?"

"Right here, Ricky. What do you have?"

"You're not going to believe this, but my headlights are illuminating the beach up ahead. There's a boat down there and what looks like six or seven guys milling around. They appear to be unloading large duffle bags and a few crates onto the sand."

"You think they're some illegals or maybe cartel drug runners?" Lonnie asked, hoping his night was about to get a little more interesting.

"I'm not sure, need to get closer for a better look."

With concern in his voice, Lonnie said, "Now hold on, Ricky. Why don't you wait a few minutes until I can get you some backup?"

Sensing she might be losing the group, Dana motioned with the remote and said, "Here comes the interesting part."

With obvious disbelief in his voice, Reyes said, "No freakin' way."

"What is it?"

"These guys aren't Hispanic. They're Middle Eas…."

"They're what? Say again, Ricky. Your transmission cut out." When Reyes didn't respond, the dispatcher tried again, "Ricky? Ricky, are you there?"

CHAPTER 54

On Farzan's order, the captain twisted the throttle on the outboard engine and the boat gently accelerated toward the shore. As the hull eased onto the sandy beach, Mazdan and Hashem, the two men in the front of the small craft, hopped out and took up positions on either side of the boat to provide security. Imad and Arman slipped over the side and began unloading the gear while Yousef Mehrdad, still a little unsteady from his wound and the boat's gentle rocking in the waves, waded ashore.

"Wait for my signal before departing," Farzan said, looking at the captain in the dim moonlight leaking through the cloud cover. "We'll be coming back to you if we need to leave in a hurry."

The captain nodded his agreement while doing his best to hide his displeasure at having to spend one more minute than necessary in the company of the Iranians. He'd hoped to be rid of the men as soon as they set foot on American soil, but that didn't seem as if it was going to be the case. As the captain of his vessel, he was accustomed to giving orders. But ultimately, he took orders from someone else. And on this voyage, his orders came from high-ranking members of the Gulf Cartel. Before leaving port, his instructions had been to provide his passengers with any support necessary to infiltrate the United States. So that was exactly what he was going to do.

"As you wish," the captain replied.

Farzan was the last member of the team to hit the beach. He scanned the area out of habit, looking for anything out of place that might indicate an ambush was imminent. He still wasn't completely sure a team of SEALs or Deltas weren't lurking in the shadows with their invisible infrared lasers dancing across his chest and forehead.

Looking up toward the road, Farzan thought he could make out the outline of a sedan and two panel vans, but with the cloud cover blocking most of the moon's natural light, it was difficult to tell for sure.

The men on the beach heard the faint sound of a chime as the passenger door of the sedan opened. The driver had disabled the car's dome light on the ceiling, and the interior remained dark. A tall man emerged from the car and stood for a moment with his hands high in the air, bending from side to side, then to the front and rear. After stretching out his tired back muscles, he lowered his arms, mindful to keep his hands open and in plain sight as he began the slow walk toward the beach.

Stopping a few feet from Farzan, the man said, "Good morning, my friends. What brings you to sunny Florida?"

So far so good, Farzan thought, recognizing the first line of the pass-phrase. "We thought we'd spend a few days at Disneyland." He waited for the man's response, which would determine if the mission was a go or if they would all die on the beach tonight.

"Disneyland is fine," the man said. "But I prefer Universal Studios."

The reply was correct, and relief, visible to the men even in the dark, fell over Farzan.

The man hugged Farzan and kissed him on each cheek before stepping back and saying, "Welcome to the United States, Major."

A wide smile spread across Farzan's face as he thought about how close they were to completing the final strike of his audacious and unprecedented operation.

The man continued, "If you don't mind, we really should get your team off the beach and load the equipment in the vans before a car comes by."

"Is there much traffic this time of night?" Farzan asked.

"Not usually. But these Americans have an annoying habit of stopping to ask if you need help when they see a vehicle on the side of the road."

The words had no sooner left his mouth when they saw the headlights of a car pull in behind the two panel vans. Light filled the interior of the sedan when the occupant opened the door, making it instantly clear to everyone on the beach that a police officer had just rolled up on their operation.

"Quiet," Farzan whispered in Farsi. He cast a glance at Mazdan, who was pulling security to the left of the group, and gave a quick nod of his head.

Mazdan caught the look and began working his way down the beach. After covering about thirty yards, he turned right and moved up toward the road. The flanking movement would allow him to approach the police officer from behind.

From the beach Farzan could see the officer's right hand clasped around a microphone clipped to the front of his uniform. A coiled black cord that ran down the front of the officer's shirt was connected to a radio on the left side of his gun belt. He could tell the man was speaking into the mic, but the distance and the sound of the waves gently rolling onto the beach prevented him from hearing what the officer was saying. Anger began to boil up from the depths of Farzan's being as he thought about the possibility of being compromised when victory was nearly within his reach – all because of the random bad luck of a policeman stumbling upon them in the middle of the night.

Mazdan measured his approach, moving quickly enough to limit the length of the transmission, but doing it in a manner that didn't give away his presence or the element of surprise. He stepped over the guardrail and moved along the shoulder, mindful of every footfall, as he closed the distance on the unsuspecting officer.

What's taking so long? Farzan thought, his eyes straining in the darkness to find some indication of the man he sent to deal with the meddlesome policeman. His anxiety increased with every passing second, and his imagination ran wild, thinking about what the officer was saying. He unconsciously tilted his head, half expecting to hear helicopters loaded with commandos approaching the beach. Then, out of the blackness, he saw a dash of movement behind the officer.

As Mazdan crept up behind the policeman, he could hear the conversation between the man and presumably his dispatcher.

"No way," the police officer said.

"What is it?" came the response over the hand-held radio.

Two steps. A mere six feet was all that remained between Mazdan and the officer. The Iranian operative pulled a folding combat knife from his pocket. Using his thumb to extend the subdued blade, he felt, more than heard, the barely audible click as it locked into place. One more step. He crouched like a jungle cat ready to pounce.

"Lonnie," the officer said, "these guys aren't Hispanic. They're Middle Eas...."

Exploding up and forward, Mazdan covered the last step in one fluid motion. His left hand grabbed the unsuspecting officer's chin and tilted his head back. The suddenness of the attack cut him off in midsentence. Mazdan's right hand was a blur as he brought the combat knife down into Reyes's exposed throat. Flesh and muscle were no match for the razor-sharp blade as it slid into his windpipe, severing vocal chords along the way to prevent an anguished scream from escaping his lips.

Once it was buried to the hilt, the assassin twisted the knife, cutting through the right side of Reyes's neck until he severed the carotid artery. Air escaped from his lungs, gurgling as it mixed with the steady flow of blood from the vicious wound. Without the vital supply of blood and oxygen to the brain, Enrique Reyes quickly lost consciousness and Mazdan lowered his limp body to the ground.

"They're what?" Mazdan heard the voice over the radio. "Say again, Ricky. Your transmission cut out. Ricky? Ricky, are you there?"

Sprinting down to the beach, Mazdan stopped in front of Farzan and the stranger who had come to meet them. "We must leave quickly, sir. The man on the radio is concerned with the officer's lack of response. He's probably dispatching backup as we speak."

The stranger turned to Farzan, "The routes have been programmed into each vehicle's satnav. Stay off Interstate 95 as you head north. It's a major corridor for the transport of drugs up and down the east coast and is heavily patrolled by law enforcement. Stick to the smaller highways and you should be fine. The journey will take a little longer, but you will be less likely to get pulled over by a state trooper looking to make an arrest."

Farzan nodded thoughtfully, appreciating the advice. The man had clearly been thorough in his preparations.

"I've also placed packets for each of you in the vehicles. They contain identification, credit cards, cash, and mobile phones. All of the documentation is clean and can't be traced back to us."

Hugging the man, Farzan said, "Thank you, my brother. Your assistance has been invaluable." As they broke the embrace, he asked, "What do you suggest we do with the body?"

"I'll take care of it. You and your men need to get moving as quickly as possible."

As the vans pulled away and the tail lights faded in the distance, the man turned and looked at the lifeless body on the ground before him. He bent down to get a look at the brass name tag pinned to the man's uniform.

"Reyes," he said to himself. "Well, Officer Reyes, I'm sorry things turned out the way they did for you tonight. It was a classic case of being in the wrong place at the wrong time."

CHAPTER 55

The group gathered in the conference room waited for Reyes's response. When it didn't come they immediately assumed the worst. Each person in the room observed a personal moment of silence, realizing they had most likely just listened to the officer's last words.

"The voice you heard in the recording belonged to Deputy Sheriff Enrique Reyes of the Franklin County Sheriff's Office," Dana said. "Prior to joining the force, Reyes served eight years in the Marine Corps. By the time his enlistment was up, he had deployments to Iraq and Afghanistan under his belt."

Joe shook his head in disgust, "The guy survives multiple tours in combat, then ends up getting killed serving his community at home. It's a damn shame."

The chief of the Counterterrorism Center, Harold Lee, asked, "Did I hear him right? It sounded like he said the men were Middle Eastern before the transmission was cut off."

Katherine Clark agreed, "I thought the same thing. What would have made him think they were Middle Eastern? It had to be dark out there and visibility would've been iffy at best, depending on the weather."

"We'll never know exactly what Reyes saw that night," Dana continued, "but with his military experience and Latino heritage, I would imagine he could distinguish a Hispanic from an Arab, even in the dark."

"Dana," Director Sloan asked, "when and where did this event take place?"

Dana took a quick glance at her notes. "The event occurred twelve days ago, sir, in Franklin County, Florida."

Carl Douglas, the chief of SAD, said, "Twelve days ago? Jesus. When was the FBI planning on sharing that information? Those guys could be anywhere by now."

"And where exactly is Franklin County?" Sloan inquired, ignoring the outburst.

Turning to the monitor, Dana hit a button on the remote and a detailed satellite image of the state of Florida filled the screen. She indicated the area using the laser pointer built into the remote. "In the panhandle, sir, along the coast of the Gulf of Mexico."

"Did the sheriff's department get anything back on the license plate Reyes called in?" This time it was Doug Kelly, the head of Director Sloan's protective detail who joined the conversation.

"According to the FBI, it was rented from a counter at Atlanta's Hartsfield International Airport. The manager was very helpful, especially after the agent from the local field office told him the case involved possible terrorist activity on American soil. He confirmed the van's plate and Vehicle Identification Number. And that's not all. The manager also provided the plate and VIN for the second van, the one Reyes couldn't see when he called in. The agent ran the credit card used on the reservation, but it turned out to be one of the prepaid kind. You know, like you'd get at Walmart or Target."

"So, no personal information is associated with it," Joe said. "Smart. Do we have any other leads?"

"One," Dana said. "The Bureau also sent us a copy of the driver's license the guy used when he rented the van."

"If these guys are as good as they've shown in the past," Clark said, "the name and address are going to be bogus, but we'll run the picture through facial recognition and see if we get a hit."

Sloan added, "Pass the photo and credit card number to NSA as well. We'll see if the whiz kids at Fort Meade can come up with anything."

Chris chimed in from the back row, "Any idea if the vans have any type of tracking equipment on them? Like LoJack or something?"

Checking her notes, Dana said, "I don't know. There wasn't anything in the FBI's report detailing the equipment installed in the vans."

"Not a problem. We can cross-reference the VIN with the manufacturer's records. Unless the rental company made major modifications to the vans, the records should give us a pretty good idea about which options were installed when they rolled off the assembly line."

"Both good ideas," Clark responded.

Paul Foley, the deputy director of science and technology said, "I can have some of my techs over at DS&T explore the options installed on the vans. With any luck, there might be one or two we can exploit to get a location, if the Iranians haven't swapped vehicles on us yet."

Lawrence Sloan sat quietly with his hands steepled in front of his face as the discussion swirled around him. He could hear the different voices suggesting various options to locate and track the Iranians, but he wasn't really listening. Instead, he was deep in thought, searching for the answer to a question that had eluded him since this all began back in Fallujah, with the assassination of Ambassador Jonathan Lewis.

Sloan fully understood the Iranians' motivation for the killings, pure revenge for the cyberattack on their nuclear program. He even understood their rationale for targeting the people who had played a significant role in the operation. The question he had been struggling to answer was how the Iranians found out Jonathan was even remotely involved in the operation in the first place. There's no way they grabbed him just because he was a target of opportunity and then hit the informational jackpot once the torture began. Someone must have talked. But who? The list of people cleared for Project Wraith was remarkably small, and they were being killed off at an alarming rate.

Sloan noticed the din of voices beginning to fade, and the change in intensity and volume snapped him back to the present. Sensing the meeting was coming an end he said, "Nice work everyone. And thank you, Ms. Criswell, for bringing this vital piece of intelligence to our attention. As I'm sure you've gathered by now, we've been looking for these Iranians for quite some time. This operation has national security implications and is currently our top priority. Please keep us informed if your friend at the Bureau happens to share any more information with you."

Dana gathered her things and left the conference room. Once she was out in the main corridor, she leaned against the wall and let out a deep, cleansing breath, happy to be heading back to her comfort zone in the Operations Center one floor below.

Sloan looked around the room and asked, "Is there anything else to discuss before we adjourn?"

Doug Kelly rose from his seat along the back wall and said, "Actually, sir, there is. You have several high-profile events this week that have been openly discussed in the press. There's the concert at the Kennedy Center, the speech at the School of Foreign Service at Georgetown University, and the hearing on the Hill with Congresswoman Drake."

"What are you getting at, Doug?"

"Sir, the Iranians have been on American soil for nearly two weeks. Unless they've been hiding under a rock, it's highly probable that they, like most everyone else in the D.C. metro area, are aware of your planned attendance at these events. I'd like to recommend you cancel or at least postpone any public appearances until we catch these guys."

"I agree with Doug," Joe said. "These guys are good, and there's no doubt in my mind they would have incorporated this information into their preoperational planning. Without the resources of a presidential visit, there's no way Doug and his agents can secure the Kennedy Center. It's just too big for a detail of this size." Joe paused for a moment before adding, "No offense, Doug."

"None taken when it's the truth," Doug said smiling. "Georgetown is a different story, though. It's a venue we're familiar with, and the smaller size works in our favor. But I still think we should consider postponing the speech, sir."

"Why is that?" Clark asked.

"Well, ma'am, as we've seen with the attacks in Iraq and Germany, Farzan and Mehrdad don't seem to have a problem with civilian casualties or collateral damage. Our presence at Georgetown would be putting a large number of faculty and students at risk if an attack took place on campus."

Clark concurred, "That's a valid point. As a parent, I know I'd be upset if my son or daughter was put in harm's way and it could have been prevented simply by postponing your speech a couple of weeks."

Sloan thought a moment, then nodded in agreement. "I agree on both counts. We certainly don't want to endanger anyone if it can

218 / David Austin

be avoided. I'll have Paula make the changes to my schedule. What about the hearing, Doug? Any concerns there?"

Kelly thought for a minute, then said, "Just one, sir. As you know, the first part of the hearing is open to the public, presumably so the congresswoman can play to the cameras by asking you a bunch of questions you won't be able to answer in an open session. It'll make you look bad in front of the media, which will earn her brownie points with her constituents and likeminded colleagues. Then, when she's done playing games and ready to get down to business, we'll adjourn and move up to the SCIF for the classified portion of the hearing."

Sloan smiled at the head of his protective detail. "You seem to have a pretty good grasp of how the game is played up on the Hill. I hope you're not planning on running for office any time soon."

"There's not enough money in the world to get me to join that circus, sir."

The lighthearted give and take made everyone in the room laugh. "I don't know if it will do any good, but it might be worth a try to ask if the entire hearing could be done in the SCIF. It's more secure, and we won't have to worry about the public presence."

"I'll get someone from Congressional Affairs to see what they can do," Sloan said. "If there's nothing else, I say we get to work running down those leads. Let's find Farzan and put an end to his killing spree."

As the group filed out of the conference room, Chris moved alongside Doug Kelly and said, "Impressive. You're not just another knuckle-dragging gun monkey, are you?"

"Nope. If I were, I'd be across the river working for the Secret Service."

CHAPTER 56

Except for a flat tire in one of the Carolinas, Farzan wasn't sure if it was North or South, the sixteen-hour drive up from the infiltration point in Florida had been uneventful. The men rotated shifts behind the wheel, stopping only for food and fuel on their trip up the east coast. As promised, the route programmed into the vans' GPS systems steered the Iranians clear of Interstate 95 and its heavy law enforcement presence.

It was just after midnight, and the Iranians were understandably exhausted when they pulled up to the two-story red brick rowhouse on Carrollsburg Place, SW. The safe house was located across the street from National's Park, the home of Washington's major league baseball team. Built on the banks of the Anacostia River, the ballpark had quickly become the cornerstone for the revitalization of a derelict and forgotten section of Washington, D.C.

Farzan liked the location for several reasons. People from all over the world lived and worked in and around the District. Add in tourists from practically every nation on the planet and members of the foreign diplomatic corps, and one could argue that Washington was one of the most diverse cities in the world. That diversity would work in the Iranians' favor, allowing them to blend in with the population while conducting their preoperational surveillance.

He also liked the house's proximity to the water and was considering incorporating the Anacostia River into their exfiltration plan. There was a pier a few blocks away, and they might be able to use the river as a viable escape route if he could acquire a boat. Farzan had already made plans to get out of the country after completing the mission, but the river intrigued him, and he figured the more options, the better.

The Anacostia merges with the Potomac about a mile and a half down river. Would it be possible to make a run down the Potomac to the point it emptied into the Chesapeake Bay and ultimately the Atlantic Ocean? But what then? They'd have to rendezvous with a larger vessel for passage to another country, where they could arrange travel back to Iran. Perhaps arrangements could be made to pay a tanker or a container ship to pluck them from the sea.

Even if they could acquire a boat, the two-hundred-mile trip from Washington, D.C. to the open waters of the Atlantic wouldn't be an easy one. While passing through the Chesapeake Bay, Farzan and his men would have to navigate the treacherous waters around Newport News, Norfolk, and Virginia Beach. The waters weren't treacherous because of currents or underwater structures capable of sinking a small vessel but because they were home to the largest U.S. Navy presence on the east coast of the United States. And it was not just the regular, blue-water, big Navy. Joint Expeditionary Base Little Creek, a small installation to the east of Norfolk, was home to the even-numbered teams of the Navy SEALs.

For his plan to succeed, Farzan knew they would have to make a clean getaway. If the Navy was alerted to their movement through the Chesapeake Bay, there was little chance he and his men would ever see the Atlantic Ocean. After giving the idea some consideration, Farzan concluded the risk of going up against the Navy was too great and decided to stick with the original extraction plan.

With the gear from the vans unloaded and stored inside the rowhouse, Mehrdad went to the kitchen and opened the pantry. He was pleasantly surprised to see it was fully stocked with groceries. Bags of rice, dried beans, and pita bread filled the upper shelves. Coffee, a variety of teas, and a five-pound bag of sugar took up most of the bottom shelf. The big Iranian moved to the refrigerator and glanced inside. He was greeted by various fruits and vegetables, two one-gallon jugs of milk, and bottles of water and fruit juices. A kettle sat atop the stove so Mehrdad filled it with water from the tap and put it on to boil. He figured everyone could use a hot cup of tea to relax after the long drive.

The other members of the team explored the rest of the house while Mehrdad was at work in the kitchen. After years of training and roughing it on operations, the men expected the usual set-up in the bedrooms, military style cots and sleeping bags. But that wasn't the case here. To their amazement, the bedrooms had been outfitted with actual beds. Delighted, each man was determined to find the person who set up the safe house and thank them for doing such a good job.

The kettle whistled as the water came to a boil and Mehrdad bellowed from the kitchen, "Tea is ready."

The men filed into the kitchen and gathered around the island, spooning sugar into the steaming cups of tea. A few added some milk before stirring the mixture until it was cool enough to drink.

Farzan sipped his tea before addressing the group. "I hope you realize the significance of what we're doing here in the Capital of the United States of America. We are literally and figuratively operating in the belly of the beast. You should be proud to be standing here among a very select group of your peers. We are going to strike a blow that will damage the very core of America's national security apparatus. And, in the course of our actions, we will be exacting vengeance for the cyberattack on our nuclear program."

Each man looked at the others around the room, acknowledging their membership in this small group on the verge of accomplishing something significant.

"Our reconnaissance of the city will begin in the morning. We know our targets, so now it's only a matter of establishing a pattern of life and selecting the appropriate attack sites," Farzan continued.

The pattern of life he spoke of referred to the normal routines people go through during the course of their day. Most people don't realize it, but they tend to set a pattern, like leaving the house at the same time or stopping at their favorite coffee shop while driving the same route to the office every day. People become creatures of habit, and the routine provides a semblance of order, which can have a positive effect on otherwise hectic or chaotic lives. But routines also make people predictable. It is this predictability, knowing where someone will be at any given time, that makes a person vulnerable to an attacker.

Mehrdad added, "Be extremely vigilant as you move around the city. We know from the briefing materials that Washington is one of the most heavily secured cities in the world. The number of local and federal law enforcement officers protecting the city is staggering. And that doesn't include the military assets in the region." He paused for a sip of tea before continuing, "For the most part, we'll be operating in close proximity to government buildings. It will be safe to assume they're all guarded and have extensive camera coverage. Remember your tradecraft, blend into your surroundings, and don't do anything to draw attention to yourselves or your actions."

The men nodded in agreement, excited about beginning the mission but understandably a little apprehensive about conducting such a bold strike in the heart of America's capital city.

Finishing his tea, Farzan said, "I want one man up at all times. We'll rotate hourly so everyone has a chance to get some sleep. Are there any questions?"

Imad raised his hand.

"Yes Imad. What is it?"

"How are we supposed to determine patterns of life if the targets spend most of their time in secured facilities or compounds? I can't imagine we'd be able to conduct surveillance on those types of locations without drawing the attention of the security forces."

Before Farzan could respond, he was interrupted by the buzzing vibration of a mobile phone.

Hashem removed the phone from his pocket and a smile spread across his face as he looked at the screen.

"What is it, Hashem?" Farzan asked.

"While we were driving up from Florida I set up several Google alerts on our targets."

"And?"

Shaking his head in disbelief, Hashem said, "The amount of sensitive information the Americans' make public is astounding. With this most recent alert, sir, we now have a location where all three of our targets will be forty-eight hours from now."

CHAPTER 57

The Original Headquarters Building's basement garage wasn't just a utilitarian underground parking lot for the CIA's senior executives. It also housed the offices of the Director's Protective Staff. The ready room was divided into two sections by a long hallway. To the right was a secure vault that served as the protective detail's office space. Desks covered with computers and multiple phones, green for internal use only and black for normal calls outside the Agency's secure system, lined three walls of the open floor plan. A good portion of the fourth wall was occupied by three enormous black safes, which stored the variety of weaponry and ammunition the detail used on a daily basis. Depending on the current risk rating and location of their protective assignments, the agents could choose from a selection of HK416 assault rifles, MP-5 and MP-7 submachine guns, and several variants of shotguns to complement their Glock 17 or 19 semiautomatic handguns.

The room to the left side of the hallway was also a large, open floorplan, but this space was designed for leisure. Oversized sofas and armchairs formed a semicircle around a sixty-inch flat screen television, giving it the feel of a man-cave or casual living room. Behind the furniture was a long rectangular farm-style table with seating for eight, where agents ate their meals, usually lunch or dinner, depending on the time of day.

Four individual restrooms, complete with shower stalls, were at the end of the hallway. Steel wall lockers, one for each agent, lined the corridor. The agents were held to an exacting standard when it came to individual physical fitness, and they made the most of the down time between movements. The Agency had two gyms, one in each of the headquarters buildings, that rivaled any of the big commercial fitness chains. Whether it was self-defense classes, long runs around the compound's wooded trail, or a trip into McLean or

Tyson's Corner for a workout at the local CrossFit, there was no excuse for being out of shape.

It was here that a small team of elite Protective Operations Specialists gathered around their leader, Doug Kelly, the special agent in charge of the DPS. "Shane, can you do me a favor and turn the TV off?"

Shane Janzen, the director's primary limo driver, grabbed the remote off an end table and hit the power button.

The threat posed by the Iranian hit squad had forced Kelly to beef up the detail, so the ready room was a little more crowded than usual. Standing before him was a group of ordinary Americans who were doing extraordinary work. He liked what he saw as he looked around the room and made eye contact with each of his agents. They hailed from places like Pittsburgh, Flint, Chicago, South Bend, Kansas City, and Los Angeles. It was a good group, and he was proud to lead them.

"I know you're all aware of the Iranian assassination team we believe to be operating here in the National Capital Region, and that we believe they're here to kill Director Sloan, Mrs. Clark, and Mr. Foley. Has everyone read the intel reports on the swath of destruction these guys have blazed across the Middle East and Europe?"

The group nodded in unison, and Erin O'Hearn, a redhead from Boston with a fiery Irish temper, said, "From the reports it appears they are very good at their job."

"Versatile, too," Doug agreed. "They've demonstrated capabilities ranging from small-unit tactics to long-range precision rifles and even EFPs. So, we need to be on our toes until these guys are captured or ventilated."

Jim Haldeman, an agent from Kansas City, spoke up, "Do we know why the Iranians are targeting three of our top officers?"

"That's above our pay grade. But it must've been a pretty serious kick to the Ayatollah's nuts for him to be pissed off enough to send a hit team into our backyard."

That last comment drew laughter from around the room. Doug continued, "So I'm assuming you've seen the boss's schedule for the day and the movement to Rayburn?"

"Yeah," Brett LaCava said, in his heavy Brooklyn accent. "Nice of Congresswoman Drake to make the hearing open to the public so the whole fucking world, to include six Iranian shitheads trying to kill us, will know exactly where we'll be this afternoon."

"If you've got a problem with Congresswoman Drake, I'd take it up with Bill and his people on the West Coast," Doug said, referring to Bill Nissen, a surfer and long-distance runner from Orange County, California.

"Not my fault, dude," Bill replied. "I'm registered right here in the good old Commonwealth of Virginia these days. But even if I was still voting in Cali, there's no way on God's green earth I would've cast a ballot in her favor."

Another round of laughter broke out in the room. Doug knew the humor was a coping mechanism to help the agents deal with any lingering nervousness or stress. Each person in the room was acutely aware of how serious this threat was and that they were the last line of defense between their charges and the assassins.

"All right," Doug said, quieting the crowd. "Back to Rayburn. As Brett so eloquently shared with the team, the first part of the hearing is open to the public. Congressional Affairs tried to get the entire hearing moved to the SCIF, but Drake wasn't having it. No TV cameras or constituents in there. So I want a few more of us than usual in the room for the open portion of the hearing."

Doug consulted the day's roster, identifying the two site advance agents, then looked at Brett and Erin. "I've already spoken with Lindsey Newell, the chief of the Capitol Police, about our concerns, but I want you to run your advance a little earlier than usual. Make sure the officers working the room have a clear understanding of the situation."

"Will do," Erin said.

Turning to Janzen, the limo driver, Doug said, "Shane, get with Erin and Brett on the route. I'd like to use the underground parking garage to minimize our exposure. Any word on the construction?"

"That's a no-go," Brett said. "I checked with the Capitol Police this morning and they said the work is a couple of weeks behind schedule. Congress can't even get their own shit done on time."

"Damn. In that case, let's plan on doing the arrival and departure at the C Street entrance. I want to avoid the horseshoe drive on South Capitol. Too easy to get boxed in, and we'd have a hell of a time getting off the X."

"You got it, boss. Let's also avoid the tunnel on 395. I know it's a convenient way to get to the Hill, but tunnels are shit for the same reason."

"Okay," Doug said. "The three of you work it out and let me know what you decide. Also, just a reminder that for the duration of this threat, Joe Matthews and his team will be pulling surveillance detection for us. They'll be keeping an eye on our arrivals and departures, looking for correlation of movement or anything out of the ordinary. Joe and his guys will be in plain clothes, no suits or lapel pins and certainly no shrouds," the coiled earpieces that are the telltale sign of protective agents the world over.

Jeanne Emerson, the shift leader, asked, "If they're not wearing shrouds, what's the commo plan?"

"Joe's guys will be using covert wireless earpieces that are tied into our radio net. Cell phones as back-up."

Jeanne nodded, making notes on her phone.

"They'll also be acting as our quick reaction force if anything goes down," Doug continued. "You all know Joe and his team from their previous tours on the detail, so if you see some guys in civilian attire running to the sound of gunfire, for God's sake, don't shoot them." Once again laughter worked its way through the assembled group. "And like I said last week when this shit storm started brewing, body armor is mandatory for all moves off the compound. If I catch anyone without it you'll be wishing you'd taken an Iranian round in the chest."

Doug paused for a minute to let everything he'd said sink in, then asked, "Any questions?" When there were none, he turned and headed for the door. "All right, then," he said over his shoulder. "I'll be up in the Command Post if you need anything."

Turning left out of the ready room, Doug entered a small anteroom and inserted a key into a panel on the wall that summoned the director's private elevator. The door chimed a minute later, signaling the car's arrival, and the veteran agent stepped inside. As he pressed the button for the seventh floor he couldn't shake the feeling that something bad was going to happen at the Rayburn building today.

CHAPTER 58

From his perch atop the Democratic National Headquarters building, Major Hamid Farzan watched the two black Suburbans idling in front of the Rayburn building's C Street entrance through the scope of his Dragunov sniper rifle. At a range of a mere three hundred and fifty yards, it would take less than half a second for the steel-jacketed projectile to cover the distance. He would be able to fire, get a sight picture on his second target, and have that round on its way before anyone even heard the report of the first shot.

Sweeping the rifle from right to left, Farzan looked for anyone or anything out of place, any sign, no matter how small, that might indicate the Americans were aware of his team's presence. He scanned the green space between C and D Streets that lay directly between his hide on the roof and the Rayburn building.

Spirit of Justice Park was split into two identical halves by South Capitol Street and formed the roof of an underground parking garage for the House of Representatives office buildings. His timing for the attack had been fortunate because the garage was closed for construction. That closure forced the protective detail to conduct its arrival and departure above ground where the targets would be exposed to Farzan's team.

Needing a break from the scope, he removed the stock from his shoulder and set it gently on the shooting mat that converted into the rifle's carrying case. To his right were several bottles of water he'd purchased from a convenience store down the street from the safehouse. Twisting the cap off of one, he took a long sip, then placed it back with the others.

Farzan pressed the push-to-talk button on a small, handheld radio lying next to the rifle. "Status report."

"This is Yousef. I'm in position."

Next came Hashem. "The western section of the park is clear."

The last voice Farzan heard was Arman checking in. "I'm at the corner of First and C with a group of tourists. All clear."

"Good," Farzan said. "It shouldn't be long now."

Reaching for a set of binoculars, he resumed his watch. He could see his men but only because he knew where to look. Their tradecraft was excellent and enabled each of them to blend effortlessly into their surroundings. Mehrdad was at the eastern corner of the Rayburn building, buying a Coke from a street vendor. Wearing a suit with a messenger bag slung over one shoulder, the big Iranian looked like any other congressional staffer on the Hill.

Arman was at the opposite or westernmost corner of the building, pretending to be a tourist. He wore jeans and a dark blue hoodie emblazoned with a big yellow University of Michigan logo across the chest. A backpack and camera dangling from a strap around his neck completed his disguise.

Positioned on the corners, Arman and Mehrdad would converge on their target from opposite ends of the building, preventing an escape up or down C Street. It would be imperative for both men to know where the other was at all times to avoid being caught in their line of fire.

Moving the binoculars' field of view to the western section of the park, Farzan saw a lone figure sitting on a bench. The man opened an insulated cooler and appeared to be taking a late lunch or early dinner break. Hashem looked every bit like a local construction worker, from his sticker-covered hard hat to the beat-up, steel-toed boots on his feet. A worn and tattered canvas satchel sat on the ground next to the cooler. If he had indeed been a construction worker, the satchel would have been filled with his personal set of tools. Today, however, it contained tools of a different trade, namely a short-barreled AKS-74U. With its stock folded, the compact carbine measured just a hair over nineteen inches long. It was a lightweight and highly maneuverable weapon. Pouches sewn into the inside of Hashem's coveralls concealed spare thirty-round magazines. Arman's backpack and Mehrdad's shoulder bag also contained items other than what they were designed to carry.

Farzan paused to take another swig of water, then raised the binoculars back to his eyes and continued observing the area. On the eastern section of the park, he saw a homeless man struggling to push a shopping cart across the grass. For a reason he couldn't fathom, the man had wandered off the paved path that encircled and intersected the park. The lush grass made it that much harder to push the overloaded cart, and he watched as the man became visibly frustrated and gave up. The effort required to push the cart appeared to be more than the homeless man was willing to expel. So he stopped in his tracks and rummaged through the cart's jumbled mass of items, the entirety of his worldly possessions. Farzan was fascinated with the man and his plight, so he decided to watch him a little longer. A grin appeared on the homeless man's face when Farzan could only assume he had found what he'd been looking for. With a triumphant pump of his fist, the man pulled a McDonald's bag from the mess in the cart and sat down on the grass to enjoy his feast.

Movement above caught Farzan's eye, so he angled the binoculars up, focusing on the roof of the building across the street from the homeless man he'd been watching. The Longworth building was another of the House of Representatives offices. Adjusting the magnification and focus, he could make out what looked like an Asian man wearing some type of maintenance uniform. He appeared to be working on a piece of heavy machinery, maybe an air-conditioning or heating unit. Occasionally the man would take a break from his work and gaze out toward the National Mall. Longworth was several floors higher than Farzan's position on the roof of the DNC Headquarters, and he imagined the man had a pretty spectacular view of the city.

Returning his attention to the streets, Farzan swept the binoculars down to the left, past Hashem's position in the park, and focused on the cars parked in a triangular lot across C Street from the idling Suburbans. Most of the vehicles were empty, but a few were occupied and deserved closer scrutiny.

A blond woman sat in a sedan reading a book. To the right he saw an elderly African American man leaning against the bed of his pickup talking on the phone. The man's free hand gestured wildly as he spoke and his facial expressions gave Farzan the impression the conversation was not going well. Moving on across the lot, he saw a man who looked like he was taking a nap in the front seat of a minivan and a woman in a sports car typing furiously on her cell phone.

Farzan's eyes settled on a navy-blue Subaru Outback parked in front of the woman's sports car. A fit looking man wearing a Washington Nationals baseball cap and sunglasses sat behind the wheel. Farzan was about to move on, but there was something familiar about the man. He was tan, but his skin had the texture of someone who spent a good amount of time outdoors, not in a tanning salon. And there was something about his hair. The man wore a hat, but Farzan could clearly see it was a deep shade of red. *Do I know you?* Increasing the zoom, he adjusted the focus and searched the driver's features for the smallest detail, trying to jog loose a memory from the recesses of his mind. *Where have I seen you before?* The feeling of not knowing gnawed at Farzan, so much so that he grimaced as if he was experiencing some type of physical pain.

Taking his focus off the man for a minute, he scanned the car, looking for anything that would help him unravel the mystery of who this guy was. A black square with a white U in the center, the logo of the ride-sharing service Uber, caught his attention. *Are you really an Uber driver? Could it be that simple?* Farzan was not one to believe in coincidences, but this had been a long, demanding operation. Maybe he was just tired – and if he was being truthful with himself – a little stressed out. Still, it just didn't feel right.

His fixation with the Uber driver was interrupted by Hashem's voice over the radio. "There's movement with the motorcade, Major."

Farzan's eyes snapped immediately to the motorcade, pushing away his interest in the driver for the time being. The rear doors of the second Suburban opened, and he watched as two agents in dark suits emerged. They moved forward and took up positions on either side of the lead Suburban, backs to the vehicle, heads on a swivel, a sure sign the arrival of their protectee was imminent.

Adrenalin dumped into Farzan's system at the sight of the activity, and he could feel his heart rate increase with excitement. "Be ready. They'll be coming out any second now. My shot will initiate the attack."

CHAPTER 59

The hearing had gone pretty much according to script. Congresswoman Drake acted as if the open session was her own personal soapbox, using the bully pulpit to rail against the intelligence community. About half way through her opening statement, Drake turned particularly venomous toward the CIA and Lawrence Sloan's leadership of the organization.

After twenty minutes of venting, Drake must have felt she had made her point and finally got around to asking questions, mostly about the actions Sloan authorized in the wake of Ambassador Lewis's abduction. Doug Kelly was shocked when she brought up the assault on the cement factory outside Fallujah and the follow-on interrogation of the prisoners. Both of those events were classified and should not have been discussed in a public forum. They were subjects for the closed hearing in the SCIF.

Kelly hadn't been in the closed session. The agents usually sat with a couple of Capitol Police officers in a small anteroom outside the SCIF's door, so he wasn't privy to what had gone on in there. But when the door opened and Director Sloan stepped out of the secure hearing room, he didn't seem the least bit upset. Over the course of his career, the veteran spymaster had been through plenty of congressional hearings. So many, in fact, that the whole exercise didn't seem to faze him a bit, regardless of the sensitivity of the content or the posturing of the politicians asking the questions.

Katherine Clark and Paul Foley, on the other hand, didn't exude the director's same calm demeanor. They looked like they could use a stiff drink, and for some reason, Kelly found that amusing. He activated the small microphone clipped inside the left sleeve of his suit coat, and said, "Coming down."

"Ten-four, coming down," Bryan Ward acknowledged from the driver's seat of the follow-car.

Nate Allen made a note of the impending movement as he monitored the radio traffic from the command post in the director's suite back at Langley. He looked over his shoulder at Tim O'Connor, Doug Kelly's deputy, to make sure he heard the transmission.

Tim nodded and said, "Do me a favor and let Paula know."

Stepping out of the command post, call-sign Citadel because it was on the seventh and uppermost floor of the headquarters building, Allen crossed the anteroom and stuck his head into the director's outer office where Paula Hanson, Sloan's executive assistant, sat. "Hey, Paula, looks like it's a wrap at Rayburn. They should be heading back in the next few minutes."

"Thanks, Nate. Any word on how the hearing went?"

"No, ma'am. Just the call that they were on the way to the cars."

Allen was headed back to the command post when he heard the distinctive ring of the secure green line. He picked up the pace and grabbed the handset on the fourth ring. "Director's Protective Staff, this is Nate."

"Nate, my name is Fred Jackson," the voice on the other end of the line said. "I'm a technical operations officer in the DS&T. I work for Paul Foley."

"Okay Fred. What can I do for you?"

"I'm sure you guys are aware of the Iranian threat against Director Sloan, Paul Foley, and Katherine Clark."

"We are. As I'm sure you can imagine, it has us kind of busy right now."

"Well, I was tasked with trying to track down the Iranians whereabouts. By using the VIN's on their rental vans, I was able to see which options had been installed when they left the factory."

Fascinating. He looked over at Tim O'Connor, opening and closing his free hand, touching his thumb to his fingers, indicating the person on the phone was a talker. *Do me a favor and get on with it, will you?*

"So," Jackson continued, not missing a beat, "They both have OnStar."

Rolling his eyes, Allen said, "I'm not sure you've noticed, Fred, but a lot of vehicles have OnStar these days. I have it on my pick-up. What's the big deal?"

"Back in 2012 General Motors unveiled a new service called Family Link. Basically, the service allowed the vehicle's owner to get text or email alerts on its location, say, when a spouse or maybe the kids arrived at a location or broke a geo-fence."

"Damn." Allen thought he might want to disable the service on his truck.

"When active," Jackson said, continuing his stream of consciousness as if he hadn't heard Allen, "the system acts like a tracking beacon."

Seeing where the tech guy was going, he asked, "And these particular vans have OnStar?"

"Yep. They both have it installed, but neither one was active. So I hacked into GM's servers and turned them on."

Whoa! Allen was happy they were on a secure line. This conversation just jumped the rails when it came to the legality of hacking into the servers of an American company, on U.S. soil no less. *Well, in for a penny, in for a pound.* "Any luck locating the vans?"

"One. Might be a glitch in the system or the equipment might be malfunctioning on the other. Not really sure at this point."

"So where is the van you were able to locate?"

It took a minute for the web portal to refresh before Jackson said, "Right now the signal is showing it's in the District. Near the corner of Ivy and South Capitol."

Hearing the words South Capitol Street got Allen's full and undivided attention.

"It looks like the van's been there a while. Like it's parked or something," Jackson added.

Allen's tone turned serious, "Fred, I need you to send me a screenshot of the van's location."

A few clicks of his keyboard later, Jackson said, "It's on the way."

Allen's computer chimed thirty seconds later, and he double clicked the file in his inbox. Seeing the van's icon on the map made Nate's blood run cold. "Listen to me very closely, Fred. I need you to continue monitoring the van, and let me know the second it moves."

"You got it."

"And there's one more thing I need you to do."

"What's that?"

"I need the location of the second van."

"But I told you earlier, its system doesn't seem to be working and…."

"And nothing, Fred." Allen said, projecting menace across the phone line. "A lot of lives are riding on your ability to locate the Iranians. Do you understand me? I don't care what it takes but find me that second van."

CHAPTER 60

The two simple words, "Coming down," spoken by the agent in charge, or Hot Seat as they're informally called, set off a flurry of activity for the agents in the motorcade. Cell phones were put away, and the local sports radio station was turned off. Agents took up positions and scanned their individual sectors. Everyone had their antennae up whenever the principal moved from the safety of a secure location, and that was especially true today.

Although it was a mere fifteen yards from the white marble entrance of the Rayburn building to the armored safety of the Chevrolet Suburban, Director Sloan, the man they were charged with protecting, would be exposed and therefore vulnerable in the ten seconds or so it would take to cover the distance.

Bryan Ward, the follow-car driver, acknowledged the "Coming down" call, then adjusted the holster on his right hip and the hand-held radio on his left. Once they were in a comfortable position, he fastened his seatbelt in preparation for the movement.

Bill Nissen and Jim Haldeman leaned their HK416 assault rifles muzzle down against the follow-car's back seat before exiting the vehicle and moving to their assigned positions.

Haldeman strode up on the left side of the director's limo, stopped at the back door, and methodically scanned the area across C Street. Moving his head from left to right, he registered a couple of people in the park, a homeless guy sat on the grass, digging through a McDonald's bag, and a construction worker on a park bench having a meal of his own. Haldeman picked up on three or four people sitting in their cars in the parking lot to his right, engaging in a variety of activities. Seeing nothing out of the ordinary, he continued his scan and waited for the next status update over the radio.

Bill Nissen observed the people coming and going along the sidewalk as he moved to the right side of the limo. His head was on a swivel, moving left to right, then back again, watching the pedestrians as they went about their business. He keyed in on certain aspects of each individual, such as their behavior and how they were dressed. Were they paying too much attention to the Suburbans in a city where black armored vehicles and agents in dark suits with lapel pins and curly earpieces were the norm and not the exception?

And then there were the hands. Were they carrying anything? Were they in their pockets? Whether it was a knife, a gun, or a suicide vest's detonator, the threat would undoubtedly come from the hands. Agents like Bill Nissen and the other men and women on the CIA's protective detail were expected to analyze these behaviors in fractions of seconds. The advance warning gained by the agent's ability to identify the tell-tale signs of an impending threat could mean the difference between life and death.

Many agents chose to wear sunglasses while they were on detail, not just to look cool, although it did have that effect, but to protect their eyes from the sun and flying debris in the event of an attack. But Bill Nissen was a big believer that you could infer a lot about a person's intentions by the look in their eyes. He also thought there were times when it was valuable for the public to be able to see his eyes. Making eye contact with someone in close proximity to his protectee let that individual know he was aware of their presence. And he was convinced there had been times over the span of his career where the tactic had prevented a person from doing something stupid. Besides, the Rayburn building was casting a long shadow over C Street today, so the sun wasn't an issue. Nissen continued eye-balling the pedestrians on the sidewalk while he waited patiently for the next radio transmission.

He saw the entourage approach through the double glass doors even before he heard the call. Reaching back with his right hand, he knocked twice on the thick, bullet-resistant door, giving Shane Janzen the signal to disengage the limo's locks. Nissen grabbed the handle with his right hand and opened the heavily armored door just enough to allow him to get a grip on the upper edge of the frame with his left. He would open the door fully, to provide an avenue for escape, once the director cleared the Rayburn building's entrance.

Jeanne Emerson was leading the procession through the lobby and Doug Kelly was in position behind and just to the right of Director Sloan. Katherine Clark and Paul Foley followed the group and were engaged in a hushed conversation.

***

Farzan set the binoculars on the mat, then reseated the Dragunov's stock in his right shoulder. Gazing through the rifle's powerful scope, he could see his target group through the Rayburn building's glass doors. The sight made his heart race in anticipation. He reached for the radio. "I can see them. They should be on the sidewalk any second."

Pausing to take his eye from the scope for the briefest of moments, Farzan looked up to the roofs of the government buildings across the way, using the American flags to gauge the speed and direction of the wind. What he saw caused a slight smile. The flags were still, hanging down limply along their poles.

Putting his eye back to the scope, he keyed the radio and said, "Yousef, Arman, start your approach, but be discreet. I don't want to tip our hand and lose the element of surprise."

"Yes, sir." Arman replied.

"Moving," Yousef said.

"Be ready, Hashem. We'll go on my shot."

"Standing by, Major."

Farzan dropped the radio on the mat and settled into a comfortable firing position. He rested his cheek on the polymer stock, then adjusted his grip slightly and thumbed the selector switch to fire.

***

Emerson nodded to the Capitol Police officers staffing the security checkpoint. "Thanks for your help this afternoon."

"No problem. Have a good one," one of the officers replied.

As she approached the doors, Emerson spoke into her radio, "Coming out."

Once again, Ward confirmed the call. "Roger. Coming out."

Almost in unison, as if choreographed over years of experience, Emerson pushed through the double doors, leading the contingent out onto the sidewalk as Bill Nissen opened the Suburban's heavy armored door and held it in place.

The openings, one leading straight ahead into the black SUV, and the other, back into the building, gave the detail two options if they detected any type of threat to the director. Once the agents passed the half-way point between the two doors, commonly referred to as the Point of No Return, they went forward into the safety of the Suburban. It was quicker than turning around and going back into the building. On the flip side, if the agents hadn't passed that imaginary halfway mark, turning back into the building was the faster option.

Jeanne Emerson paused a moment to let a few pedestrians pass, then moved forward and took Nissen's position at the door. "Thanks, Bill."

"No sweat."

Easing out of the way, Nissen moved to the right and stopped at the gap between the rear of the limo and the front of the follow car. He was facing east, watching the people on the sidewalk moving toward him, when one guy in particular caught his eye. The man was wearing a business suit and had a messenger bag slung diagonally across his chest. He was big, like a weightlifter, and looked like he could have been of Middle Eastern descent. At first glance, he seemed like any other staffer or government worker, but there was something about his demeanor that didn't feel right to the veteran agent.

The threat detector in Nissen's head instantly kicked into gear, and he ran through the mental checklist that would identify the guy as friend or foe. He started at the top. The guy's dark eyes stared in their direction, intensely focused on the group exiting the Rayburn building. Strike one. Next, his hands. His left hand gripped the bag's strap across his chest, not unusual in and of itself. But his right hand was buried deep inside the messenger bag hanging along his hip. Strike two. The man shifted his gaze and looked directly into Nissen's eyes, and he immediately knew the guy was trouble. Strike three.

Nissen stepped into the center of the sidewalk, placing himself between the man and Director Sloan's entourage. He raised his left hand, palm out, gesturing for the man to stop when he heard a voice come through his earpiece.

"All units, this is Citadel. Be advised, one of the Iranians' vans has been located. It's parked approximately two blocks from your location. The hit team may be in your area of operations as we speak."

CHAPTER 61

"We need to go quickly, sir," Doug Kelly said, placing a hand on Director Sloan's shoulder and increasing their pace toward the limo. Kelly didn't waste time answering the radio call because he knew the rest of the detail heard the transmission and would be responding according to the untold hours of training spent preparing for this eventuality. Instead, he focused on the door held open by Jeanne Emerson, the safety of the armored Suburban's interior beckoning to him.

Farzan took a deep, cleansing breath to control his heart rate and the adrenalin coursing through his veins. He watched the double doors part and a female agent lead the contingent out onto the sidewalk. Lawrence Sloan was five or six feet behind the woman as Farzan centered the scope's reticle on his head and took one more calming breath. His index finger began taking the slack out of the trigger and he felt the rifle buck against his shoulder as it expelled its steel core, high-velocity round. He watched through the scope with anticipation, waiting for the impact as the projectile covered the distance in about a third of a second.

Kelly swore he could feel the presence of the bullet as it passed inches from his head. He heard a dull thud, sure it was the impact of the round hitting flesh and bone. His suspicion was confirmed by a woman's terrified scream a second later. Instinct and years of training kicked in at the realization his detail was under attack.

He used his left hand on Sloan's shoulder to control his protectee, then pointed to the Suburban's open door with his right hand. The action gave the director a visual indicator to go along with the verbal command. "Into the truck, now!"

Sloan followed Doug Kelly's order and ran to the open door. The sudden burst of movement by Sloan's agent caught

Farzan's eye, and he immediately knew he'd missed his intended target. Something as simple as changing their pace had caused the bullet to pass directly over the CIA director's head, and strike the man Farzan knew to be the deputy director of science and technology instead. The steel core round hit Paul Foley on the bridge of his nose and blew straight out the back of his skull, spraying blood and brain matter over the people unfortunate enough to be walking behind him. The bullet continued on its downward trajectory and hit a woman in the abdomen. She collapsed to the ground next to Foley.

Kelly managed to steal a quick glance at the sidewalk before following Sloan into the Suburban. He caught a glimpse of Paul Foley's lifeless body on the ground with a pool of blood expanding around what was left of his head.

Jeanne Emerson slammed the door and yelled, "GO! GO! GO!"

Hashem, the man dressed as the construction worker, had thrown down the remnants of his meal and retrieved his carbine from the canvas tool bag. He shouldered the weapon and took aim at the follow car's driver. From his position in the park, he had an unobstructed view of the agent behind the wheel and opened fire, emptying the thirty-round magazine in seconds. The bullets passed through the Suburban's unarmored door, killing the driver instantly. Bryan Ward's body slumped to the right and came to rest on the truck's center console.

With automatic gunfire erupting all around the Suburban, Shane Janzen accelerated away from the chaos. As he pulled out into traffic, he saw a man on the sidewalk firing at them flash by on the right. Round after round pounded the passenger side of the Suburban, the impacts sounding like someone swinging a sledge hammer against the side of his truck.

Farzan couldn't believe his eyes. He'd missed one of the easiest shots he would ever take. Frustrated and embarrassed, he let out a scream that sounded like the wail of a wounded animal. *How did the agent know to move at that exact moment?* The echo of the gunfire reverberating off the white marble façade of the Rayburn building refocused his attention, and with his eye back on the scope, Farzan resumed sweeping the area, looking to reacquire his targets.

For Bill Nissen, everything seemed to happen in slow motion as the attack erupted around the motorcade. He heard a woman's scream behind him but ignored it. She was somebody else's problem. His responsibility at the moment was the big man advancing on him. He saw the man's hand emerging from the messenger bag as his own right hand swept his suit coat out of the way and settled on the familiar grip of his Glock 17. Nissen drew his pistol and yelled, "Gun!" as the big man began pulling his own weapon out of the bag.

The curved thirty-round magazine of Mehrdad's carbine caught on something inside the bag and he knew the American agent would beat him to the draw. With the weapon still in the bag, he pointed the muzzle in Nissen's direction and pulled the trigger. The un-aimed shots missed their intended target but managed to take down a couple of pedestrians who'd been slow to seek cover.

Mehrdad ripped away the remains of the shredded messenger bag and extended the rifle's folding stock, ready to fire another burst at the agent. Nissen managed to get off two shots of his own which caused Mehrdad to flinch as he pulled the trigger. One of the Iranian's rounds caught Nissen in the left shoulder but the other two missed wide. Mehrdad didn't see where they went but heard a shriek and saw a woman he thought might be Katherine Clark, the deputy director of operations, fall to the ground.

Nissen managed to stay on his feet, but the momentum of the impact spun him around and exposed his back to his attacker. The Iranian took advantage of the opportunity and put three rounds into the agent's back before he could turn around. The trauma plate in Nissen's vest absorbed the first two but the third round went high and passed through the carrier's soft armor. The 5.45-millimeter bullet severed Bill Nissen's spine just below the base of his neck, and he collapsed in a heap like a puppet whose strings had been cut.

Foley was down, and Mehrdad was somewhat confident he'd hit Clark, even if it was by accident. He was just beginning his search for other targets of opportunity when he noticed two men in blue uniforms emerge from the Rayburn building. He was about to turn and engage the police officers but they both fell before he could fire. A second later he heard two cracks from Farzan's Dragunov echo through the streets.

Mehrdad's presence, along with the gunfire at the other end of the block, sent a wave of panicked pedestrians running directly at Arman. The Iranian operative yelled and waved the muzzle of his rifle to the left and right, trying to get the crowd to clear a path.

They didn't seem to notice him or heed his warnings until he fired into the onrushing stampede, parting the crowd like the Red Sea, as four people dropped dead on the sidewalk.

John Roberts was the first member of Joe Matthews' team to react, and he sprinted toward the action. Several people fell, four, maybe five in all, as the Iranian fired indiscriminately into the crowd of pedestrians. *Motherfucker!* He was furious with the man for killing the innocent bystanders. Roberts wanted desperately to put an end to this guy but didn't have a clear shot. There were just too many people in the way.

As the Suburban sped away with their prize, Mehrdad noticed a man running up behind Arman. He wasn't in uniform, like a police officer, but wore plain clothes, jeans and a light jacket. But it wasn't the man's wardrobe that caught his attention. It was the fact that he was running to the sound of gunfire, not away from it like everyone else. Then it dawned on him.

"Arman!" he screamed. "Behind you!" but Arman's ears were ringing from the reports of his rifle and he couldn't hear a thing. He was so focused on what was going on in front of him that he had absolutely no idea there was a threat to his rear.

With a clear backdrop and no civilians in the way, John raised his weapon to the back of the man's head and pressed the trigger. The jacketed hollow-point exited through Arman's nasal cavity and he collapsed on the sidewalk as blood flowed from the gaping wound in his face.

John pressed the transmit button on his radio, "One Tango down."

CHAPTER 62

Joe Matthews tapped his fingers impatiently on the steering wheel as he sat in the car with the Uber decal on the windshield. After that initial shot, all hell had broken loose, and the air filled with the high-pitched staccato of assault rifles. The sound of the volleys changed as one or more of the attackers switched his rifle to fully automatic. The rifle fire was intermingled with the single pops of the agents returning fire with their handguns. Capitol Hill had become a war zone.

Desperate to find the sniper, Joe asked, "Anyone see where that initial shot came from?" Two more rifle shots boomed through the streets. "Kev, can you see anything from up there?"

Dressed in the maintenance uniform, Kevin Chang looked through a set of high-powered binoculars from the roof of the Longworth building. "Stand by. Thought I saw a muzzle flash on a rooftop across the way." He zoomed in on the spot and saw a rifle's barrel protruding from behind an air conditioning unit. "I see him. Or rather the weapon. Looks like a Dragunov." Pulling up a map of the area on his smartphone Kevin identified the building. "He's on the roof of the Democratic National Committee's headquarters."

"Do you have a shot?"

"Negative. I don't have an angle from my current position." He bent down, picked up a soft-sided case, and sprinted to his right. "Moving to the southwest corner of the building. I should be able to get some suppressive fire on him from there."

"Do it!" Joe fired up the car's engine. "Chris, you're with me." Slamming the car into reverse, he backed out of the parking space and made a right onto Delaware Avenue.

Mike McCredy – disguised as the homeless guy in the park – saw the construction worker across the way fire a full magazine into the side of the follow car. Springing to his feet, Mike grabbed two

trash bags out of the shopping cart and threw them aside. They had
been concealing a soft-sided case similar to Chang's. Peeling the
Velcro edges apart, he slid his right hand into the bag and withdrew
an HK MP7A1 submachine gun. He shouldered the weapon and
centered the optic's red dot on the shooter but didn't break the
trigger.

People were running in every direction, doing their best to
escape the carnage. And unlike the Iranians – who had no qualms
about inflicting collateral damage – Mike and the other Americans
would not put innocent civilians at risk. He wouldn't take the shot
as long as there was a chance he might hit one of them.

Reverting back to his days as an All-American linebacker, he
slung the weapon and took off at a sprint. Leaping off the elevated
grass lawn, he cleared the six-foot-wide sidewalk and landed in the
street's bike lane. Putting his hand up to warn oncoming traffic, he
managed to dodge three cars fleeing the scene and crossed South
Capitol Street. As he neared the other half of the park's retaining
wall, Mike pushed off with his left leg and soared up and forward,
easily clearing the three feet to the elevated lawn. The feel of the
grass underfoot calmed him as he went left, darting around the
circular fountain in the center of the park.

Hashem looked around a concrete planter he was using for
cover in the middle of the park. He had seen one of the agents dive
behind the low wall that formed the boundary of the park, so he
stood slowly searching for an angle that would give him a clear shot
at the American.

As Mike approached from behind, he willed the man to
remain focused on Haldeman. *Just concentrate on Jim, and don't
look behind you.* Looking past the man for the briefest of moments,
he made eye contact with his fellow agent so Haldeman would know
the homeless guy bearing down on the shooter was one of the good
guys.

Putting his hand on the ground to maintain his balance as he
circled the fountain, Mike leaned low to his right. The move
reminded him of a technique he had used to get around an offensive
tackle or tight end on his way to the quarterback. He seemed to pick
up speed as he came out of the turn, then straightened up and headed
directly for the Iranian. As he'd been taught as a linebacker, Mike
ran through his target and hit the man squarely between the shoulder
blades with every bit of strength he could muster.

Completely blindsided by the hit, Hashem let out a pained groan as the air was forced out of his lungs. His head slammed into the concrete planter, flattening his nose across the right side of his face. The impact broke Hashem's jaw and shattered his teeth with a sickening crunch as he fell to the ground.

Mike was knocked out cold by the viciousness of the hit and collapsed on top of the Iranian.

Haldeman scrambled over the wall to the two unconscious men. He pulled out some flex-ties and secured the Iranian's hands before turning his attention to McCredy.

"Mike, you with me?" he asked, giving the big man a gentle shake of the shoulders. "Mike…?"

McCredy groaned as he rolled off the Iranian and sat up, trying to shake the cobwebs out of his head. He looked over and grimaced at the bloody mess the man's face had become after smashing into the planter. "Did I do that?"

"Yeah, hit him like a Mack truck and knocked yourself out in the process."

"Damn," Mike said still shaking his head. "Haven't done that in a while. Is he still alive?"

Haldeman checked for a pulse but the man's heart was still. "Doesn't look like it. The whiplash might've snapped his neck or he may have suffered a skull fracture when his head hit the planter. Hard to tell."

Keying his radio, Jim said, "This is Haldeman, I'm with McCredy. Another Tango down."

With Director Sloan evacuated and the other agents engaging the attackers, Special Agent Jeanne Emerson turned her attention to Paul Foley and Katherine Clark. Foley was closer, so she moved to him first. After a quick glance at irreparable damage to his head she moved on to another patient, one she could treat.

Emerson spotted Katherine Clark fifteen feet away. She was clearly wounded, but Emerson could see she was conscious and alert. Blood drenched the left side of her charcoal grey skirt and pooled around her hip. Emerson rushed to the DDO, knowing she had to get her out of the line of fire before treating her wounds. She bent down to grab Clark by the shoulders and drag her into the Rayburn's lobby when Clark yelled, "Jeanne! Behind you!"

Looking back, Emerson saw the enormous Iranian fire a burst from his assault at John Roberts. *Damn, he's big,* was the first thought that ran through her mind. Then, *Oh, shit!* as his rifle ran dry and he transitioned to his handgun. They made eye contact and at that moment, she knew the next rounds he fired were coming her way. Emerson turned her back to the man, shielding Clark with her body just as his handgun barked twice. The trauma plate in her body armor absorbed the two bullets, but the force of their impact cracked a couple of ribs and knocked the wind out of her. She slumped forward across Clark's upper body, feeling as if she'd been hit in the back with a baseball bat.

Emerson found herself on the verge of passing out. *Come on, Jeanne,* she thought to herself, fighting off the blackness of the approaching tunnel vision. *If you pass out now you're both as good as dead.*

She managed to inhale a deep breath, even though the action sent jolts of pain through her broken ribs, and the tunnel vision began receding. Emerson hoped the man assumed she was dead and would look for other threats before finishing off Clark. That momentary pause was all the time she needed.

More concerned with Roberts and the other agents, the Iranian didn't notice Emerson's hand disappear under her suit coat. In one fluid motion, she drew her Glock 19, turned toward the big Iranian, and snapped off a quick shot.

She'd intended to put at least two rounds in the center of his chest but found she couldn't raise her arm that high as a lightning bolt of pain radiated from her back and traveled up to her shoulder. The recoil of the shot she'd fired reverberated up her arm and found its way back down to her broken ribs. Jeanne gasped and almost dropped the pistol as the ensuing agony registered in her brain.

No one was more surprised than Emerson when she heard the man scream out in pain. Her round had hit him squarely in the hip and shattered his pelvis. His roar was a combination of agony and fury as he reached out for a parked car to lean on in a last-ditch effort to stay on his feet. Emerson tried to raise her arm high enough to put a few more rounds into him, but the pain was too great and her arm fell limply to her side.

She transferred the pistol to her left hand, raised the weapon and pressed the trigger twice, sending two rounds into the man's chest.

CHAPTER 63

Grimacing as she got to her feet, Emerson walked over to her attacker, covering him with her handgun the entire way. Even though he was unconscious and bleeding from the gunshot wounds, she could see his chest rise and fall with uneven breaths.

Wincing through the pain in her hip and abdomen, Clark raised up on her elbows to get a better look at the man. "Is he still alive?"

Emerson lined the sights up on his forehead and contemplated pulling the trigger. "For the time being."

Clark collapsed onto her back, exhausted from the effort. "Good. Don't kill him. We need to make sure he survives so an interrogation team can extract every bit of information stored in that big head of his, if it's still intact after bouncing off the sidewalk the way it did."

Removing her sights from the man's head, Emerson replied, "Yes, ma'am," both relieved and thankful for Clark's interruption.

She'd gone to a dark place, even if it was just for a moment, and the sound of Clark's voice had coaxed her back from the edge. Jeanne Emerson was a highly trained field agent who used her skills and talents to protect people. She was not a cold-blooded killer, even though she'd considered putting a bullet between the unconscious man's eyes a few seconds earlier. Following through on a decision like that would mean she was no better than the men who had attacked her motorcade today and killed innocent civilians unfortunate enough to get in their way.

"And Jeanne…."

"Yes, ma'am?"

"Thank you for saving my life."

Emerson was about to respond when she heard footsteps running up from behind. She spun around and leveled her pistol, ready to take on the next attacker.

"Whoa! Easy, Jeanne," the man said, raising his hands, palms out. A Glock 17 was in his right hand, but he made sure it was pointed at the sky so she wouldn't see it as a threat. "It's me...John."

She kept the weapon leveled for a second then lowered it to her side. "Sorry. I didn't realize it was you."

"No problem." He nodded toward the unconscious body splayed out at her feet, "I saw what you did there – with the big guy. Awesome job."

"Thanks," Emerson replied, not sure how to react to the compliment. "John, could you do me a favor?"

"Anything. What do you need?"

"Could you slap some flex-ties on him? My back is killing me."

With the Iranian's hands secured, John began going through his pockets and the messenger bag, looking for any useful intelligence.

Emerson moved gingerly to the rear of the follow car and opened its clamshell doors. Looking over the top of the back seat, she caught a glimpse of Bryan Ward's body slumped across the center console and said a quick prayer for her friend and fellow agent. Without thinking she reached for the medical bag with her right hand, and the action sent another bolt of pain through her back. Emerson took a deep breath to give it a chance to pass, then closed the doors and returned to treat Clark's wounds.

The wail of sirens filled the air as a phalanx of first responders descended on the Rayburn building. "Hang in there," Jeanne said, packing combat gauze into the holes in Clark's hip and side to control the bleeding. "EMTs will be here any minute."

What the hell is taking so long? she thought. *We're in the middle of Washington, D.C., for Christ's sake.*

Time seemed to slow down during the firefight, and Emerson felt as if the battle had gone on forever. But the whole engagement had lasted only a little over five minutes – a mere three hundred seconds – from the first shot that killed Paul Foley to the last two rounds Emerson fired into the Iranian's chest.

Clark looked up at Emerson. "Jeanne, ask John to come over here. I need to talk to the two of you."

Roberts joined the women and took a knee.

Clark motioned for them to come in closer so no one would

hear the conversation. "I think the guy Jeanne shot is Farzan's right-hand man, Yousef Mehrdad. If he gets processed into the criminal justice system, the courts will provide him with legal counsel, and we'll never get the chance to conduct a proper interrogation."

Emerson and Roberts nodded in agreement but weren't sure what she wanted them to do about it. Any number of police agencies – local, federal, and at this point they wouldn't rule out some military units – were rolling up on the scene as she spoke.

"Grab the first ambulance crew you can get your hands on. Get the EMTs to load Mehrdad, then have them take you directly to Langley." Clark reached up with her left hand and motioned to Roberts, "Give me your phone." Without a word, he slid it out of his front pocket and handed it to her. "I'll call Langley and ensure Medical Services is prepared for your arrival. Doc Hamilton will have the surgical suite ready when you get there."

"What if the EMTs refuse?" Roberts asked.

Dialing the number, Clark said, "Be persuasive."

CHAPTER 64

The Suburban rocketed down C Street with its emergency lights flashing and the siren blaring. Janzen made a right onto Washington Avenue, then asked over his shoulder, "Where to, Doug?"

"The White House," Kelly responded, knowing there was not a more secure facility nearby.

Janzen slammed on the brakes, allowing a Honda Accord to clear the intersection, then turned left on Independence. He grabbed the radio's mic and said, "Citadel, this is Shane."

"Go for Citadel," Nate Allen replied from the command post at CIA headquarters.

"We were hit exiting Rayburn." Janzen swerved into the left lane to avoid some slow-moving traffic. "I have Doug and Director Sloan. We're heading to the White House." He changed lanes again, this time moving right to cut across the National Mall on Third Street.

"Son of a bitch," Allen muttered, before replying, "I'll contact the Secret Service and let them know you're coming. Stand by."

While Janzen was doing double duty up front, Kelly was busy checking Sloan for injuries. Every protective agent worth his salt knew the story of John Hinckley's assassination attempt on President Reagan. Jerry Parr, the Secret Service agent in charge of the president's detail that day, had piled into the back of the limo just as Kelly had done with Sloan a few minutes earlier. Similarly, Parr had directed the agent driving the limo to head back to the safety of the White House. It wasn't until Parr noticed President Reagan was having trouble breathing and saw bright, frothy blood in his mouth that he realized the president was injured and redirected the driver to George Washington University Hospital. Parr was credited with saving the president's life that day.

Running his hands along Sloan's torso, Kelly asked, "Are you injured, sir? Feel pain anywhere?"

"I...I think I'm okay," Sloan replied unsteadily.

Kelly pulled his hands from inside Sloan's suit coat and was relieved to see they were clean. No blood. He checked Sloan's arms and legs in the same fashion in case he was in shock and didn't realize he'd been wounded. Kelly breathed a sigh of relief each time his hands came back clean, confident the director wasn't injured.

"Okay, sir. Do me a favor and strap in," Kelly said as he climbed over the center console and took his position in the right front seat of the Suburban.

Sloan turned and looked out the rear window. When he didn't see the familiar sight of the follow car behind them, he asked, "Doug, where is everyone else?"

Kelly shifted in his seat so he could look directly at Sloan. "We haven't heard any radio calls, so they're probably still engaged at Rayburn."

"Shouldn't we go back for them?"

"No, sir."

"Why not?"

Kelly appreciated Sloan's concern for his people, especially those willing to put their lives on the line for him. "As you may remember from our training sessions, there is a division of responsibilities." He paused a moment as Janzen hit the brakes and made a hard left onto Constitution Avenue. "In the event of an attack, my responsibilities, along with Shane here, are to cover and evacuate you from the scene. Which is what we're doing right now." He paused again, this time to ensure the director comprehended what he was saying.

"I remember."

"So, while we're evacuating you," Kelly continued, "the rest of the detail is addressing the threat."

"Addressing the threat? What the hell does that mean?"

"It means, sir, that they're probably in the middle of a gunfight with those goddammed Iranians as we speak. And the last thing they need right now is to hear me on the radio asking for a status report."

Sloan fell silent, deep in thought as he said a quick prayer for the men and women fighting for their lives back at the Rayburn building.

Kelly turned back to the front as they stayed right and merged onto Pennsylvania Avenue. They'd just crossed Sixth Street, passing the Newseum and the Capital Grille, when they heard Nate Allen over the radio.

"Shane, it's Nate."

Kelly answered, freeing up his driver to focus on the traffic. "Doug here, Nate. What do you have for us."

"Bad news, boss. The JOC denied your access." The Joint Operations Center was the Secret Service's command post at the White House. All protective details arriving at the White House validated their credentials and had their entry cleared through the JOC.

"The agent I spoke with said POTUS is in the middle of a function on the South Lawn. No way they're willing to open the gates, especially if there's a chance you're being pursued."

Fuck! Kelly thought, but immediately chastised himself. He knew he'd make the same decision if the shoe was on the other foot. "Alright. We'll bypass the White House and come straight to headquarters. Let the officers at the Parkway gate know we'll be coming in hot."

"Will do."

They passed the U.S. Navy Memorial, made a left on Ninth, then a right that put them on Constitution. Traffic was heavy this time of day, so Janzen took to the middle turn lane and rode it all the way down the Mall.

Kelly looked to his right as they passed the Ellipse and could see the crowd gathered in front of the White House for the event the Secret Service agent had mentioned to Nate. He couldn't imagine the Service would allow the president out in the open, now that they were aware of the attack on Director Sloan. They'd most likely have the White House on lockdown until the attackers were neutralized one way or another.

Janzen shot right, avoiding a couple of people crossing Seventeenth Street. The move drew the ire of the other commuters, who leaned on their horns and screamed obscenities at the bullet-ridden Suburban as it sped by.

"How could they not see and hear us coming?" he whispered under his breath. "With the lights and sirens going we're like a fucking UFO flying down the street."

Doug leaned over and said quietly, "How about we ease up

on the speed a little? It doesn't look like we're being followed, and I'd hate to have a wreck, or obliterate a tourist on the way back to HQ."

Janzen eased back on the gas as they approached the Potomac River. A quick trip across the Roosevelt Bridge and they'd be back in the friendly confines of Virginia. Then it would be less than a ten-minute run up the George Washington Parkway to the CIA's back gate.

He almost began to feel that things were starting to go their way.

CHAPTER 65

Kevin Chang reached the southwest corner of the Longworth building, ripped open the soft-sided case, and threw it aside. With his assault rifle up and ready, he searched the DNC headquarters' roof for the sniper. Finding the spot where he'd seen the barrel earlier, he cursed. "Joe, I still don't have a great angle. I can see a little more of the sniper but not enough for a kill shot."

The car's tires squealed, doing their best to maintain traction as Joe made the right onto South Capitol. He carried too much speed into the turn, and the back end tried to come around on him. Joe countersteered to neutralize the spin, then hit the gas and accelerated down the street. "Just get some rounds on him to take his focus off the detail."

"Copy." Kevin's thumb flicked the selector switch to single fire and he pressed the trigger, raining controlled shots down on the position. He saw the sniper flinch, then slide back farther behind the protection of the air-conditioning unit. "I don't think I hit him, but he pulled back to cover. He's off the gun."

"Good job," Joe replied. "We're getting close. Keep him pinned down just a little bit longer."

The sight of Yousef lying motionless on the ground infuriated Farzan and he sighted the rifle on the woman, determined to avenge his friend. He was taking the slack out of the trigger when a chunk of the roof kicked up in front of him. Startled, he took his eye away from the scope to look for the cause of the disturbance. It wasn't long before more impacts began chewing up the rooftop all around him. With his elevated position, the only place the rounds could be coming from was somewhere above him. *Of course. The maintenance man on the roof of the Longworth building!*

Farzan pushed off with his elbows and crawled backward, retreating farther behind the air-conditioning unit to get away from the incoming fire. Once he was safely behind cover, he reached out and grabbed the Dragunov by its stock. As he pulled the rifle back, a steady stream of rounds tore into the shooting mat where he had been lying just moments earlier. Farzan knew he had to disrupt the shooter's fire if he was going to get off the roof alive.

Judging from the angle of the incoming fire, Farzan knew the man had moved from where he'd first seen him on the roof of the Longworth building. Thinking about the structure of the building, Farzan pictured in his mind where he thought the shooter would be. Confident he had an idea of the man's location, he backed a little farther behind cover, then pushed himself up onto his knees, and waited. If he was patient, the man would have to reload and that's when Farzan would make his move.

That pause in the firing came a moment later so he lifted the Dragunov and rested it on the top edge of the air-conditioning unit. He looked through the scope, and just as he thought, spotted the man on the left corner of rooftop. Thinking back to the beginning of the attack, Farzan knew he'd fired three rounds, leaving him seven, one in the chamber and six in the rifle's box magazine. He fired off a quick shot that went high, over the man's head. Lowering his point of aim, he fired off the six remaining rounds in quick succession. The heavy projectiles tore into the balustrade lining the roof's terrace, sending the man diving for cover as he was showered with bullet fragments and chunks of white marble.

With the man off his gun, Farzan grabbed his backpack by one of the shoulder straps and darted out from behind the A/C unit. He threw open the roof's access door and stepped into the stairwell overcome with stunned disbelief. The attack had started off so well. His men were positioned properly, and the element of surprise had been on their side. Or so he had thought. Something or someone had alerted Director Sloan's agent to the threat. The surgical strike he'd planned so carefully had fallen apart and now he and his men were engaged in a full-scale firefight in the middle of Washington, D.C.

Halfway down the stairs, he stopped for a moment and retrieved a mobile phone from his pocket. Scrolling through the contacts list, he found the name he was looking for and thumbed the call button.

Mazdan answered on the first ring. "Yes, Major?"

Farzan's head bowed and his chin fell to his chest, but he managed to keep the disappointment out of his voice. "Foley is dead and Clark is severely wounded, but Sloan managed to escape. I'm breaking down my position and will be evacuating the area."

"What about the others? Are they evacuating as well?"

The loss of his men was beginning to sink in, and Farzan took a deep breath. "I'm afraid not. Hashem and Arman were killed in the attack."

"And Yousef?"

"I'm afraid he is dead as well."

There was a long pause as Mazdan processed that last bit of information. He could understand or even accept the loss of Hashem and Arman. They were good operators, but there were times when fate favored the enemy, no matter how skilled or highly trained men were. Yousef, though, was different story. He was the Alpha male and recognized as such throughout the Quds Force. He was the one person on the team who seemed to be invincible.

"I'm sorry, Major. I know how close the two of you were."

"All of our losses today have been tragic. But this is not the time to mourn them."

"Yes, sir. What would you like us to do?"

"Are you and Imad in position?"

"We are. Just as we'd discussed."

Farzan nodded to himself in the stairwell. "Good. I believe Director Sloan's Suburban is heading your way."

"Only the single vehicle?"

"Just the one. Hashem disabled the follow car before he was killed." There was a pause. "Do you have everything you need?"

"Yes, sir. We'll be ready."

"Once you complete the mission, initiate your exfiltration plan. Good luck, Mazdan." Farzan disconnected the call and slid the phone back into his pocket. It was time to leave, and he headed down the stairs, taking them two at a time.

CHAPTER 66

Joe Matthews drove like a man possessed, determined to put an end to this madness once and for all. He managed to avoid a Toyota Prius by the slimmest of margins, but the maneuver forced him into the left lane…and oncoming traffic.

The image of a Chevy Malibu filled the windshield and he searched for a crease in the traffic that would allow him to avoid the imminent head-on collision. Finding a sliver of daylight, Joe swerved to the right while the panicked driver in the Malibu did the same. The cars passed so close to one another that he saw a flash of the driver's blond hair in his peripheral vision and even caught the bouquet of the woman's perfume. He subconsciously took a second to try to identify the fragrance, right up until the moment their side view mirrors collided, sending razor-sharp pieces of glass and plastic into the passenger compartments of each car.

Joe recoiled away from the impact and instinctively put his left arm up to protect his face from the debris. Feeling the sting of a hundred wasps as the shards embedded themselves in the top of his hand and forearm, he snarled, "Son of a bitch!"

He took a few seconds to survey the damage to his arm. What he saw reminded him of a porcupine, with glass and plastic splinters instead of quills. Having seen enough, Joe grabbed the steering wheel with his injured left hand and began pulling the fragments out of his skin.

"You okay up there?" Chris asked over the radio. "Want me to take the lead? I was the one who dreamed of becoming a professional racecar driver, remember?"

"I'm fine," Joe said, wincing as he worked on a particularly large shard of glass wedged under the skin on the top of his hand. "And just because you wanted to be a racecar driver doesn't actually make you one."

"Ouch! And I thought we were friends."

The pain in Joe's hand was excruciating, and his eyes filled with tears as he continued trying to remove the big piece of glass. It was slick with blood, and he was having a tough time getting a good grip on it. Joe hit the brakes hard and veered over into the left lane to take advantage of an opening in the traffic. The quick steering adjustment caused his fingers to slip off the blood-soaked shard, and he groaned as the twisting motion pushed it deeper into his flesh. He wiped his right hand on his jeans, trying to remove as much of the blood as possible, then gripped the piece of glass with his thumb and index finger.

Joe took a deep breath, then steeled himself for the pain he knew was sure to come. *"Okay,"* he thought. *"Do it quick...like ripping off a Band-Aid."*

With one mighty tug, the shard came free, tearing at the skin on its way out, and Joe let out a scream that filled the car. Blood poured from the open wound, so he slid his hand between the seat and the back of his thigh, to stem the flow.

Using his shoulder to wipe the tears from his eyes, Joe looked at the jagged piece of glass. Immediately, his thoughts were filled with ideas of places he'd like to stick it in Farzan. He looked at it a few more seconds before throwing it out the window.

"So, what's the game plan?" Chris asked over the radio, taking Joe's mind off the pain in his left hand.

Checking the map displayed on his smartphone, Joe said, "Make the next left onto Ivy. Pull in a little way, then hold your position."

"Roger," Chris said, as they passed under some rarely used elevated train tracks and merged onto Canal Street. He made the quick left onto Ivy and asked, "What are you going to do?"

"I'll go around and block Ivy from the New Jersey Avenue side. It's the only way in or out of the DNC headquarters by vehicle, so we should have him boxed in."

Chris thought the plan was sound, except for one thing. "What if he goes out the back? We can't cover the entire thing by ourselves."

Joe shot down Canal to the point where it changed into E Street. "Yeah, you're right. We need more people."

He dumped just enough speed to let an oncoming delivery truck get through the intersection at New Jersey Avenue, before getting back on the gas. He sped past a blur of row houses, then slowed as he approached his turn. Joe didn't want to alert the sniper or any lookouts he might have posted, so he blended in with the other traffic before making the left onto Ivy.

Joe pulled into a spot along the curb about forty yards from the DNC's main entrance and took a deep breath before pressing his radio's transmit button. "All units, I need a headcount."

His stomach churned as he waited on the responses, not knowing if any members of his team had been killed or wounded in the attack. The relief was palpable, as one by one, he heard the voice of each man check in. *Thank God.* Now that he knew everyone was alive and well, he needed to find out if they were available to help cordon off the building.

"John, what's your status?" Joe asked, turning his injured hand over to inspect the gash. It hurt like hell, but the bleeding had stopped for the time being.

"Tied up, boss. Jeanne Emerson and I are in the middle of something for Mrs. Clark."

Moving down the list to the next member of his team, Joe said, "Kevin?"

"Still on the roof. Give the word, and I can be there in ten minutes."

"Hold what you've got," Joe said. "If you have a good view of the back of the DNC building, we may need to keep you up there in an overwatch position."

"Roger that, standing by," Kevin replied. "You know where to find me."

Moving on to the last member of his team, Joe asked, "Mike, how about you? What's your status? Are you up?"

Joe heard Mike's radio break squelch but couldn't make out a word he was saying. The response was garbled and sounded like a drunk was transmitting over their net.

Finally, McCredy replied with a semi-coherent, "Uh, sorta." The unsteadiness in his voice was apparent to everyone listening to the radio.

Concerned for his teammate, Joe asked, "You okay, Mike?"

Jim Haldeman's voice broke in on the conversation, "Joe, it's Haldeman. I'm with Mike."

"Is he wounded?"

Trying to decide how he was going to explain McCredy's

condition, Haldeman said, "Not in the classic sense of the word. He came flying across the park at full speed and launched himself into the Iranian shooter. The collision was so violent Mike was knocked unconscious. He's awake, just a little woozy. Probably has a concussion."

"What about the shooter?"

"Mike destroyed the guy. He's down for the count."

Joe nodded and smiled. He pictured Mike's hit like an NFL highlight on ESPN, then said, "Jim, can you cover the back of the building for us?"

"Sure thing. Be right there." Before leaving he reached over and grabbed Mike's shoulder. "Just lean back and take it easy. Help will be here any minute."

With Haldeman in play, Joe decided to have Kevin stay put on Longworth's roof. He had a good view of the DNC building from his elevated position and would be able to give them a heads-up if he spotted any movement.

While they waited for Haldeman to get in position, Chris asked, "Want to go in and start searching for Farzan or wait for him out here?"

"Let's hold tight out here," Joe replied. His injured hand was throbbing and starting to swell so he opened and closed it, trying to work out the stiffness that was setting in. "Besides, the building is too big for the two of us to clear by ourselves. It would be way too easy to miss him. And if we did make contact and there were a lot of people around, he might feel cornered and take hostages."

"Well, then, outside it is." Chris replied.

Jim Haldeman sprinted across D Street and headed for a six-foot privacy fence separating two row houses on the corner. Grabbing the top of the wooden slats, he propelled himself up and over the fence, then stood perfectly still as his feet settled into the backyard's soft grass. He hoped the owners didn't have a big, angry dog, and to his pleasant surprise, the yard was quiet and empty.

He hustled across the yard, letting himself out through a gate, and stepped into a communal garden bracketed by spaces for the owners' vehicles. As luck would have it, the parking area was directly across the railroad tracks from the DNC building. Jim looked around for a minute until he found a spot that provided a good view but allowed him to stay out of sight. He took a second to catch his breath before letting Joe know he was in position.

CHAPTER 67

Shane Janzen took the right-hand exit ramp off the Roosevelt Bridge and merged onto the George Washington Memorial Parkway. The twenty-five-mile stretch of highway runs along the banks of the Potomac River from Mount Vernon to the Capital Beltway. It provides daily commuters with spectacular views of the District, Georgetown, and the Potomac River, making the four-lane divided highway one of the most scenic byways in Northern Virginia.

The CIA's headquarters in Langley borders a good stretch of the GW Parkway and has its own entry and exit ramps which lead to the compound's back gate. Agency personnel take advantage of that easy access to the Parkway when heading into the District for meetings at the White House, State Department, or countless other government agencies.

Doug Kelly continually checked the rearview mirror for any signs they were being followed. So far, he hadn't seen anything that would lead him to believe that was the case. He'd noticed a few commuters giving the Suburban some hard stares, mostly out of curiosity or probably astonishment. Black SUVs were a dime a dozen in the nation's Capital, but one riddled with bullet holes was not a sight they typically saw on a daily basis.

Except for the drone of the big eight-cylinder engine and the tires running along the Parkway's smooth pavement, it was quiet inside the vehicle. Director Sloan was on a secure call with the CIA's Operations Center, and Kelly listened in as Sloan asked pointed questions of the staff and analysts, then issued marching orders based on their answers. From what he could hear of the one-sided conversation, it sounded as if Harold Lee and Carl Douglas, the chiefs of the Counterterrorism Center and special activities division, were also patched in.

Kelly's smartphone vibrated, diverting his attention from the director's conversation, and he saw Jeanne Emerson's name illuminated on the display. He had a feeling the news wasn't going to be good so he took a deep breath before answering the call. "How bad is it, Jeanne?"

"Pretty fucking bad, Doug. We've got three KIA, Paul Foley, Bill Nissen, and Bryan Ward."

The news hit Kelly hard. Three dead. The Agency hadn't lost that many people in one day since 2009, when seven employees and contractors were killed by a suicide bomber in Khost, Afghanistan.

"Mrs. Clark is wounded," Emerson continued. "Took a round in the hip and another in the side. She's lost a lot of blood but should be okay. The EMTs are taking her to George Washington University Hospital."

"Well, at least there's a little good news," Kelly said, turning to look out the window. As he thought about the men who died today and the families they were leaving behind, the spectacular views along the route didn't give him quite the same pleasure they otherwise would have.

"There is some more good news if you have a minute."

"At this point I'll take all I can get."

The Suburban passed under Key Bridge and the office buildings of Rosslyn cast a shadow over the Parkway. The campus of Georgetown University was across the Potomac on their right. *Not much farther,* Kelly thought.

"We killed two of the attackers and wounded another. Mrs. Clark says the guy still breathing is Yousef Mehrdad."

"Do we have him in custody?" Kelly asked, excited by a break that might finally have gone their way.

That last statement got everyone in the Suburban's attention. Janzen looked over at Kelly with a questioning look, and Director Sloan paused his conversation and asked, "What is it, Doug?"

Doug filled Sloan in on his conversation with Emerson, then said, "Jeanne, I'm putting you on speaker with Director Sloan and Shane." He hit the button on the smartphone's display. "So, do we have him in custody?"

"In a manner of speaking. I shot him twice in the chest, but he's still alive. He's one tough son of a bitch."

"Is Mehrdad on the way to GW Hospital as well?" Sloan asked.

"No, sir. John Roberts and I are in an ambulance on the way to headquarters with him. Mrs. Clark called Doc Hamilton and had him get the surgical suite prepped."

A smile crossed Sloan's face for the first time since this whole ordeal began. *Well done, Katherine.*

"Mrs. Clark was concerned he'd lawyer up or claim diplomatic immunity if he was arrested, and we wouldn't get a chance to interrogate him."

"This way he's kept out of the legal system," Sloan said, finishing Emerson's thought. "Once he is stabilized, we'll transfer him to a safe house and nurse him back to health. Then the interrogation will begin, and he'll be persuaded to share everything he knows with us. I'll let Dr. Hamilton in on the importance of our patient, so he can ensure Lieutenant Mehrdad receives the best possible care."

The traffic thinned out as they cleared the congestion of Rosslyn, so Janzen gave the Suburban a little more gas and accelerated up the Parkway. The trip had been uneventful since they left the Rayburn building, but he'd feel a whole lot better once they were back on the headquarters compound.

Kelly re-entered the conversation and asked, "Any word on the sniper, Jeanne?"

"Not yet. He was set up on the roof of the DNC Headquarters building. Kevin Chang put some effective fire on his position but doesn't think he hit him. Joe Matthews, Chris Ryan, and Jim Haldeman are going after the sniper as we speak."

As they approached a scenic overlook on their right, Kelly saw three vehicles parked in the lot and eyed each one for threat indicators. All the occupants were out of their cars looking down toward the boathouse on the D.C. side of the river. Kayakers and rowing crews regularly launched from the dock or Fletcher's Boathouse just across the Chesapeake and Ohio Canal. No one at the overlook seemed to be paying any attention to the traffic speeding by, so Kelly dismissed them as threats. There was a second overlook about a half mile ahead, and he would repeat the process if there happened to be any cars or people present.

Kelly looked back to see if the director had anything else for Jeanne. Sloan shook his head and returned to his call with the Ops Center. Taking the phone off speaker, Kelly said, "Anything else, Jeanne?"

"Not right now. I'll send you a text if anything comes up."

"Okay. See you back at headquarters." He disconnected the call and set his phone in one of the center console's cup holders, then reached for the microphone clipped to the dashboard. Pressing the transmit button, he said, "Citadel, this is Doug."

Nate Allen's voice came back immediately, "Go, Doug."

"Nate, we're about five minutes out. Can you let the officers at the Parkway gate know we're getting close?"

"Will do. See you in a few."

CHAPTER 68

There was something about the lone vehicle and the two guys milling around at the second overlook that made the hair on the back of Kelly's neck stand up. Then it dawned on him. Their vehicle. The only vehicle in the lot was a solid-white panel van, just like the ones the Iranians were using. For a split second, Doug considered he was being a little paranoid, which wouldn't be totally unreasonable after everything they'd gone through in the last fifteen minutes or so. But the innate feeling that something bad was about to happen only got worse as they approached the overlook.

"See the van, Shane?"

"Yep. It's a dead ringer, isn't it?" Janzen checked his mirror and moved over into the left lane, creating some space between themselves and the overlook.

Doug cursed their current position while simultaneously appreciating the Iranians' planning skills. The four lanes of the Parkway near the first overlook were divided by a median. It was interspersed with trees, but there was still plenty of room to pull a U-turn and head back toward the District in an emergency. But the road narrowed as it approached the second overlook, and the grassy median was replaced by a steel guardrail. There wasn't an opportunity to exit the Parkway or reverse direction until they hit Route 123, also known as Dolly Madison Boulevard, which was another two and a half miles up the road. They were locked into their current direction of travel and would have to go past what they both believed to be part of the Iranian assassination squad.

"Let's hit it hard and fast."

"Cut their reaction time and make us a harder target," Janzen agreed. Pushing the gas pedal to the floor, he said, "I like it."

The Suburban's engine roared as it approached ninety miles an hour. They were moving fast, but the Iranians were faster. Kelly saw one of the men bend over to pick something up but couldn't tell what it was because he was shielded by the panel van. He was prepared to see the man re-emerge with some type of weapon, an assault rifle or an RPG. But when he stood up, Kelly saw the man held nothing more than a length of rope. He followed the rope across the road with his eyes and noticed it was attached to something metallic. The man sprinted away from the road and the object deployed across both lanes.

Kelly blurted the first thing that came to mind, "Spike strips!"

"We should be okay," Janzen said. Our run-flats will keep us mobile long enough to get back to headquarters."

Run-flat wheels consisted of a solid ring of hard rubber or another composite compound that was attached around the rim of the wheel. If the tire lost pressure, the ring would support the wheel and allow the vehicle to be driven until it reached safety. These types of wheels were commonly installed on most vehicles used by protective details to transport their VIPs. Each of Director Sloan's vehicles in the CIA fleet were equipped with the run-flats.

Assuming that would be the case, the Iranians had prepared accordingly and modified the spike strip by attaching small blocks of plastic explosive along its length in six-inch intervals. Each block was approximately the size of a pack of gum and was activated by a pressure-sensitive detonator.

The Suburban hit the device at speed, and the spikes worked as advertised, puncturing both front tires. Before Janzen or Kelly had a chance to register the whoosh of escaping air, they heard several loud pops as the explosive blocks detonated under the chassis.

The small explosion mangled the right front wheel, rendering the run-flat technology useless. The results were even more destructive on the left side of the SUV where the wheel was sheared from the axle. The rogue wheel careened across the Parkway, clipped the steel guardrail and shot up into the air, tumbling end over end into the oncoming traffic. It bounced off the hood of a sedan whose driver happened to be paying more attention to his smartphone than the road, then smashed through the windshield of a pickup truck three car lengths back.

A fraction of a second later, the Suburban rolled over the remnants of the spike strip, shredding its two remaining tires. The run-flats on the rear wheels worked like a charm, and under normal circumstances would have kept the SUV running for miles. But the sudden loss of tire pressure and lack of traction made the rear end of the Suburban unstable, and it swung around to the right, sending the armored vehicle into the guardrail at a forty-five-degree angle.

The impact crumpled the front end of the truck and sent it into a violent counterclockwise spin. Anything that wasn't strapped down flew through the cabin like ingredients in a blender. Classified documents spilled from Director Sloan's briefing books and fluttered around the cabin, causing snow-like white-out conditions. Emergency equipment, heavy-duty jacks, and medical kits, routinely stored in the Suburban's rear compartment, were always strapped down for this eventuality. Nobody wanted to be saved by the vehicle's armoring only to be killed by an object flying around inside the truck like an unguided missile.

At this point Kelly could only grab the "chicken handle" mounted on the frame and yell, "Hold on!"

As the centrifugal force assaulted his senses, Sloan felt as if he were on one of those spinning rides at the county fair. He'd loved those rides as a kid but wasn't caring for the sensation very much at the moment. The Suburban spun back on the road and into the traffic approaching from the rear at seventy miles an hour. Continuing across both lanes, the SUV would have gone over the edge and dropped at least a hundred feet to the rocky banks of the Potomac River, if not for the trees lining the right side of the Parkway. Forming a natural guardrail, the trees saved the men's lives, even if it was only for the time being.

Sloan's seatbelt had kept him in place for the most part, but the force of the collision with the trees slammed him against the armored door. Pain exploded in his shoulder as his collarbone splintered. The agony registered in his brain and then raced back down his arm into the fingertips of his right hand.

Kelly was buckled in as well, but the sudden stop whipped his head to the right, and it bounced off the bullet-resistant window leaving a red smear the size of a softball. Blood oozed from the wound and dripped onto the starched collar of his white dress shirt, staining it a deep crimson. His unconscious head slumped forward with his chin resting on his chest.

"Son of a bitch," Janzen groaned softly, taking a second to check himself for injuries and gather his senses. His neck hurt like hell from the whiplash, but other than that he seemed to be in pretty good shape. He looked over at Kelly, and immediately feared the worst. Doug's breathing was so shallow that Janzen thought he was dead. He checked for a pulse and was relieved when he felt a heartbeat. It was faint, but it was there.

Janzen unbuckled his seatbelt and turned to check on Director Sloan. Lying in a heap against the door, and moaning in pain, the extremely fit, vibrant man suddenly looked old and fragile, and the sight saddened Janzen. It reminded him of how his grandfather looked in his last few weeks, as lung cancer ravaged his body.

Back in the detail's command post, the monitor on Nate Allen's desk exploded with flashing lights and audible alerts. Vehicles belonging to the CIA's fleet, especially those used by the director's detail and other senior staff, were equipped with tracking devices and a myriad of sensors. One of the sensors monitored impacts and automatically sent a distress signal to the CP when it was activated. The audible alert from this sensor was a unique, high-pitched beep, and Allen knew what it was without even looking at the screen.

Tim O'Connor, the deputy chief of the Director's Protective Staff knew the sound as well and asked, "Who is it, Nate?"

Without looking up from the monitor, Allen said, "It's the boss."

"Where are they?"

"According to the tracker, they're on the Parkway, about five miles from HQ."

"Moving or stationary?" O'Connor asked, even though he knew the answer. Barring a malfunction, the alarm would not have gone off if the vehicle was still mobile.

"Stationary. Let me try to raise them on the radio. Doug, this is Citadel. Do you copy? What's your status? Doug? Shane? This is Citadel. I say again, what's your status?"

Janzen pressed the transmit button. "Nate, it's Shane. There was a secondary attack on the Parkway. Doug's unconscious and the director is injured. The truck is disabled, and we need immediate assistance."

Tim O'Connor picked up his desk phone and called the U.S. Park Police, the law enforcement agency responsible for patrolling the George Washington Parkway, and requested all available units to be dispatched to the location. His next call was to the Fairfax County Fire and Rescue station just down the road in McLean. He could hear the sirens of squads leaving the station in the background before he hung up.

"Hang in there, Shane. Park and EMS are on the way. How badly is the director injured?"

"His shoulder is banged up. Maybe broke his collarbone," Janzen said, turning around to face Director Sloan and see if anything else had begun hurting since his initial assessment.

Movement out the back window caught Janzen's eye, and he noticed two men approaching the Suburban. One of them carried something that looked like the jaws of life firefighters use to extract people from vehicles. But there was something about the men's demeanor that didn't make him think they were there to help. The compact AK-style assault rifles each man sported confirmed that assumption.

"Uh, Nate, whoever you have responding better hurry. I've got two Middle Eastern guys headed my way, and I don't think they're friendlies."

CHAPTER 69

Farzan's heart pounded, and his ears still rang from the Dragunov's reports as he leaned against the cinderblock wall in the stairwell. He took a minute to control his breathing and bring his heart rate back down to an acceptable level, then edged closer to the door and listened for any unusual activity that would indicate the building was crawling with federal agents or police officers.

So far, so good. Everything seemed quiet on the other side of the door, just the normal sounds and conversations one might expect to hear in the lobby of a busy office building. Farzan used his sleeve to wipe the sweat from his forehead, then brushed the dirt and debris from his clothes, and tucked in his shirt. After mentally checking his appearance to ensure he would blend in with the other people in the building, he took a deep breath, slung the backpack over his shoulder, and stepped through the door. Relieved he wasn't immediately swarmed by police or shot through the head, Farzan smiled at the receptionist. Pretty, with long blonde hair, she smiled, too.

Standing off to the side of the lobby, he casually observed the activity outside through the entryway's glass doors. Just the rhythm of a normal work day as people went about their business. A few officemates chatted on the sidewalk, taking a break from the drudgery of their cubicles while relishing the change of scenery and a breath of fresh air.

Cars came and went, slowly passing in front of the building's entrance, then exiting onto Canal Street or New Jersey Avenue, depending on which way they were heading. One by one, Farzan scanned the vehicles in the parking lot across Ivy Street, looking for watchers who would positively identify him to a kill or capture team as soon as he stepped outside. Once again, he failed to find anyone or anything out of place.

His train of thought was broken by the sound of a woman's voice. "Excuse me. Is there anything I can do for you?"

He turned to see the blonde receptionist looking at him, probably wondering why he was hanging around the lobby.

"No, thank you," Farzan said, making a show of checking his watch. "I'm just waiting on a friend. Unfortunately, he seems to be running late." He hoped the story would buy him a little time, but he knew he'd have to move soon. The man who fired on him from the roof would have given the police his location, and they had to be on the way. In fact, Farzan was surprised they weren't here already.

He gave it a few more minutes, then, without seeing anything out of the ordinary, decided it was time. He pushed through the glass doors and descended the five steps to the sidewalk.

Chris Ryan's voice crackled in Joe's earpiece. "I think our guy just exited the building. He's wearing blue jeans, a grey, lightweight jacket, and a black tactical backpack on his left shoulder."

"Is he moving?"

"Not yet. He's taking a minute to check the area. I'll let you know when I have a direction of travel." Thirty seconds later, Chris came back, "He's heading your way on foot. Want me to dismount and follow?"

"Yeah, but hang back a little. Don't spook him."

Pausing to take one last look around the area, Farzan turned left and headed toward New Jersey Avenue. As he approached a delivery van parked near the service entrance, he glanced at the reflection in the windshield. Using it to see if anyone was following him, he saw a man get out of a parked car and cross the street to the sidewalk. The man looked tall and fit, even in the distortion of the reflection. That, in and of itself, was not concerning, but it was enough to pique his interest.

Farzan pulled out his smartphone and pretended to send a text message, stalling for time until he could see where the man was heading. If he turned left and entered the building, then it would have been a false alarm. *But if he goes right and continues following me, he'll have to be dealt with.* Looking up from his smartphone, Farzan checked the windshield's reflection and saw the man bypass the building's entrance.

"Aw, shit," Chris muttered before pressing the transmit button on his covert microphone, "Joe, I think I'm blown. He stopped in front of that white delivery van to your right to look at his phone and may have seen my reflection in the windshield."

While Joe wasn't thrilled that Chris had been spotted, he realized they were running surveillance on a highly trained operative. As much as he hated to admit it, Farzan did have a say in what happened next. "Okay. Stick with him. I'll approach from the front once I have eyes on."

Farzan put the phone back in his pocket and continued walking at his normal pace. The man wouldn't be alone, his backup would be nearby. Farzan gave the other cars parked along Ivy a hard look. One or two of the closest vehicles were occupied, but the people inside didn't fit the profile of an operator, so he dismissed them as potential threats. He continued down the sidewalk in a nonchalant manner, not giving any indication he knew he was being followed.

Chris said, "There's the bend in the street. Once he clears the van you should have a pretty good view of him."

Joe waited impatiently for Farzan to appear in his field of view. His injured hand hurt like a bitch, and the swelling was moving into his fingers, making them feel like sausages.

There, on the right. A car parallel parked along Ivy with a single man in the driver's seat. Farzan didn't look directly at the car, using his peripheral vision instead so the man wouldn't know he saw him. Farzan took his tradecraft seriously, and his surveillance-detection skills had done their job up to this point.

But when he noticed the Uber decal on the windshield, his head snapped involuntarily to the driver. Their eyes locked, and he knew instantly why the man had seemed so familiar when he'd observed him through the scope of his sniper rifle. *Munich!* That was the man who had pursued them after the Voigt assassination, the same man who had wounded Yousef as they sped away from the scene. The time for being sneaky was over, so Farzan turned to get a good look at the man tailing him. He was tall with long sandy-blond hair. Yes, these were the same two men from Germany. *But how?*

Joe saw the man come around the van and continue up the sidewalk. For some unknown reason, the man broke protocol and looked directly at him. All thoughts of the pain in his hand evaporated. "I'll be damned."

"What is it? Chris asked.

A rage began to boil as if someone had stoked a furnace deep inside his gut. "It's Farzan." Joe turned off the ignition and exited the car. "I'm on foot and moving to cut him off. We've got some unfinished business with that son of a bitch."

"Roger that. Just give the word when you're ready to take him down."

Farzan's mind raced as he looked around for an exit to the situation he suddenly found himself in. As he neared the end of the building, a plan began to take shape. Located inside the DNC Headquarters, the National Democratic Club's outdoor seating spilled into the alley between the club and a neighboring townhouse. Several tables were already occupied with regulars interested in getting a headstart on happy hour.

The man to his front crossed the street and took an angle to block his escape. Farzan could tell the man behind him was moving faster, closing the distance to coincide with his partner's arrival. For a brief second, Farzan considered entering the club, hoping to get lost in the crowd and make his way out a back door. He changed his mind after a few seconds of deliberation because he'd never been inside and didn't know the layout of the interior. He assumed it had a back door but what if it didn't? He'd be trapped. No, it was not a good idea. But he could use the club as a distraction to occupy the American operatives long enough to make his escape.

Without breaking stride, Farzan swung the backpack off his shoulder and reached inside the main compartment. When his hand emerged from the bag, it held a black cylindrical object. He pulled the cotter pin and casually tossed the flash-bang grenade into the throng of people milling around outside the club. The cylinder bounced once, rolled under a table and came to rest against a woman's purse before it went off.

Meant to stun and disorient rather than maim or injure, the bright flash and loud boom of the flash-bang sent people diving for cover. Those closest to the blast sat on the ground screaming hysterically or wandered around aimlessly in a daze. Curious patrons streamed out of the club with smartphones in hand, anxious to be the first to livestream video of the incident.

Their reaction was even better than Farzan had hoped, and he smiled inwardly. Even though he despised this generation's fixation with posting every moment of their lives online, their need to document the event would work in his favor. More people meant more chaos. He reached for another flash-bang and launched it into the ever-growing crowd. Most of the people seemed to believe the event was over after the initial explosion, and Farzan was amused at the looks on their faces when the second device went off. The simple increase in the number of people gathered on the sidewalk magnified the hysteria exponentially. Smartphones dropped by their startled owners littered the ground and were crushed as people ran in every direction.

Using the bedlam to his advantage, Farzan pushed through the crowd and darted left into the alley between the club and townhouse.

CHAPTER 70

The pandemonium caused by the flash-bangs wreaked havoc with Joe's plan to capture Farzan. Screaming people ran in every direction, not realizing the bright flashes of light and ear-splitting booms weren't designed to cause injury. Fearing for their lives, the panicked mob stepped on or over each other in their haste to be anywhere else at the moment.

The time for stealth was long gone, so Chris sprinted to the spot he'd last seen Joe. He found his friend standing on the hood of a sedan and shouted to be heard over the panicked screams, "I lost him in the crowd. Any idea where he went?"

Looking over the scrum from his elevated position, Joe caught a glimpse of Farzan's grey jacket and black backpack and pointed toward the alley. "There!"

Chris took off down the alley in pursuit, catching a flash of grey before it melted into a group of people and disappeared around the corner.

Joe leapt off the hood, running to catch up and asked over the radio, "Jim, do you copy?"

"I'm here. What do you need?"

"Farzan's in the middle of a group of people running through the alley. Do you have a visual from your vantage point?"

"Yeah. They're turning to my left, your right. The area behind the townhouse dumps out on to New Jersey Avenue."

"Dammit," Joe cursed under his breath. He was hoping it was a dead end and that Farzan, along with everyone else, would be corralled like a bunch of wild mustangs in a box canyon. "Can you get up to street level from your position? We need to maintain a visual on Farzan. I don't want to lose him again."

"On my way."

Sure the operatives wouldn't be far behind, Farzan stole a

glance over his shoulder and saw them round the corner into the alley. He reached into the bag once more, pulled the pin from a third device, and lobbed it nonchalantly over his shoulder.

Joe and Chris heard the metallic clink, clink, clink of what they thought was another flash-bang bouncing across the pavement. But when they saw the device, it wasn't the oblong cylinder they were expecting. Instead, it was an olive drab sphere the size of a baseball. Both men yelled, "Grenade!" and scrambled away from the bouncing ball of death.

Joe rolled behind a car and banged his injured hand on the pavement. He grimaced in pain, cradling his arm as he hunkered down next to the front wheel, using the engine block for cover.

Chris's only option was a dumpster to his left. He wasn't sure if its metal walls were thick enough to keep the grenade's fragments from penetrating, but in a situation like this, beggars couldn't be choosers. He flung the dumpster's plastic lid open and dove in, landing face first in the middle of several bags of stinking garbage as the grenade detonated. The sound of the explosion reverberated inside the metal container and hammered Chris's eardrums. The assault on his inner ear and the odor of the rotting garbage was just too much, and he emptied his stomach, vomiting in great heaves.

Joe flinched as the grenade went off, sending its razor-sharp steel fragments in every direction. The shards penetrated the vehicle's bodywork but didn't go any farther than the engine block. It was a totally different story at the rear of the car, where the fragments went through the rear quarter panel, passed through the trunk, and came out the opposite side. Joe looked at the ragged holes in the bodywork and knew he'd chosen his cover wisely. He held his position for a few more seconds before breaking cover, waiting to see if Farzan would follow up with another grenade or a barrage of gunfire.

He frantically searched the alley and the area around the dumpster but couldn't find any sign of Chris. Joe's hearing was still recovering after the roar of the explosion, but he swore he heard what sounded like someone retching. Yet as hard as he looked, Chris was nowhere to be found. Finally, Joe moved to the dumpster and peeked in over the edge. The sight of his friend, alive and uninjured, heaving his guts out sent a great wave of relief crashing over his body.

"Good God, you reek!" Joe said, recoiling in horror from the stench.

Chris looked up with vomit running down his chin and offered a weak, "Fuck you, buddy."

They burst out laughing at the absurdity of the situation. The moment passed as quickly as it had come, and Joe turned serious. "Whenever you're ready, sweetheart. We've got a bad guy to catch."

Chris swung a leg over the edge and climbed out. He leaned against the dumpster, still a little unsteady on his feet, and gave it an appreciative pat. The metal box was pockmarked from the grenade's shrapnel, but none of the fragments had penetrated. It had held, and in doing so, saved his life.

Regaining his legs, Chris used his sleeve to wipe his chin. "Let's go get that bastard."

Joe pressed the talk button on his radio. "Jim, what's your status?"

Breathing heavily from the run, Jim said, "I'm on the sidewalk on the west side of New Jersey Avenue. I heard another explosion. You guys okay?"

"Yeah, we're fine. Any sign of Farzan?"

A frenzied group of people burst onto the sidewalk fifty yards to Jim's right. A guy wearing a light-grey jacket and a black backpack had his head on a swivel, taking in his surroundings. "I see him. He's here." Jim's hand instinctively went to his weapon as Farzan slid the backpack around to his front and reached inside. Jim was quick on the draw and had his weapon up with a good sight picture on the Iranian's chest. He moved toward Farzan in a tactical crouch but couldn't take the shot because of the other people milling about.

"Stay put, Jim. We're on the way," Joe said, as he and Chris sprinted down the alley.

"Don't do anything stupid," Chris added.

Joe looked over. "Not helpful."

As Jim closed the distance, a middle-aged lady wandered in front of the Iranian. Momentarily shielded from Jim's view, Farzan took full advantage of the situation and pulled a short-barreled AK-74 from his backpack.

CHAPTER 71

With everything going on in the command post, Nate Allen thought this might be what it felt like to be an air traffic controller as he pressed the transmit button. "Brett, Erin, this is Citadel. What's your current location?"

Brett LaCava was behind the wheel of the Ford Expedition, so Erin O'Hearn answered the radio call. "Just got off the Parkway and are heading to the gate."

"I need you to reroute to the director's limo immediately and be prepared to engage hostiles when you get there."

O'Hearn hit the lights and sirens and said, "Ten-four, Nate. Hang tight, Shane. We'll be there in three."

CIA police officers held outbound traffic at the gate to clear the way for LaCava as he massaged the brakes, dumping just enough speed to make the left onto the ramp. He was immediately back on the gas, summoning all the horsepower the SUV could muster and it rocketed onto the Parkway. He wove through the traffic like a NASCAR driver working his way to the front of the pack.

O'Hearn removed her MP7 from its carry bag, extended the stock and fore-end grip while simultaneously calling lanes for LaCava. The left lane opened up, so she used the temporary break in the traffic to ready his HK416 assault rifle.

Shane Janzen was busy attending to Director Sloan. It was obvious his collarbone was broken, and Janzen thought his shoulder might have been dislocated as well. But in his current predicament, he could only try to get Sloan into a comfortable position and wait for help. He was about to start working on Doug Kelly's head wound when he noticed the flashing lights of a Park Police cruiser. The officer maneuvered the patrol car through the backed-up traffic and came to a stop about twenty yards from the disabled Suburban.

Underwhelmed by the response, Janzen grabbed the mic, the

frustration in his voice coming through the transmission. "A Park Police unit just pulled up." When he didn't see a phalanx of other responders converging on his position, he continued, "One unit? That's all they could send? Are you fucking kidding me? Where the hell is the cavalry?"

Nate said, "Hang in there, Shane. Help's coming from all over. She just happened to be the closest."

The marked unit's arrival also drew the attention of the Iranians, and they advanced on the patrol car. Janzen knew the officer didn't stand a chance. The worst part was knowing he couldn't do a damn thing to alter the outcome. As much as he wanted to get out there and help her, he could not unlock the Suburban and give the men access to Director Sloan.

The officer saw the two men approaching and reached for her patrol rifle. She struggled to release the clamp that secured it in the rack as her eyes focused on the men and their weapons. "Goddammit!" she screamed in frustration, mesmerized by their muzzles' black holes that seemed to be staring at her like dark, evil, eyes.

Abandoning the quest for her own rifle, the fight or flight response kicked in and she chose flight. Forcing herself to break the visual lock on the imminent threat advancing on her, she turned around and looked out the rear window, searching for an escape route through the bumper-to-bumper traffic. Finding none, she panicked, slammed the car into reverse and mashed the gas pedal to the floor.

The patrol car was moving, but not nearly fast enough to outrun the bullets the Iranians' had unleashed to chase it down the Parkway. Anger flowed through Janzen's veins as he watched round after round pepper the patrol car's windshield.

With the officer's left hand on top of the steering wheel, the twisting of her torso as she turned to look out the rear window had her body armor out of position. As a result, the left the side of her ribcage was exposed to the fire. One of the rounds found its mark and tore through the soft tissue of her armpit, obliterating both lungs and her heart as it passed through her chest cavity. She was already dead by the time a second round went through the back of her head.

Janzen saw the officer's head snap forward, and a red spray cover the cruiser's rear window. Her dead hand clutched the steering wheel and pulled it to the right, as her body slumped across the passenger seat. Janzen watched in horror as the front wheels canted, aiming the back end of the car toward the road's edge.

With her foot still firmly pressing on the accelerator, the patrol car jumped the low, stone retaining wall and shot between two trees like a kicker splitting the uprights. The car seemed to hang, suspended in the air for a moment, before it fell tail first to the river below.

"Motherfuckers!" Janzen screamed, banging his fist on the dashboard.

Having dealt with the meddlesome police officer, the Iranians refocused on their primary objective inside the disabled Suburban. The two men walked up to the limo's back door and peered inside, positively identifying their target. Satisfied they had the right vehicle, Imad pulled security while Mazdan took off his backpack and set it down. He unzipped the pack and, struggling a bit with its weight, removed an object, then set it gently on the ground.

From his vantage point in the driver's seat, Janzen got a good look at the object, and his heart skipped a beat. He was no explosives expert but like all the agents on the protective detail, he had attended plenty of familiarization courses on a wide range of IEDs. And he would wager a substantial sum of money that this object was an Explosively Formed Penetrator.

Being inside the Suburban when the EFP went off would not be a survivable situation. Janzen's time of barricading himself, Director Sloan, and Doug Kelly inside the armored truck was rapidly coming to an end. He drew his Glock and press-checked it to make sure a round was in the chamber. If help didn't arrive soon, he would have to deal with these two shitheads himself. "Nate, we're running out of time here. I think these guys are getting ready to plant an EFP on the limo."

"Brett and Erin should be there any second. I'll get Fairfax County's Bomb Squad rolling along with a couple of our EOD techs."

Before Allen even finished the sentence, an SUV Janzen recognized as belonging to the detail's fleet came screeching to a halt on the opposite side of the parkway. The sight of his friends bailing out with their weapons at the ready was an incredible boost to his morale.

Erin O'Hearn kicked her door open and went to the front of

the vehicle. Brett LaCava followed her lead, climbing across the center console and passenger seat to keep the truck between himself and the Iranians.

Moving behind a sedan abandoned by its owner, Imad yelled, "Contact front!" and unloaded a full magazine into the Expedition. The volley's initial rounds went into the truck's front tire, and it exploded with a whoosh of air. The remaining rounds worked their way up the side of the vehicle as the muzzle rose, punching ragged holes in the quarter panel. Oil, antifreeze, and wiper fluid pooled under the CIA vehicle as the rounds ripped through the engine's hoses and reservoirs. Imad dropped down behind the sedan and slapped a fresh mag into his weapon.

With his partner's suppressive fire keeping the Americans' occupied, Mazdan lifted the EFP, lined it up with Director Sloan, then leaned forward and attached it to the Suburban. The magnets on the bottom of the device made an audible thunk as they bonded with the door's bodywork.

Janzen shifted around in his seat, trying to get a good look at the front of the device. He was trying to determine if it was on a timer or command detonated. The Iranians would have to get out of the blast radius before it went off, unless this was a suicide mission. But that hadn't been their MO up to this point.

The sound of gunfire filled the air again as LaCava took advantage of the brief lull in the action and started sending some rounds of his own at the guy behind the sedan. O'Hearn was desperate to get an angle on the other guy, the one working on the limo's door. She moved to the rear of the Expedition and took a quick peek around the back end of the truck. "Dammit!"

A minivan with a panic-stricken father and two kids strapped in their car seats was directly in her line of fire. She yelled and waved with her off hand, trying to get the dad's attention but it was no use. The guy was vapor-locked and unresponsive. For an instant, she considered firing a shot across the hood to snap him back to reality but thought better of it.

O'Hearn's focus on the family in the minivan was broken when she heard LaCava yell, "Reloading!" over the gunfire.

She returned to the front of the Expedition and shouted, "Covering!" Leaning around the front of the SUV, she fired controlled bursts at the Iranian while LaCava reloaded his rifle.

"I'm up!" Brett said, popping back up over the hood, looking for targets.

Erin ducked back behind the front wheel and thought about how many rounds might be left in her own magazine. It wasn't easy to keep track in the middle of a gunfight, so she yelled, "Reloading!" *Better safe than sorry.*

"Covering!"

She hit the mag release but missed the partially loaded mag as it slid out of the MP7's pistol grip and clattered to the pavement. Erin cursed her clumsiness, but without hesitation went directly to her belt for a fresh mag. With her weapon ready, she looked down to retrieve the magazine she'd dropped since it still held some rounds.

Noticing the gap between the road and the Expedition's frame, an idea popped into her head. She lay down on her stomach, then rolled onto her right side and tucked the stock into her shoulder. Looking through the weapon's red-dot sight, she still couldn't see the man firing at Brett, so she adjusted her position and scanned to the left, searching for the guy planting the device on the Suburban when a pair of legs filled her optic. She could see only the backs of them from the knees down but decided something was better than nothing.

"Gotcha, motherfucker." Erin said, as she centered the red dot on the man's left calf and pressed the trigger.

CHAPTER 72

Working feverishly to connect the EFP's detonator, sweat dripped from Mazdan's forehead, causing his eyes to burn. He wasn't sure if the excessive perspiration was from the temperature or the stress he was experiencing at the moment, but he paused just long enough to wipe his brow with his shirtsleeve.

When he was back in Ahvaz training for the operation, the Quds Force explosives instructors had run him through the process countless times, and he had never had an issue after the first few attempts. Under the controlled circumstances he had been able to complete the connection with his eyes closed. But today, in the middle of a firefight on U.S. soil, the Iranian operative was finding the task more challenging than he'd ever imagined. He rubbed his sweaty palms on the front of his pants before resuming his work.

"How much longer?" Imad yelled to be heard over the gunfire. The sirens in the distance were a sure sign the police were rapidly converging on their position. "We're running out of time, and I'm getting low on ammo."

"Another minute or so," Mazdan said as the firefight raged around them. "I'm almost finished."

Once the EFP was armed, he and Imad would break contact and detonate the charge. They hoped the explosion would be enough of a distraction to keep the agents and other first responders occupied while they made their escape. The two Iranians needed as much of a head start as they could manage, if either of them hoped to survive this encounter.

A jet was waiting for them at the Hagerstown Regional Airport, roughly eighty miles away in Maryland. Mazdan checked his watch and frowned. They had an hour and fifty-three minutes to get to the airfield, and the plane was going to take off, with or without them. If he and Imad missed the flight, they'd have to evade the authorities on their own until alternate arrangements could be made. The thought of being left behind heightened his sense of urgency, and he went back to work arming the device.

Mazdan was just about finished when he felt his left leg jerk.

He looked down and saw a red stain spreading across the material of his pant leg. His initial reaction was, *I've been shot. It doesn't seem to hurt as much as I thought it would.* He had never been wounded before and was pleasantly surprised at the lack of pain, which was due largely to the massive amount of adrenalin pumping through his veins.

Determined to complete his task, he forced himself to concentrate, as the sound of gunfire echoed through the woods surrounding the Parkway. He had just put the final touches on the detonator when a second blow slammed his leg against the Suburban's armored door. The bullet passed through the thick muscle in the center of his calf and came out his shin, splintering his fibula. Before the pain even registered in his brain, a third high-velocity round punched through the soft tissue behind his knee. The bullet fragmented when it hit bone, sending tiny bits of shrapnel tearing through the joint. With his destroyed leg unable to support his weight, Mazdan collapsed next to the truck, screaming in agony as he stared in disbelief at the hideous wound.

Ducking behind the sedan as rounds from the American agents snapped overhead, Imad looked over and saw his friend writhing on the ground, clutching the remnants of his leg. If the bleeding wasn't controlled his comrade would be dead in a matter of minutes. "Mazdan, use your tourniquet!"

"I...I can't. It's in the car with the rest of my gear."

Imad considered throwing his own tourniquet across the divide but decided to hang on to it. There was no guarantee Mazdan would catch it, and even if he did, he might not be coherent enough to put it on properly. Instead, he eyed the distance between them and did the calculations in his head, trying to decide if he could reach his wounded friend without being cut down by the Americans' fire. He came to the conclusion that he had to try. After all, if the roles were reversed, he hoped Mazdan would do the same for him.

Imad stole a quick glance at the EFP attached to the Suburban's door, "Is the device armed?"

Fighting through the pain Mazdan nodded. "It is." He reached into his pocket and withdrew a silver cylinder with a red button on top. He held it in the air as if he were proud of his accomplishment or possibly getting ready to throw it, Imad wasn't quite sure which.

Just as Imad was about to break cover and attempt to rescue

his friend, two shots from O'Hearn's MP7 rang out in quick succession and he looked on helplessly as Mazdan's head blew apart. His raised arm fell to the ground and the lifeless hand opened, releasing its grip on the detonator. The metal tube rolled gently across the pavement and came to a stop halfway between the two men. Once again, the calculations started running through Imad's head. If he could get to the detonator, he might still have a chance to blow the charge and attempt his getaway.

Weighing his options, he knew he really didn't have a choice. He was running low on ammunition, and the authorities were getting closer by the second. Staying put wasn't an option – he would be killed or captured for sure. But if he could blow the charge, there still might be a chance he could get to his vehicle and make a run for the airport. Imad reached for his last full magazine and reloaded the assault rifle. He took a couple of deep breaths to steel himself, knowing the next few seconds would make or break the entire operation.

Thumbing the selector switch to full auto, Imad popped up and rested his elbows on the hood to provide a stable firing platform. His rifle barked as he sent four short bursts in the direction where he had last seen the two American agents. With their heads down, Imad turned and sprinted to the detonator. The broken glass and shell casings dug into his knees as he slid to the spot like a baseball player going into second base. He reached for the detonator, the mission's success mere inches away.

A brief flash of movement caught his eye, and Imad realized he'd just made a fatal mistake. In the chaos of the firefight, he'd forgotten there was an uninjured agent in the CIA director's vehicle. He saw the door open and the agent exit the Suburban, the muzzle of his pistol leading the way. Imad's eyes darted from the agent to the detonator, then back to the agent. He was caught in a no-man's land. Too far away to reach the detonator, and out of position to get a shot at the agent. In that split second Imad knew he was finished.

Shane Janzen didn't hesitate. With his sights lined up perfectly, he took advantage of Imad's hesitation and pressed the trigger three times. He sent two jacketed hollow point rounds into Imad's chest and followed up with a third to the bridge of his nose. The Iranian fell onto his back with sightless eyes looking up at a bright blue Virginia sky.

CHAPTER 73

The herd of people Farzan had used to cover his escape came to a halt in the middle of the sidewalk. Believing they were out of danger, many were bent over trying to catch their breath, while others with varying degrees of shock setting in milled around aimlessly unsure of what to do next. Realizing they had survived the encounter, a few even appeared giddy and were hugging and high-fiving each other. The euphoria they were feeling was going to be short-lived.

Joe burst out of the alley with Chris hot on his heels and looked on in disbelief at the events unfolding before his eyes. Unconcerned with the innocent civilians caught between himself and the American agent, Farzan moved the selector switch to full-auto and opened up on Jim Haldeman.

An elderly man attempting to pull a young woman out of the line of fire was rewarded for his heroism with two bullets to the chest. The woman he was trying to rescue was hit in the shoulder. The impact of the bullet caused her to fall awkwardly and her head bounced off a truck's bumper. She hit the ground hard and lay motionless with her legs on the sidewalk and her upper body splayed into the street.

A D.C. Metro patrol unit arrived on the scene and screeched to a halt, but Farzan dumped half a mag into its windshield before the officers could even get out of the car. The cops ducked behind the dashboard as the barrage shredded the interior of the vehicle. The officer behind the wheel threw the patrol car in reverse, deciding this fight was more than he had bargained for, and backed out of the kill zone.

With Farzan distracted by the police officers, Joe raised his pistol, aligned his sights, and fired two shots into the Iranian's back. Farzan grunted and fell forward onto his hands and knees. For a brief moment, Joe thought this murderous ordeal might be over. But those thoughts were dashed as he saw the Iranian straighten, then turn and empty the rest of his magazine at them.

"Sonofabitch!" Joe cursed, ducking behind a minivan.

Chris got real skinny behind an old oak tree, hoping to hell it was thick enough to stop the rounds. "He must be wearing body armor. Headshot the asshole next time."

"No shit, Sherlock."

Sticking his head around the tree, Chris saw Farzan get to his feet and take off across New Jersey Avenue, avoiding traffic like a rodeo clown dodging bulls. "He's up and running!"

The block across the street was triangular, with row houses lining all three sides. Each street had only one or two alleys that provided access to the backyards. Farzan spotted an opening to his right, hurdled a low wrought iron fence, and disappeared into the alley.

Joe yelled, "Don't lose him!" as he and Chris took off in pursuit.

Jim was running to catch up and didn't notice the car approaching from his right. Catching it in his peripheral vision at the last minute, he dove for the safety of the opposite sidewalk. The front end of the car clipped his foot, snapping his ankle and sending him helicoptering though the air. He bounced off the hood of a parked car and went headfirst into a boxwood hedge. Haldeman called out over the radio to let Joe know he was out of the fight.

Chris was the first to cross the street and easily cleared the fence. His leap wasn't as graceful as Farzan's, but he wasn't looking for style points.

Joe wasn't far behind. "Hold at the entrance. Let's not rush into an ambush."

Even though there was a cloudless blue sky overhead, the low angle of the sun, combined with the clustered rooftops and canopy of trees, shrouded the alley in darkness. Joe edged his Glock around the corner of the house, careful not to silhouette himself in the fatal funnel, and used the light mounted under the frame to illuminate the alley. Seeing it was clear, he whispered, "Moving."

"Move," Chris replied in a low voice.

They each took a side of the alley and moved forward, stopping at the far end of the houses. Joe pied the left corner and scanned the back yard. "Clear."

Chris did the same to the right. It was clear as well.

The row houses were old, maybe built in the fifties, so each house and yard were unique. The fences that surrounded them were as varied as the homes themselves. Some were no more than four-feet tall and made of chain-link while others were built from six-foot wooden two-by-fours for privacy.

Joe noticed movement to his left and got his head around just in time to see Farzan going over one of the lower chain link fences. He pointed in the Iranian's direction. "That way!"

The Iranian sprinted through the yard, racking his brain for something, anything, that would get the Americans off his trail. A solution came to him as he glanced at the home's patio. Continuing past the house, he hopped one more chain-link fence to gain some additional distance from his pursuers, then ducked behind a storage shed. He took up a prone position and inched forward on his stomach until only his head and assault rifle were exposed around the corner. As he waited on his prey, he hoped the hasty plan would work.

When the Americans came into view, he saw they were moving cautiously but still quickly enough to keep from losing him in the maze of houses. He would use their haste to his advantage. Only a few more steps, and they would be in the kill zone.

Farzan's heart pounded in his chest and sweat dripped from the tip of his nose as he lay in wait for the men to pull even with the patio. His eyes darted back and forth from the men to the patio. When he was satisfied they were within range, he angled his rifle and fired a single shot.

He was up and running before the explosion's echo faded, racing through the adjacent yards as debris from the blast rained down around him.

CHAPTER 74

Flat on his back gasping for air, Joe was trying to figure out what the hell just happened. Slowly, his head began to clear and he remembered hearing a shot. Then, a fraction of a second later, an ear-splitting explosion. He rolled his head to the left and looked to the spot where he believed the blast had originated. Black scorch marks were visible on the patio and the remnants of a grill were strewn about the yard. *Must've shot the propane tank,* he thought

The shockwave had slammed him into a tree, and he may have blacked out for a minute or two. It was impossible to tell. As he took deep breaths, trying to re-introduce air back into his lungs, he had the sudden realization that his hands were empty. Looking around frantically, he spotted his gun on the ground about three feet to his right.

He sat up to retrieve the weapon, but stopped halfway through the motion when a searing pain shot through his left side. Feeling as if someone had cut a hole in his torso and poured lava into his ribcage, the burning sensation ran slowly through his hip and all the way down his left leg.

Joe figured he had broken a rib and moved his hand to support the area before making another try for his gun. As his hand neared the painful spot it brushed against something hard. He looked down to find a jagged piece of metal embedded in his side. The gruesome sight ignited a wave of nausea and he fought to keep his stomach from emptying its contents. *That's no broken rib.*

Joe knew he needed immediate medical attention, but he was also aware he didn't have that luxury at the moment. He couldn't let Farzan get away.

Doing his best to stabilize the object, Joe dug his heel into the soft grass and pushed off with his right leg, sliding along on his rear end. It took a few repetitions, but he was eventually able to make his way over to the pistol.

Armed once again, he reached for his side, sliding the fingers of his left hand above and below the piece of metal to hold it in place. He holstered his pistol, then leaned on a tree for support, paused a moment to take a couple of breaths, then gently rose to his feet. As he stood, the movement sent a fresh flow of lava running through his body. A muffled cry escaped his lips and tears filled his eyes as the searing pain nearly buckled his knees. When he was fully upright, Joe wiped his eyes and looked around frantically for Chris.

He found him lying in a pile of leaves in a corner of the yard where two sections of fence came together. Pain racked Joe's body as he eased down to one knee, and checked for a pulse. Joe said a silent prayer of thanks when he found one.

Chris had a gash along the left side of his head, probably caused by the grill's lid which was on the ground a few feet away, and his clothes were soaked with blood where he'd caught a few pieces of shrapnel.

Joe keyed his radio, "All units, Chris is down! I need EMS at my location right fucking now!"

Nate's reply from Citadel was immediate, "Roger that. I'm pinging your phone's location and will get an ambulance rolling."

"Use Chris's phone instead," Joe ordered. "I'm going after Farzan."

With help on the way, he pressed his left hand to his side, took a deep breath to steel himself for the pain he knew was coming, and stood. Despite his best efforts to stabilize the piece of metal, it shifted with the motion, and sent pain shooting through his abdomen. Joe broke out in a cold sweat and thinking he was on the verge of passing out, stumbled back against the fence for support. *"Just take a minute, give the pain a chance to subside,"* he told himself. When he was confident he wasn't going to lose consciousness, he pressed forward and hobbled off in search of Farzan.

Heading north through the tree-covered yards, Farzan looked left and right, desperate for an exit that would get him back onto the street. From his map study before the attack, he knew the Capitol South Metro Station on D Street was no more than a hundred meters away. He planned to make for the underground and lose himself among the crowds of commuters and tourists. But first, he would have to find his way out of this maze of yards.

He continued straight ahead, hoping the row of houses

paralleling D Street would have some type of street access. If they didn't, he'd have to break into one of the homes and use it as a pass-through to the street. Moving deeper into the block, he noticed fewer of the chainlink fences that had marked previous yard's borders and a gradual change to the taller, wooden privacy fences.

Looking up and down the row, Farzan cursed his luck – and lack of options. He could go back the way he came and look for an alley on one of the side streets. But that would take him toward the Americans if they hadn't been disabled by the explosion.

Or he could continue forward and go through one of the houses. But which one? Because each of them had one of the tall privacy fences, he had no way of telling whether or not they were occupied. Having to deal with the homeowner or a family would undoubtedly get loud and messy. And with the phalanx of police officers flooding the area, he would prefer a stealthier course of action.

Choosing a quiet looking house, Farzan approached its gate and listened for any sounds that would indicate the owners were home. All he could hear was the traffic noise along D Street and the wail of sirens, as first responders continued their descent on the Rayburn building.

Rolling the dice, he decided to give this house a try and was pleasantly surprised to find the gate unlocked. Stepping inside, he swept the yard and the back of the house with his rifle. He breathed a quick sigh of relief when he found it was empty, except for some patio furniture and a small storage shed.

Farzan closed the gate behind him and had taken only two steps toward the house when he heard the back door open. Caught out in the open, Farzan froze, willing the woman to close the door without glancing into the back yard. Luckily, she had her back to him, as if she were speaking to someone in the house. *Then why open the door?*

A second later, his question was answered. Farzan's heart skipped a beat as a Rottweiler weighing upward of a hundred pounds or more stepped through the door. There was a pregnant pause as he and the behemoth locked eyes. Having decided the stranger's presence on his territory was not welcome, the dog let out a low growl and bared a mouthful of teeth, a not so subtle warning designed to keep the intruder from advancing any closer to his master's house.

Ever so slowly, Farzan stepped back toward the gate. He had every intention of retracing his steps and trying another house. But the movement, as subtle as it was, acted like a starter's gun and ignited the protective instincts in the Rottweiler's DNA. The dog charged, covering the distance between them with a speed and agility Farzan hadn't believed possible for such a large animal.

When the dog was no more than six feet away, it crouched low and lunged. Farzan shouldered is rifle but the beast was on him before he could get a shot off. Its thick legs and huge paws hit him in the chest and knocked him to the ground.

As Farzan tried to bring the rifle to bear, the dog's mouth clamped onto his left forearm. He screamed in agony as the dog wrenched its head back and forth, as if it were trying to rip the arm off at the elbow. Farzan howled again as he felt the bones in his arm shatter under the pressure of its vise-like jaws.

In desperation, Farzan grabbed the rifle with his good arm and smashed its stock across the dog's back. He continued raining blows on the Rottweiler until it finally released his arm. But the dog wasn't done with him quite yet. Finding a new target, it quickly began attacking Farzan's ankle with the same level of intensity. He screamed again as the dog repeated the back and forth action on his lower leg. Abandoning the rifle, Farzan drew his pistol and pulled the trigger three times. The dog yelped and released its hold on his leg, then staggered a few steps and collapsed on the grass.

Using his good arm and leg, Farzan pushed himself away from the dog and leaned back against the fence. Looking down at the ragged wounds, he never would have imagined this was how his day would turn out.

CHAPTER 75

Joe stared at the gates and felt like a contestant on a game show, trying to decide if Farzan was behind door number one, two, or three.

From his left, Joe heard someone say in a low voice, "Are you with the cops?"

Joe turned and saw an elderly black man standing on his back porch. Curiosity must have gotten the best of him, and he had to come out to see what was causing all the commotion.

"Something like that," Joe offered. "You didn't happen to see a guy come by here in the last couple of minutes, did you?"

The man nodded and pointed to a gate two houses to Joe's right. *Door number three.* "He went in that one. It's the Cunningham's. Nice family."

"Think anyone is home?"

Looking at his watch, the man said, "Probably. She's a stay-at-home mom and the kids should be back from school by now."

"Shit," Joe muttered.

The man noticed the blood soaking Joe's left side and said, "You're bleeding pretty bad, young man. Want me to call an ambulance?"

Joe looked down at the piece of metal and gave him a weak smile. "Not quite yet. There's some unfinished business I need to take care of first. You should go back inside. Stay away from the doors and windows. It may get a little ugly out here."

The man's demeanor visibly changed, and he said, "I spent twenty-three years in the Army. Served three combat tours in 'Nam. It doesn't get uglier than what I saw over there."

Realizing he'd insulted the man, Joe said, "Sorry, sir. No offense intended. I was in the Army myself. Saw combat in Iraq and Afghanistan along with a few other places. It's just…this guy I'm after has already killed a lot of people, and I don't want to see anyone else get hurt."

The man peered into Joe's eyes, recognizing the look of a fellow combat vet. Even though they were separated by a couple of generations, the two men were brothers in arms. He nodded his understanding and turned to go back inside. Before closing the door, he said, "Give him hell, son."

"Will do, sir."

Joe limped weakly toward the home the man had indicated and unlatched the gate. He held his position for a moment, listening for any signs of activity. Hearing nothing, he raised his pistol, and pushed the Cunningham's gate open. Stepping inside, his eyes were immediately drawn to a discarded AK-74 assault rifle. Next to it, a massive Rottweiler whimpered softly in a blood-soaked patch of grass.

The old man had been right – Farzan had definitely come this way. Joe just hoped Mrs. Cunningham and her kids hadn't suffered the same fate as their dog.

As Joe moved deeper into the yard, he heard the unmistakable sound of the gate closing behind him. Turning around, he saw Farzan on the ground, leaning back against the fence. He'd been hidden by the gate when Joe pushed it open.

"You!" Farzan roared, as he raised the Makarov and snapped off a quick shot.

Joe spun to his left, doing well to avoid the bullet, but the torque on his body forced the jagged piece of metal deeper into his abdomen. The pain took his breath away and he fell to his knees. Releasing his grip on the Glock, Joe's hands instinctively moved to protect the injured area. The pistol bounced once in the thick grass then disappeared into a pile of leaves.

Totally defenseless, he wondered what was taking the Iranian so long to fire the kill shot. That's when he heard Farzan cursing up a storm in Farsi and realized his pistol must have malfunctioned. With his left arm rendered useless by the Rottweiler's attack, he was having a hell of a time clearing it with his one good hand.

"That's what you get for using a piece of shit Makarov, Hamid."

Hoping to find his pistol, Joe took a quick glance around, but it was nowhere in sight. Knowing he'd be dead if Farzan got his weapon back in working order, Joe sucked up the pain and dove on top of the Iranian. He ripped the useless pistol out of Farzan's grip and threw it across the yard.

Now that there were no weapons involved, Joe's hand-to-hand skills gave him a distinct advantage and he went to work. Catching Farzan on the side of the head with a vicious elbow strike, he rolled the stunned Iranian onto his back and straddled his waist as he continued the assault with a barrage of haymakers. Excruciating pain radiated through his side with each punch he threw, but Joe ignored it, determined to put an end to Farzan once and for all.

The Quds operative's hands were up, offering some defense to the pummeling, until one of Joe's punches landed squarely on his injured forearm. Farzan screamed in agony as he felt the broken bones grind against one another. The useless arm dropped limply to the side.

Now that he was fighting one-handed, Farzan was in desperate need of a way to protect his head from the onslaught. Keeping his right arm up to absorb the damage from Joe's lefts, he then tucked his chin to his chest and canted the unprotected side of his head into his left shoulder.

The subtle shift of his head allowed Farzan to catch a glimpse of the shrapnel sticking out of Joe's side. He hadn't noticed it at first, but from this angle, it was hard to miss. Sacrificing his guard, Farzan accepted a glancing blow to his cheek, then drove a right hook into Joe's ribcage, just above the wound.

Joe groaned as the pain rushed up and down his left side. Instinctively, he tucked his left arm in tight to protect his flank as Farzan continued attacking the injured area. But the tactic backfired as each blow slammed Joe's arm against the hunk of metal. Every time his arm hit the shrapnel, its jagged edges cut deeper into his torso.

The world began to darken around the edges as tunnel vision set in, and Joe knew he was on the verge of passing out. For a moment, he considered how easy it would be to give in and let the darkness envelope his damaged body like a warm blanket. The pain would be gone, and he could finally rest, no longer required to travel the world averting one catastrophe after another. Let someone else have a turn chasing the bad guys for a change.

Joe felt himself listing to the left as he tried to fend off unconsciousness. The sensation reminded him of a dream he'd had as a kid. He' been playing in a field with friends when he'd fallen into a well. But instead of splashing into the water, or hitting the bottom of a dry hole, he just continued to fall. And the farther he fell, the smaller the light at the opening became, until he was completely shrouded in darkness.

The strength in Joe's powerful arms was sapped and the punches he'd been throwing had become ineffective. They were no longer the powerful blows of an operator, but more like those of a belligerent drunk in a bar fight.

Seeing his opponent falter, Farzan took advantage of the opportunity and grabbed the piece of shrapnel with his good hand. He shook it violently, using the jagged edges like the teeth of a saw. The Iranian delighted in Joe's screams each time it tore through flesh and muscle.

Seeing victory within his grasp, Farzan taunted his opponent, "It looks like you've fallen short once again. I've been at least two or three steps ahead of you at every turn, and now your final defeat will take place here in your homeland. Fitting, wouldn't you say?"

"Is this it?" Joe thought. *"Is this how it's going to end?"* The thought infuriated him, but the injury had taken its toll. There was nothing left in the tank.

Now that he had the upper hand, just killing the American wouldn't satisfy his desire for revenge. No, Farzan felt the need to inflict some additional pain as compensation for the death of his teammates. He struck the piece of shrapnel with the palm of his hand, driving it further into Joe's side. The Iranian grinned, "How does that feel? Does it feel like failure? Perhaps this is the cost you must pay for killing so many of my team."

A white-hot lightning bolt of agony shot through Joe's body and exploded in his brain like fireworks on the Fourth of July. The intensity of the pain obliterated the darkness, and Joe entered a state of clarity beyond anything he'd ever experienced. He opened his eyes and stared down at Farzan with a look of pure fury.

The Iranian immediately realized he'd made a terrible error in judgement. The American had been teetering on the edge of unconsciousness, moments away from succumbing to his injury. It would have been an easy kill for Farzan if he had only let nature take its course. But what he saw as he looked into Joe's deep blue eyes was sheer determination. A will to survive. A will to win.

Through gritted teeth, Joe said, "I'm not done yet, Hamid.

There's one more member of your team I'm going to kill."

Joe wrapped both his hands around Farzan's, and without breaking eye contact, pulled the shrapnel out of his side. Blood poured from the wound as it broke free, and he let out a scream that echoed through the trees. The darkness tried once more to overwhelm him, but Joe pushed it aside, the thoughts of the people Farzan had killed fueling his rage.

With two good hands to Farzan's one, Joe used his superior strength to guide his newfound weapon over the Iranian's face. Blood dripped from its tip, dotting Farzan's cheek, nose, and forehead as their arms shook with the exertion.

Farzan's left arm was useless, the damage from the dog's attack too extensive. So he locked his good elbow, trying to buy enough time to come up with another plan of attack.

Seeing what Farzan was up to, Joe released his grip with his right hand and fired it into the inside of Farzan's elbow, forcing the joint to bend. Regaining his two-hand grip on the shrapnel, he leaned forward and put his chest on top of his hands, using the full weight of his body to drive the jagged piece of metal downward.

Farzan's eyes widened, realizing what was about to happen. "No...n-n-no! You don't have to do this!" Farzan pleaded, as the ominous looking weapon inched closer and closer to his right eye.

Joe was disgusted with the Iranian's cowardice now that the tables had turned. "Mercy? Is that what you're asking for?"

With the tip of the metal hovering mere centimeters from his eyeball, Farzan admitted defeat, and barely above a whisper, said, "Yes."

Joe snarled, "Like the mercy you showed Ambassador Lewis back in Fallujah? Or Friedrich Voigt and his security team in Munich? How about Officer Jesse Reyes when you came ashore in Florida? Did you show him any mercy when you nearly cut his head off?"

"Wait...." Farzan started to protest, but he was cut off as Joe drove the shrapnel through his eye socket and into his brain. Joe sat still, staring down Farzan's lifeless body for another thirty seconds or so, desperately wanting to be convinced it was over.

The exertion and blood loss finally took their toll, and he rolled off the Iranian, ending up flat on his back next to the wounded Rottweiler. With the last of his remaining energy, he reached for his radio's transmit button. "Nate, you still there?"

Back in Citadel, Nate bowed his head and said a short prayer. "I'm here. Man, it's good to hear your voice."

"I...uh...I could use that ambulance right about now."

"I'll get one rolling right away."

"Hey Nate...."

"Yeah, Joe?"

"Could you do me a favor and see if there's some type of emergency vet service in the area?"

"Vet service?"

"Yeah. I partnered up with a pretty badass Rottweiler to take down Farzan. He's been shot and needs medical attention."

Nate chuckled. "I'll see what I can do."

Joe reached over and slid the dog's collar around so he could see his name tag. He grabbed a handful of fur and scratched the whimpering dog behind the ear. "Hear that, Carl? Hang on just a little bit longer. Help is on the way – for both of us."

Epilogue, Six Months Later

After surviving emergency surgery at CIA's Langley Headquarters, Yousef Mehrdad was transferred to a safe house outside of Berryville, Virginia, to begin his recovery.

The sprawling two-hundred-fifty-acre estate had been in the Agency's real estate portfolio since 1963. To the casual observer, the property resembled other wealthy farms or ranches spread across this patch of Virginia horse country. But to those few in the know, the large manor nestled among the rolling, grassy hills was an integral part of the CIA's national security operations.

It had hosted conferences for sensitive, behind-the-scenes negotiations with leaders from countries whose citizens wouldn't approve of a public relationship with the United States, much less the CIA. Defectors from the Soviet Union to modern-day Russia, North Korea, and China had passed through the estate's doors for debriefings before being resettled elsewhere in the country. And it had even been used once or twice as a makeshift black site to interrogate high level al-Qaeda or ISIS operatives.

With Mehrdad's recuperation complete, the Berryville estate transitioned from a rehabilitation center to a state-of-the-art interrogation facility.

From the very beginning, the Iranian operative had been a tough nut to crack. He had resisted to the best of his abilities, but deep down, even he knew the one unalienable truth of interrogation. At some point, everyone breaks. And his breaking point came after thirty-eight days of perhaps the harshest enhanced interrogation ever performed by the CIA.

Mehrdad had earned the respect of his interrogators, psychologists, and doctors over that five-and-a-half-week period, but at the end of the day he was still the enemy. And as an enemy of the United States, he was in possession of information the CIA planned to exploit. The Quds operative's information was valuable because it was still actionable.

Thanks to a bit of disinformation leaked by unnamed Agency officials, news reports of the brazen daylight attack in downtown

Washington, D.C. indicated the entire Quds Force assassination squad had been killed. Unaware Mehrdad was in CIA custody, the Iranian government had no reason to alter their protocols. As a result, the information in Mehrdad's head was still as valid as the day he left Tehran.

When Mehrdad finally did break, he provided information on a number of current and upcoming operations. While the information had some value, it was also fairly routine for an interrogation of someone of his skillset. He was a foot-soldier who executed plans and orders. Up to a point, nothing Mehrdad had shared with his interrogators had been earth-shattering. But then he told them about the torture session with Ambassador Jonathan Lewis and how he came to know of the existence of an operation named Project Wraith.

Still recovering from their injuries, Director Sloan and Katherine Clark made the trip to Berryville to conduct this portion of the interview personally. It was during this session that Mehrdad provided Sloan with the golden nugget of information that had eluded him since this whole ordeal began in Fallujah – how the Iranians found out about Project Wraith in the first place. As it turned out, they had help, and it came from inside the U.S. government. When asked to identify the person who betrayed the United States, Mehrdad told them he didn't have the name, he knew only that the person was an aide or somehow connected to a powerful congresswoman. It wasn't a positive identification, but it did give Sloan and Clark a pretty good idea of where to start looking.

When the interrogation team was confident they had bled Mehrdad dry, he was hooded, then outfitted with blacked-out goggles and soundproof earmuffs. He was completely isolated from his environment as a rendition team drove him to a nearby airstrip where he was loaded aboard one of the Agency's Gulfstream G-550s. An hour later, the plane landed at a covert facility in southeastern Virginia. The door opened, and the crisp night air was cool on Mehrdad's skin as he was helped down the plane's stairs and ushered into the back of an SUV.

His hood, goggles, and earmuffs were removed when the vehicle reached its destination, and even though it was dark, his eyes still took a minute to adjust. He saw they were in a dense forest. Looking down, he found himself standing at the edge of a large rectangular hole. Realizing what was about to happen, he closed his eyes and took a deep breath, inhaling the pleasant scent of the pines as the bullet entered the back of his head.

***

A charcoal grey van with an electronics store's logo plastered on its sides backed into an alley a block from a nondescript brownstone on the corner of Fifth Street and Independence Avenue SE.

From the driver's seat, John Roberts looked on as a car pulled up outside the brownstone. The District was known for its wide variety of nightlife, but even the most die-hard party-goers had to call it quits at some point. The car wasn't a cab, so he figured it might have been a friend or one of those ride-sharing services like Uber or Lyft. A man matching the description of the brownstone's owner exited the car and waved to the driver. He turned and fumbled with his keys as he staggered up the steps.

Roberts hailed Mike McCredy on the radio, "Stand by. The target just arrived."

"Roger. Thanks for the heads-up."

The homeowner threw the keys into a bowl on a small table in the entryway, checked to make sure the door was locked, then headed to the kitchen for a nightcap. *A beer,* he decided. *I've already had enough of the hard stuff tonight.*

As he reached for the refrigerator, a hand shot out from the darkness and clamped down over his mouth, preventing a scream from shattering the silence. The homeowner struggled, but it was no use. Whoever had him was strong, and even though he worked out regularly, the lack of sleep combined with the amount of alcohol he'd consumed left him at a distinct disadvantage. The next thing he felt was the sharp pain of a needle in the side of his neck. Then everything went dark.

Todd McCutcheon awoke with a start. His mind was foggy, but he remembered something about being attacked in his kitchen. Had he been dreaming? Admittedly, he'd had a lot to drink last night, but his alcohol intake had never resulted in a dream as crazy as this. He looked around the austere room, then down at his hands, confused as to why they were shackled to an eye-bolt screwed into the table.

He looked up, and for the first time, noticed there was a woman sitting across the table from him. She wore a white blouse under a navy-blue cardigan with a string of pearls around her neck.

Looking at him over a pair of reading glasses perched on the end of her nose she said, "Hello, Mr. McCutcheon."

The sight of Katherine Clark, the CIA's Deputy Director for Operations sitting across from him instantly cleared any remnants of the drugs or alcohol that had been in his system. Even though McCutcheon had a pretty good idea of why he was in this predicament, he wasn't sure how they had found out about his involvement with the Iranians. Playing dumb, he asked, "What's going on here? Where am I?"

"I'll be the one asking the questions, Mr. McCutcheon. Your responsibility in this endeavor will be to answer them."

Unused to being spoken to in this manner, he decided to take an indignant tone. "Mrs. Clark, you obviously know who I am and who I work for. If you don't let me out of here immediately, I'll have your job...."

McCutcheon's rant was interrupted as Clark leaned across the table and slapped him across the face. The blow wasn't intended to injure the prisoner, only to get his attention and set the ground rules for who was in charge as they moved forward.

The slap sent a wave of pain through her left side and she winced ever so slightly. It would be the only indication she would show this piece of trash that his actions had impacted her in some way. Clark took a moment to smooth her blouse and cardigan, using the gesture to give the pain a chance to subside.

She continued, "Yes, Mr. McCutcheon. I am well aware that you are Congresswoman Cynthia Drake's chief of staff."

Hearing Drake's name bolstered his confidence. "Then you must also know the amount of power and influence I wield in this town. And that I will use every bit of it to expose whatever the hell this is and...."

Another slap, this one on the opposite cheek, cut him off. Clark paused again, a little longer this time, to let the discomfort pass.

"When you say, this town, where exactly do you think you are, Mr. McCutcheon? In the time you've been unconscious, we could have transported you to any point on the globe. You could be at a black site in Poland or in the basement of a government building in Washington, D.C. You have no way of knowing where you are or how long it has been since you were taken from your brownstone." She paused for effect, letting the reality of the situation sink in.

"You can't keep me here indefinitely. Someone…hell, the congresswoman herself will realize I'm missing. For all you know she may have called the police already."

Acting as if she hadn't heard a word he'd said, Clark pulled a folder from a briefcase next to her chair and placed it on the table. "Mr. McCutcheon, this folder contains evidence of the crimes you're accused of committing."

"Crimes? That's absurd. I haven't done anything."

"The most serious of those crimes is treason. You do realize treason is punishable by death, don't you?"

"Treason? Death penalty? Are you out of your mind, lady?"

Clark opened the folder and removed a sheet of paper. She slid it across the table for McCutcheon to see. It was the coversheet for a classified file. "Top Secret – Eyes Only" was printed across the top in bold red letters. A red stripe ran diagonally from the top right corner to the bottom left. Two words were in the center of the sheet – PROJECT WRAITH.

Then, as if to drive the point home, she spread glossy eight-by-ten photos across the table like a dealer at a Las Vegas blackjack table. They were gruesome crime scene photos of all the people killed in the attacks. She shook her head in disgust, "Do you have any idea how much blood is on your hands?"

McCutcheon flinched, almost recoiling from the evidence as the blood drained from his face. Losing some of the bravado, he tried to counter, "I don't know anything about what happened to those people. Why would you show me something like that?"

"You may not have pulled the trigger or set off the explosive, but you enabled those who did. In my book – or any court of law for that matter – that makes you just as guilty. So why don't you stop wasting my time and yours, and tell me why you did it?"

Clark was so confident in her statements that McCutcheon didn't see much reason to keep up the charade. Besides, he was proud of his actions and relished the chance to confront this woman who was such a big part of the institution he was trying to bring to its knees. Leaning back in his chair, he asked, "How did you know it was me?"

A slight smile creased her lips at the confession. "How we know is not important. What I'm interested in is why. And if Congresswoman Drake was involved in your activities."

McCutcheon scoffed dismissively, "Cynthia? God, no. She had nothing to do with it. Don't get me wrong, she hates those of you in the intelligence community almost as much as I do. She doesn't have what it takes to conduct any meaningful action. Scoring points and using her power to join the ranks of the political elite were more important to her than crippling your illegal organizations."

"So you decided to take matters into your own hands," Clark said, more of a statement than a question.

"Someone had to. I had been researching the rumors about Jonathan Lewis and his involvement in a top-secret operation for years, wondering why someone from the State Department would be involved in something so classified. The more I dug, the more it seemed he had something to do with the Stuxnet attack on the Iranian nuclear program. Cynthia could only think about how she would use the information to ruin Lawrence Sloan and preen in front of the cameras at the hearings. But I wanted more. It was important to me that the CIA, among others, felt the type of pain they'd been inflicting across the globe for decades."

Katherine Clark looked at him impassively as he continued for another forty-five minutes, detailing how he'd concluded Jonathan Lewis was involved in the cyberattack and how he went about passing the information to the Iranians. When he was done, she retrieved the documents and photos from the table and returned them to her briefcase.

Using a cane to support her healing hip, she stood and said, "Thank you for your honesty, Mr. McCutcheon. This concludes our session. Some men will be in shortly to take you home."

A buzzer sounded, and the door opened. Before she left, McCutcheon said, "I'll bring the full force of the House Permanent Select Committee on Intelligence against you and your cohorts. I'll see you behind bars if it's the last thing I do."

"I very much doubt that will be the case, Mr. McCutcheon," Clark said, as she left the room.

Two days later an article ran on the front page of the *Washington Post*. According to the story, Todd McCutcheon, chief of staff to Congresswoman Cynthia Drake, had died from an apparent self-inflicted gunshot wound to the head. His death was ruled a suicide after the police found a note on the kitchen counter. From the contents of the note and classified material found in his home and on his computer authorities determined Mr. McCutcheon was spying for a foreign power. The country he was working for was not publicly identified because of the ongoing investigation.

Fallout from the resulting scandal cost Congresswoman Drake the leadership position on the House Intelligence Committee and effectively put an end to her political career.

***

Tehran, Iran

General Amjad al-Massoud, the commanding officer of the Quds Force, took a pack of cigarettes from his tunic as the black Audi staff car pulled out of the Joint Chiefs of Staff of the Islamic Republic's headquarters building and headed west on Abbas Abad Street. He turned to the other man in the back seat and offered him a cigarette. "Where shall we dine tonight, Malek?"

General Malek Ashkan commanded the Quds base in Ahvaz and had been Hamid Farzan's boss. Losing Farzan and his team had been unfortunate, but Ashkan chalked it up to the cost of doing business. The team had been extremely successful, right up to the point they had all been killed, and Ashkan would use that experience to make his next hit squad that much better.

"I hear Divan is excellent. It's consistently rated one of the top five restaurants in Tehran."

With the decision made, the driver turned right, taking the northbound ramp onto the Modares Highway. He merged into traffic, and seeing the left lane empty, drifted over and picked up speed. The best way to stay on the general's good side, he knew, was to beat the drive time he'd promised and get them to dinner ahead of schedule. Classic under promise and over deliver.

A motorcycle's single headlight appeared in the rearview mirror, catching the driver's attention. It was approaching fast, weaving in and out of traffic, until it pulled up alongside the Audi. The driver admired the rider's skill, but as a rider himself, it was nothing compared to his appreciation for the man's jet-black Honda CBR 1000RR sport bike.

A tap on the window tore al-Massoud's attention away from the conversation, and he noticed the motorcycle for the first time. The bike's passenger raised his visor to reveal a pair of icy blue eyes. A strand of dark red hair caught between his forehead and the helmet, blew in the wind. The man took a small piece of paper from the pocket of his riding jacket and stuck it to the window with two-sided tape. In Farsi, the note read, "Compliments of Lawrence Sloan."

The generals looked at one another in confusion as they heard the metallic thunk of something being attached to the car's door. The man saluted before flipping the visor back into place and tapped the helmet of the man piloting the motorcycle. At the signal, the biker downshifted and hit the throttle, sending the bike rocketing up the highway.

Taking the next off-ramp, the motorcycle went left and came to a stop on the overpass. Watching the traffic below, the man on the back of the bike removed a mobile phone from his pocket and pressed a speed-dial button. The call connected and the Explosively Formed Penetrator detonated, sending its copper projectile through the back seat of the general's sedan. The destroyed Audi slid along the highway, passing under the men on the motorcycle, before coming to a rest in the far-right lane.

When the medical examiners arrived on the scene they were horrified by the devastating effect the weapon had on the human body. Generals al-Massoud and Ashkan had been cut in half, their hips and legs still sitting perfectly in place, while their torsos were collapsed on top of one another like the upper and lower halves of a pair of mannequins.

Satisfied with their work, the men on the motorcycle continued across the overpass and reentered the highway going southbound. Over the helmet to helmet intercom, Joe Matthews said, "Pretty fitting that was the same EFP Farzan's guys put on Sloan's limo."

"I do love me some irony," Chris said, the smile on his face hidden by his helmet's visor.

"Can't this thing go any faster?" Joe asked. "I'll buy the first round if you get us back to the bar before last call."

Twenty minutes later they pulled up to a wooded compound in central Tehran, and Chris beeped the horn twice. Guards opened the iron gate just wide enough to allow the bike access and the two operators entered, setting foot on the sovereign property of the Embassy of the United Kingdom.

Chris looked at his watch. "Made it with time to spare. Looks like you're buying."

***

Northern Virginia

Barbara Lewis sorted through the mail as she walked up the driveway. Today's delivery was fairly routine, a few bills and offers on interest rates too good to be true from a couple of credit card companies. She closed the garage door and entered the house through the mud room. Stepping into the kitchen, she put the bills with the others waiting to be paid and set the credit card offers aside for shredding later.

A plain white envelope, about the size of a greeting card, caught her eye and she wondered how she'd missed it earlier. There were no stamps or postal markings, no return address, just her name written across the front with remarkable penmanship. She flipped the envelope over and examined the back, but there were no clues to the sender's identity there, either. Barbara took a steak knife out of a drawer and used it as a letter opener. The envelope did contain a card, but it wasn't made by Hallmark. Instead, the gold embossed seal of the Central Intelligence Agency was centered on its outer flap. With trembling fingers, she opened the card and read the handwritten message. She read the card again, then clutched it to her chest:

Mrs. Lewis,
Our fire and brimstone has hit its mark.
Sincerely,
Lawrence Sloan

Made in the USA
Coppell, TX
26 January 2020